Sex, Lies, and Video Poker

Sex, Lies, and Video Poker

An Erotic Novel About Gambling

by Bob Dancer

Compton Dancer Publishing
Las Vegas, Nevada

Sex, Lies and Video Poker
An Erotic Novel About Gambling

Published by: Compton Dancer Publishing
Las Vegas, Nevada
www.bobdancer.com

ISBN: 0-9727592-9-8

Interior Design and Production: R.L. Rivers

WARNING

Some of the characters in this novel really get it on like bunny rabbits, and their activities are described more explicitly here than is typical in mainstream novels. I asked them to tame it down a little and they told me to mind my own damned business.

Some readers will be offended by the explicitness, and I'm sorry they're unhappy.

But they were warned up front!

To Shirley

The process of writing an erotic novel can place more strain on a marriage than you might think. I am extremely grateful that Shirley never lost sight of the love we share with each other.

Monday
November 29, 1999

One advantage to living alone is you always know what you'll find when you get home. The bottle of wine you were saving for an unspecific special occasion will still be right where you left it, foil and cork intact, and skimpy lingerie won't have suddenly appeared.

Almost always, anyway.

When I came home from a Body Pump class a little after noon, I heard music in my bedroom. "Killing Me Softly" by Roberta Flack, the kind of music played on a soft-rock love-song kind of station, probably KJOI, and I always listened to country music on KZLA. I had company. The uninvited kind.

I stepped through the bedroom door and observed a nicely constructed lady, gloriously naked, lying face up, legs spread immodestly, snoring quietly next to an empty wine glass and mostly empty bottle of 1987 Robert Mondavi Reserve Cabernet that had been unopened this morning. Her face was turned away from me.

I hadn't shared my bed with anyone since Paula and I split up two years ago. And although I dated some, nobody was worth bringing home. And while I'd never before seen this particular woman undressed, there was no doubt in my mind who it was. Her hair color, slenderness, and height provided me with some clues, but her huge breasts and the fact that she'd been drinking were the clinchers. It was Meg.

Seeing Meg naked caused some involuntary, and not altogether unpleasant, twinges in my you-know-what. But they were short-lived, quickly replaced by a number of questions. Such as, why was she here? Did she intend for me to observe her this way or did she just get drunk and forget whose condo she was in? Did she have any romantic ideas in mind? If so, and if I told her no (which I most certainly would, because sex with Meg would improve my life in the same way that a crazed porcupine would enhance a convention of soap bubbles), would that create an even stickier situation? Hell hath no fury and all of that?

The answers to these questions wouldn't be answered until she awoke. Since Richard was in Phoenix, there was no hurry for Meg to be anywhere else. Besides, I had work to do and for now I decided to let sleeping dogs lie. Or rather, let a sleeping sister-in-law lie.

While the delicto was still quite flagrante, though, I decided to check her out. I'd always wondered if Meg's most conspicuous assets were home grown or store bought. No harm in looking, I supposed, although it'd be best just now if she remained asleep. I'd never been the Peeping Tom type (not counting that time with my next-door neighbor Patty when she was 15 and I was 14, though I'm fully convinced she put on that particular show on purpose). I was a healthy heterosexual male and the desire to look closer was simply irresistible.

Upon visual examination, I decided hers were real rather than Memorex. Although she was only in her early forties, gravity isn't kind to the enormously endowed. Silicone jobs would be firm and sticking right out there, according to my experience anyway, and these weren't. Not that this answered any of the pressing questions of the moment, but hey! Inquiring minds want to know.

I was surprised to see Meg undressed, but I wasn't surprised to see her. She had permission to be here, although I could see we'd need to have a talk about boundaries. Meg had the "key" to my condo, which was actually a code for a keypad. She also knew the code that disarmed the burglar alarm. Richard, as well as being Meg's husband, is my older brother and all three of us are partners in a jewelry business. Meg often takes things back and forth. And although Meg drinks too much and can be a nuisance, having her as a courier is a big help and, until today anyway, there had never been a problem with her having access. Although I trust her, I wasn't stupid about it. The large safe in my workshop held quantities of cash, gemstones, and precious metals and she didn't have access to that.

Richard runs the retail outlet, called Georges' Gorgeous Gems, open Wednesday through Sunday and located between the post office and an Albertson's in a decent-sized shopping center in Culver City, California, ten miles southwest of downtown Los Angeles. I came up with the name as a play on "Gorgeous George," a male wrestler from decades ago. People come in wanting to talk to George, but George is actually our last name: Chris (that's me), Richard, and Meg George. It's always amusing to watch Meg explain how the apostrophe placement in the name indicates more than one George. For two reasons. First, she's actually quite bright, but many people seem to believe that there's a negative correlation between brain-size and breast-size, and Meg takes unabashed advantage by using a little-girl voice. And second, of course, most people looking for jewelry aren't paying attention to apostrophes.

With Meg behind the counter, women find their husbands less reluctant to enter the store, while the men try as hard as they can to look Meg in the eye while she's talking. The men buy their wives nicer things than they would otherwise, because they feel a little guilty for enjoying the view, and maybe because they're trying to impress Georges' Gorgeous salesgirl to boot. And while Meg is an eyeful, and mildly flirtatious, she never seriously hits on the husbands. Also for two reasons. First, because annoying the wives would seriously cut down on business and second, because Richard keeps a shotgun and two pistols hidden at different places around the store, each loaded for bear. He's very protective of his assets and he has a jealous side that you don't want to know about. I was reminded of this as I looked again at his wife passed out and naked on my bed. Richard just might kill somebody over his wife's honor some day. I'd just as soon it wasn't his own brother.

My part of GGG is to design and fabricate a lot of the jewelry. A three-bedroom condo sounds pretty large for a single guy, but one of the bedrooms is my jewelry-creation workshop, one bedroom is my office, and one bedroom is my bedroom.

I never planned on being a jewelry designer. I'd always been a hotshot baseball player and it got me a scholarship to UCLA. I figured out in my sophomore year, however, that I'd never make it in the pros. An outfielder hitting 260 in college ball and possessing average-at-best speed, power, throwing for distance, and throwing for accuracy would never make the pro scouts drool. I had to be damned good to receive and keep a scholarship to a major university in the first place, but I was nowhere close to being good enough to move on to the next level. Still, I had an athlete's body, my daddy's good looks, and a full scholarship, so I didn't have to worry about money or female companionship. Once my dream of being a rich and famous ballplayer dried up, I basically majored in getting laid. I might not have been pro material or a star academically; I also didn't have much direction, but I was very successful at not sleeping by myself.

Richard is a year older than me. He was also a student at UCLA when and where he met and fell in love with Margaret "Meg" Herman. Meg's father, Isaiah "Ike" Herman, is a successful jeweler in the San Fernando Valley who wants to eventually pass on the family business to his only child. Sweet voluptuous spoiled-rotten Meg.

Ike's dictum was that if Meg wanted to inherit, she and whoever she married would have to get four-year college degrees first, then some accreditations from the Gemological Institute of America. The GIA, a school based in Carlsbad, California, teaches people all sorts of things about jewelry—design, production, evaluation, selling, whatever. Ike would pay for all of Meg and company's education, but it had to be done. To Richard this was a no-brainer. Marry a wet-T-shirt-contest winner, become a millionaire, and live happily ever after.

Richard and I thought it'd be cool if I got a piece of the windfall too. Not including Meg, of course. Richard and I had both "shared" Rosalind not too long before Meg and we almost ended up killing each other. It brought out the monster hiding within Richard. I didn't need it spelled out for me any clearer than that, and that was before he started buying guns.

Ike had accepted me into his family more easily than Richard, so it was no problem convincing Ike that it'd be better if Richard and I were partners. So Ike paid for my GIA classes too. My bachelor's degree was in geography, which was rather useless since I didn't want to be a travel agent or a geography teacher, but it was the easiest major to complete at the time that Ike agreed to finance my future.

At the GIA, Richard specialized in retail sales and I took classes in gemstone cutting, jewelry design, and jewelry fabrication. Then Ike gave us a $250,000 deferred-payment loan to start the business, with a promise that if Richard and Meg were still married in ten years, the loan would be forgiven. Not many wedding presents are designed to be shared equally with the best man, but this one qualified.

And speaking of the blushing bride, I heard her in the bathroom. Country music was coming from my workshop, and since radios don't usually turn themselves on by themselves, she probably figured out I was there. I was hoping she decided to put something on before she came in.

Technically, I got what I hoped for. She had on see-through lacy thong panties and nothing else. Her nipples, I noticed without meaning to, were hard. Uh oh. This could be awkward.

"Hey, Chris. I'm lonely. Richard works too hard and travels too much. What do you think I should do about it?" She was using her little-girl voice. I had to admit it was damn sexy.

"Meg, you look tastier than Rum Raisin Häagen-Dazs ice cream and that's as tasty as it gets. But I can't do it."

"Why not?" she said, daring me. "Are you afraid?"

"Damn straight. Richard's my brother, my partner, owns big guns, and knows how to use them."

"He'd never find out from me. Would you tell him?" she teased.

"Of course not, because there'll be nothing to tell. My dick says yes yes yes, but the rest of me is running for cover."

She put her arms around me. "How 'bout just a few kisses then? Wet ones. And you can touch me wherever you like. I know you've wanted to for a long time."

I removed her arms, gently but with intention, and eased her away. "Please, Meg. This could jeopardize the rest of our lives. Why don't you get dressed, then pour yourself the rest of the wine and bring me some water from the cooler? There's something I want to talk to you about."

Meg went out quietly enough. I was relieved at the reprieve. I needed neither a wrestling match nor a weepy woman on my hands. And the truth is I'd never seriously lusted after Meg or her mammaries. They reminded me more of udders than anything sexy. Maybe if I'd been raised on a farm, they'd be more attractive.

Besides, seeing them up close today more than satisfied any curiosity I ever had. Even so, explaining any of this to her or pissing her off in any other way wouldn't improve my life at all. I'd try to finesse it. Maybe I'd luck out.

In the meantime, I needed to think of something to talk to her about.

She returned, dressed, looking more embarassed about being caught trying to cheat on her husband than angry about being rejected. She handed me a glass of water.

"Take a Jacuzzi today?" I temporized, not really knowing what to say. She nodded. My condo is equipped with a good-sized tub with jet nozzles and the whole works. She and Richard don't have such a tub and she likes the relaxation. In the two and a half years I'd lived here since Paula and I sold our house, Meg's taken several soaks, whether I was home or not. We've never told Richard she did this.

"I've started taking a dance class," I told her. "It's called West Coast Swing and it's a lot harder than I expected. I'm pretty much over moping about Paula and ready to enjoy being a bachelor again. I figure I'll enjoy life more once I find a steady girl, and maybe dancing will help me meet somebody interesting."

"You've always been a bachelor," Meg replied, slightly annoyed. I think Meg, like many married women, felt that any man going through life as a bachelor was getting off too easily. Which is why she'd tried to fix me up a few times.

"Yes and no. For fourteen years with Paula, I was perfectly monogamous. Our relationship lasted longer than many marriages. In many ways, our breakup was as painful as a divorce."

"You never told me much about why you two broke up. Tell me now and I'll keep my distance." She grinned sheepishly, which was as close to an apology as I was likely to get out of her. And while I'd never been much for sharing my personal life with Meg, if I could get out of this predicament with a few minutes of conversation, that'd be cheap enough.

"It's never one thing or one person's fault, but we argued a lot about gambling. As you know, I like to play blackjack."

She nodded as I continued. "On the second shelf over there you can see ten books or so. I've read every one and I'm a pretty good player. Sometimes I win and sometimes I lose, but overall I'm about even or a little ahead. Paula said I was quite a bit behind and she was scared about it."

"Scared? In what way?" Meg asked. "Were you gambling for a lot of money?"

"Not really, but it grew over time. When I started, I'd bet $3 a hand. Just before Paula and I called it quits, I was betting between $10 and $25 a hand. As you know, I was clearing close to a hundred grand a year and my share of the business is worth a bundle. Plus, we owned our own house free and clear. So, relatively speaking, I figured that $25 a hand was pretty modest."

"Betting $25 a hand doesn't sound like too much to me," Meg agreed, as if her opinion on this matter had relevance.

"Paula believed that anyone who went to Vegas more than four times a year was a compulsive gambler. And compulsive gamblers end up going through all of their own assets, and the assets of their loved ones, and everyone dies broke."

"So that's why you never married? Because she thought she'd end up broke?"

I ignored Meg's comment. "Whenever I tried to show her the sections in the books that explained how what I was doing was making me an actual favorite over the casino, she dismissed it all as a ploy designed to sell books. She didn't believe that anyone could end up beating the casinos."

"She's right that the casinos didn't get to be so big because they paid off a lot of winners."

"That's true. Most people *do* lose. But there's a huge difference between casinos winning off *most* players and casinos winning off *all* players," I replied. "There's considerable skill involved and most people don't have it."

"Poor baby," Meg said. "Your relationship was doomed."

"One nice thing about gambling in Vegas," I continued, "is they give you free stuff like rooms, meals, and shows. It's a lot more fun to share this with somebody. Hopefully, I'll meet someone sooner or later who appreciates this kind of a vacation."

"Sounds good to me," Meg said coyly. "I'll go with you."

"That'd be fine," I said, choosing to take her words at face value and ignore the not-too-subtle flirtation, "as long as the trip includes Richard. But still, I'd be looking for someone to make our threesome into a foursome."

"I bet you would. Do you need to practice your West Swing Coast, or whatever it was? I'd be happy to work on it with you."

I could use the practice, but this had way too much potential for her to get amorous again. "I'd love to, Meg, but I've got to get some stones cut. I promised Richard I'd have three new pieces before we open up on Wednesday."

"Okay. Well, I have to run. Thanks for the wine and the chat." Apparently, she had no more use for me today, now that her Plan A didn't work and I turned down her Plan B too. I didn't want to think about her Plan C.

"Bye, Meg. Catch you around."

I thought of several double entendres. "It was nice seeing you." Or, "Something was different about you today and I can't quite put my finger on it." But I decided to let well enough alone and allowed her to just leave.

Thursday
December 2, 1999

I've been devoted to physical fitness since I was quite young. This commitment has rewarded me immensely. It got me a scholarship to college, as much success with the ladies as a guy could want, and likely better health and a longer life thrown in. Eighteen years after I played my last game of college ball, I'm still at the gym more than twice a week.

My workout schedule varied. I liked to get my aerobics by hiking in the hills on weekends. Recently, I'd been taking a Body Pump class at the gym. This was an hour of working on one specific body part for five minutes at a time. For example, to exercise the biceps, we'd usually do about 150 curls. We'd hold a barbell in front of us, arms extended downward, palms forward, then lift the barbell by bending at the elbow. You could do full curls, bottom half only, top half only, and the same mix with a reverse, wider, or narrower grip. The instructor called out the sequence in time with the music and everyone in class performed the routine simultaneously. The barbell itself weighs 10 or 11 pounds, and there were numerous 11-pound, 5.5-pound, and 2.2-pound weights to put on each end of the bar. Those might sound like odd weight amounts, until you see they're labeled 5, 2.5, and 1 kilograms, respectively.

I usually liked to attend the 10 a.m. classes, which tended to be less crowded. But today, a discussion with Richard about what jewelry he bought in Phoenix while he was gone prevented me from going to the early class. So I took the 5 p.m. class instead. It's more crowded and you have to arrive early before they run out of weights, but since it was the only class that fit into my schedule, I took it.

Today's class was tough. I added 4.4 pounds during both the chest presses and the squats. Might not sound like much, but when you're already close to your personal maximum and you do it 150 times for each exercise, it added up. After the class ended, I set about putting my weights away, but I was dragging. I'd left all of my energy in the classroom—which is the name of the game if you want results.

The "bench" we use for the bench presses is the same one they use for the step class. Before I could put mine away, a pretty redheaded lady asked me to leave it where it was; she intended to use it for the step class that would begin next. "Fine with me," I muttered tiredly.

I then realized that I'd seen her before. "Don't you drive a tan BMW?" I asked. "I think we live in the same condo complex."

"No way! Mine's not tan," she replied with a laugh. "If it was called tan it would have been two thousand dollars cheaper. Mine is called Kalahari Beige Metallic. And you drive an off-white Lexus, don't you?"

"Nope. Mine's Alabaster Metallic and an extra two grand for the paint color sounds about right." I returned the chuckle. "My name's Chris. Hope you have a good workout."

"Thank you. I'm Annie. See you around."

As tired as I was, I noticed she was beautiful in a wholesome sort of a way. About the right age relative to me for dating purposes, trim figure, and no ring on the fourth finger left hand. But the way she spontaneously laughed when we were talking about car colors made her truly irresistible. I'd had way too many women when I was younger to believe in love at first sight, but this lady sent sizzles that I hadn't experienced for at least 20 years. It'd be far-fetched to believe that Annie wouldn't have a boyfriend if she wanted one, but until I knew for sure, I could hope. I had to find out more about her, somehow. But it couldn't happen today. I was already out of the exercise room and the step class was about to begin.

I went into the locker room and put on a different colored shirt. I sat down on a stationary bicycle, several rows deep among the exercise equipment that faced the glassed-in exercise room, and began to pedal slowly. I didn't need any more exercise. I wanted to watch Annie while she didn't know she was being watched—also the reason I changed shirts to complete my "disguise."

Some ladies really dress up for exercise class. They invest in numerous different, color-coordinated, Spandex outfits—frequently in bright colors. They're there to be seen—perhaps using the gym as a singles club. Annie, on the other hand, dressed in thigh-length navy shorts and a pale-blue tank top. Both probably cotton. Appropriate for an exercise class, clean and pressed, but designed for functionality rather than appearance. She performed the routines precisely, attempting to do each exercise the way it was designed.

I watched for 10 minutes, then left. When I got home, I found an old John Denver CD and set it to play "Annie's Song" over and over and over again. "You fill up my senses like a night in the forest." Whoa! Could I be a goner already?

Monday
December 6, 1999

The 6:30 p.m. Friday class, the day after I first spoke to Annie, was called kick boxing. I showed up and looked around for her. She wasn't there, but I took the class anyway. The Saturday 6:30 class was called medium impact aerobics. I tried it again. No Annie. The next night, Sunday, there were no evening classes, and today, Monday, at 6:30 they had advanced step and sure enough, Annie showed up for a workout. "Hey Annie Kalamazoo Beige," I called out.

It was just a simple line, but I was proud of it. When she originally told me "Kalahari Beige," I knew the name must have been inspired by the Kalahari Desert in southern Africa. My Geography major was finally good for something! Attempting to be clever, I debated whether "Kalamazoo Beige" or "Cowabunga Beige" was funnier. I kept going back and forth, and Kalamazoo was what finally came out.

She laughed again. I was re-smitten. "Hey Chris Are-You-A-Bastard metallic." We both grinned. This was great. She remembered my name, but holy shit! She instantly came up with the perfect rejoinder to a line I'd practiced for three days. I've always admired the combination of beauty and brains, but this lady seemed to measure off the charts in both categories.

I positioned my step on the other side of the room from Annie's. The way you rotate around the step, you can observe the moves of anyone else in the class at least part of the time. I could tell Annie had taken the class from this teacher enough to recognize her code names for various patterns. For example, "Charlie three" meant to do what other teachers call the "Charleston" pattern three times in a row. I never did figure out "around the world with a hitch" completely. For the most part it didn't matter. You kept moving, got your heart rate up, and did the best you could.

As we left the class, I confessed the truth to Annie, primarily because she probably already knew. "I haven't taken much step before."

"I could tell. Did you like it?"

"I could take it or leave it. The real reason I'm here is because I enjoyed your laugh so much the other day that I was hoping to run into you again so I could invite you to join me for a drink or a snack. Maybe you'll laugh again."

Annie looked at me without speaking for 15 seconds, which was 10 seconds too long. My heart sank. "Tonight's totally out, because I have to go back to the office. And I should warn you I rarely go out on dates."

"Why not?"

"The whole dating scene generally bores me."

My disappointment showed, and so, I imagine, did my surprise. A beautiful girl like this who didn't date? Too boring? I wondered what the real reason was. And then I realized that if she had a husband or boyfriend, she would have phrased it differently than "rarely go out." That meant that with a little perseverance, I might have a chance. God! I'd only spoken to her for a minute and was already on an emotional roller coaster. And then she surprised me again.

"However, I recently made a resolution to try to get to know some of my neighbors. While this isn't exactly what I envisioned, perhaps we can let that slide on account of the fact that you almost killed yourself in class just now to see me again. Does dinner on Friday interest you? Strictly as a Dutch-treat neighborly visit?"

"Is the Pope Catholic? Do you have a place in mind, or should I choose?" I asked.

"Choose away."

"Nick's, on National east of Sepulveda. Do you know it?"

"That's a fine choice," Annie announced. "Does seven o'clock work for you?"

"It's a date!" I responded, and then caught myself and added with a smile, "what I mean is, it's a neighborly visit."

"Very good," she smiled back. "And I'll be here Thursday night at six-thirty. And at Nick's on Friday. I'll be coming from work, where we dress pretty casual, so don't knock yourself out."

"I've never really thought about what I should wear when trying to impress a neighbor. I'll work something out."

She rewarded me with one more laugh and was gone.

Tuesday
December 7, 1999

"We've received an offer to buy the business," Richard told me as he and Meg sat on the couch in my living room while I was in the chair I usually used for reading. "I think it's worthy of consideration."

"Tell me more," I said.

"For $750,000 cash, George Miamoto will buy the lease, the store fixtures, the name, and the customer database. He'll choose the inventory he wants to keep and pay us wholesale. We agree not to open up another jewelry store within ten miles for three years."

"He'll have to move the apostrophe from behind the 's' to in front of it, of course," Meg added, fixing me with a sparkling gaze that put me immediately off guard. I wished she'd tone it down when Richard's trigger finger was nearby.

"What about the equipment in my workshop here?" I asked, keeping my voice level.

"He doesn't know about that and it isn't included." Richard so far seemed unaware of Meg's innuendos. "We'll need to put a value on it and it'll affect the split between the three of us, which as we all know is one third apiece."

"'Among' the three of us," Meg corrected. As was normal for them, when Meg corrected Richard's English, he scowled, and when Richard scowled, I always preferred to be elsewhere.

"Our books show we have a half-million in inventory. Can we actually get that?" I asked.

"I think so," Richard estimated, "but you never know until you actually try. I figure each of the three shares is worth four hundred grand, give or take. I've been tired of the jewelry business for a long time. My degree is in education. I want to give teaching a try."

"I know you've hated the store. How do you feel about this, Meg?"

"I've got mixed feelings. I like selling jewelry and I'm good at it and I know a lot of the customers. I think Miamoto will find that without me, the sales figures will drop dramatically." She had her hands behind her head with her elbows thrust back, stretching the front of her bright red sweater. I wasn't sure whether she was teasing me again or just emphasizing that her sexiness was a major asset for the store. The net effect of her actions was to make me uncomfortable. Fortunately, Richard remained oblivious to his wife's behavior.

"Are you interested in seeing if Miamoto wants to hire you as a sales person or manager or something?" I asked.

"No. If I were still there, people would think it's the same store. They'd expect the same discounts we've given them and to fix stuff for free that they bought six years ago. You must have fixed Sophie Stein's pin ten times."

"Besides, if Miamoto had to honor such implicit guarantees, he'd want to pay a lower price," Richard observed.

"Right. Also, Daddy is sixty-eight and wants to slow down. He's been bugging me to come run his store. So I'll still have a job doing what I like. Richard will be happier and Daddy will be delighted. That only leaves you to consider, Chris. How does this strike you?"

Her head was turned so Richard couldn't see her face, but I could. She slowly ran the tip of her tongue full-circle around her lips.

"Basically as a big surprise," I said trying to keep my cool. "I didn't know you were seriously looking for buyers. I'm sure I'll be fine, although I haven't really thought about my options yet. At age 39, I'm not quite ready to retire."

"No reason you'd have to," Richard said. "What you do is primarily in your workshop. GGG is a major outlet for you, but not the only one, and not irreplaceable."

"I agree. I sell about half of my output at GGG, but it shouldn't be too hard to find other stores to carry what I can make."

"I can help you take your stuff around to other stores until you find enough buyers," Richard offered.

"Actually, I've been thinking of getting out of L.A. anyway. Someplace hot. Maybe Palm Springs or Phoenix. I don't know yet. I'm good at what I do and I can create a home-workshop setup anywhere. I can sell things on eBay. In the meantime, I'll have plenty of cash so I can take time off if I want." I suppose I had talked myself into it.

"It sounds like we're in agreement," said Richard. "The question now is whether to accept the current offer or to counter for an extra hundred thousand. Extra money would be nice, even split three ways, but chasing him away risks getting our tits caught in the wringer."

I noticed Meg cringe at Richard's language. He'd never been a guy to mince words or worry about what would be a politically correct way to say something. I'd heard him ask more than one guy we knew whether or not their wives gave head! Meg was disgusted by this side of Richard, but bringing it up again wouldn't do any good.

"I don't have strong feelings about it," I said. "If Meg thinks we should go for more, I'll let the two of you explain to me why and I'll vote one way or the other. But if Meg agrees with you, or doesn't care, we might as well make it unanimous."

Meg shrugged, which I took to mean that she and Richard were on the same page before they got here.

"Then I take it that means we contact a lawyer and accept the current bid."

They both nodded.

"By the way, Meg," I continued. "Your father gave us seed money for the business. Does he figure he's entitled to any part of the sales price?"

"Nope. Daddy said it's all going to come to Richard

and me anyway. And, probably, to you too because you're his favorite. As far as he's concerned, since Richard and I are still married, we've paid back the loan."

"What kind of earnest money did Miamoto put up with his offer?" I asked. When Richard shook his head, indicating this wasn't included, I continued, "I think we should get at least fifty thousand as a non-refundable deposit once we go into escrow. If he's serious, that shouldn't be a problem. And if he's not serious, we don't want to mess with him."

Richard wrote a note. "Good point. I'll discuss with our lawyer the best way to do that."

"Make sure you let me see the lawyer's contract before you send it to Miamoto," I requested. "I'm still in a bit of shock at the idea of no more GGG. I'll probably come around in a few days, but I need a least a little time to organize my thoughts. Okay?"

"I'll bring the papers by as soon as they're ready," Meg promised, with a smile full of a promise I didn't want. It occurred to me then that living in a different city from Meg might prolong my life. Let her trap some other guy in her web. I knew she'd never trap me, but I could never know if Richard would be so certain of that.

Thursday
December 9, 1999

Ike took my bishop with his pawn and announced, "Mate in two."

I studied the position for two minutes. Ike's pronouncements were frequently unreliable, but this time he had me. Two moves earlier he'd uncovered a flaw in a trap I thought I'd set for him. My "inspired" sacrifice had been shown to be unsound. I reached over and toppled my king—conceding. "You're the better man today, Ike. Congratulations."

Ike and I played chess together once a month or so. It had been what he liked to call a tradition since Meg and Richard married. Neither of us was a very good player, but we were approximately equally bad. I'd sort of adopted him as a father figure, since I had no parents of my own. We alternated locations. Tonight was at my condo, so we ate the Jewish deli that Ike brought. Next time would be at his home and I'd take over some Chinese, probably. Sometimes I'd bring some other sort of food for variety, but whatever it was, we'd eat while we played two out of three games. Tonight Ike won the first two, so we didn't play a third.

Ike beamed. He frequently lamented that his memory wasn't what it used to be and he took each chess victory as an affirmation that he hadn't lost all of his mental marbles just yet. At the same time, he was always gracious in defeat. He loved me like a son and I suspect that he wished that I was the one Meg married, rather than Richard.

"Do you think we're getting a good price for the store?" I asked him.

"Probably," he answered with a shrug, "but who knows

for sure? Jewelry stores, like pieces of jewelry themselves, sometimes create a lot of emotion. Somebody falls in love with a place, there's no telling what they'll pay. At least this way, the offer came to you and you don't owe a commission to a broker for finding a buyer."

"Are you sad that Richard is getting out of the jewelry business?"

"A little," he replied, "but he has to live his own life. My dreams included lots of grandchildren, even from you and Paula would have been okay, but it never happened. At least it hasn't yet. I don't think any guy could be good enough for my Meg, especially a *goy*, but they've been together a long time. All in all she has a pretty good life, so how can I complain?"

Friday
December 10, 1999

I made reservations for 7. I was dressed in a navy blazer over a red silk T-shirt, tan slacks, and dark-brown freshly polished shoes. It was my sharpest "casual" outfit. Dressing well was the first step in my newly created Good Neighbor Policy.

Annie showed up in blue jeans and a well-worn Ohio State University sweatshirt. She saw me and frowned, "I told you we dress casually where I work."

I beamed at her and said, "You look wonderful to me. Let's eat."

After we were seated at a table, we ordered a glass of wine each and told the waitress, who identified herself as Heather, that we needed time to study the menu.

Meanwhile, Annie started to fill me in about herself. She told me she worked at the Rand Corporation in Santa Monica. I'd heard of it, of course. It's a world-famous think tank where brilliant minds do all sorts of research projects. "I can tell you I work with computers," she explained, "but I can't be more specific than that. Unless, of course, you have the suitable security clearance and a demonstrable need to know."

"Reminds me of the magician who, when asked to explain a trick, tells the crowd, 'I could tell you, but then I'd have to kill you.' The audience always laughs at this, and then some plant in the audience yells, 'Tell my wife!'"

"That's cute," Annie said, "and I wouldn't want to have to kill you. My work is challenging, I set my own hours for the most part as long as I meet deadlines, and I love it. What kind of work do you do?"

"I was a jock in college and didn't get serious about studying until someone promised me a lucrative future.

My brother, his wife, and I are equal partners in the jewelry business, which happened after his father-in-law agreed to pay for us to get as many GIA accreditations as we wanted, as long as we graduated college first."

"What's GIA?" she asked. "It sounds like one of the acronyms we have floating around at work all the time."

"It's the Gemological Institute of America," I answered. "Probably the most famous school on gemology in the world. They teach you how to design, create, sell, and repair jewelry."

"I've never heard of a college for jewelers," Annie remarked, "but it makes sense."

"Richard runs the retail store, his wife is the chief salesman, and I cut stones and make pieces in a workshop in one of the bedrooms of my condo. And, like you, I get to set my own hours as long as I meet deadlines."

"That's one of the best things about my job," Annie concurred.

"Recently, I've started to sell jewelry over the Internet on a new site called eBay. I've been doing quite well."

"Interesting," Annie said. "How long have you lived in Pacifica Terrace View?"

"About two and a half years. I moved there after an almost-divorce and took a three-year lease. I haven't decided yet whether to renew or move somewhere else."

At this point, Heather came by and asked if we were ready to order. Although I'd eaten at Nick's enough to be able to pick easily, Annie hadn't opened her menu. "Tell us again what your specials are," I requested, and Heather described the halibut, the osso bucco, and a steak-lobster combination.

"I'm going to order the halibut," I told Annie, but of course Heather heard too. "If you want to take more time with the menu, I'm in no hurry."

"Actually the halibut sounds good to me too."

Heather asked the obligatory "soup or salad?" and the "baked potato or rice pilaf?" questions, then left. Despite the interruption, Annie picked up the conversation right where we left it.

"What's an almost-divorce?"

"Paula and I never married, although we lived together for twelve years. We segregated our finances into hers, mine, and ours categories, because she had a considerable trust fund over which she was very protective. That was fine with me. We both worked, and the jewelry business generated plenty, eventually."

"Why'd you split up?" Annie asked.

"I liked to go to Vegas every few months, while Paula saw it as highly irresponsible to gamble at all. My biggest loss ever in Vegas was three thousand and it was my money."

"That doesn't sound like so much," Annie commented, surprising me a little, "for an occasional vacation. Some hobbies cost more than that."

"And it wasn't always losses. I had lots of winning trips, but Paula saw gambling as a progressive disease. She believed that if we got married and I got access to her trust fund, I'd gamble it all away and she'd be left penniless. She was super-vigilant making sure that never happened."

"Was giving up going to Vegas an option to keep the almost-marriage going?"

"If I thought that would've helped, I'd have considered it. I'm not saying for sure I would have done it, but I would've at least thought long and hard about it. But she and I never agreed on money. She was weird."

"What do you mean?" Annie asked. "Give me a for instance."

"This sports coat, for example, was one of my last clothing purchases while we were together. It cost $240, and I could easily afford it. She told me I could've gotten a sports coat for a lot less. I agreed, but this one fit me very well and I thought it looked sharp."

"It does look nice," Annie agreed, "and $240 doesn't sound outrageous."

"Sometimes she'd snap at me if I spent a buck-forty-nine a pound for Gala apples when you could buy Red Delicious for ninety-nine cents. It didn't matter to her that I thought that Galas tasted better."

"So that's why you split up? Apples?"

I smiled. "That, and other stuff too."

Annie looked at me, waiting to hear about the other stuff, which I didn't feel like explaining. We were just neighbors, after all, and I'd have reminded her of it if she inquired further. But she just asked, "Are you still in contact with her?"

"Sort of. It was an amicable almost-divorce, I suppose. She's with another guy now and she still calls up and asks for a discount on jewelry periodically, but that's the extent of the relationship."

"How'd you talk her into the Lexus?" Annie asked with a smile. "Couldn't she find a Yugo in a color she liked?"

"I bought the Lexus immediately after she left, sort of like a release valve."

Heather brought the fish and took away the salad plates.

"Now, your turn, neighbor. How long have you been at Pacifica?"

"About two years, and there was nothing 'almost' about my divorce. I married Tony Ferrari right after I received my masters at OSU while he was getting his MBA. His father owns the Ferrari Furniture stores. Have you heard of them?"

"You mean the 'Elegant furniture for persons with taste' store?" I echoed the frequent television ad.

Annie laughed. "Ah, so you've seen the commercials."

"Sure, who hasn't? Exquisite furniture, beautiful people, and often a Ferrari sports car in the background. Are the two companies really related?"

She snorted. "They claim to be, but I think it's all hokum. Anyway, Tony started out running the Westchester store, then opened new ones in Pacific Palisades and Brentwood."

"My turn to ask the indelicate question. What led to the nothing-almost-about-it divorce?"

"One day I stopped into one of the stores unannounced, something I virtually never did, and discovered Tony and his big-boobed bimbo of a secretary enjoying some afternoon delight in his office. I had, and have, zero tolerance for that sort of thing."

I started to say that I did too, but I could see by the set of her jaw that my opinion was totally irrelevant in this matter.

"I saw my lawyer the same afternoon. Tony claimed that it was all a misunderstanding. That it wasn't what it looked like at all."

"Did he have any interesting explanation for what it really was?"

"Don't know. There was no way I'd believe anything he said over what I saw with my own eyes. I never went back to our house other than one time to oversee the movers packing my things."

"I see," I said, although I didn't really. Misunderstandings have been known to happen. I had a flashback to the afternoon when Meg threw herself at me. What if Richard had come in then? Would he really believe that the only touching that took place was me pushing her away? But there was no percentage in me arguing with her about it.

"He kept the house and the stock in the company, and gave me a cash settlement. My attorney said I could get more if we went to court, but friends told me that a drawn-out divorce usually only benefits the lawyers. One reason I don't date much is I think that most guys will cheat on a woman eventually."

I got that message loud and clear. This woman was still hurting from two-year-old pain. Attempting to defend my gender would keep the conversation heavy, which wouldn't get me anywhere I wanted to go. I was about to change the subject, but she did first.

"I'm curious, and I don't want to put you on the spot, but what can you tell me about this ring?" Annie slipped what appeared to be an engagement ring off her fourth-finger, right hand. "I've never had it appraised, and I've always suspected that Tony bought a cheap one."

I took the ring, blew on it, and hedged. "Well, the light here isn't the greatest, and I don't have a loupe with me."

"What's a loupe?"

"A type of magnifying glass used by jewelers. I have a hand-held ten-power loupe, which is the standard for evaluating diamonds, but it's sitting on my workbench."

"Why'd you blow on the ring?"

"To see if it was a diamond or cubic zirconium. If the condensation doesn't disappear almost immediately, you have a CZ. This stone is a genuine diamond," I concluded, handing it back.

"Is it a good one?"

"The size is probably two carats."

"How do you know?"

"Experience mostly. You can't evaluate the carat weight precisely unless you remove it from the setting. I'm evaluating it mostly by size. A one-carat diamond has a diameter of about 6.5 millimeters, while a two-carat diamond has a diameter of a little more than 8 millimeters. Since I measure stones all the time, I can eyeball it pretty closely."

"How about the quality of the stone?"

"I can't precisely judge the perfection of the stone, but it's not bad. If it had big inclusions or was cloudy or yellow, I'd be able to see that, even in this light and with no loupe. The setting is simple, but that's acceptable for a diamond solitaire. That ring likely cost over $5,000 wholesale."

"Oh," she said quietly, lost in thought. "I'm surprised."

"Tony may have misbehaved at the end of the marriage, but he didn't skimp at the beginning."

So far this discussion wasn't going the way I'd hoped. I'd hoped for a light moment before I sprung the real question of the evening, but light moments seemed scarce just now. I plunged ahead anyway. "Do you like to dance?"

"Dancing is a skill I always wanted to have, but I was never with a guy who wanted to do it with me. Why do you ask?"

Before I could answer, Heather came by and asked if we were finished eating. I'd pretty well cleaned my plate and Annie had eaten slightly more than half of hers. No surprise, really. Annie was probably 5'2" and couldn't weigh much more than a hundred pounds. No way could she stay that size if she ate full portions at restaurants. Neither of us wanted dessert, but I ordered coffee and Annie asked for hot water with lemon.

"I'm just about finished with a six-week class in beginning West Coast Swing. I'd learn better if I had a practice partner. Perhaps one who lived in the neighborhood."

Annie smiled warily. She had been talking not too long ago about guys being deceitful, so I could imagine she was suspicious. "That's probably true. Go on."

"Well, if this neighbor practiced for an hour or two with me, then took the last class in the first beginner series this coming Tuesday, she could decide whether it might be worthwhile to sign up for the second beginner series, which starts the following week, also on Tuesday. With a little between-class practice, she and I would develop some dance skills."

"That sounds nice for you, assuming you could find the right neighbor," Annie admitted with a grin, finally warming up again. "But do you think the neighbor would get enough out of it to make it worth her while?"

"Well, I wouldn't bring this up unless I believed that both the neighbor and I might agree we had some potential together after the six-week series. I'd promise not to press her for any decision involving romance until the series was over."

"A real honest-to-goodness promise?"

"Oh yes. I'm a real Boy Scout when it comes to trust." I lifted my right hand and gave scouting's three-fingered "On My Honor" sign. "That'd give her an almost two-month feeling-out period before she had to decide whether she wanted to beat off my advances or not. My guess is that neighbor could collect a lot of information in seven weeks of classes, including driving back and forth, and seven practice sessions. And, if at any time either one of us decided we didn't want to progress to being more than neighbors at dance class, at least we'd both have learned some dance steps in the process."

Annie smiled, but she didn't say anything.

"Of course," I kept the pitch going since we were both enjoying this, "should this neighbor decide she couldn't keep her hands off me and wanted to up the stakes before the series was over, I'd be willing to consider that if and when it happened."

"If and when, indeed," Annie laughed. God, I loved that laugh. "As a programmer, I appreciate the need to handle all contingencies when you're laying out a proposition. Is this dance class very expensive?"

"Not really. It's ten bucks for an individual class and forty if you sign up for a six-week series. I'd insist on paying for the first class, and then the neighbor could decide whether she'd feel more comfortable being my guest for the series or paying for it herself. It'd be well worth the extra forty dollars to be able to practice what I learned."

Just then, Heather presented the bill. "Speaking of money, I was serious about tonight being Dutch treat. How much do I owe?" she asked.

"It's forty-nine sixty-two before the tip. How does thirty apiece sound to you?"

"Perfect," she said, then reached into her wallet and extracted a $10 and a $20. "And just how did you plan on deciding which neighbor to introduce to West Coast Swing?"

"My first choice by far would be one with red hair, green eyes, and an infectious laugh, if I ever could find one like that."

"On the off chance that you're referring to me, let me commit now to practicing for a few hours this coming Sunday night and attending the class on Tuesday. On the drive home from that class, I'll let you know whether it feels comfortable to sign up for a six-week series. How's that sound?"

"Like I've died and gone to heaven. In a neighborly sort of way."

Tuesday
December 14, 1999

The class was in Bellflower at a place called Swingtime Dance Studio, which was a 45-minute drive down the 405 to get there by the seven o'clock class because rush hour lasts late. Bellflower was in the southeast corner of Los Angeles County. Greater Los Angeles is *huge*, and crisscrossed by never-ending freeways, most of which are busy at least some of the time. It would become a half-hour drive for the class starting next week at 8:30. Traffic was a constant consideration when you lived in the Los Angeles basin, and a major reason I was considering leaving town.

Annie and I practiced what I'd shown her Sunday evening to the warm-up music prior to class. The teacher, Michele Adams, greeted Annie. "It's not often we get new blood the last week of a series, but there are more guys than gals here and we can use a lady. You're a little behind the others, but you should be able to catch up in a few weeks if you and Chris practice together. It'll help his dancing too." A friendly greeting, and I was glad for the encouragement that we should practice together.

On this night there were ten men and nine women. To start with, we partnered up and placed ourselves in a sort of a square around the room. I started with Annie, of course, and this left one man solo. After six minutes, Michele said, "Ladies down one," and all the women rotated clockwise to the next guy. Every five minutes or so, we rotated again. Over time all the men got to dance with all the women.

In this particular class, we learned a new sugar push, a move where the man pulls the woman in to him, then pushes her away while still holding on. It might sound simple, but Michele spoke about tension in the arms, hand grip, foot pattern, shifting your weight, posture, and a few other things as well. Most of the class had heard this at least once or twice before, but it was all new to Annie, who desperately tried to take it in.

At the break I asked Annie how it was going for her.

"I'm amazed at how complicated this is. There's *so much* to remember. I'm used to being one of the smarter ones in class, but here I'm struggling."

"This is the sixth week. Almost every other person here has been through five of Michele's classes before. There's a lot of repetition. Anything you don't get tonight she'll cover again next week. And even if you understand some of these steps perfectly tonight, she'll cover them next week too, because somebody else won't have gotten it."

Annie smiled grimly, not quite convinced.

I continued, "My theory is that anyone who can figure out what 'around the world with a hitch' means in an advanced step class ought to have a leg up, pardon the pun, on everyone else in this class. The important question is are you enjoying yourself?"

"Oh yes. You've got yourself a passenger for the next six Tuesdays. Congratulations."

"Wonderful. That's all I want for Christmas."

On the drive home, Annie asked me if I had plans for Christmas, "since you brought it up." I told her I usually just exchanged gifts with Richard, his wife Meg, and Meg's father Ike, but sometimes that happened on Christmas Day and sometimes it didn't. We used to celebrate Hannukah when Ike's wife Esther was still alive, but now everything happens around Christmas.

"Taking you to Richard's house for Christmas would be making a statement that's premature at this point. But if it's not rainy, Christmas would be a good day for a hike. Care to join me?"

"Let me think about it," she replied. "Does Sunday night at seven still work for you for dance practice?"

"Sure does. And thanks for a wonderful evening, neighbor," I said, giving her hand a little squeeze as I walked her to the door of her condo.

"Same to you, neighbor," she said with a giggle. "And I'll probably go to step on Thursday. Good night."

A good night kiss, or more, would've felt very nice about then. But a deal's a deal. And if I ended up with this girl, waiting an extra six weeks would be small change.

Saturday
December 25, 1999

Annie and I got together Christmas morning to go hiking. I told her I knew all of the trails in the Santa Monica Mountains within 20 miles from our condos and this was what I did instead of step class.

I wore my well-worn hiking boots and carried water, first-aid kit, and lunch for two in my backpack. Annie wore tennis shoes and didn't mind carrying her own water in a daypack that Paula left behind. Wearing something belonging to my "ex" didn't seem to bother her.

We climbed up a trail that actually started in the middle of a housing development in Pacific Palisades. It gained elevation slowly for a few miles while it wound back into the hills. Then there was this killer section where it gained more than a thousand feet in less than a mile. The trail is one-person wide and I led the way up the steep part, non-stop at a good clip. I could hear Annie's breathing behind me, but I didn't turn around. When I reached the summit, I put my pack down and took a rest. She wasn't far behind me, having kept right up.

"Were you showing off or just trying to kill me?" she asked, panting heavily, while shrugging off her own pack and taking a swig of water from the bottle I passed to her.

I grinned. "I was just thinking about that advanced step class I suffered through while trying to meet you and figured it was payback time. You could have asked me to slow down, you know."

"Nope. That would have been admitting that I couldn't keep up. I'm enough of a competitor that it'll take more than a little old hill like this one to make me cry uncle. Does this trail lead anywhere specific, or does it keep going through these hills forever?"

"This particular trail gets us to Topanga Canyon State Park about a mile from here," I told her. "At the park, you can pick up three or four other trails that lead to various places. For today, I'm figuring that the park is a good turnaround place. I go hiking a couple times a month and this one is shorter than average for me, but steeper. Next time, we'll try one of the other trails."

"Sounds good."

At the park, we washed our hands, picked out a picnic table, sat down, and ate lunch. I'm not a chef, but I did pick up two turkey wraps (a sort of sandwich) and some fruit at Trader Joe's, and brought along a half-bottle of wine. It was nice.

"Is the Y2K problem a concern at Rand?" I asked. "And tell me to bug off if you can't talk about it. I'm curious, sort of, but not at the expense of national security."

Annie smiled. "I can answer that without giving any secrets away. We've tested everything more than once and it doesn't appear to be a problem. You never can be sure, though, until it actually happens and everyone else around the world is making their adjustments. Several of the senior programmers who've been there for a long time, including me, are on 24-hour call for the entire time that it switches from 1999 to 2000 anywhere around the globe—which of course happens over 24 hours—and then we have to be available to fix whatever has gone wrong, however long that takes. Most of our research deals with domestic stuff, but some has international implications, so we have to be ready. I need to be within two hours of the office until it's decided that no crisis situation exists."

"You make it sound like it's doubtful that you'll be called in," I concluded.

"We think so and hope so. It's sort of like wearing a seat belt. It probably won't be necessary this time. But in the rare event it *is* necessary, then we're protected by our readiness. I'll probably go in anyway and work on other things. If I have to be tied down, I might as well be productive, so I can take some free time later. The company's good that way. Depending on how much you need to meet with others, you can pretty much set your own hours."

"How much do you need to meet with others?"

"Not a whole lot, usually, but I really can't tell you more than that. Do you have plans for the millennium?" she asked.

"I'm invited to Las Vegas by a casino, but I've heard on the news that Vegas is so sinful it might be an inviting target for terrorists, so I'm staying home. And I'll probably hike up here again if it's not raining. You're invited, of course."

"I'd have to be within distance to get to Rand quickly. Just in case."

"We could take a hike where if we used two cars and left one at each end, we'd always be less than an hour from one of them. Depending on where we were when the call came, you might have to take my car. But I'm willing to trust you. Besides, I know where you live," I said with a grin.

"Silly," she said. "Actually, that might work. Speaking of trust, though, I have some indelicate questions that I wouldn't ask of just a casual neighbor."

"Fire when ready, Gridley," I responded. "Who was Gridley, anyway?"

"That's a discussion for another day," she said seriously, with a similar set of her jaw to what I observed when she explained her divorce. "My questions concern sexual fidelity. Have you ever been sexually unfaithful to a woman?"

Talk about a loaded question! I was on the hot seat and I knew it. "At the risk of sounding Clintonesque, the exact answer to that depends on semantics," I responded mildly.

"That's a load of crap! You either did or you didn't. Which is it?"

"Probably not."

"What kind of answer is that? That's like saying you're a little pregnant."

"Oh no. Not at all. I'll be happy to swear under oath that I've never claimed to be a little pregnant." I was attempting to lighten the mood. It wasn't working.

"Look. You can refuse to answer the question, but don't equivocate. I'm intolerant of lies on this subject."

I took a deep breath and dove in. "Let me try to answer your question. Paula was the first woman I ever made a serious commitment to. And I kept that commitment. So did she, as far as I know. Whatever our problems were, sexual cheating wasn't on the list. Before Paula, however, I was a student in college and there were many different women. I never made such a promise to any of them, although a few times there was a misunderstanding of sorts."

"Misunderstanding?" Annie jumped at the word. "That's a pretty convenient euphemism at times."

"Annie, we're talking about ancient history here," I said quietly. "I wasn't a sexual saint in college. But I made that commitment to Paula in 1984 and she's been the only woman since then."

"Really? There haven't been any since you split up?"

"The reason I haven't had any sexual partners since Paula is because I've been looking for the one. I'm almost forty and my priorities are different than they were as a horny college student. I could've scored plenty if I'd been looking for brief liaisons. But I haven't. I've had maybe five dates in the past few years, but nothing has clicked. Until now. And that's the truth." I stuck out my tongue and blew air noisily over it the way Lily Tomlin would do with her little-girl character, Edith Ann, on the old "Laugh In" television show. I was hoping it would take some of the tension out of the moment.

It did. Annie smiled. But then she got serious again. "That's a good answer. And it sounds truthful. Thank you. It's important to me. Shall we start back now?"

"Sure."

We cleaned up our picnic trash and walked in silence, single-file. The steep section was downhill this way, which is much easier, but it's easy to slip and you have to pay attention. When we got to where we could walk side by side, I said, "For some reason, I'm able to give a lot of trust to at least some people. I trusted Paula completely and it was fine with me if she went out for lunch with former beaus, which she did three or four times over the twelve years."

"Uh huh," Annie said. I wasn't sure if she was listening or lost in thought. This was a complicated woman with some serious pain. I was lost in my own thoughts. Nobody's perfect, but I was seriously wondering whether a relationship with her was worth the effort it would require. But I looked over at her again and decided I wouldn't give up until I knew for sure.

Back at the car, I drove to the nearby Self Realization Fellowship Temple on Sunset near the Pacific Coast Highway. "Ever been here?" I asked and she shook her head. "You're in for a treat."

The Temple is a peaceful place. It was founded years ago by a holy man from India, Paramahansa Yogananda. It contains a good-sized lake surrounded by gardens and places for meditation, along with a bookstore and gift shop. The monks (which might not be the right word) teach classes and hold services. After my breakup with Paula, I took several calming half-hour strolls around the lake. During our walk I took Annie's hand. When she took my hand in both of hers and brought it to her lips for a brief kiss, I started to breathe easier again. It was turning out to be a Merry Christmas after all. We continued to hold hands as we walked slowly along. At the exit, I slipped a $20 into the donation box.

Before we got into the car, Annie took both of my hands in hers and examined them. "Your hands have character. Very strong. Belonging to a working man."

"They've always been valuable tools to me, both in sports and now at work. They're certainly not pretty. I work around sharp tools and stones with edges on them. If you look close, you'll see my hands have hundreds of scars on them."

Annie looked and nodded.

"And I can never get them completely clean. Grinding and polishing gemstones creates gritty, sandy powder—sometimes coarse and sometimes fine. And you use water when you drill or cut, which creates this messy sludge. It gets into the pores after a while, and scrubbing doesn't remove all of it."

"I see," Annie said, observing my right hand closely as I drove with my left. "Are you self-conscious about them?"

"Not for the most part. My hands say who I am and what I do. And I do good work. Still, I was a little hesitant to sign up for dance class, because of my hands. Some women, you know, prefer their men to have smooth white-collar hands instead of rough blue-collar ones. Are you like that?"

"I don't think so. You clean up well, at least when motivated. Whatever our future holds, I don't think your hands will be an issue."

Back in the car I gave Annie a small box. "A little Christmas offering for my favorite neighbor."

Her eyes widened in excitement as she unwrapped the box. Inside were earrings made of green stones with red speckles—dime-sized oval stones hanging by a small gold chain from a dot of the same stone that was attached to the ear stud.

"How lovely and unusual!" she exclaimed. "What kind of stone is this?"

"It called bloodstone chalcedony, or sometimes by the name heliotrope."

"Heliotrope!" she exclaimed. "I've heard the word before, but I've never known what it was. Just a color with an exotic name. Sort of like periwinkle or chartreuse."

"I think the color heliotrope is reddish purple," I told her, "but the heliotrope stones are green and red. The green in those particular stones matches your eye color. The red matches your hair. I didn't cut the stones, but I did make them into the earrings. I hope you like them."

"I do! And you really picked out the color and designed them specifically for me?"

I shrugged like it was no big deal. I was pleased, though, that she noticed the effort I had gone through to create something special for her.

She reached up, pulled my head down, and gave me a big kiss. After ten seconds or so, we disengaged. "Thank you, Chris. I've had a lovely Christmas. But it's not over. I got you something too. It's rather large and it's at my condo, so you'll have to come in to get it. And despite the fact that things are progressing nicely, you can't stay too long. Agreed?"

"Agreed. Unless you tie me up and force me."

When she laughed again, my mood brightened considerably. At her condo, which appeared to be the same floor pattern as mine, she led me to a large gift resting against her living-room wall, wrapped in three different kinds of Christmas paper. "I didn't have enough of any one design and I was running late. If it really bothers you, though, you can wait until next year and I'll have it wrapped better."

"Fat chance," I muttered and went to rip the paper off. To my surprise, it was an unframed mirror. I didn't know I needed one, and certainly not this size. "For the ceiling over my bed?" I quipped.

"No, goofy. It's for dance practice. For a lot of these dance moves, posture and exact hand position are important. I use the mirrors at the studio and at the gym and thought it would help here too. The wall next to your black-leather chair would be good. Though if you don't want it at your place, we can hang it next to my fireplace and practice here."

"Wow! How nice!" I exclaimed. "I like the fact that you're investing in us staying together. Next to my black chair will be perfect." I took her hand and pulled her until

I was sitting on her couch and she was on my lap. "I'll behave, sort of. But such a nice present deserves a nice kiss."

She enthusiastically kissed me back. She ran her hand over my chest muscles, which of course gave me permission to return the favor. I didn't, for some reason, although I wanted to. After thirty seconds I broke it off. "I better go now. If I don't, you might not respect me in the morning."

"I agree you should go. Thanks for being so patient, Chris."

At home it was cold-shower time, which washed away most of the sexual tension. But not my pleasure with a day well spent. After hanging the mirror so we could use it the next day for practice, I went to bed and fantasized about how it would have been had we spent the night together.

Tuesday
December 28, 1999

"What's with the mirror?" Meg asked. She and Richard had come by to discuss the sale of the store again. "You decide you need to spend more time looking at yourself?"

"Something like that," I answered. "When you're as good-looking as I am, you need to take advantage of every opportunity to use a mirror."

"I need a drink before I throw up," Meg announced as she headed to the kitchen. She brought back two cans of Diet Pepsi for her and Richard and a glass of water for me. She only drank wine at my place when Richard wasn't around.

"Actually, I'm taking a West Coast Swing class, and I practice with a dance partner every Sunday evening. The mirror was a Christmas present from her to check our posture and stuff like that while we practice."

"This one serious?" asked Richard.

"Well, I wouldn't call the West Coast Swing as serious as the tango or the waltz, but clearly more serious than the Watusi or the electric slide."

"C'mon, asshole. Give," ordered Richard. "Is this woman likely to be around for a while? You going to introduce her to us, or what?"

"Probably, but it's still early and I don't want to jinx anything by talking more about it now."

"Fair enough," Richard dismissed the subject. "Have you thought any more about the sale of GGG?"

"Yes I have. I'm willing to go ahead with the sale as discussed. Have we determined how serious Miamoto is?"

"Not sure," said Richard. "Miamoto insists he's serious, but he won't give us enough information to run a credit check. He has, on the other hand, given us a fifty-grand non-refundable deposit and we've set up an escrow account. He has until January 31 to come up with the rest of the money. I'm optimistic, but I'm going to keep showing up at the store until the sale is finalized."

"How about advertising?" I asked. We ran regular ads in the *Los Angeles Times*, the Culver City papers, and the telephone books. "It doesn't make sense to keep spending money on the future of something that will belong to somebody else."

"I agree, sort of," Richard responded. "This week we're advertising for the after-Christmas sale, and that's important. I'd rather sell jewelry at a discount from retail than let it go for wholesale to Miamoto. But starting the first of the year, I plan to reduce the advertising to almost nothing. If the deal falls through, we can start it up again."

"How about my stuff? We have a lot of my pieces at the store. Should I keep producing at the same pace?"

"Oh yes," said Meg. "My vote is you keep going whole hog. If the new buyer has any sense at all, he'll take everything you have and ask for more. I'll order some for Daddy's store. Your things always sell. We'll have to decide on the date when the loose stones, raw material, work in progress, and finished pieces stop being community property, so to speak, and start being your property."

"That won't be a problem. Different subject. Are any of our computer programs subject to the Y2K problem?"

"I don't think so," Richard responded. "All of our programs are from major vendors and we're up-to-date on the upgrades. They've all addressed this sort of thing. The only time you're supposed to have a problem is when you have home-grown programs. And we don't."

"Very good. Anything else?" I asked.

"Of course there is. We brought over your Christmas present," Meg told me, handing me what looked like a Christmas card. "Here."

It *was* a card, but included was a coupon book for twelve monthly car detailings.

"Cool! Especially since I now have a weekly passenger in the Lexus," I said, giving Meg a brotherly hug and Richard a handshake. "Thank you. And it just so happens that I got something for you too. Or maybe that's you two too, although it's not a tutu."

I gave them a catalog for Norwegian Cruise Lines, with a homemade gift certificate entitling them to any seven-day cruise they wanted. "You guys have been stuck minding the store, partly for me, for too long without taking even a week off. Pretty soon you'll be able to. On me. Merry Christmas."

Meg turned excitedly to Richard. "Can we go to Alaska? I've always wanted to."

Richard smiled broadly. "Why not? Thank you, Chris." They both hugged me, with Meg maybe forgetting that her husband was watching and me keeping my hands at my sides because I definitely did *not* forget. After a while, they left.

I was pleased with my gift-giving so far this year. Only three presents, but each of the people were special to me. And I'd see Ike next week.

Wednesday
January 5, 2000

"Checkmate!" I exclaimed. "Twice in a row! I may never lose a game this whole millennium."

"In your dreams," Ike said, picking up the last piece of barbecued pork with his chopsticks. Ike may have been raised kosher decades ago, but barbecued pork was still his favorite Chinese dish, and I always made sure I ordered some whenever I stopped at Hunan Garden on the way over. "It's just these new chess pieces are confusing to me. But I'll keep them anyway."

Ike lived in Toluca Lake, an upscale community abutting North Hollywood and Burbank in the San Fernando Valley. Toluca Lake was close to various motion-picture and television studios, and many celebrities lived there.

Ike and Esther moved there in the mid-1950s, and that's where Meg was born and raised. Although the house was now too large for Ike by himself, too many memories continued to live there with him, and he'd never move. With the assistance of a once-a-week housekeeper, gardener, and Meg's regular "care" packages to her beloved father, he was fine.

We were playing on Ike's Christmas present from me—a replica of an eighteenth-century Russian chess set. He now had five totally different sets and each time we played at his house we used a different one. Ike was proud of his collection and the chess sets were always on display.

Ike had given me a top-of-the-line gemological microscope. I'd been using the one I purchased used back when I was a student at GIA. It was okay, but I'd been thinking of upgrading. Ike read my mind and gave me one that sold for more than five grand. It was awesome!

"Only the best for you, my boy," he told me. "You're

an artist. An artist can only be as good as his tools."

I thanked him profusely, of course. It was nice to have a father who was proud of me. I felt so blessed that I decided to broach a delicate subject with him.

"I want to ask for your guidance in a sexual matter," I said. We'd never discussed such matters before. This could be interesting.

"I'm a sixty-eight-year-old man. I'm almost dried up down there. You're a young stud. Why do you want my advice?"

"I don't believe that for a second, Ike. At your age, unmarried women outnumber the men two to one. And a man who owns a jewelry store? You must be getting more action than anyone in the entire synagogue. Is it Mrs. Cohen or Mrs. Goldberg who can't keep her hands off of you?"

"Okay, so maybe there's still some lead in my pencil," Ike told me with a smile. Actually, he had a huge grin on his face. Maybe being acknowledged for his sexual prowess was as satisfying to his ego as winning a chess match. "But you're no spring chicken in these matters yourself. What do you want to know?"

"I met a woman named Annie. She's absolutely perfect, except ..."

"There's always an 'except,'" he told me. "And the better you get to know her, the more excepts you discover. If you keep waiting until you find one without an except, you'll be waiting until the *next* millennium."

"I agree. I really want to believe that this one is worth the effort, but I'm trying to decide if she's a lost cause. She believes her ex-husband ran around on her, so she's now convinced that *all* men will run around on their women. And she appears to be militantly vigilant, looking for signs of indiscretion."

"So, did you keep your pecker zipped up with Paula?" Ike asked.

"Sure did. I never once strayed in that regard. I *thought* about it, though."

"That doesn't count," Ike advised. "So if you didn't cheat on Paula, you probably aren't going to cheat on Annie. So you've got nothing to worry about. If that's her only except, you're home free."

"I'm not so sure. With Annie, it's not being guilty that counts. It's her *thinking* you're guilty that matters. It appears that when she sees something she doesn't like, she doesn't stick around long enough to hear the other side."

"So don't get anywhere close to a situation that could be misunderstood. Come on now. How often have women thrown themselves at you without you welcoming the action?"

"Not often. Almost all of my sexual conquests have been initiated by me," I said quietly. No way in the world was I going to discuss Meg with her own father. Ike still thought his princess walked on water.

"So you're worrying about something pretty far-fetched. If she's all that perfect otherwise, go for it. And if you change your mind, ask her if she likes sexy senior-citizen jewelry store owners, will you? I'd love to meet a woman where that's her only except."

I laughed. "Sure, Ike, if I decide not to pursue Annie, I promise to put in a good word for you."

Ike nodded his head like he was happy with the way the conversation went.

"Actually, Ike, your advice has eased my fears. Thanks a lot. And thanks again for the microscope."

"My pleasure," he told me, beaming.

Tuesday
January 11, 2000

"Nice earrings. Get them anywhere special?" I was driving us to dance class.

"Nah. Just from some guy in the neighborhood who's trying to hit on me," Annie deadpanned. Then she started laughing. "Actually, I love them, Chris. It's just that sometimes when somebody dangles a line fishing for a compliment, the urge to chop it off is too strong to resist."

Well, that felt better. For a moment she did have me going again. She continued. "I decided they're a good length for dancing. I've been watching the earrings of the gals in class and the ones that swing a little look best. Thank you again. It still bowls me over that you made them especially with me in mind."

"You're welcome again. I was actually thinking color, size, and shape when I designed them. I didn't consider the utilitarian question, 'Where will she wear them?' I guess we'll find out tonight if I mounted the stones and attached the mountings to the gold chain well enough to hold up during dancing."

I guess we'd exhausted this subject, as Annie changed course completely. "You've mentioned you run a jewelry store with your brother. Do you have any other family?"

"Not the usual kind. I grew up in Southern California with Richard as my only sibling. We were very lucky in the parents department. They came to most of my high school athletic contests, and there were a *lot* of them in several sports, and *all* of Richard's stage presentations, of which there were relatively few. They died in an automobile accident while Richard and I were in college."

"That must have been tough."

"There's never a good time to lose parents you love,

but everything considered, it was probably for the best. Richard and I were fully grown and capable of fending for ourselves, and earlier that year we learned that both Mom and Dad had pretty severe health problems. We got their best years and didn't have to watch them go through painful deaths. Richard and I decided that maybe the accident was a sort of joint-suicide pact, or maybe suicide-murder. There was never a suicide note found, but Richard and I believe that this was probably engineered by my father as a gift to the two of us. That's one possibility consistent with their love for us, and that's the one we choose to believe."

"Wow! I guess I don't know whether to be sorry for you that you've lost them or happy for you that you can remember them so fondly."

"Be happy. It'll be nineteen years this summer. I still think of them both frequently, and Richard, Meg, Ike, and I still visit their gravesite every July seventeenth."

"I know about Richard. Who are Meg and Ike?"

"Meg is Richard's wife, and a full one-third partner in the jewelry business. She's our chief salesperson. I'm the jewelry designer and creator and Richard's the overall business manager, although it's a small business, so we've all done a little of everything. They've been married since college and Meg is as much family to me as Richard is."

This was a highly filtered version of Meg. There was no way telling Annie about Meg's alcoholism and flirtatiousness would help me get to where I wanted to go.

"Ike is Meg's father. I guess he's the most special person in my life. He always wanted a son, and I wanted a replacement father, I guess, so we sort of adopted each other. We use a monthly chess match as an excuse to get together and we've never missed a month in seventeen years. Paula accepted Ike easily, and if you and I end up getting serious, you should know up front that Ike's part of the package."

"I don't see that as a showstopper. What's he like?"

"He's this little old Jewish widower who lives for his

daughter Meg, his jewelry store, and me—probably in that order, although he liked my Christmas present this year so maybe I moved up on his list. He's full of wisdom, but much of it is Yiddish wisdom and that's a different perspective from how I grew up."

"He sounds nice. You're fortunate to have each other."

"I agree. Oh. And this is funny. I told him about you. He said you seemed so perfect that if I ever decided I didn't want you, I should put in a good word for him. I was supposed to check out if you liked 'sexy senior-citizen jewelry-store owners,' and that's a direct quote. I promised to put in a good word for him, and now I've kept that promise, but I don't want you to consider it too carefully just yet. I'm still actively considering trying to keep you for myself."

"You are, huh?" she asked while we were pulling into the parking lot. Then she asked coyly, "And just what did you tell him that made me seem so perfect?"

I stopped the car in the parking lot to Swingtime, put my finger gently on her nose, and said, "Be careful when you go dangling for a compliment. I've heard that sometimes somebody just has to chop off your dangle with an axe."

Every time I heard her laugh was a new pleasure.

In tonight's class we learned a new tuck turn, a pattern whereby the woman passed on the man's left side rather than his right. It didn't look like a major difference, but it was. Normally, the man spun the woman clockwise when she came out of the tuck. This time he spun her counter-clockwise, and to make it work right, the spin had to come slightly earlier than it did in the regular version. Most of us had quite a bit of trouble with it, but by the end of the evening I had it. And if I could lead it, Annie could follow. It was clear that our practice sessions put us ahead of many of the other students.

On the way home I asked Annie about her family.

"It was not as idyllic as yours. I never knew my father, who died when I was three, and my mother never spoke about him or even kept pictures. I've always suspected he was abusive toward her. Unlike me, she was a very timid woman and she didn't remarry until I was twelve. My stepfather liked to peek into my bedroom window when I was changing clothes. Sometimes he'd even barge into the bathroom when I was taking a bath."

"That must have been awful. Did you complain to your mother?"

"I did, but she said that as long as Claude only looked, it wasn't too bad. She begged me not to rock the boat, because she had no confidence she could ever find another man. I threatened him with a knife if he ever touched me. He never did, but he continued to violate my privacy. When I got a scholarship to college, I found ways to stay at school twelve months a year. I didn't invite them to my wedding. I don't know or care if they're alive or dead now."

I looked over at her and noticed the same set of her jaw that she had when she spoke about Tony or infidelity. I laid my hand on top of hers while I turned my attention back to the driving. "You've had it tough. I wish I could take away some of your pain."

We drove along quietly, each lost in our own thoughts. I could see part of why she was so distrustful of *men*, but I didn't have a clue whether she'd ever be able to trust me. I didn't want the evening to end on such a somber note, but when we'd reached our condos the silence was still overbearing. I didn't know if a joke was appropriate, but I felt I had to try something.

"Do you know what the fish said when he swam into the wall?"

The question startled Annie out of her reverie. She mused about the question, smiled, and then shook her head.

"Dam."

It was a pretty corny joke, but she smiled anyway. It wasn't a full laugh, but then again the joke didn't deserve one. She gave me a big hug at her doorstep and said, "Thanks. I needed that."

As she shut the door, I reflected that my little joke was more of something a neighbor might use to bring someone out of a funk than something a boyfriend, or whatever was the right term now, might say. Still it felt perfect. I was feeling pretty proud of myself as I walked the 200 yards to my own condo.

Tuesday
January 18, 2000

"I dropped my dop stick today," I told Annie as we started off for class. "That's unusual for me."

"Your dip stick? You were working on your car?"

"No. My dop stick. I use it like a handle to hang on to stones while I'm working on them."

"I've never heard of them. How do they work?"

"The ones I use are approximately the size of an emery board. They're made of wax. They come in different colors depending on their shellac content and how hot you need to get them to make the wax melt. Usually I use black ones, which require a fairly high melting point."

"Do you heat the stones or heat the dop stick?"

"Depends. Usually you heat the stones themselves using a dop pot, where you use a light bulb to heat the stones. But some gemstones, like opal, are heat sensitive and special techniques are required."

"Is dropping a dop stick a major disaster?"

"It can be. Some gemstones are fragile and dropping one can shatter it, depending on how it hits, whether a dop stick is attached or not. Other stones are more resilient. Today I was working with some pink topaz in a marquis cut, which means it's shaped like a football, and one of the points chipped off when it hit."

"Did that ruin the piece?"

"No. But it changed it. I had some gold findings and I placed one on each end. It turned out well enough. There's enough variety in what I do that this just looks like another variation on a theme. It was time-consuming, but not a disaster."

"Do you get mad at yourself when those things happen?"

"Sometimes. They do seem to happen more often when I'm in a hurry and facing a due date. But this one was all right. It was a 'don't worry about the small stuff' situation."

At Swingtime, we learned a new whip pattern. In swing, whips are patterns that generally take eight counts to complete, whereas most of the other patterns require only six. Nearing the end of my second series of classes, I now knew four different whip patterns, including the one from tonight. Not a lot, but I suppose that knowing four is better than knowing only three.

"I'm curious about something," Annie asked me on the way home from dance class. "It might sound critical, but I actually mean it in a complimentary way."

"What is it?" I asked warily. The start of this conversation didn't exactly give me a warm and fuzzy feeling.

"It's about your house, or rather your condo. For a bachelor, it's actually pretty clean. And one of your rooms is an industrial workroom of sorts—which probably generates lots of dust, sludge, slurry, or whatever. Not the kind of stuff you want in your kitchen or bedroom."

"You're right. The gemstone-cutting business is a messy one. I keep the door to the workshop closed, wear a lab coat, and change shoes every time I go in or out. I have slip-ons so it isn't a major problem. I also have washable one-size-fits-all booties for the rare visitor."

"Good thinking."

"Plus, I have a girl who comes once a week. Since you come over on Sunday evenings for dance practice, she now comes on Sunday afternoon. If you visit on another day of the week, you'll see a difference, but it won't be terrible. I prefer living in clean surroundings."

"Me too. And as I said, it was more of a compliment than a criticism. I just wanted to know how you did it."

"Thank you for noticing. I do what I can."

"Was it tough to get a girl to come over on a Sunday?"

"Not really. Teresa has been with me since shortly after I moved in. She doesn't speak good English, so we haven't had long conversations. Her husband works on the condo gardening crew. They're trying to bring over the rest of their family from Mexico. They're probably illegal aliens, which, as you know, is a hot political button here in California. Teresa's an excellent worker, though. I'm glad she has room for me."

"How'd you find her?"

"The week I moved in I asked a neighbor lady who was getting her mail when I was getting mine. She said Teresa does a lot of the condos at Pacifica and everyone thought that was a type of security. If Teresa ripped anyone off, we'd all find out about it and she and Carlos might be deported or have to start somewhere else. And if anyone gave her a hard time or didn't pay, she'd tell the rest of us."

"Sounds like a good system."

Wednesday
January 26, 2000

Tonight was the first night of Intermediate West Coast Swing I, taught on Wednesday nights by Phil Adams, Michele's husband. Annie and I were having such a good time with our hobby, we kept going, even though we hadn't been out social dancing yet.

Right after the Beginner II class ended last week, I invited Annie to Las Vegas for Super Bowl weekend. I'd received an invitation from the Luxor, one of the casinos where I'd played $25-a-hand blackjack. She told me she'd let me know on the way to class tonight. I was awaiting her decision. With this girl, I never knew what was coming.

After twenty minutes of small talk about jewelry and whether Bush's lead in money-raising would make him unbeatable in the primaries, she broached the subject. "Frankly, I'm worried," she told me on the drive to the studio. "So far all our togetherness has been three hours or less at a time. It's a whole new ballgame when we'll be together 15 hours a day for three days in a row. On the other hand, I'd like to go to Vegas with you, and the Super Bowl is a good excuse, especially since the Rams are in it," she continued. "Seeing you enjoy your hobby would also be interesting."

I was still waiting for the verdict. To relieve my own tension I tried a joke. "Give it to me straight, doctor. I can take it."

"Tell you what. Separate rooms this trip, and if it turns out that we can spend more than three hours together at a stretch, and I don't see why we couldn't, then two weeks later, I promise to give you a Valentine's Day to die for, if you can fit it into your schedule."

"A Valentine's Day to die for? You mean just us, together somewhere, clothes off, lights out, party time? No more waiting for you to make up your mind? Is that what you mean?" We had just pulled into the parking lot outside of the studio.

"Close. But not exactly," she told me, coyly. "Would it be such a terrible thing if we left the lights on?" I reached for her and, laughing, she dodged me by exiting the car.

We introduced ourselves to Phil, paid for the class series (still Dutch treat), and went out onto the dance floor to warm up.

Although it was clear that he and Michele were teaching the same dance, Phil emphasized slightly different things and Annie and I both needed to pay attention. Tonight's pattern was a sugar push with both man and woman learning different syncopated steps. A syncopation is when you alter the number of steps or perhaps the timing, but still end up in the right place at the right time. West Coast Swing is *full* of syncopations.

At the end of the class, Annie and I stayed and watched the Intermediate II students warm up. It was easy for us to see how much more proficient they were than the students in our class. One woman, who was particularly good, came off the floor and stood by us while she was temporarily without a partner. I asked her how long she'd been taking swing.

"Maybe two years, and I take a more advanced swing class on Sunday mornings," she answered. "In the second Wednesday night class, you get students who keep coming back over and over again. We like Phil and the other students. If you're working your way up to being at our level, welcome. You'll find you learn faster when you dance with partners who know what they're doing."

"We're Annie and Chris and we've just started the Intermediate I class," Annie said. "It'll be at least two months before we take the Intermediate II class for the first time."

"That's great. I'm Susie. And it really doesn't matter

much how good you are today. The fun is in dancing and getting better. And for most of us, there's always more 'getting better' to go. I know people who've been taking lessons from Phil and Michele for ten years and have no intention of stopping anytime soon."

Susie had been scanning the crowd while she was talking to us. She was friendly enough, but she'd rather dance than talk. "Nice to meet you, and if you'll excuse me, I'm being beckoned from across the room by Paul. Bye." She walked away and Annie and I decided to leave.

When I started the car and drove off, I asked, "So tell me what you think we'll learn about each other in two weeks that we don't know now?"

"We haven't fought yet," Annie told me.

"You want to fight?" I asked with amazement. "And that will help you decide if we ought to have sex or not? That doesn't sound like a sensible way to obtain the information. What am I missing?"

"Of course I don't want to fight, you goof. But we're each bright, successful, and have formed different ideas about the best way to do things. What I want to know is when we disagree, how do we resolve it? Can you stand up to me? Can you stand me standing up to you? Tony was a guy who had to be the smarter one at *everything.* And he wasn't. But I had to let him think he was to keep the peace. I don't want to go through that again."

"Have you decided what we're going to fight about?" I asked. Until this moment I'd been really looking forward to this weekend. Now I was on that roller coaster of doubt again.

"Not really. I have some ideas about where some differences might occur, but I don't want to mention them unless they actually happen," Annie told me.

"It feels like you're planning to ambush me."

"Not exactly, but I can see that it looks that way now. Let me try to explain it better," Annie went on. "I was definitely *not* looking for a boyfriend a month and a half ago when I asked you to leave your step at the gym."

"That makes us even," I wisecracked. "I wasn't looking for a boyfriend either."

She ignored the crack. "I was happy with my life. I didn't have a checklist of what characteristics the perfect guy would have, but if I did, you would have scored pretty high: a smart guy I could trust, had a nice sense of humor, who kept himself fit and was successful."

"Not to mention handsome, adorable, hung like a horse, and modest," I chimed in.

"Right," she laughed. "Something like that, anyway. In the past six weeks, we've danced, hiked, gone to the gym, and had to hold back our hormones big time. It's a lot of fun. And I want it to continue."

"I sense a 'but' on its way."

"I'm afraid so. Everything we've done so far is perfect and life isn't like that. We haven't spoken at all about politics, to give you one example. How much should the U.S. spend on defense? When should and shouldn't abortion be allowed? Should immigrants get full citizen benefits? Should limits be put on gun ownership? And what about when environmental concerns get in the way of progress? Most adults have strong opinions about at least some of these things. What happens when you and I end up on different sides? When I want to donate $2,000 to a political candidate you can't stand for some reason, what happens then?

"Now, I don't expect any of these issues to arise this weekend, but let's talk about some that will. You've invited me to Vegas basically to be a decorative observer while you do your thing. Okay. I can do that sometimes. But I'm a lot more than decoration. I happen to be mathematically gifted and am paid big bucks for my technical expertise. Gambling, like it or not, is applied mathematics, and that's my subject more than yours. It might turn out that I know more about parts of it than you do. What happens when I tell you that one of your ideas is wrong—and I prove it to you mathematically? A lot of guys get pretty defensive when a woman tells them they're wrong.

"This might be the first time some stress will be thrown at us. My fervent desire is that we find a way to let me be me and let you be you, and both of us can be comfortable with that."

She'd been hitting me with the stick, sort of, and then she gave me one hell of a carrot. "If we can make that happen, two weeks later over Valentine's weekend, you'll find yourself with a very willing sex partner, willing to do just about anything you desire, except if it causes pain or involves a threesome or moresome. Other than that, anything goes. What do you say?"

What could I say? I couldn't imagine it being that hard to avoid conflict. And Annie at my sexual beck and call? Oh my. I might not be ready to commit to forever and ever amen, but I was certainly willing to do it her way for another couple of weeks.

"It's a deal, Annie. I'm really looking forward to a weekend in Vegas with you. And don't forget your dance shoes. It might not be a sexual date, but it's still a date and we need to practice our dancing anyway."

Friday
January 28, 2000

We decided to drive. We lived on the west side of the Los Angeles basin, and Interstate 15 to Vegas, the best way to go, is considerably east of L.A. Rush-hour traffic on Friday starts at two or so; to avoid it, we left at noon.

"I'm planning to play 20 questions so I can know more about you. Tell me to mind my own business if you like, but I'm curious as to how much money you're taking and how much you'll be betting," Annie asked me shortly after we hit the Santa Monica Freeway heading east.

"I have four grand on me, which is more than I've ever taken. I have a checkbook and ID and I expect I could cash a check if I had to. But I'd be surprised if I lost that much. I usually win, actually. I like to bet $10 a hand to start with, and if things start to go well, I bump it up to $25. That way I can take advantage of winning streaks and pay the minimum during losing streaks. I think money management is a major key to winning at blackjack."

"Do you need to bet a certain amount to qualify for the benefits this weekend?"

"I don't think so. My host told me that if I played my regular amount, everything would be cool. He said he could pick up the second room, but that would reduce my food comps to the coffee shop—which is actually quite good—and the buffet. If we share a room next time, that'll either let us have a nicer room or some nicer meals."

"This will be fine, I'm sure," said Annie. "How many hours do you plan to play?"

"They give me rewards based on four hours a day with a $25 average bet. I bet less than that sometimes, so I'll probably need to play more. Usually I play six or eight hours a day when I'm by myself. My host knows I'm with a new girlfriend and that I might play less this time."

"Well, I don't want to be a nuisance," Annie said. "I have no particular agenda this weekend other than for us to enjoy ourselves, and root like hell for the Rams on Sunday. Were you a Rams fan when they were based in L.A.?"

"Yes," I answered. "I've lived in Los Angeles my whole life and have always rooted for the Dodgers, Rams, and Lakers. Somewhat less for the Angels. I never particularly warmed up to the Raiders when they were here. But as an ex-jock, I really like sports. Do you?"

"Pretty much," she answered. "I can listen to the TV announcer and understand what he's saying, so I don't need you to explain football to me. And I'm really looking forward to the game and will probably cheer very loudly."

"Would you have watched the game anyway?"

"Wouldn't have missed it. Vegas or no Vegas. You could not have talked me into a hike this Sunday afternoon."

"That's great. Who do you think is going to win?"

"I'm a Ram fan, so I hope Warner passes for lots of touchdowns. But I doubt there's a good bet to be made on the game."

"Why not?" I asked. "Surely it's possible to be smarter than the other bettors, isn't it? Especially for a math whiz like you?"

"Possibly." She didn't seem to respond to my teasing. "I haven't really studied sports betting. But it seems to me that there's so much information out there, the line is probably pretty accurate. And if so, the fact that the sports books make you lay eleven to win ten is too big of an edge to overcome, no matter which team you bet on. Otherwise, why would the casinos give away their food and rooms in order to get bettors to come to town?"

"I didn't look at the line. I assume the Rams are big favorites. Right?"

"Yep. Seven points. That's quite a bit, although nowhere near a record."

I was amazed. This lady appeared to be very savvy

gambling-wise. I'd been expecting to show her the ropes in Vegas—being the older and wiser one, so to speak, hoping it would impress her. But just because she knew about sports betting didn't mean she knew squat about blackjack. That was my real strength, anyway.

"So you're not going to bet on the game?"

"Something small, maybe. I've heard that having a little something on the game adds to the excitement, so I'll bet ten bucks on the Rams. That'll be enough."

"Are you sure you can afford it?" I kidded.

"It's a stretch, but I think I'll be able to swing it," she smiled. "Seriously, I don't plan on betting this weekend, but I do have two grand on me just in case the urge becomes irresistible. Another question. The Luxor has a lot of blackjack tables. How do you choose the one for you? Do you have a favorite dealer or something?"

"I've come here several times and I recognize most of the dealers. There's some I've never beaten, so I'll avoid them. I like to sit at third base, which means the left side of the table."

"What difference does it make?" Annie asked. "Does that change the odds somehow?"

"Oh yes," I tell her. "When you've seen idiots at third base ruin the game by taking the dealer's bust card, you learn that that's the most important position at the table. Since I play pretty well, I like to play third base in order to protect the whole table."

"I see," Annie said. "Do you stay at the same table or do you move around?"

"I move. Whenever I lose three hands in a row I change tables. That keeps me from long losing streaks at the same table. Most people who've had really bad days stay at the same table and get their heads handed to them. Not me. I move so my luck will change."

"May I make a special request?"

"Of course," I said quickly. "What would you like?"

"The football game starts at three o'clock or so on Sunday, and at most games they have all-you-can-eat junk food, like hot dogs, ice cream, popcorn, and the like. Both of us eat better than that. I'd like one fancy meal this weekend, and I'd like it to be my treat. I've been to the Mirage before and Kokomo's is pretty good. May I suggest we walk to the Mirage and have lunch on Sunday at Kokomo's, on me? Please? Then we can walk back and watch the Rams kick some Tennessee butt."

"Okay. But if you pay for a nice meal now, you'll have to let me pay for a meal in two weeks. It's only fair."

"I see your point," Annie said. "Except I think it won't cost us anything. I've got a friend who works at the Mirage. I think I can talk her into a free meal at Kokomo's, which will probably be a lot nicer than the coffee shop at the Luxor."

"Okay," I agreed. "We can eat at Kokomo's. If you can get it for free, great. Otherwise, this whole weekend's my treat."

Friday
January 28, 2000

Even the Invited Guest line was pretty long at check-in, but it went fast enough. Our two rooms were on the sixteenth floor facing south, which gave us a view of the brand-new sparklingly golden Mandalay Bay. Since the Luxor is a big pyramid, the elevators are in the corners of the building and are called "inclinators." The rooms themselves have a lot more floor space than ceiling space, because the outside wall slants dramatically.

We got to the rooms about five and decided to go down to play. We'd eat later. We found an empty table. The dealer had the decks spread out across the layout. I had Annie sit at third base and I sat next to her. I gave the floorlady my player's card for rating purposes and told her that Annie was just watching and wouldn't be playing. The floorlady said that this wasn't a problem, as long as the casino didn't get really busy.

I started by betting $25 off the top for the first ten hands. I'd read a book called *Comp City*, where the author, Max Rubin, said that often the person in the pit only records your first few bets. Later on you can lower your bets and still get credit for the bigger ones, so that's what I did.

Except tonight my ship had come in. I won the first three hands, and probably 15 out of the first 20. I like to increase my bet when things are going well, so soon I was soon playing two separate hands of $25. One of my bets was placed in front of Annie, so even if the table filled up, they wouldn't ask her to move.

After about three hours, I asked Annie if she was ready for dinner. She was. I cashed out more than $1,200 ahead. Life was good.

"It's nice when things happen the way they're supposed to. We were able to control the table because of where we were sitting, and it paid off. That's what blackjack is all about," I told Annie after we were seated at a table at the Pyramid Cafe, Luxor's 24-hour coffee shop. I had received a VIP line pass when I checked in, so the wait hadn't been long at all.

"Why did you increase your bets?" she asked me. "It's your money and I'm certainly not trying to act like a nag or anything of the sort, but you said you were going to bet between $10 and $25 a hand, and you ended up averaging more than that. Was it the fact that you were winning?"

"Yep," I replied. "That's exactly what it's all about. Did you learn anything about the game by watching me?"

"Some of your plays were different than I thought made sense," she said, "but obviously you were very successful tonight. Remember, though, this weekend isn't about me playing. It's about me watching you play. And I'm glad I'm here and I'm glad you're winning. Are you going to play after dinner?"

"I don't think so. Three hours at a $40 average bet is certainly more than four hours at $25. So I thought we'd see if we could find a place where they played suitable dance music."

"That sounds nice to me."

The Luxor lounge had a small dance floor and a good band with some 60ish black male performers who sang Motown music. A couple of the songs were about the right tempo, so Annie and I got out there and did our thing. The floor was crowded and the West Coast Swing takes up quite a bit of room, so we got bumped a bit. Still, our first venture into social dancing at a nightclub was a success.

Upstairs at Annie's door, she kissed me, hugged me, and told me that she was having a good time and that everything was on course for Valentine's Day. I would've liked to barge into her room and have my way with her for several hours. But I didn't mind turning around and heading back to my room, either.

There's something about being ahead $1,200 that makes *everything* beautiful.

Saturday
January 29, 2000

The wake-up call came at 7:15. Way too damn early. I'd changed my mind and gone down to play after dropping Annie off at her room and got only about three hours of sleep. But we had an 8 o'clock breakfast date, and a "test weekend to see if we can travel together" was a bad time to break dates. So I rolled out of bed, showered, shaved, got dressed, and was on the phone to Annie at 7:45. She said she was on schedule and would knock on my door in about ten minutes.

One room separated Annie's room from mine. Which was a good thing. There's a huge psychological difference between a woman you're lusting after being on the same floor and right on the other side of a wall. If she were next door, I might try sending Morse code signals through that wall!

I opened the door to Annie's knock and was knocked out! "Oh my God!" I exclaimed. "Look at you! Turn around."

Annie twirled, then did a little curtsy with a bend of her legs and a tilt of her head, posing for me, with an ear-to-ear grin. She was wearing a knock-your-socks-off outfit. It wasn't sexy at all—although in truth *anything* she wore would've appeared damn sexy to me right then. It was a simple long-sleeved blouse opened a modest two buttons from the top. And slacks. Normal sorts of accessories. That was it.

What made this outfit special were the colors. Her silk blouse was exactly the same color as the green in the earrings I'd given her. Her reddish linen pants matched the red speckles in the stones, which she was also wearing. Her belt and shoes were dark green. An entire outfit designed around one pair of earrings, and the outfit fit her like it was made for her.

"I guess this means you like the earrings," was the wittiest comment I could come up with.

"Good guess."

"This is awesome. How on Earth did you find clothes that matched and fit so well?"

"Do I have to tell you my secret?" she asked. And then, bursting to tell, she did.

"I'm delighted with the way it turned out but it really wasn't that hard. I have a dressmaker who's done some things for me, and she's also making a dynamite dress for me for Valentine's Day, by the way. Anyway, I gave her an earring, told her what I wanted and how much I was willing to spend, and said, 'Make it happen.' She did. It took a couple of fittings, but voilà! I'm glad you like it."

"I do. Very much. I've designed jewelry for outfits before, but I've never known of anyone designing an outfit for my jewelry. I'm honored."

She gave me a hug and a kiss and we started toward the inclinator.

"And when we get home," I added, "please let me borrow your belt. I'll find an interesting way to put some of the same stones on the buckle. Not a lot of them, because you're a petite lady and I wouldn't want the buckle to overwhelm the outfit, but a few would look nice, I think. Okay if I give it a try?"

She stopped walking and gave me a long hug. "I'd like that a lot."

Hand in hand, we walked out of the inclinator and into Pharoah's Pheast, the Luxor buffet. It wasn't crowded. I guess most people go to bed too late on a Friday night in Las Vegas to wake up early Saturday morning. Still, there was a small line, so I pulled out my line pass again and we were selecting our food within five minutes of arriving. I wouldn't have minded standing in line a little longer, though, because holding hands with Annie felt great. We were in that glow period at the start of a love affair where any kind of touching feels like a million bucks.

Even excluding her clothes, Annie looked like a spring

flower. Smiling, a bounce in her step, we probably already looked like lovers, instead of soon-to-be lovers. "I feel wonderful!" she exclaimed, which anyone with eyes already knew. "I'm happy to be here and I'm happy to be here with you." As she set her tray down, she looked at me. "You don't look like you slept too well. Something wrong? I'd have expected a big winner like you, especially one who's about to get the girl, to look perkier than you do right now."

"Yeah, you'd think so," I responded. "And I'm fine. It's just that after I dropped you off at your room last night, I was too excited to go to sleep. So I came downstairs and played for six hours. I actually didn't get much sleep."

"I understand," Annie said. "Years ago Tony and I'd come to Vegas together and sometimes we would stay up the whole first night. It's either the desert air or the gambling fever that does that to people."

"Yep," I agreed, "it's that damn desert air."

"Perhaps if I'd been playing, I'd have wanted to stay up too. Anyway, you're up and we're at breakfast. Whatever you want to do for the rest of the day is fine with me. If you need to nap either now or this afternoon, feel free. I brought along a new John Grisham novel that I'm dying to get into, so don't worry about me being left in the lurch."

"Oh yeah? Which book is that?"

"*The Testament*," she told me. "It's been out a year or so and was the most interesting title in the new-books section of the library yesterday morning. Do you like John Grisham?"

"Yes, although I've only read a few. I read one about a little boy seeing a murder and another one about a black man hiding in the courthouse closet and killing two white guys who'd raped his daughter."

"Yes," Annie said. "*The Client* and *A Time To Kill*. Those were two of his early ones. I think I've read them all. He just might be my favorite author. I read enough computer and math journals to choke a horse and it's nice just to read for escape sometimes."

"I'm going to the omelet station," I told her. "Can I bring you one?"

"No thanks. I'm a cereal and yogurt kind of girl. But go ahead. I'm fine."

When I returned I saw that Annie had ordered more coffee for me and hot water and lemon for her.

"So how'd you do in the wee hours? Is your hot streak still sizzling?"

"Unfortunately, no," I answered. "I couldn't buy a hand. I usually busted. On those rare occasions when I did end up with a 19 or a 20, the dealer would get a 20 or 21.

"Even though I was only betting $10 or $20 at a time, I dropped $1,100. I intentionally quit when I got down to being just $100 ahead for the trip. Hopefully, my few hours of sleep has stopped the outflow."

"Are you angry?" she asked. "I don't imagine that losing is any fun for you."

"Nah, I'm not angry. I think 'frustrated' is more the right word. When you play every hand correctly and you just lose, lose, lose, you could definitely say it's no fun."

"I sympathize. Now let's talk about the rest of the day. Do you need to play some more or are you done for this trip? Do you need to nap before you play or are you ready to go out there and get your money back? My only request today is to have an hour-long walk with you somewhere."

"I want to play some more right after breakfast. After maybe two hours, I'll decide whether I want to nap first and then walk or walk first and then nap. And I'll probably play some more. Then we can get a few more dances in tonight."

"Goody," Annie said. "I could learn to like coming to Vegas with you."

"Tomorrow's schedule is pretty well filled with going to the Mirage in the morning, the game in the afternoon, and driving back home."

"That all sounds good to me. I'm ready to hit the tables when you are."

The blackjack tables were surprisingly empty for a

Super Bowl weekend. Unfortunately, my luck hadn't changed. The first table I selected took 10 minutes to fleece me out of $300. The second was better, but not much. It took 25 minutes for me to lose 'only' $250. This sucked.

At our third table, it was empty when we sat down. But by the time the dealer finished shuffling, a tall thin man with a big stack of black chips and a half-full bottle of Heineken sat down in the middle of the table and placed one black chip on each of two spots. At first base, an obvious newbie with his wife as a "backseat driver" bought four red chips with a $20 bill.

The first two hands were winners for all of us. The dealer started each hand with a five up and ended up busting both times. So I upped my bet to $25. Time to get my money back. The skinny guy in the center of the table was now playing two black chips on each square, burping regularly, and the novice at first base was still betting $5 a hand. He and his wife were excited to be ahead $10.

On the third hand the dealer again started with a six. Our nickel bettor had an ace six, and stood. The best play was to double. Second best was to hit the hand. Standing was the third best play. Oh well. It was his money. The big bettor in the center split eights on the first hand, then doubled down when he drew a two to his eight. "Give me some pictures," he demanded of the dealer, who obliged with a queen and a jack. On the second hand, he stood on his 19. His three hands were 20, 18, and 19, and he had a total of $800 bet. I was dealt two face cards and stood pat, of course.

The dealer flipped over his down card, a seven, and said "14." He then drew an eight, announced "22," and started to pay us off. Dealers pay third base first, so he matched my green chip with one of his own, and I withdrew both of them. I knew the dealer had made an arithmetic mistake and hoped he'd get on to the next hand, destroying the evidence. He paid the guy in the center with eight black chips, who remained impassive. This guy may have noticed what had gone on, or maybe he was too drunk. Who knew? Over at first base, when the dealer was paying off the five dollar bet, the player's wife spoke up.

"Why are you paying us? Don't you have 21?" she asked the dealer.

When the dealer examined his hand again, he muttered "Oh, shit," and called over a supervisor, who looked at the layout. She saw me with no chips bet, the guy in the center with $800 bet, matched by an $800 payoff, and the guy at first base with his single red chip matched by a payout of another red chip.

"Sorry, folks," she said, "but when this is brought to my attention, I must enforce the rules. Take the money," she told the dealer. The dealer took the sixteen black chips and two red chips and placed them in the tray.

"My mother always told me to tell the truth," the lady who had spoken up said, defensively.

The man in the center looked at her and said. "Lady, I'm stuck $22,000 in the last two days and your big goddamned mouth just cost me sixteen-fucking-hundred. And you're not even *in* this stupid-ass game. Why don't you take your pissy-faced morality and go play somewhere else before I say something that you *really* don't want to hear?" And then he belched.

The nickel player and his wife looked to the dealer and the supervisor for some sort of support against this barrage of profanity. The casino employees just stood there impassively. Finally, the player addressed the supervisor, "Are you going to allow him to speak to my wife like that? What kind of place is this, anyway?"

"Generally speaking, people not in the game have no right to speak up. So while your wife's arithmetic was correct, most players would agree she was out of line. And while I wish that Henry hadn't used quite such colorful language, I understand his point completely. Don't you?

"I'm certainly not kicking you out or anything, but maybe it would be better if you played at another table. Okay? Would you like John to give you a green chip for your five red ones? It's easier to carry that way. And I'll give you a comp for two lunch buffets, just so there's no hard feelings. How's that sound?"

The player and his wife took the comp and left quietly. The supervisor then gently scolded Henry. "You're chasing away my customers, Henry, not that I blame you. Can I get you another Heineken?"

Henry nodded and the game continued. It apparently went unnoticed that I had ended up $50 ahead when the dust settled. Had I left my initial bet and the dealer's payoff in the betting square, the supervisor would have demanded that the dealer take it too. But since there was nothing in the square when she looked, she probably assumed I'd busted on the hand. Not that this was a likely scenario with the dealer's up card being a six. But I didn't say a word. Neither did the dealer. It was impossible for me to know whether the dealer knew and chose not to speak up or he was so flummoxed by his mistake and the aftermath that he just didn't remember. In any case, I bet another green chip for me and a five-dollar toke for him.

The game continued, and the dealer apologized softly to both of us as soon as the supervisor went away. He apologized again when he dealt himself a blackjack, a 20, and a four-card 21. I left as Henry was letting loose another stream of profanity. I wouldn't have phrased it like Henry did, but I certainly wasn't any happier.

As we settled into another table, Annie whispered, "I think Henry might have been a bit irritated."

I laughed, which took away some of my own anger. This wasn't going the way I'd planned at all. I really wanted to impress Annie with how well I played, and here I was, losing my shirt.

The new table was no better. Ten minutes and another $140 down the tubes, I told Annie I was ready for a break. "Fine with me," she said.

"Where would you like to walk?" I asked her.

"I don't much care," she said. "Since we're walking back and forth to the Mirage tomorrow, why don't we walk either to the Orleans or the Hard Rock? Not that I have any desire to go inside—either one would just be a place to turn around. But before we go out, I want to change shoes. I brought some walking shoes that'll be more comfortable."

Ten minutes later we were walking toward the Hard Rock. It was fairly chilly, but we both had jackets and kept up a good pace, so we were fine. Once we had crossed the Strip and were walking east on side streets, I asked her, "What'd you think of the whole situation on the dealer mistake? Had you noticed the dealer misplay?"

"I was a math major in college. My professors would be ashamed if I thought that six, seven, and eight added up to 22. *Of course* I noticed. And the way you played it impressed me very much."

"Really?" I said, rather proud of myself, even though I didn't have a clue just why.

"Yep. Pulling your bet back immediately, just in case, paid off. I think most players would have left the bet there and ended up $50 poorer. I know you must be losing close to $1,000, but it would have been $1,050 if you hadn't made that heads-up play."

This was interesting. I was feeling a little guilty for pulling a fast one. She not only noticed I was doing it and figured out why, but praised my little subterfuge, rather than condemning me for it. This lady was more complicated than I thought. And obviously paying attention to what was going on.

"But tell me something. If the supervisor had looked you in the eye and asked you what your bet had been, what would you have said?"

"I would have told her the truth," I answered. "There's a difference in my mind between not volunteering incriminating information and bald-faced lying. What would you have done in that position?"

"About the same, for about the same reason."

I'm not sure that this agreement was anything to be proud of, but knowing we were on the same page felt right.

"Were you surprised when the supervisor took Henry's side in the dispute?" I asked Annie. "He was pretty over-the-top vulgar by some standards."

"That's a tough one," Annie said sarcastically. "From the casino's point of view, you have one player who's lost over $20,000 and wants to keep playing with a pile of black chips in front of him while drinking three beers an hour. And you have another player on a budget who'll lose $40 max on this trip. It's hard to figure out which one the casino wants to keep, isn't it?"

"Sorry," I said, "As they might say in one of your John Grisham novels, I withdraw the question."

But I had another serious question on my mind. I'd stayed up all night and soon would have to lie down for three or four hours. This was probably a pretty dumb move for someone wanting to prove to Annie that trips together would be fun. And the stakes were high. Whether or not I was going to have a willing sex partner in two weeks was far more important to me now than the thousand dollars I'd just lost. Had I blown it already? So I asked her.

"You're being a good sport about agreeing to fend for yourself for several hours while I nap this afternoon. Is it really okay? Or deep down are you so annoyed that this messes up my chances for happiness in two weeks?"

She laughed. God, I loved the way she did that. She could've asked me for anything in the world just then and I'd give it to her if I could. Just to hear her laugh.

"Don't worry about it," she told me with a hug as we walked along. "I know what it's like to enjoy a hobby. You like to play blackjack and you don't get to Vegas very often. So you play a lot when you get here. No big deal. Plus," she added, "the rules of engagement this weekend are tough on both of us."

"Rules of engagement? We're about to become engaged? To be married? Are you sure? I had no idea. This is all so sudden."

"No, you goof," she laughed. "Maybe the 'rules-of-engagement' term comes from reading too many Tom

Clancy novels. What I mean is that we're so, so close to being lovers and this weekend we aren't allowed to do what we both want to do. Since Tony's betrayal and my disgust with men in general, I'd given up on sex. I really never thought about it. Even reading novels, I'd skim over the sexy parts quickly. But for the last couple of months, I've found my mind going in that direction repeatedly. I don't know if you're masturbating now to relieve the pressure, but I am. For the first time since before I was in college, I'm playing with myself. I want you, Chris. I really really want you. But there's some stuff we need to talk about at the Mirage tomorrow. After that talk, I'll probably be able to make up my mind."

"Why wait until tomorrow?" I asked. "We've got nothing better to do for the next hour than to talk about whatever you want. Exactly when I start my nap doesn't matter very much."

"No. It's got to be face to face, and I want you well-rested when it happens. Humor me, please," she requested. "And I know it's probably irresistible to try to figure out what I want to talk about, but I'd be willing to bet that you won't be able to do it no matter how hard you try. So just don't try, if you can help it."

"Any suggestions about how to turn my mind off about that?"

"Oh sure," she said with another laugh. "Just think about all the things we're going to do to each other in two weeks. And that that's the goal for both of us. Please don't think I want anything less."

"Okay, one wet dream coming up."

"That's fine," she said. "Enjoy yourself. And however good your dream is today, in two weeks it'll be better. I promise."

"Okay, two wet dreams coming up."

She laughed again. God, I loved that laugh.

Sunday
January 30, 2000

We started for the Mirage about nine in the morning. It's about two miles, I guess, from the Luxor. But walking anywhere along the Strip takes awhile, especially on Super Bowl Sunday. We got there, looked at the white tigers, and continued inside. "Let's play a few hands of blackjack," Annie suggested. "This was one of the places I played years ago."

"Why not? This *is* my weekend to play," I said. "Do you have a particular table in mind?"

"Yes. I like the hand-held games rather than the shoes. They have some nice double-deckers sort of near the guest-room elevators."

We found the tables. There was one with a $25 minimum, and all the others were for more. Some were for $500. But nobody was at the quarter-minimum table, so I sat down and gave the dealer two $100 bills to change, then pushed a green chip into the betting circle.

In a shoe game like I played at the Luxor, the cards are dealt face up and the players aren't allowed to touch them. In the two-deck game, the cards are dealt face down and the player must pick them up. On the first hand, I caught an eight and nine and immediately tucked them under my bet, which is the way you signify you don't want any cards. It didn't matter to me what the dealer had. I had to stand on a seventeen. The dealer started with a three, turned over a four, then drew a six, three, and five for 21 exactly. Damn!

I placed another $25 chip out there. This time I received a seven and a four. I would double this against any dealer up card except for an ace. The dealer had a four, so I went ahead and doubled by placing a matching green chip in the betting circle. The dealer gave me a card face down and I didn't peek. The dealer turned up his own seven. Uh oh. I might be in trouble. My relief at seeing him draw a three was short-lived as he then drew a seven for another 21. I still had a chance, if my down card was a picture. But it wasn't. It was a five. Two hands, down $75 against a dealer too lucky to live. I told Annie I was ready to go.

"Then make this bet for me," she told me. She handed me a $100 bill and said, "Bet it all. I'm with my favoritest guy and feel lucky."

"But Annie! The dealer has gotten 21 twice in a row. You should bet small."

Annie bet big anyway and was dealt a ten and a six. The worst possible starting hand! And the dealer dealt himself an ace. Unfair! "Insurance?" the dealer asked.

"Don't insure this lousy hand," I advised. "It's not worth it."

"My daddy sold insurance and it sounds good. How much does it cost?" Annie asked the dealer. I was stunned. I thought Annie knew nothing about her father. Why was she lying?

"Half your bet if you want to insure the whole thing. That's $50," the dealer informed her.

Annie pulled another $100 out of her purse and nodded. The dealer took the offered bill and replaced it with four green chips, after calling out, "Breaking a hundred!" He placed two of the green chips directly in front of Annie's bet and placed the other two close to Annie. He then slipped his cards into a mirror device that told him whether he had a 10-card underneath. He did. He flipped over a king and pushed Annie's insurance back into the box where she had her original bet.

"Let's go, Annie. That's *three* 21s in a row for this guy. You can't beat such stupid luck."

Instead she said, "This is fun," while piling the two green chips on top of the black one. "Just a few more hands."

Annie picked up the card this time. She used both hands, and the dealer informed her that players were only allowed to touch the cards with one hand. She apologized. She showed me her cards, a three and a six. The dealer showed a two.

"I want to bet more. Can I insure or double or split or something?" she asked the dealer.

"Annie, you're only supposed to double a nine against a dealer three through six. This is a two. It's a bad bet," I told her, embarrassed that she was out of control. I wanted to protect her from herself, but clearly she wasn't taking my advice. Time to shut up, I guessed.

"You can double for any amount up to $150," the dealer informed her. "If you do, you get only one card."

"Great," said Annie. She pulled another $100 bill out of her purse and used the two green chips in front of her. That meant she was making a $300 bet on a bad play. The dealer gave her a card face down, then turned over his down card, a queen, and drew another queen and broke. He gave Annie three black chips, and she squealed in delight.

"Can't leave now! I'm on a roll!"

She bet two black chips and was rewarded with a blackjack. But the dealer also had an ace and asked if she wanted insurance. "Oh yes," she said. "Tell me again how I do it."

"Just say 'even money,'" I told her. I thought everyone knew you should take even money on blackjacks. It was her first correct play of the day.

She showed the dealer her cards and he nodded and paid her another two black chips. He had a six underneath. On the next hand, Annie received an ace and a nine. She told the dealer she didn't want any more, and he showed her how to tuck her cards. She ended up beating his 18. He paid her another two black chips. On the next hand, the dealer and Annie tied and the dealer began to shuffle.

"Phew! What a great ride!" Annie exclaimed. "But let's

go eat now." And then she asked the dealer, "What do I do with these?"

He took her chips and "colored her up" to two purples, worth $500 apiece, after starting with $200 or $300, I wasn't sure. Amazing! She won $700 or $800 in five minutes while making lots of mistakes. While I, after playing so well yesterday, got my head handed to me. Unfair!

After we cashed in the chips, Annie remarked, "It's better to be lucky than good."

"I couldn't agree more," I muttered. Though I felt sure she missed the sarcasm.

"That was *great*! I feel so *alive*!" she gushed. Despite my losing streak, her pleasure was infectious. I felt pretty good too.

"Let's go see my friend," Annie bubbled. "Maybe she'll feed us."

We made our way over to the Club Mirage. Annie approached a well-dressed lady named Carol, who greeted her. Annie introduced me to Carol and asked if we might be able to eat at Kokomo's. "Of course," said Carol. "Do you need me to make a reservation?"

"No," Annie said. "I made those Friday. I figured it might be busy today."

"Right you are," Carol said. "I'll call this over. Just go and enjoy your meal. Nice meeting you, Chris."

We thanked Carol and went to the restaurant, where we were seated in about ten minutes. "Ever eaten here before?" Annie asked. "It's one of my favorites."

"What happened just now?" I asked. "Carol can give free meals in expensive restaurants to her friends without losing her job? I don't understand."

"Don't worry. I'll explain everything. Let's order first. And you might as well order a lot, because I have a lot to tell you." She looked over at me with a twinkle in her eye. "The truth is, I've been holding out on you."

"No kidding! I *know* you've been holding out on me," I told her. "That's why we have separate rooms."

She laughed. "That too, but that's not what I'm talking about. The next hour will determine our future."

Before she could go on, our waiter, Carlos, came over, introduced himself and Marie, who'd also be serving us, and told us the specials of the day. As far as I was concerned, this was rotten timing. Although we were here to eat, I cared more about whether I was going to get laid soon than what food I was going to force down in the next hour. Cheerio's would be perfect if Annie was part of the package, while steak, lobster, and caviar would be insufficient if she wasn't. Still, I got through the ordering process graciously enough and then told Annie, "All right already, Annie. I'm ready for you to lay it on me."

"Okay," she said, "brace yourself. I'm going to tell you that you've been saying things that aren't true. I'm going to prove to you that you've made a lot of mistakes. And I'm going to suggest an entirely different way of doing things. Nobody likes to be told that they're wrong. But I need the space to be smart. I need to know that you can accept the fact that I'm smarter than you are about some things that are important to you. Like playing blackjack."

"Get real," I scoffed. "You didn't even know how to pick up the cards, or take insurance, or that insuring a blackjack is called 'even money.' You took insurance at a terrible time and you doubled down when you shouldn't have. You just plain got lucky. Skill had nothing to do with it."

"That was just an act. I fooled you. Maybe I fooled them. Let's first talk about the games at the Luxor. What rules do they have?"

"They deal shoes and you can double after split. Sometimes they hit soft 17 and sometimes they don't. Is that what you mean?"

"Yes. What else?" When I shrugged, she continued. "They also allow you to resplit aces and surrender after the dealer checks for blackjack. I didn't see you surrender at all, and there were several times it was warranted, even for a basic strategy player. A player 16 against a dealer 10 is the most frequent case, although there are others. The six-deckers, where they stand on all 17s, have a house edge of 0.26%. The eight-deckers, where they hit soft 17, have a house edge of 0.49%—which is almost twice as much. Yet you went back and forth between them willy-nilly. Any serious player would have stuck to the much smaller house edge, and known about surrendering.

"Now at the Mirage, the house edge was smaller, primarily because it's a two-deck game rather than a shoe. You give up resplitting of aces and late surrender, but the fewer decks more than makes up for it. It's been awhile since I added it up, but I think it's 0.19% against you.

"Think back to the first hand you played here. You had an eight and a nine and the dealer had, in order, a three, four, six, three, and five. Do you remember?"

"Of course. The dealer lucked out and got a 21 exactly. I was pissed."

"And I was excited that seven cards had come out without any 10s or aces. Highly unusual. And the player now had an advantage. Time to increase the bet, for any player tracking the cards. But you kept the same bet. Do you remember the second hand?"

"Yes," I said. "The dealer pulled another 21 and I got beat again on a double down."

"Yes," Annie agreed, "but your cards were a seven, four, and five, while the dealers were a seven, four, three, and seven. That's fourteen cards played with no 10s or aces! Time to get a *big* bet on the table. You wanted to leave, but I insisted that we play my $100.

"I was dealt a 10 and a six against the dealer's ace and he asked about insurance. You looked at the 16 and didn't want to insure a bad hand. I looked at the odds. A double-deck game starts out with a 104 cards, of which 32 are 10-valued cards and 72 aren't. But we'd seen 16 non-10s against only one 10. That meant there were 31 10s and 56 non-10s, which is a ratio of about 1.8-to-1 and they were offering 2-to-1 odds. It was a *great* bet.

"On the next hand, I doubled a nine, consisting of a three and a six, against a dealer two. You were right that you should only double against three through six when the deck is normal, but we had a highly positive deck. Doubling against the two was the correct play by far.

"On the next hand, it was a closer play on whether to insure or not when I had a blackjack. By this time, we'd seen five 10s and 21 non-10s. Now there were 27 10s still in the deck and 51 non-10s. I'd have insured that even if there were 53 non-10s. Since there were only 51, it was a pretty strong play.

"This morning here at the Mirage, I looked at the fact that the dealer drew so many little cards as *wonderful* news, because the big cards were still in the deck and that's when the player has the edge. Time to bet *big*. You looked at those same cards and thought it was *awful* news, because you'd lost two little bets in a row. Time to *leave the game*. This is a substantial difference of opinion."

Carlos and Marie arrived with our lunch. And just in time. Annie'd been bombarding me and I needed a breather. Although I would have played every hand different than she did, I had to admit that her explanations made sense. She certainly knew her numbers and I now knew she'd seen right through my "expertise." I'd been intending to *impress* her with my blackjack prowess, and instead now I found out that she'd evaluated my play and determined that I wasn't as good as I thought I was.

The weird thing was, I didn't even realize I was so mediocre! I had to admit, it was scary having the girl of my dreams point this out to me. What if she thought I was a liar? What if she concluded that, since I wasn't up to her standards as a blackjack player, I wasn't up to her standards period?

"I believe that all competent players would have made the same plays I did, and tried to get more money on the table," Annie continued after our servers left. "I used the 'ditsy-redhead' act to accomplish that. But the fact that I *won* or tied every one of my bets, even though they were correct, was quite fortunate. I'm a much better player than you, but luck plays a dominant factor in each session. Plain and simple, I was lucky today. You were lucky on Friday and unlucky yesterday."

"Okay," I conceded. "Obviously, you're a better player than me. A lot better. Are you saying I need to become a blackjack expert for us to have a future together?"

"Absolutely not!" she exclaimed. "That's not why I'm telling you these things at all. I could happily be your girl even if you didn't change your blackjack skills or habits one iota. Let me go on and it will all make sense, I think. I can tell you now that fact that you admitted without choking that I was a lot better player than you counts for a lot. You're at least halfway to a touchdown."

"That's good," I said with a grin, starting to feel better. "I'm really looking forward to scoring. Keep going."

"You told me you usually won at blackjack," Annie said. "I'm telling you that that wasn't accurate. I've observed your play for several hours. There's no way in hell that you're a winning player. Not even close."

"I don't think you can be so sure," I said. "I don't even know for sure myself."

"I believe you," Annie said. "And that's why I said you weren't being accurate rather than call you a liar. There's a difference. But I'm certain your claim to be an overall winner can't be valid."

I leaned back, arms folded. I had never seen her so offensively argumentative before. Yet she kept returning to the fact that things were going well for us. Who could tell? Maybe I'd be able to figure things out soon. In the meantime, there was no advantage in speaking.

"You're frequently playing a game where the house has about a half-percent edge, and your misplays probably cost you another half-percent," she asserted. "Over a weekend when you play a few hundred hands, giving up a percent to the house can sometimes be overcome by just plain being lucky. But over dozens of such trips, that one percent will eat you up. Guaranteed."

"But I avoid losing streaks by changing tables. And I

bet more when I'm winning. Those things must count for something," I told her. "Your mathematical models might be pretty spiffy, but I'll bet they don't take those things into account."

"Changing tables has absolutely nothing to do with changing your luck. Changing your bet based on whether you won or lost the hand before is totally ineffectual in changing the percentage against you. Let me show you. Assume you're heads-up against a dealer off the top of a new deck in a single deck game. They shuffle the cards well and in this casino, they deal without burning a card. You're dealt a six, seven, eight of mixed suits and the dealer gets a 10 and a nine. There are still 47 well-shuffled cards that you haven't seen yet. You with me so far?"

I nod.

"Okay now. Assume at the next table over the same cards were dealt, except it's now the dealer who gets the six, seven, eight and the player who gets the 10 and the nine. The exact same 47 cards haven't been seen by anyone. I ask you, by just looking at the two packs of 47 cards, could anyone in the world tell which scenario had just taken place? That is, whether the player won or the dealer won?"

"Uh, no, I don't think so."

"Then how can you justify betting more in the first case than in the second? Since the decks are indistinguishable from each other, the odds of you winning the next hand must be exactly the same," she concluded. "Smart players base the size of their bets on the composition of the unplayed cards, not on what just happened."

"Maybe you're right. But what about sitting at third base and protecting the table? What's that worth?"

"Absolutely nothing," Annie insisted. "For every time the order of the unplayed cards when it gets to third base is a 10 and then a five, there's exactly the same number of times when it's a five and then a 10. Sometimes what the player at third base does helps the table, whether it was right to take a card or not, and sometimes it hurts, whether it was right to take a card or not. It all evens out, and players who choose third base to influence the results are just fooling themselves. There are some strong reasons for preferring to sit at third base, but protecting the table isn't one of them."

"What are they?"

Annie waited until Marie picked up our empty plates and left the check.

"First, if you sit at the end and have good eyesight, you can see all the cards without moving your head. That makes it possible to track the cards without being obvious about it. Sitting in the middle of the table forces your head back and forth and that's easier for the floorpeople to spot. Second, the more cards that have been played before you make your play, the better you can do in some close decisions. Both of these reasons are somewhat counterbalanced by the fact that floorpeople *know* that good players prefer third base."

"So is it better to have the advantages and make the pit more suspicious or not have the advantages?"

"Good question, Chris. Every expert player has to answer that for himself, and different players come up with different conclusions. I like to sit at third base, because a lot of non-experts like sitting there for reasons like protecting the table. Since the floorpeople can't know for sure why I'm sitting there, I always felt the advantages outweighed the disadvantages. There's a lot of erroneous information floating around among gamblers. It's a case where you have to pick your guru, rather than listen to everyday players."

"Who are your gurus?"

"Peter Griffin, Arnold Snyder, and Stanford Wong, primarily. Although I studied Thorp's work along with that of Revere and Uston, among others. Not one of these writers supports any of the theories you espoused. I've looked at the blackjack titles on your bookshelf. You have these same books. If you're going to continue playing blackjack, perhaps you should read them again. You'll save yourself thousands of dollars if you do."

I felt like I'd just been scolded. It *had* been a couple of years since I'd read these books, and I hadn't read them that carefully. I valued being an intuitive player far more than I wanted to be a by-the-book robot. Although Annie was about the most beautiful and sexy robot I'd ever been close to, I knew I couldn't play like she did. It just wasn't me.

"I seem to be attracted to women who don't appreciate my gambling," I said quietly as Annie signed the comp slip and I left a tip. Walking back to the Luxor to watch the game, I was pensive, and a little hurt. I tried not to show it, smiling and maintaining my end of the conversation as she chattered on about blackjack and the Super Bowl. But it definitely felt like Annie was trying to pick a fight for no good reason at all. Just because she was a math whiz, did she have to lord it over me?

Sunday
January 30, 2000

When we were in front of Bellagio. Annie started in on me again. "I agree with Paula that you were probably a net loser at blackjack, but I hardly believe you were out of control or that your losses were excessive. At least if this weekend is typical of your betting patterns.

"Assuming you play at a 1% disadvantage and your average bet is $25, your average loss per hand is 25¢. If you play 50 hands per hour, your average hourly loss is $12.50, and a four-hour session costs you $50. And for that you can get a free room or two and some modest meals? Not bad. I suspect you're sometimes betting larger for the Luxor to be giving you such stuff. But overall you're getting amenities for substantially less than retail. And doing something you enjoy."

"I probably get credit for betting more than I do," I suggested. "Max Rubin says in *Comp City* that the floorpeople pay more attention to your *first* few bets than they do to your later bets."

"And Max is right," Annie agreed, "so long as the casino only sees your act a few times and you're consistently betting more whenever you start out at a table. But this trip you probably changed tables 15 times, so several of the floorpeople got to see you more than once. And if you lost at the previous table, you bet small at the current one whether this was the first time the floor person saw you or not. If you've done this on several trips to the Luxor, my guess is that they have your average bet pegged pretty accurately."

"I guess some of my trips I bet more than I did this time," I admitted. "And I did lose $6,000 once, instead of what I told you. You can really determine how much I bet by the rooms they give me?"

"Sort of," Annie said. "When I played years ago we bet more and received more. But getting two rooms and low-level meals for four hours of quarter play sounds excessively generous of the Luxor. I don't see how they can afford to do that."

"Why don't you play any more?" I asked, resisting the temptation to add, "since you're such a hot-shit blackjack player." After all, despite my embarrassment at being shown up, I still kept my eye on the prize—and that was sex with Annie.

"Because Tony does," Annie answered quietly. "I came here several times after we split up and ran into him. It was too painful. Especially when three months after he married Betty Boobs he was here with another amply-endowed woman. He's a pig!"

"Betty Boobs?"

"That's what I called her. As near as I could see, she had no redeeming qualities whatsoever, other than huge breasts. Tony started bugging me to get implants in the last six months we were married. I wouldn't do it. I couldn't see how it would change anything important. I might've done it, I suppose, if he'd been a loving husband, but at the time he was rarely home. For some reason, he seemed to come to the belief that if he was with a woman with a less-than-spectacular chest, it reflected negatively on his masculinity. I was no longer good enough for him in the attractiveness department. As I said, he's a pig."

"And a blind one at that. Does that mean you don't come to Vegas any more or you hate the Vegas experience?"

"Oh no," Annie laughed. "I come about ten times a year. And I stay in nice suites and eat in nice places—like Kokomo's. I just changed games. Now I play video poker instead of blackjack."

"You play slots?" I asked incredulously. "I thought the one-armed bandits were for people with big checkbooks who were too dumb to learn blackjack."

"Video poker is not the same as slots," Annie said with a smile. "And if you look me in the eye and tell me that I'm too dumb to play blackjack, I'll probably have to re-evaluate *your* intelligence."

"I don't think that, and even if I did I hope I'd be clever enough to keep it to myself just now. I believe that you're the best blackjack player I've ever met, even if you don't give proper credit to people who play by methods not approved by your gurus. Can you actually win at video poker?"

"Oh yes, and the comps are incredible. In two weeks, we'll be staying in a suite at the Golden Nugget that probably sells for $600 a night or more. And we'll eat at their best restaurants. And we'll be playing a game where I have the advantage 24-7. And there'll be a slot tournament where I could win thousands more. I'd say that that's better than the deal we have at the Luxor this weekend, wouldn't you?"

"Sure. Does this mean that I've passed your test and that I can have my way with you over and over and over and over again in two weeks?"

"Yes," she said, then stopped in the middle of the sidewalk and gave me a big kiss. The couple directly behind bumped into us and the guy said, "Get a room!" But it was cool. "And I'm hoping you'll be in the mood to do it early and often."

"So is Carol really a friend, or is the Mirage one of the places you play?"

"She's an executive slot host, which is a professional friend, sort of. We like each other well enough, but we've never had any contact outside of the casino. She gave me the meal because I've played enough there that I have a bunch of accumulated comps. I'd never put her in a position where she could lose her job for giving me something I didn't deserve."

"And you really win at this video poker game?"

"This is my first trip in 2000, and as you know, I'm up $700. In 1998 I was up $23,000 and in 1999 I was up

$8,000. I play a game where the biggest jackpots are $20,000 all at once, so one jackpot can make a big difference in your annual score. But if the games stay the same as they are now, I'll probably be up between $30,000 and $40,000 this year."

"How do you figure?"

"Because I plan to come to Vegas more often. I receive at least two or three invitations a month to come here. I've decided to start accepting more of them."

"Would you require me to learn to play video poker in order to be your boyfriend?"

"Not hardly. You can play whatever game you like. But if you want to come to Vegas *together*, and I have a choice between putting my brain on hold while watching you play a losing game and staying in standard rooms and eating at buffets, or me playing a game that I love and have the advantage at and can play while staying in luxurious suites and eating at high-quality restaurants, well, what would you suggest I do?"

I wanted to suggest she try to refrain from taking such delight in proving she was smarter than me. Instead I said, "I see what you mean. So to be with you, I either need to learn video poker or sit and watch you play, and play a little blackjack at the same hotel you're playing video poker at?"

"Right—so long as you're well-rested and can screw my brains out when I come upstairs! You can play blackjack at the Nugget, of course, but you'd be playing at a disadvantage and you wouldn't get any benefit from your play. We'll already be receiving as much as we want of their top-of-the-line benefits. You earning a buffet or two wouldn't add anything at all."

"How long do you think it would take me to become proficient at video poker?"

"I'm not sure. It depends on how seriously you apply yourself. I have a guru in this game too, and he spells out the information clearly enough if you're serious about picking it up. You might want to skim the information before our trip in two weeks so you can understand what I'm doing while I play. Later on, you can decide whether it's a game that catches your interest."

"What was it about our lunch at Mirage that told you I was a satisfactory companion to share your love nest?"

"First, that when I said you weren't always accurate and didn't know squat about this hobby you're bragging about, you didn't get highly defensive—or offensive, either. I'm sure I haven't convinced you about everything, but at least you took it well. Second, you knew I was smart, but I intentionally got in your face and *proved* I was smarter about *your* hobby. I had to see if you could take it—basically, let me be me. Whether you actually agree that I'm smarter at blackjack or are just biting your tongue so you can get laid, I don't know. But it worked. Congratulations. And third, you're at least willing to try something that's important to me. You're not a total stick-in-the-mud. But as I said, I'm not quite sure of your motives at this point."

"My motives are almost entirely lustful and lascivious," I told her as we reached the Luxor again.

"Sounds good to me," she said. "Let's go watch the game."

Sunday
January 30, 2000

We decided to drive home after the game. Now that I knew that Annie was far more expert about blackjack than I was, I had no desire to play again. At least not until I studied the game. Or maybe came back to Vegas without her. Or maybe switched to video poker.

"That might be the all-time best Super Bowl," Annie gushed, pretending to be a sports announcer, as we started southward on Interstate 15. "The Rams, with their overpowering offense, only manage field goals on their first three possessions, yet still end up with a sixteen-zip lead. The Titans tie it late in the game. The Rams then score on a seventy-three-yard Warner-to-Bruce bomb with less than two minutes left. Tennessee races down the field and on the last play of the game is one yard shy of the tying touchdown. Very exciting."

"Right up there football-wise, anyway. Certainly my personal all-time best," I concluded, "if you include who I watched the game with."

"Me too," Annie agreed. "I'm glad we saw it together."

"I've been thinking about the blackjack earlier today at the Mirage," I told her. "Do you mind if I ask you questions about it?"

"Not at all. Fire away."

"It seems to me that the count you used for insurance purposes was just a 10 versus non-10 count. I don't remember how to do any particular kind of counting, but I seem to recall that the 10 count isn't very good for betting and playing purposes. If that's so, why do you use it?"

"Very good," Annie told me. "Your recollection is correct. The 10 count is only good for insurance purposes, and that's why I use it. But it's also the only thing I use it for."

"But there are other reasons to keep a count, aren't there?" I asked.

"Sure there are. I also keep what's called the Hi-Lo count, where I add one for every card between a two and six inclusive, and I subtract one for every 10 or ace. I used to use a more complicated count, but I couldn't do it and keep an insurance count at the same time, so this is what I ended up mastering. It's been a couple of years since I played it, but this weekend I was able to keep both counts through an entire eight-deck shoe. I could probably play a pretty competitive game now if I wanted."

Wow! I'd challenged her because her count wasn't particularly well-respected, and she agreed and said that's why she keeps *two* counts. Annie was either a convincing bullshitter or one smart lady. I was betting on the latter.

"Okay," I told her. "There's no doubting that your intellectual skills and game-playing skills are superior. Probably genius level. I don't know. Is video poker a game where you have to be super bright to succeed?"

"No, not at all. But I'd guess that most of the successful players are smarter than average."

"Why do you say that?"

"Because the strategy for 9/6 Jacks or Better has been published and is available to all who want it. It's really not that hard. Besides, the available computer software corrects you when you're wrong. So you can practice at home until you're perfect. I figure it's masterable by at least half the population if they put their minds to it."

"That means half of the population are incapable of learning it perfectly?"

"Something like that, but that's just a guess. And half the people who don't play it perfectly can learn to play well enough so that they can get vacations at a discount off of retail. It's impossible to come up with an accurate figure for how many people who don't play perfectly do so because they aren't bright enough or because they just haven't practiced enough.

"But if you compare that to the far less than one percent of the population who can keep two count systems in blackjack the way I do, there's no contest on which one is easier. I'd say a hundred times as many people are capable of playing winning video poker than are capable of playing winning blackjack."

"And you're including me in the category of people who can win at video poker?"

"Oh yes," she answered. "No doubt about it. I don't know if I could teach you to play winning blackjack or not. But I'm a thousand-percent positive I can teach you to play winning video poker. And I hope you'll let me."

"Why is it so important to you?"

"Because it's an investment in *us*," she explained. "I'm not in this for two sex-filled weekends and then nothing. One reason I've made you wait so long to get laid is that I wanted to be sure that you were in this for more than that too."

"Oh, I am! But I must say that two sex-filled weekends sound better than one sex-filled weekend. What hurdles will I have to jump to get three?"

She smiled, shook her head, and basically ignored my question. "Going to the gym is a hobby we both have. And I've started hiking because of you, and we're taking dance classes together partly to be with each other. We both love to go to Vegas."

"So four things to do together are better than three?"

"Sure. Plus the fourth one is considerably different than the others. They're mostly physical. This is mostly intellectual. And it's the first bond that started out as my idea instead of yours."

"If I'm supposed to be focusing on the intellectual instead of physical aspects with respect to our weekend in two weeks, I must belong in the slow reading group."

She laughed. "You're a goofball. I'm looking forward to the sex too."

I was glad she was in a good mood. I wasn't crazy about all these relationship hoops she was making me jump through, but at that point I still figured she was worth it. Of course, I mused, all women are perfect lovers when you're in the fantasizing stage. Only time would tell how perfect this one turned out to be. But I couldn't worry about that now. I was close enough to a touchdown that, hoops or no hoops, I wasn't going to drop the ball now.

She was lost in her own thoughts too. After ten minutes or so of silence, I asked her why she picked video poker for her next game. It didn't seem to me like video poker and blackjack had much in common.

"What they have in common is that the smart player can make money at both of them. To me the fun of Vegas comes from beating the house."

"So your favorite part of this weekend was winning $700?" I asked.

"Being $700 ahead is small change to me, and essentially irrelevant. I gambled for five minutes and got lucky. But this weekend wasn't about gambling. It was about finding out about you."

"Okay. I won't congratulate you for winning $700. Instead I congratulate you for winning me," I kidded.

"Thank you very much. And now that I've found out what I needed to know, I do feel like I've won a prize."

"Thank you very much," I told her. "We're almost to Primm. We can stop there, check in, and I'll show you exactly what prize you've won."

She laughed. "Stopping at Primm is an excellent idea—in order to use the restrooms. As for the rest of the prize, I guess I'll just have to wait."

As we got back into the car after the brief break, I asked Annie, "Who are your video poker gurus?"

"Bob Dancer definitely heads the list. He's the only one I've heard of who publishes completely accurate strategies. Every other video poker writer takes the view that perfection is more trouble than it's worth and that their 'almost-perfect' strategies are close enough."

"And you agree with Dancer?"

"Unquestionably. The game I play is called Jacks or Better. It happens to be about the easiest video poker game in the world to play perfectly. On the $5 machines I play, Dancer's strategy is probably worth a buck an hour more than some of the others."

"That doesn't sound like much if his strategy is a lot more difficult," I observed.

"It is to me, and the strategy isn't that hard. You can judge for yourself. I have his report on the game ready to give to you. Also his computer tutorial."

"He's a computer programmer too? No wonder you're drawn to him."

"He didn't program *Bob Dancer Presents WinPoker*, but he does endorse it and promote it. It's the best program out there for video poker, by far."

"Do you know this Dancer guy?"

"I've never met him, but he and his wife Shirley frequently end up at the same events I go to. They're hard to miss. If there's a dance floor at the awards banquet, they'll be up there. And thanks to you dragging me to dance lessons, I now know that one of the dances they do is the West Coast Swing."

"Will they be at the Golden Nugget in two weeks?"

"I have no idea. It wouldn't surprise me either way. I've seen them at some Golden Nugget events, but sometimes they're not there."

"If it's such a lucrative event, why wouldn't they be there?"

"Probably three or four casinos are running good events that weekend. It may well be that they've decided a different one is better, for whatever reason. I'm not in their circle, so I just don't know."

"Is their circle hard to get into?"

"Probably not," Annie said, "but I really haven't tried. I haven't attempted to make friends in Vegas. Probably two-thirds of the people at these events come as couples, but of the other third, males outnumber females ten to one."

"Sounds to me like you'd be welcome with open arms."

"For sure," Annie told me. "At the risk of sounding

immodest, I'm sure I'd be considered a real catch for one of these guys. I'm much younger than the others who have the bankroll for this game. I've got enough of my own money to qualify for the tournament. And looks-wise, well, guys have been hitting on me since I was 13."

"I don't doubt that for a second. Why haven't you let it happen?"

"Because I don't want gambling to be the *only* thing or even the *main* thing a relationship is based on. I wanted to find a guy I had other things in common with first. Teaching somebody I like to play video poker is relatively easy. Teaching somebody who likes video poker to take an interest in dancing, physical fitness, art, hiking, and whatever else might be a little more difficult."

"I'd like to commend you for the intelligence you're showing in your plan of attack," I told her. "I think you've ended up with exactly the right guy."

She giggled. "So do I. Too bad his humility is so debilitating."

I laughed. "Do you expect me to become proficient at this game in two weeks? Is that possible?"

"Those are separate questions. I don't *expect* you to become proficient in that short of a time period. I do *hope* that you'll at least take the few hours to read the Dancer report once to give you an idea. Exactly where you end up between reading the report once and absolute proficiency is totally up to you and will be fine with me."

"But I *could* get pretty good in that period of time if I tried?"

"It's definitely possible to become decent with these tools relatively quickly, but you'd really have to commit yourself to it. That probably means 20 or more hours of practice on the computer. Even then there'll be some holes in your knowledge."

"Okay, we'll see. I promise to read it at least once."

"Thank you," she said squeezing my arm. "This means a lot to me."

"I've played a lot of live poker. That's got to be a tougher game, so I should be able to pick up this video poker pretty easy. Right?"

"Yes, live poker is more difficult. But they're not the same. Video poker has its own complexities."

"How are they different?"

"Well, in live poker, a royal flush is just the best straight flush. In video poker, a royal flush returns 4,000 coins and all straight flushes, whether 5-high or king-high or anywhere in between, return 250 coins. Very different.

"The hand ranking is the same, at least in Jacks or Better. In other video poker games, sometimes four 2s, 3s, and 4s are worth more than four 5s through kings. Sometimes four aces are worth more than a straight flush."

"Are those the only differences?"

"Hardly. The essence of live poker is you have several decisions about whether to check, bet, call, raise, pass, and there's probably some I left out. Bluffing is part of live poker. In video poker, there's only one bet per hand. And once you make that bet, which is usually five coins, you're in the game until the end. And you can't successfully bluff a video poker machine.

"Another big difference is that in video poker you can determine *exactly* the correct play, because it's straightforward mathematics how often you'll get a straight, a flush, a full house, etc., and you know going in what those are worth. In live poker, you can figure out how likely you are to get each of these hands, but you won't know if they'll win the pot until it's over. And sometimes it can be *very* expensive to find out. There are other differences as well, but that'll get you started."

"I see. It's clearly more complicated than I originally thought. I think I'm about talked out for one weekend," I told her. "There's a lot of things about video poker and you and me I need to think about. Why don't you pick out a CD that looks good to you and we'll listen to music for a while."

"Sounds like a plan," Annie said and chose a Linda Ronstadt-Aaron Neville CD. Most of my CDs are by country-western artists, but not all. She picked out the one that had "I Don't Know Much But I Know I Love You." I liked the choice.

We drove in relative silence for the rest of the trip, listening to CDs and having an occasional brief conversation about inconsequential things. When we finally reached our condos, I walked Annie to her door. "May I come in?" I asked. "This weekend deserves a nice goodbye kiss, and I don't want to give the entire neighborhood a thrill."

"Sure," she said. "I'd like that."

We sat on her couch and our mouths came together furiously. Her hands found my chest, and mine found hers. She didn't stop me when I reached my hand under her sweater and unhooked her bra.

We kept it up until I absolutely needed relief. I pushed her back on the couch, laid on top of her, and pushed against her while both of us were still dressed. Soon I came, with a loud groan. She held me tight and said, "Eleven more days and it'll be great for both of us. I can't wait."

I hadn't had any "dry screws" since before Paula, 15, 20 years ago. They capture most of the physical release of the "wet" ones, although not nearly the emotional satisfaction. I felt a bit like a horny teenager, coming in my pants. But Annie obviously wasn't offended by this. And it would now make waiting eleven days more bearable.

On my way out, she handed me the *Jacks or Better Report* and the computer disk *Bob Dancer Presents WinPoker*. They were on the table right by the door, so she'd obviously been planning, or at least hoping, to give them to me before we left for Vegas. She told me she had to work late the next two nights, but would see me at six on Wednesday to drive to dance class.

"There's no need to unpack now," I told her, "so give me the belt buckle on Wednesday," I reminded her.

"I don't know whether to be impressed that you remembered the belt, or offended that images of my tender body didn't drive that thought completely from your mind."

Monday
January 31, 2000

The phone rang at a little after eight in the morning. It startled me. I was in the middle of another dick-in-hand Annie dream and I didn't want it to end. Too bad. It was Richard. He was in somewhat of a panic and burst right into it. "Miamoto is having problems getting financing. His lawyer insists it's a momentary setback and wants an extension to the option. He's willing to pay for it."

"Can this discussion wait five minutes?" I asked. When Richard said yes, I told him to call me back then. I got up, turned on the coffee, went to the bathroom, then did some jumping jacks to get my blood and brain cells moving. Richard graciously waited a full 10 minutes before calling again. When he did, with Meg on the extension, I was ready.

"Give it to me again from the top," I told him and he did. "What kind of extension does he want and how much is he willing to pay?" I asked.

"He wants to pay a non-refundable $25,000 for another month, the money to be applied to the sales price," Meg told me. "That gives him an extra month and gives us nothing, assuming the deal goes through."

"You two have already been discussing this, right? Bring me up to speed."

"Richard wants to take the offer. He doesn't want to lose the sale. I want the sale too, but it's really inconvenient to wait a month. Daddy was expecting me to start tomorrow. I think Miamoto should be made to pay a penalty for messing up our plans."

"I tend to agree with you, Meg, but I'm also with Richard. We don't want to chase him away. How about we counter by asking for a non-refundable $50,000, which expires at the end of February, of which $25,000 will apply toward the purchase price and $25,000 is because we're going to have to scramble to delay this a month. How does that sound?"

"I like it," said Meg.

"If it works, great," said Richard. "If it doesn't work and he runs away, then I'm going to feel like John Bobbitt after Lorena got through with him."

"We all want the sale to go through," I said, "and we can't know what he'll say until we put the offer on the table. I think it's worth the risk. Even if he refuses, there's a good chance we can go back to his original offer."

"You guys both agree," Richard whined. "That's two votes. It doesn't matter what I think."

Meg fielded this one. "Come on, honey, you know we've always compromised until we got unanimity on major decisions. We're not going to change that on our last big vote. It's no fair that to say that if it works, you're in favor of it, but if it doesn't, then Chris and I stuck it to you."

"Tell you what, Richard. Let's ask for a non-refundable $75,000 now, still with the $25,000 penalty and $50,000 to be applied. That gives him room to counter at $50,000. Then he'll feel he got a good deal and we have what we want too. Okay?"

"Okay, I'll try it," Richard said somewhat begrudgingly, "and I hope you're right. But if you aren't, I won't hold it against you. I agree I'm part of the decision too."

"Perfect. But make sure you let him counter before going to our fallback position," I said. "I've read enough lawyer novels to know we don't want to negotiate against ourselves."

"Good," said Meg. "Richard will call the lawyer back and we'll keep you posted. Anything else to talk about?"

"Nothing unusual," I told them, "but today's the last day of the month and as you know, I always use the 15th and the last day to end my eBay auctions."

"How much you got out there this time?" Richard asked.

"Around $10,000," I told him. "The bids could end up higher or lower than that. It's a little more than usual for me, but not by much. I emailed over the numbers last Thursday in case either of you wanted to check out the action."

Nobody had anything else to say, so Meg announced with a giggle, "Meeting adjourned," and we all hung up.

Tuesday
February 1, 2000

Miamoto ended up accepting the first offer. His lawyer sent a cashier's check for $25,000 by courier to Richard and one for $50,000 couriered to the escrow office, along with instructions that were faxed over to Richard to make sure he concurred. He did.

I was glad the deal was still alive, mainly for Richard and Meg. But for me too. I still wanted to get out of Los Angeles. Even though the air quality near the coast where I lived wasn't bad, my occasional forays into the poisonous smog of the city really irritated me. And I'd had enough of L.A. traffic. Of course, there was no way I'd leave Annie, unless all the magic between us evaporated once we finally got around to doing the dirty. That was possible, though I doubted it. In some ways every relationship feels magical before you sleep together. As Ike said, they all have their excepts.

Yesterday after the gym, I surprised myself by taking a long nap. Long Vegas weekends tend to exhaust me anyway, but going through Annie's bizarre "pass-or-fail" test was even more tiring. Even though I didn't know what the test was or how to study for it, I desperately wanted to pass it and apparently I had. As far as I could see, there was no reason Annie and I couldn't spend the night together after class on Wednesday.

Since I got all the eBay sales to the post office this morning, and had plenty for February 15, I decided to tackle Jacks or Better. It couldn't be that hard. I installed *WinPoker* onto my computer and started to play. The first hand I was dealt a pair, which I held. The second time I had a four-card flush, which I held. This was easy. The third hand was 7♥8♠A♦9♣T♠ and I guessed the 789T.

Right again. Piece of cake.

The fourth hand I got Q♥J♠5♣7♣8♣. The high cards or the clubs? Who knows? I tried the QJ and the computer flashed "*Major Error!!!* Cost: 3.49 cents." That didn't sound so major to me, until I realized that the game assumed I was playing for quarters. If we were playing for $5 like Annie said, this would be 20 times that, or almost 70¢. Still not too bad. I wondered if all of the errors came with three exclamation points.

Soon I was dealt A♣T♣2♦6♠5♠. I held the AT. This time, in small timid letters, I got "*Minor Error!* Cost 0.43 cents." Only one exclamation point this time. Presumably, there was some sort of middle-sized error with two. I decided not to try to find it. I assumed it would find me.

The good news was that it found me right away. I was dealt J♣K♠T♣8♦5♣ and held the JT. The sign said "*Moderate Error!* Cost: 1.24 cents." The bad news was that not only did I have the wrong answer and not know why, I felt I was being gypped out of an exclamation point. Oh well. Life is full of tragedies.

I got some hands right again, then was dealt 3♦4♦7♦K♠J♠. This was no problem. I'd already learned that straight flush draws were more valuable than high cards. When I held the diamonds, this time I got "*Major Error!!!* Cost: 18.38 cents." Oh dear. This was trickier than I thought. I decided to go read the report.

It took me less than two hours to read it through the first time. By the time I'd finished, my head was swimming. High cards, low cards, gaps, flush penalties, straight penalties, and a bunch more. It didn't seem like it would be impossible to learn, but it was clear that I couldn't absorb it all in one sitting.

Wednesday
February 2, 2000

"Mandy made me a dress for the Valentine's Day awards banquet. It's a burnt-red color. She had a square left over for you to put into your pocket. Will you wear this in the pocket of your navy blazer?"

We were driving down to Swingtime. I held the pocket swatch so I could see it without taking my eye off the road. "Of course. But I'll have to figure out a different shirt. The red shirt I had on when we went to Nick's wouldn't go well with this. But it's no problem. I have time to get another one. This matches your earrings, it seems to me. I don't suppose that's a coincidence?"

"No," Annie admitted. "Those earrings are the only jewelry anyone's ever made for me. They're special."

"I'm glad you feel that way. And don't forget to give me your belt when we get home tonight. Also, I'd like to make up a necklace for your outfit, but I need to know how long to make it and what shape. Will you try the dress on so I can examine the neckline?"

"It was going to be a surprise."

"I already know the color, the fabric, when you're going to wear it, and that you'll be well satisfied sexually at the time. That's not exactly what I'd call a huge surprise. And if you let me see it, I can do a better job on the necklace."

"Okay. But the dress is delicate. We can't be doing any serious necking while I'm wearing it."

"It'll be a struggle, but I'll force myself to undress you before we undergo said necking. That sound any better?"

She laughed. "That sounds a *lot* better. But it's not going to happen. Eight more days until we do that. I'll figure out a way to show you the dress when we get home." In spite of all the sexy things we were talking about, it was still her laugh that turned me on the most. Then she gently put both of her hands around my right arm.

"Chris, it's really sweet that you're designing jewelry for me and going to the extra trouble to make sure I look special. No one's ever done that before for me. Thank you thank you thank you."

"You're welcome welcome welcome. I'm looking forward to taking the belle of the ball to the big dance. And trust me, no one's ever invited me to a weekend like you've promised either."

"I can hardly wait. For a lot of reasons." And she punctuated this last sentence with an arm squeeze.

The studio has two separate classrooms, and Michele would be teaching a waltz class in one of the rooms while Phil taught swing in the other. As we came up to sign in for the class about 15 minutes early, Michele was speaking to Phil and happened to look our way. "Hey Chris," Michele greeted me, "Annie's always been beautiful. But now she's positively glowing. What have you been doing to her?"

"You know, swing dancing affects different people in different ways. It must be pre-class glow," I explained, tongue in cheek. Annie giggled. Phil smiled and nodded his head. I took it as a sign that he approved of my taste in women, and that if Annie was happy, I must be doing something right.

In tonight's class we learned a new tuck turn. This was my fourth. I found myself cataloging the patterns so I could remember them. When Annie and I'd danced at the Luxor, I'd gone through my catalog of patterns over and over again. My repertoire of steps was growing, but it still wasn't very large. Going through the entire list systematically allowed me to display everything we knew, so the repertoire didn't seem quite so small.

Tonight's tuck turn required a different hand position than we'd learned before, where the woman performs a figure four with her left leg in the middle of the pattern. Tonight's pattern was mostly for the women, with the guys just standing there as the "frame" while the women painted the picture. Phil introduced a new sugar-push footwork pattern just for the guys at the end. It was less than what the women got, but still it was something and I couldn't complain. We also reviewed the patterns we'd gone over the previous two weeks. Learning from Phil was definitely a slow process, but the students who'd been doing it for months looked really good. Annie and I would be there soon.

On the ride home, I asked Annie if I could tell her a somewhat lengthy story, and she said to go ahead.

"In my junior year in high school, Holly Bennett was the love of my life. Apparently, I was interesting enough to her too, so we started going out. On the second date, I got a chaste kiss from her. On the fourth date, we French kissed for half an hour. When I tried to put my hand on her breast, she stopped me until the sixth date. On the 10th date her bra came off. On the 15th I got a hand job. And finally on the 25th date or so we went all the way. Since I'd never had sex before Holly, and every night we went a little bit further, this was continually exciting."

"Let me guess where this is going," Annie interjected. "You're seeing similarities between Holly Bennett and me. Correct?"

"Yes. And I'm not a 17-year-old virgin anymore." My words came out with a little more force than I intended.

"Are you angry?"

"'Angry' isn't the right word. I'm confused. This waiting eight more days doesn't make any sense to me. We've both decided that this is what we want to do. We're both very, very ready for it. Why wait? I just don't understand."

"The real reason is important to me. At the same time, though, it's silly and I didn't plan on telling you."

I drove on saying nothing. She, too, remained silent. I figured she was going through some internal debate on whether to tell me this important reason.

"Just telling you will change the dynamics of a perfect situation in a way I don't want it changed."

I continued to drive quietly. She seemed to be arguing with herself. Maybe I'd win an argument where I wasn't even a direct participant!

"Okay, here goes. Next Thursday, February tenth, is my birthday," Annie told me, then looked at me as though that explained everything.

I couldn't help it. I started laughing. Big-time belly laughs. I had to pull the car over to the shoulder of the freeway for safety reasons. I was laughing so hard that tears were blinding me.

Annie looked at me like I'd lost it. When I finally calmed down, she said, "I had no idea what reaction to expect from you. I didn't consider that one at all. What's so funny?"

I started laughing again and said, "Holly Bennett," and just kept laughing.

Flashing lights in my rear-view mirror instantly cured my laughing fit. I hit the button to lower my window and put both hands on my steering wheel where they could be seen. I assumed this was just an inquiry about why I was on the shoulder of the freeway, but I didn't want to give a motorcycle cop any reason to be jumpy.

"Everything okay here?" the CHP officer asked.

"Yes, sir. Everything is fine."

The officer noticed my wet eyes, and the grin starting to creep across my face again. "Have you been drinking, sir?"

"No. It's been three days since I had anything to drink."

He shone his flashlight around the inside of the Lexus, then leaned in and asked Annie, "Have you been drinking, ma'am?"

"No sir, officer," Annie replied pleasantly. "We're just on our way home from dance class."

He frowned, as if thinking this was a pretty flimsy story. "License, registration, and proof of insurance," he said to me. It wasn't a question.

The officer took my papers and returned to his bike

to call in the information. Apparently, this was just routine. I wasn't worried. My last ticket was three years ago, and I went to traffic school to boot. Annie and I continued our chat while we waited for my license and registration to be returned.

"I didn't figure out Holly Bennett's methodology until I discussed the matter with Kyle Spencer and Arturo Jimenez, who were next in line for Holly's affections. Kiss and tell to be sure, but Holly was the first conquest for all of us and we never could figure out just why things ended. I started dating Holly in early October. She told me her birthday was November fourth. Dick started dating Holly shortly after New Year's, and she told him her birthday was February fourth. For Arturo, Holly's birthday was June fourth."

"So she moved her birth date around so she could get presents from each new beau. And always the fourth of the month so she could remember. Pretty clever," Annie observed. "Are you doubting my birthday is February tenth? Would you like to check my driver's license and registration?"

"Not really," I said. I then faked holding a Groucho Marx cigar, waved two fingers, and said with a leer, "But I would like to use my dipstick to check your oil."

She laughed and I continued. "I was tickled by the coincidence that we'd just been discussing a similarity between you and Holly and then the subject of birthdays comes up. I hadn't thought about Holly and her convenient birthday strategy for years."

The officer returned my documents, told me everything was fine, and to be very careful when I merged into traffic. I told him I would and pulled out.

"I still don't see what your birthday has to do with whether we spend the night together or not."

"Birthdays are very special to me," Annie told me. "Two years ago I got myself the Beemer on my birthday and last year I sprung for a hugely major upgrade on my home computer. This year, I had my heart set on having you."

"That's not what we're talking about," I told her. "We're

driving to Vegas and you're *going* to have me. Probably more than once. But I don't see what that has to do with tonight."

"Because what I really want for my birthday is you *for the first time*. In six months time, I'm hoping that we'll have made love so many times, whether we've had ninety-seven orgasms by then or a hundred and seven will be totally irrelevant."

"Can we try for one fifty?" I quipped.

"But the first time is one to remember," she told me. "There's a lot to the Golden Nugget suite that I haven't told you about yet. What would make the evening absolutely perfect for me is for it to be our opening act, sexually speaking."

"Why didn't you tell me your birthday was coming up?"

"Sort of the opposite reason from Holly, I suppose. I didn't want you have to run around getting me a present. It's not 'things' that I want from you, although I will take that necklace you talked about, thank you very much. It's those little items like love, honesty, humor, empathy, stuff like that."

I drove along quietly. This was the first time I'd heard her use the word "love." While it was not the same as "I love you," it was close. And I was at least close to being in love with her too. How could I keep arguing with her?

"So what you really want for your birthday is for me to tie a knot in my dick tonight and wait eight more days?"

"Tell you what. I'm a reasonable woman and am willing to meet you halfway. If you can tie a knot in your dick, we don't have to wait."

"Perhaps that was a slight exaggeration," I conceded.

"It doesn't have to be a whole knot. Even a half-hitch will do," she grinned.

"Perhaps that was a major exaggeration," I conceded further.

"In that case, yes, what I really want for my birthday is for us to wait."

I pulled the car into my garage and leaned over to

kiss her. "If you absolutely can't wait," she told me between kisses, "we can do it tonight as often as you can get it up. I won't stop you and I won't hold back on you. But it will be much, much better for me if we wait."

As we walked to her condo, I knew she'd get her way. I wouldn't have figured out the birthday fixation in a million years, but one thing I'd learned about women is that when you keep them happy, they find a way to keep you happy.

When we got inside, Annie modeled her dress. It fit her perfectly, of course, since it was tailor-made. I asked if she had some thread I could have and some scissors I could borrow. She did. I draped the thread around her neck, figured out the best length for the necklace, cut the thread, and put it into my pocket. Later, I'd use it as a pattern.

Then I asked her to bring me her belt buckle. She did, then said, "Don't go away," as she ran into the bedroom. I waited on the couch. When she returned, she was in thigh-length shorts and an Ohio State sweatshirt. Bare feet. She was clearly comfortable with having me there while she was in her grunge-around-the-house clothes. All in all, a good sign, I figured. She plopped herself down next to me and moved easily into my arms as our lips found each other. I could grow used to this!

It didn't take my hand long to move underneath her sweatshirt. To my surprise she wasn't wearing a bra. She moaned lightly as I fingered one of her nipples. I knew that if I kept this up, she wouldn't get the birthday present she wanted.

I stood up, with her still attached, and then sat her back down on the couch. I moved to an adjacent chair and held up my hand in a sort of a "stay" gesture.

"I need to say a few things," I told her. She nodded and leaned back on the couch.

"This feels too damn good, Annie," I told her. "I want you really bad and everything about you says you want me too. So something's got to give. The only way for us not to have sex for eight days is to keep our distance. I can call you every night and we can go to dance class, but if we see each other any more than that, we're going to end up naked."

She frowned, but nodded. "You're right. But I'm so close right now. Please touch me while I come!" and she lay back on the couch.

I rushed over, knelt next to her, and placed my hand between her legs on the outside of her shorts. She put both of her hands on top of mine, pressed down hard, and pulsed her hips upward, groaning. As she ground into my hand, I pressed my pelvis into her hip. She won the race. Loudly. She called my name and moved her hands to hold me tightly.

But now I was too far gone to stop. I withdrew my hand and, still dressed, moved on top of her. I thrust hard against her, pelvis to pelvis, and less than a minute later, I, too, found relief.

I moved us both to the floor and held her. Annie-sized couches aren't made for Chris-sized people to stretch out. "That was date number 24," I told her.

"I understand your point," she told me as we both lay there panting. "Loud and clear."

Thursday
February 3, 2000

Between the dress details and the should-we-or-shouldn't-we talk, I neglected to tell Annie that I'd been practicing video poker. I'd already fulfilled my promise to her to read the report once. But I like strategic games and I like to win. Also, I found this one interesting, at least so far. I read the report again. This time it was easier. But understanding what a report says and knowing how to play every hand are two different things. I went back to *WinPoker*.

I played 200 hands over about an hour and made 13 mistakes. The good news was that when the computer told me I was wrong, I could look at the report and determine the right play. The bad news was that I wasn't able to figure it out *before* the computer decided how many exclamation points to give me.

But I was getting better. I'd try it again tomorrow. Today I wanted to work on Annie's jewelry. Heliotrope isn't an expensive gemstone, so I could easily give her several pieces. The problem was in matching colors. The reds and greens in the stones are all similar, but I wanted to pick out exact matches if I could. When I gave her the earrings to start with, I purposely saved five matching stones for color comparison. Those were more than enough for the belt buckle, but I'd need to get more for the necklace. For this I had to go downtown.

The Jewelry District in downtown Los Angeles is located almost entirely along Hill between Fifth and Eighth streets. While there are some stand-alone stores, several multi-story buildings are filled with hundreds of little shops specializing in some sort of jewelry: diamonds, loose and set, chains, watches in all price ranges, chains, gold, silver, platinum, chains, all sorts of gemstones, chains, and a variety of other items. Some were open to everyone, others only to the trade. I knew my best chances for good heliotrope were two shops inside the St. Vincent Jewelry Center between Sixth and Seventh, and another one at the California Jewelry Mart across the street. If these three failed to yield enough good stones, there was one decent possibility each in the International Jewelry Mart and in the Jewelry Theater Building, which were both on Seventh. I tried St. Vincent first, primarily because it gave me two pops at the prize in one place.

Also, I'd called Ari Gurel yesterday and asked him to bring a supply of rough heliotrope today. I also asked him to show me his already cut-and-polished heliotrope. On any given day, Ari and his wife Yasmin only remove a sample of their inventory from their safe to display on the store shelves. I told Ari I'd be in at about eleven and would be looking to buy a sizable quantity of heliotrope if I could match colors with what I had.

"Why heliotrope, my friend?" he'd asked. "That's not your usual."

"New girlfriend," I told him. "Red hair and green eyes."

"Ah yes," he said. "Something like that can easily move you out of your usual territory. What size stones?"

"They're for a necklace. Probably in the eight- to ten-millimeter range. I'm thinking oval rather than round. Perhaps a bigger one for the centerpiece."

"Do you want them predrilled as beads?"

"I wasn't thinking of using beads, but let me see what you have. Maybe I'll go that route."

"Very good. See you at eleven."

Ari was off to the bank when I got there, but Yasmin showed me several hundred stones. By comparing them to what I had, together we picked out about 20 that were possibilities if I were to make the necklace in exactly the same style as the earrings. But I decided that they would be too large for a woman of Annie's size to wear with that particular dress. Even though I wouldn't be using them for this project, I decided to take all of them, in case I wanted to do something else later. The cost was small and the colors matched perfectly. Yasmin also had a few pre-strung strands in exactly the right colors, which I also took. And I bought two softball-sized chunks of rough stone. Heliotrope is easy to work with. It'd be simpler to cut new stones than drive down here to buy some.

She then showed me the gold spacer balls they carried to string between the stones. They weren't quite right, so she suggested I try store number 314 in the same building, which had a wider selection. I didn't know who ran that store, but I was pretty sure that if Yasmin recommended them, they'd turn out to be Israeli. Dozens of nationalities could be found in the Jewelry District, but they tended to stick together with their own kinsmen. If I'd first stopped at a store run by a Korean, he would have recommended other Koreans to supply anything he didn't carry. But since I was familiar with the Jewelry District and their suppliers anyway, I knew I'd try the shop of two Armenian brothers, Aram and Tigran Kurabian, before I followed any of the recommendations.

"Have you strung beads before?" Yasmin asked.

"No. Why? It doesn't look that hard."

"It isn't. But good quality strands of beads have hand-tied knots between each bead. That way, if a strand breaks, at most you'll lose one bead."

"That makes sense."

"It isn't hard. But it takes time. if you leave this job to the last minute, make sure you leave time for the knotting too."

"Thank you, Yasmin. That's good advice."

It turned out that my purchase of stones and pre-strung beads wasn't that large, and I apologized for making them bring out all these stones for such a small sale. By this time, Ari had returned from the bank. He told me not to worry about it and to be sure to invite them to the wedding.

At the Kurbabians' shop, I found spacer balls I liked, bought them, and was finished with my Annie shopping. Then I combined the trip with my regular once-a-month resupplying. I needed to stock up on several other stones, along with gold and silver findings for a month's supply of jewelry assembly. I'd decided to make Annie a necklace even before I knew that it would be worn with her dress. I didn't have a definite length or shape in mind before last night, but then she showed me her dress. Sometimes things just fit together so well!

Sunday
February 6, 2000

"Do I have to wear a chastity belt in order to practice dancing tonight?" she asked me in a teasing voice when she came over to practice our recently learned moves.

"No, but I'm hoping that you ate lots of garlic for dinner, although I don't think that'd stop me once I got started."

I stopped the innuendos short by turning on the dance music. One of our favorite practice songs was "The Bop" by Dan Seals. It's slightly slower than usual for swing numbers, but when you're practicing, slower is better. Although we did get a little practice in, we found ourselves groping each other and stealing kisses. I turned off the music and went and got us each some water from the cooler. A cold shower would have to wait until later. I was glad when Annie asked if I'd been practicing on *WinPoker*.

"Yes, actually, quite a bit."

"Are you using the Error Log feature?"

"I don't even know what that is."

"I know your office is your private space, Chris. The door's always closed. But if you let me get close to your computer, I'll show you."

"Well, I would've had my office in better order if I'd known you were going to see it." Truth was, I'd been working on some financial data that I wasn't ready for her to see. Not that I didn't trust her, but who knew what she could infer from the numbers on my screen? "Let me tidy up a bit first, okay? Can't have you thinking I'm a typical bachelor type."

"Too late to worry about that," she called out with a smile in her voice. "And don't worry about it not being a showplace," she said. "An office should be however you need it to be in order to get your work done. Get into *WinPoker*, click on 'Training Modes,' then click on 'Advanced.'

When I did that, the pay schedule was compacted and new information appeared in the upper-right-hand corner. It showed I'd played 2,215 hands and had made 84 errors. It also calculated my return at 98.64%. My errors cost me $37.65.

"You've been very busy. I'm impressed you're working so hard on this."

"Is it a good score?" I asked, hoping for praise, actually.

"For your first two thousand hands, it's excellent. But you need to get better. We haven't talked about the slot club yet, but you need to get at least 99.8% accuracy just to break even. You've made seven times more errors than there can be."

This wasn't the response I was hoping for. But she wasn't done. "The key to getting better, I think, is to not keep making the same mistake over and over again. That's where the Error Log comes in."

"Show me."

"Okay, click on 'From Error Log,' and then 'View.'" I complied. "The first error you see is the last one you made. Do you remember it?" It was A♣Q♥T♥7♠4♥.

"Yes," I replied. "I chose the QT and the computer said that the AQ was correct. I didn't notice the flush penalty before I played the hand."

"Yes. You can see the word 'HELD' above the queen and ten and the word 'HOLD' below the ace and queen. That tells you what you actually held and what you should have held. Now click on the forward arrow."

I did and the hand Q♥J♠5♣7♣8♣ appeared, with 'HELD' above the high cards and 'HOLD' under the clubs. "That should be the first mistake you made while practicing."

"Yes," I agreed. "I hadn't read Dancer's report yet. I

now know that 3-card straight flushes with no high cards and one gap are move valuable than unsuited high cards. I never make this mistake any more."

"Excellent! That's what studying is all about. If you go through the rest of the errors, you'll see the hands you have problems with. I suspect you'll see one or two kinds of errors over and over again. By reviewing just those hands, with the correct play shown, you'll be well on your way to eliminating your errors."

She took both my hands in hers. "You're doing very well, Chris. I'm very pleased with the effort you're putting in to learn my hobby. And you know why I'm not smothering you in thank-you kisses."

"Yes. And it's nice to know that you think I deserve them. You mentioned the slot club. Is that something I need to know about?"

"Absolutely. But not immediately. As long as you're going to be following my lead on where to play, you don't need to know. But if you want to learn to choose good plays for yourself, you'll have to eventually learn about it."

"Do you have time to tell me now?" I asked.

"Yes. I have the time, but not the 'no power.' I better go now, so I can still have the birthday present I want."

"I understand," I told her. "I want you too." I put my arm around her waist and ushered her to the front door. "Go. We'll talk about slot clubs on the way down to Swingtime Wednesday night."

Although it was early and I'd cleaned up just a few hours before, as soon as she left, it was time for a shower—as cold as I could stand it—and bed. Cold shower notwithstanding, I rubbed against the mattress while imagining being with her. It wasn't my sexual release of choice, but at the moment it would have to suffice. Sometimes you have to do what you have to do.

After a brief rest I went back to the Error Log. In the early part of the log, I'd missed all sorts of hands. The last 20 errors, however, were all moderate or minor. I could definitely see improvement. And it had been at least

200 hands since I'd made an error of any sort.

I saw a button to clear the log. I pressed it and all the counters reset to zero: zero hands played, zero errors. I started to play again to see what my level was. I logged an even 1,000 hands and made one error. From K♥T♥9♠3♣5♥, I held KT instead of just the K. I knew the rule, which was the K is preferred to the KT if there is both a 9 penalty and a flush penalty, but momentarily forgot about it. It was a minor error costing 0.19 cents, and my return was listed as 99.98%. Not bad. A couple more days of this practice and I'd be ready.

To think. The only reason I started to learn this game was for good sex. Turned out I liked it!

Tuesday
February 8, 2000

"At least I got off the bagel for the millennium," Ike told me. He'd won one out of the three chess games we played. A "doughnut" was a zero score, the term frequently used among bettors. But Ike was Jewish, so his doughnut became a bagel.

"Ike, I need some financial advice. You in the mood to put on your accountant yarmulke?"

"What? You need I should give you a loan? Your credit's always good with me."

"Nothing like that, Ike. In fact, it's the opposite."

"Very good. I didn't think I needed to borrow money, but who knows? What interest rate did you have in mind?"

I laughed. "Not that either. I have almost a half-million dollars now, mostly in mutual funds, and I'm going to get a bunch more from the sale of GGG. I want some advice on what to do with the money."

"It's good you should think of these things now. I believe a man should first find a good wife, then buy a home, then plan for his children's education, and then plan for his own old age. In that order."

"Okay, but back up a little and leave the wife and kids out of the discussion, since I don't have any. And even buying a home. Right now I don't even know whether I'm going to be staying in L.A. I'm more asking you whether I should be in stocks, bonds, CDs, or some other financial instrument. All of a sudden I've got more money than I know what to do with. How do I figure this stuff out?"

"You're going to move away from here?" Ike sounded surprised. "I need you to play chess with me so my sets don't get dusty. But it's okay. Don't worry about me. I'll be a little lonely, but all right."

"Ike, sometimes you remind me more of a Jewish mother than a Jewish father. I'm talking about leaving Los Angeles, not leaving the planet. I'm still going to be in the jewelry business, so I'll probably come to the Los Angeles Jewelry Mart once a month or so. We can arrange our chess matches around those visits. But what should I do with my money?"

"Thank you for asking, but maybe I'm not the best guy for advice. The stock market is very high now and has been going up for years. Sooner or later it will come down. I've put most of my money in bonds and real estate investment trusts, but it's only a guess. If the stock market tanks in the next year or so, I'll be a genius. If it goes up for five years before it tanks, I'll be a schmuck. And my crystal ball fails to tell me which scenario is more likely.

"Also, Chris, for me it's different. I'm 68 and I've got more money than I'll ever need. It's just a matter of how much I'll pass on to Meg and a few others. But you're younger. You should still be trying to accumulate, rather than just preserve. The stock market has historically been a good place for accumulation, but maybe it's not so good now. I wish I could help you more, but I just don't know."

"I understand nobody knows for sure. But what's your best guess."

"My best guess is gold. I'm a jeweler and a Jew, so I think of these things. Gold is at about a 10-year low right now. That's my number-one pick for you. But it's not a guarantee."

"Gold bullion? Gold futures? Gold funds?"

"For gold bullion we're talking about a thousand pounds in your safe. I don't think so. Gold futures are more of a short-term gamble and you have to know what you're doing. Gold funds are the way to go, in my book. Is your account still with Charles Schwab?" I nodded and he continued. "There's probably a Charles Schwab gold fund. And if not, they can help you get into another one."

"Thanks, Ike. I understand it's just a guess, but you've been helpful. I'm more willing to trust your guess than mine."

Wednesday
February 9, 2000

As soon as we pulled out of my garage on the way to Swingtime, I asked Annie to tell me about slot clubs.

"Okay," she said, "but it's going to require me talking non-stop for about ten minutes. It's almost as hard to learn everything about a slot club as it is to learn 9/6 Jacks."

"Fine with me," I told her. "I'll try to remember it all, but if I forget, I'll let you tell me again this weekend while I'm trying to generate enough energy to ravage you again."

"Fair enough, although I think I'll be offended if you want to think about a slot club at a moment like that."

"I've never heard of a woman being jealous of a slot club before," I kidded. "I suppose anything is possible in Las Vegas."

Annie was silent for longer than I thought she should be. When I glanced over at her, she was staring at me hard. I didn't know why, so I tried to ease us past this slight impasse. I smiled, touched her hand, and prompted, "Slot clubs?"

"Every slot club has different rules," Annie began. "They're all similar, but where the player can find an advantage is in the differences. So you have to study each one."

She took a deep breath and continued. "The Golden Nugget awards points based on the number of dollars played through their system. Every $75 of play earns you a point, and points are worth 50¢ in cash, plus a certain value in comps. That comes out to 0.67%. When you add that to the 99.54% that 9/6 Jacks returns when you play perfectly, the competent player can receive 100.21%. You with me so far?"

"So far so good," I said, "although how much the 0.21% advantage is really worth must depend on how many dollars you can get through the machine."

"Exactly," she encouraged, finally warming up to the subject. "I play about 600 hands per hour, which on a $5 machine adds up to $15,000 per hour. A 0.21% advantage means a little over $30 hourly."

"Wait a second. If you multiply $5 by 600, you only come up with $3,000."

"That's right," she said. "In most video poker games we bet five coins, but we use the size of a single coin to describe the game rather than the total bet. So on a $5 game, each bet is $25, and 600 of those bets per hour add up to $15,000."

"I see," I said. "I should have known I wasn't going to catch a math major in an arithmetic mistake. But I didn't realize I'd be betting $25 a hand. I thought I was only going to be betting $5. Isn't it scary to bet so much?"

"Not to me. And you bet $25 at a time in blackjack. At least sometimes."

"Yes. But I'm betting 60 or fewer hands an hour, not 600. This will be a lot more money on the barrelhead than I'm used to."

"True enough. It takes some getting used to. I've heard enough about your personal finances to know you have a big enough bankroll to survive at this level. But there's no hurry for you to jump in. You're welcome to gamble with my money for a few trips until you're used to the swings. After you have a few trips under your belt, *then* you can decide how comfortable you are. In the meantime, let's continue the slot club discussion."

"Okay. A 0.21% advantage on $15,000 means a little more than $30 an hour. That doesn't sound like very much. My guess is you earn much more than that at Rand."

"I do," Annie said, "but the $30 comes with a lot of extras. The comps you commanded from playing blackjack at the Luxor were pretty good. But wait until you see what I get from playing video poker."

"Like what?"

"At the Golden Nugget, you collect your comps and cashback at the same time. So a dinner for two at Stefano's, which is one of their two best restaurants, costs you 100 points, but they give you $50 at the same time.

"They have a menu of the prices for various things. A standard room with no food costs you 76 points a night, I think. A room with the works for food and beverage costs you 300 points. The Tower Suite we'll be staying in costs 1,000 points a night, but they also give you $500 cashback for every one of those nights."

"Let's see now. A thousand points means $75,000 of play, is that right?" I calculated. "Even if it's the best room in the house, that seems like a lot. Wouldn't it be better to take a smaller suite with less risk? After all, the big prize for me this weekend is making love with you. It seems to me that doing it in a regular suite would be much the same as doing it in a luxury suite. And at much less risk."

"I understand your point. And risk is another conversation we'll have before we get to Vegas, but it'll have to wait until we're finished talking about slot clubs. For now, please just trust me. I'm not asking you to put up any of your own money this weekend. Even if it looks real scary to you just now, I can afford the swings and I'm very successful at this game."

"Okay, let's go on then. It takes $75,000 of play per night, and you can play $15,000 per hour, so that means five hours a day of gambling is required. Correct?"

"Correct. Plus I have over 10,000 points 'in the bank,' because I've played more than the minimum on previous trips. So it's not necessary to play a certain amount every trip."

"Is that how you got them to give you a free meal at Kokomo's?"

"Yes. The Mirage's slot club and comp system is very different when you get down to specifics, but it's the same general idea. I have a bunch of comps accumulated at the Mirage and the Venetian, plus the Golden Nugget, of course."

I turned the car into the Swingtime parking lot. "How much is 'a bunch?'"

"I don't really know," she said. "Essentially unlimited, I suppose, as long as they're for one or two people and I continue to play. If I asked for 50 tickets to Siegfried and Roy all at once, I'm sure they'd find a way to nicely tell me 'no.'"

I pulled into a parking space and killed the engine. "Is this slot tournament part of the slot club?"

"Not exactly. On the way home I'll tell you how that works."

We held hands going into the dance studio. This was actually the first time we'd done this in front of people who knew us and it felt rather special. No one at the studio even noticed, probably. It was clear to anyone with eyes that Annie and I were a couple. We always came in together, left together, and danced with each other on the breaks. Everyone who'd given it any thought probably assumed we'd been an item for some time.

In tonight's class we learned a form of swivels, which is a move where the man and the woman are pivoting in opposite directions at the same time. A major key to this move is keeping the proper amount of tension in the arms. Annie picked it up right away, but I found it elusive. I figured we could try it in Vegas over the weekend, but if I still didn't have it, I'd ask Phil to review it next week. Which he was probably planning to do anyway, because I wasn't alone in my struggles.

"So tell me about slot tournaments," I prompted as I headed for the freeway to return home.

"They're a way to reward good players. This event is a rather low-level tournament where 150 people or so will compete for something like $30,000."

"And how do you get to be one of the chosen 150?"

"It's not that hard, actually. It does require a certain amount of play and the ability to get to Vegas on a Friday, which lets a lot of people out, but most players who *ask* to be invited *are* invited."

"So I could be invited?"

"No. You have to have a significant amount of play. But in four more weeks, they'll hold another one of these tournaments. And that one will pay more money to fewer people. If it's not full, we can probably get you in, if you play enough this weekend."

"Do you think I'm ready to play?" I asked. I hadn't shared with her that I'd practiced more since Sunday and today I'd actually played an even 1,000 hands with no mistakes at all.

"Certainly, as long as you let me supervise you. By the end of the weekend, we'll be able to evaluate how close you are to being ready to play unsupervised."

"I wasn't sure whether this weekend would be both of us playing or just me watching you," I said, "but I am interested. Assuming I played the normal amount for one of these tournaments, how much could I lose if things went bad?"

"I'd say for the entire weekend, if you had no luck at all, ten grand would be about max."

"Holy shit!" I exclaimed. "I thought I had the advantage. And I could really lose that much?"

"It's possible, but not really likely," Annie responded flatly. To her this was a math class and she had no emotion attached to the money. "This is a game where the mean and the median are different, and both are different from the extremes. Are you familiar with those terms?"

"They both mean average, don't they? But if they're different from each other, I don't know how. Tell me."

"Okay, let's say we decided that putting 1,000 points on your card would likely get you an invitation. That's $75,000 worth of play, and a .2% advantage means that you're the favorite by $150. You with me so far?" she asked.

"Yes. So far I can do that in my head, sort of," I told

her. "Multiplying 75 by two and getting 150 is easy. But there's a lot of zeros, and I'd have to think about what 0.2% means. Although I trust your math, I wouldn't know whether it was $1,500 or $150 or $15 or even a buck and a half unless I either used a calculator or a pencil and paper."

"Understandable," she said. "But for now, trust me that it's $150. That's called the mean. If you played the 3,000 hands necessary to earn the 1,000 points lots of different times, your net score would be $150 per time."

"Okay. That's what I'd call an average," I said.

"Correct. And that's a number that's easily calculated. The median is the number where half the time you'll lose more than that, and half the time you'll lose less," she explained, "and this number isn't so easily calculated. From experience, I'd say that number is around $1,600 in the hole. Half the time you'd lose more than $1,600 and half the time you'd lose less. Actually, you'd probably hit minus $1,600 on the nose a few times, but you get the idea."

"I can see that minus $1,600 is a lot different than plus $150. Why are the mean and the median so far apart?" I asked.

"Because you only get a $20,000 royal flush every 67 hours or so. At the end of those 67 hours, assuming you get exactly one royal, your score will be pretty close to the mean, once you include the cashback. But for most of the five-hour sessions along the way, which is how long it takes to play $75,000 through the machine, you're going to be losing."

"Okay," I said. "A $1,600 loss doesn't sound so bad, although a $150 win sounds better. Where does the $10,000 come from?"

"That represents the worst-case scenario. In other words, if you played out these 3,000-hand sessions maybe 1,000 times, what's your tenth worst score? That number will probably be around $10,000 in the soup."

"Losing $10,000 wouldn't bankrupt me by a long shot, but it sure would piss me off big time."

"I understand," she told me. "I suspect most people would feel that way."

"So if I'm not ready to take that risk, I shouldn't play?"

"Actually, that's just one weekend. It can add up to more than that over several weekends. It's not probable, but it is possible."

"That much risk is probably a showstopper for me. I thought I was ready to play. But I guess I'm not."

"As I alluded on the trip down here, what if I bankrolled you until you play enough to get comfortable with the amounts of money involved?" she asked. "I'm comfortable with the risk level. And after we do this for two months or six months or whatever, you'll probably decide you want to bankroll yourself. After all, you'll have the advantage."

"Why would you do this?"

"Call it another investment in us," she said, and then back-tracked a bit. "I haven't thought it all through yet. Let me sleep on it tonight and see if it's something that makes sense for me too. Meanwhile, you think about it as well."

We were just pulling into my garage. "Okay," I told her. "Meanwhile, I've got a special request for tomorrow. All in all, I think I've been a good sport about waiting and I deserve some special consideration for that."

"I don't know," Annie told me with a smile. "Don't you think having a hot-to-trot sex partner for three days is sufficient consideration?"

"When you put it that way, sure. But I want … well, why don't I just tell you what I want and you tell me if it's something you could do."

"Okay. Make your request and I'll consider it."

"Very well. On the drive to Vegas tomorrow, I want you to wear a full skirt, just like the one you have on now. That very skirt would be fine, although I know you have a blue one in a similar style."

"That doesn't sound like much of a request. So I assume there's more. Correct?"

"Yes," I said. "Under your skirt I want you to wear nothing at all."

She squealed in surprise. "Whoa! I wasn't expecting that! But I can do it, under one condition."

"And what might that be?" I asked.

She leaned over, kissed me warmly, and gently started stroking me. I was already hard from the discussion of her not wearing any underwear. "However much you want to," she said, "you can't masturbate tonight. I want you to save it all for me."

"Agreed," I said with a struggle, "24 and a half."

She squealed again and immediately jumped out of the car and ran, laughingly, to her condo. It occurred to me that I just might be the luckiest guy in the world.

Thursday
February 10, 2000

We'd agreed to leave about three o'clock. Annie had a one o'clock meeting and she promised to drive home immediately afterwards. We decided to take her car. I needed to have my car at the dealership for some scheduled maintenance and this seemed to be a good time to do it.

When she knocked on my door at 2:50, Annie was wearing her blue full skirt. With folded-over white socks underneath tennis shoes. Definitely no panty hose, and maybe nothing at all. Impossible to tell just by looking. I immediately found myself wondering whether or not she was a natural redhead. I assumed she was, given her pinkish coloring and plentiful freckles. It would change nothing important if I learned she wasn't, but all day my mind had been on her exact color, texture, and curliness. I was 39 years old going on 18.

I took her in my arms, lifted her off the ground, and twirled her slowly while I sang, "Happy birthday to you, happy birthday to you, happy birthday dear Sexy, happy birthday to you."

"You remembered," Annie sighed, batting her eyelids at me for effect.

"How could I forget? I've been trying to give you your present for weeks now."

I placed my suitcase-on-wheels and a garment bag into her trunk, tossed my leather jacket into her back seat, climbed into the passenger seat, and buckled up. We looked at each other with Cheshire-cat grins, and she headed for the eastbound onramp of the Santa Monica freeway.

"I've really been looking forward to this weekend," I told her.

"Me too! Only a few hours more until, well, you know."

"So we both have something to wait for," I told her as I placed a small wrapped box on the between-the-seats console, "you can't open up your birthday present until you're absolutely naked." In this particular box were only worthless rocks, in case she opened it early 'against orders.' I shook it and the rocks rattled around.

"Anyone ever call you a bastard before?" she asked with a smile.

"Never someone having a birthday," I replied. And then, as though it wasn't a change of subject at all, "Tell you what," as I reached over and took the wheel. "I'll steer for now and you extract your arms from your sleeves. Then while you steer, I'll see if I can figure out how your bra unhooks."

She grinned. She was wearing a stretchy kind of short-sleeved tank top and it took her a full minute to remove her arms. I assume she could have done it in ten seconds had she wanted, but it was at least four hours to Vegas and you can only do each thing for the first time once. Why not draw it all out a bit?

I placed my hand on her tummy. Although the sky darkens early in mid-February, it was 3:15 and broad daylight. We had to use *some* discretion. "First, I'll have to see if I can find the clasp," I said as I took her entire right breast in my right hand and flipped my thumb gently over her hardening nipple.

"Did it ever occur to you that that's an unlikely place to find a clasp? Do I have to teach you *everything?*"

"I'm just checking to see who's having more fun. So far it seems to be a tie."

I repeated the procedure on her left nipple until that too was hard. I then outlined the front of her bra with my finger. She didn't say anything, but she didn't stop smiling and she kept her eyes on the road.

In fact, there was no doubt in my mind where her bra clasp was. I'd practiced dancing with her dozens of times. Although a hand-to-hand grip is the usual case in West

Coast Swing, the man's right hand in the middle of the woman's back is common enough. I don't know about other men, but I always allow my hand to notice whether or not a woman is wearing a bra, and if so, whether the clasp is in the back. Every time so far, Annie was and the clasp was.

"Lean forward, please," I requested. She did and I smoothly unhooked the clasp. I felt lucky that it popped quickly. What guy hasn't experienced the awkwardness of having it take several minutes, or even not being able to do it at all? Usually the girls thought it hilarious, but I was quite happy to avoid that situation this time. I slipped the bra off of one shoulder at a time and moved the strap off her right arm. She did her left arm by herself and flipped it into the back seat.

I'm not much of a tit man, I guess. Smaller than Annie or bigger than Meg, once I've petted for a few minutes I'm ready to move on to the good stuff. But she was breathing rapidly and shallowly and no way was I going to stop. I kept one eye on the road and the other hand ready to grab the wheel in case she lost control. "Rub my leg," she requested hoarsely.

I aimed to please! I started at the bottom and stoked her shin. She spread her legs as wide as she could while keeping one foot on the gas pedal. I gently scratched her inner thigh and she moaned quietly. As I kept it up she whispered, "Hurry up!" I ignored this and kept stroking her thigh, each time getting closer to the top. She took my hand and moved it directly to her moistness. As I'd requested, she wasn't wearing panties. I used the fingertips of my left hand to stroke what I hoped was the right place, while I took the wheel with my right. She squeezed my left arm with both of her hands and kept saying, "Yes. Yes. Yes." I really wanted to watch her face, but keeping my eyes on the road seemed prudent just now.

Soon she exhaled in a burst and pushed my hand away. Her breathing took about 30 seconds to return to normal. She sighed deeply, put her hands back on the wheel, and said, "Thanks. I needed that."

Neither one of us spoke for about five minutes. Something magical had just happened. It wasn't major sexual progress over what we'd done earlier, rather a Hollyesque move forward I suppose, but it was our first sexual contact on D-Day. Or was it F-Day?

She broke the silence first. "That was nice. Thank you very much. I think I might be in love with your left hand. Anything I can do to return the favor?"

"Not just yet. I don't really get off on hand jobs, and while you stroking me would feel wonderful, it would end up making matters worse, unless we stopped somewhere to finish. But I'll gladly take a rain check and allow you to return the favor big time in a few hours. For now I'd like to just sit back and quietly enjoy feeling better than I've ever felt before."

"You got yourself a deal," she said and turned on the CD player.

Thursday
February 10, 2000

Annie pulled off the freeway at Barstow, which was still over 100 miles from Vegas. "I'd rather you drove the rest of the way," she told me.

"No problem." We got gas and used the restrooms, and I pulled out onto the highway. She picked up the "present" and shook it again.

"I'm naked under my clothes," she told me. "That's close enough." She started to unwrap it, slowly enough so that I could easily stop her if I wanted to. But since I knew it was box of rocks, I actually *wanted* her to disobey instructions.

But I had to put up at least a token fight. "Annie, you can't open that yet. It's against the rules."

That didn't come close to stopping her, nor did all the Scotch tape I'd used so she'd have to struggle to get it open. "If I break a fingernail on this, you'll be sorry," she told me as she worked on it.

"It wouldn't be my fault. I told you not to do it."

She finally lifted the lid and looked at the pebbles. She turned on the overhead light to peer closely at them. Though they looked rather ordinary to her, she also knew that I worked with gemstones, so she asked, "Are these stones unique in some way?"

"Well, last weekend I helped my brother remove a tree stump from his yard, and these were on top when we finally got it moved."

"So they have no value at all?"

"Nope, unless you get sentimental about tree stumps."

"Then why did you give them to me as a present?"

"I didn't, actually. I asked you not to open it until later, didn't I? Plus, you told me you didn't want nice things from me for your birthday, so I figured that this ought to tickle you to death."

She laughed.

"I seem to have created a monster. Perhaps I shouldn't have held out on you so long."

"On that we're in total agreement."

After that, Annie fell silent again and I started to wonder if I'd done the right thing with the pebbles. Oh well, what's done is done. I slipped in a CD and drove the BMW toward Vegas.

Finally, I said, "Shall we stop at Baker? We can look at the thermometer before we find a room. It'll inspire me." Baker calls itself the "Gateway to Death Valley." Although I'm sure there are a lot of old mines and other things of interest to explore in the area, to me it's always been just a place to get gas on the way to Las Vegas. It has this thermometer that's supposed to be the biggest in the world. Hard to know if the claim is valid or not.

"Keep driving," she said. "Did you think any more about you gambling this weekend with either your money or mine?"

"I did. I think I want to experience a few weekends of play before I risk $10,000. How would it work if I played with your money? Assuming, of course, that you still think it's a good idea."

"I do. Each entry in next month's tournament is probably worth $400. If we can get you qualified while playing a game where we have the edge, that'd be a good deal."

"I can see that, but I'm still not convinced about the risk-reward equation."

"That's fine. I'm comfortable with the risk. But there are some things we need to agree on up front."

"Like what?" I asked.

"Some of the return is in cashback," she told me. "That $150 average win was made up of $500 in cashback accompanied by a $350 loss on the machine. I'm going to recommend that you leave the $500 'on account' in case you want comps down the road, but when you do finally start to gamble on your own account, we need to remember that that $500 is mine."

"No problem. What else?"

"There may be tax consequences. Every time you hit a straight flush or a royal flush, you'll get a tax form called a W-2G. Do you keep a gambling log on your blackjack wins and losses?"

"No."

"I didn't think so."

"Why not?" I felt defensive again.

"Because you said you weren't sure if you were an overall winner or loser. So I figured you didn't keep track, not even for tax purposes."

"Well, in case you're concerned, I pay my taxes. I just figured that my wins and losses evened out in the long run, so I never bothered reporting anything."

"That's fine. Many blackjack players don't. But with video poker, there are the W-2G tax forms so it's smart to keep good records. When we get back to L.A., I want to set up a gambling log to accurately record your wins and losses. We'll include the $1,200 you lost two weeks ago."

"Why do that?"

"Lots of reasons, but the main one I'm concerned about here is you pay taxes on your net win, which is a whole different thing than your W-2Gs. If you end up owing taxes for wins while you're gambling on my money, I'll take care of it.

"If you win anything in the tournament next month," Annie continued, "let's agree to split it. Under this setup, you have no chance of taking a loss and you get half your winnings from special events. Not to mention the comps lavished on you by the casino and the sex goddess."

"Sounds like a perfect deal to me. Especially the goddess part. Are you sure you're not taking the worst of it by being my financial backer?"

"I'm positive. This isn't about money to me. It's about doing things together. Winning or losing an extra few thousand won't make a difference in my lifestyle."

As we passed Whiskey Pete's and the other casinos just across the Nevada border, Annie gently scratched my shoulder and asked me if I'd do her a favor. "And what would that be?" I asked.

She moved her hand to steady the steering wheel. "I'd like you to unhook the belt of your pants, unzip them, and let me play with you." I thought it better to wait until we were in the hotel room, but refusing her might spoil the mood. So I decided to tough it out as best I could. I unhooked my belt, undid the button at the top of my pants, and pulled down the zipper. I then took the wheel and waited, simultaneously wanting and not wanting to feel her touch.

"Thank you. I'll try not to make it too painful on you." After a brief giggle, she added, "If I can help it." She pulled my shirt free all the way around, then gently caressed my chest. All over at first, and then she flicked her fingernails first over one of my nipples, then the other. After going back and forth a few times, she playfully and gently tugged at my chest hairs.

She hadn't touched my crotch yet, but I was already at full extension down there. I found myself squirming with my entire body. I lifted my left leg and moved it as close to my right as I could, futilely trying to caress myself with my own legs. I hadn't noticed the speedometer in a while, but Annie did. She commented that if I kept driving on the freeway at 35 miles an hour, it'd take longer to get there than I wanted. I sped up.

Annie then stroked me over the top of my underwear. I wanted to close my eyes and go with the flow, but I forced myself to keep my eyes on the road as I gently moved against her hand. We'd already passed the offramp for Jean. I hoped I could make it the rest of the way. "Pull down your underwear," she ordered.

"This is not a good idea. Not at 65 miles an hour."

"Do it!" she ordered in a forceful voice I hadn't heard before. "I'll steer."

So I did. My shorts and pants were halfway down my

thighs and I felt ridiculous. And that was *before* she placed the pebbles in my pubic hair, balanced on top of my erection.

"What the hell is that for?"

She started scratching my chest and whispered melodically. "Would you like me to assist you in getting your rocks off?" she asked mischievously. And then she started stroking me.

"Cute," I said. "Nice play on words. And yes, I want the pebbles out of there, but I don't want you to make me come."

She continued her stroking. I groaned. "The bucket seats won't let me use my mouth just now. I hope you'll let me taste you when we get to the hotel."

I groaned louder. "Please stop," I begged finally. "It's getting very hard, pardon the pun, to concentrate on the driving. This weekend will be a lot more fun if we're alive to experience it."

"Good point, pardon the pun," she said, removing her hand, removing the pebbles one by one to make me unsure if she was going to resume the stroking, then sitting back. "But don't zip up just yet. We've got about 15 minutes, and if your breathing returns to normal before we get there, I just might decide to administer a second application."

Interstate 15 passes right next to the Las Vegas Strip, and we saw the huge casinos off to our right. I knew the Golden Nugget was downtown, which was a few miles farther up the highway.

"Take the Charleston offramp," she instructed. "I've never tried to steer with a joy stick before. Let's see if it works," she said as she reached over and placed her hand on my currently half-hard member. "When I pull this way, it means get over in the right lane."

I obeyed. "Do I want Charleston East or Charleston West?" I asked.

"Either one. They both get you there."

"How can that be?" I asked somewhat nervously,

because I had to make a turn in a half-mile and I was traveling at 60 or so. "It can't be right to go either east or west. At least one has to be incorrect."

"Oh, so you think you're in a position to argue?" she asked mischievously, while she gave a tug or two. "Seems to me that control is at least somewhat in *my* hand at the moment."

"Okay, okay." I tried to focus, but the information was streaming in at highway speed. I could see the yellow "Golden Nugget" lettering up ahead on the right, which had to be east since we were traveling north, but I was traveling too fast for the Charleston East offramp so I had to go west. She'd been tugging away, which I suppose was her attempt to direct my steering, but my hormones wouldn't let my brain kick in enough to figure out the code.

"When I pulled back on the joystick like that, I was trying to tell you to slow down."

"Oh. I thought that meant I was supposed to lift my front tires off the road. And I don't know how to do that in somebody else's car."

"Poor baby," she cooed, "am I making it *hard* on you?" Sure enough, taking the Charleston West offramp worked out just fine, although there were several turns involved, necessitating instructions via her hand in my lap. Each time I figured it out correctly, she cheered and giggled simultaneously.

When we pulled into the Golden Nugget self-parking garage, I lowered the window to take a parking ticket in order to raise the mechanical arm. An old man running the attendant booth on the other side of the ticket machine happened to glance down and see Annie's hand in my crotch. He gave me a thumb's-up and a big grin as we entered the garage.

Once parked I struggled to get myself put together again: tucking, zipping, buttoning, and refastening the belt. "We better wait here for a few minutes. I've got a hard-on that won't go away."

"We better *not* wait," she corrected. "If we stay here I *guarantee* the problem won't disappear for a while." And she started to stroke me again.

"Okay, we can go."

After retrieving our bags from the trunk of the BMW, I draped my leather jacket over my free arm—hiding the evidence, so to speak. Waiting with us for the elevator to take us down to street level where we could walk across to the casino was a 60ish couple.

"Aren't you cold?" the woman asked me. "It must be in the forties. Why don't you put your jacket on?"

"I guess I'm just the hardy type," was the best I could come up with. Annie was close to me with her back to the other couple. I could feel her body shaking with laughter. By the time we entered the elevator, she was able to turn around with nothing more than a friendly smile on her face.

As soon as we walked into the casino, we passed adjacent to a large glass-walled room with a tent-like roof. There were slot machines in one corner, lots of tables and chairs, and decorations in a "hearts-and-flowers" theme.

"That's where the tournament and the awards dinner will be held," Annie pointed out. "There was a sign-up reception tonight, but we couldn't make it without me leaving work earlier. It would've been nice, because they shoot a photograph and I'd like to have one of us, but it couldn't be helped. In the warm-weather months they take the roof off of this place and it's part of the sunbathing area next to the swimming pool. But from October to March or so, it's covered and used as a multi-purpose ballroom."

Annie led the way to VIP Check-in. "Welcome back, Miss Ferrari," the VIP hostess, Marie, said. "I see you're in a Tower Suite for three nights this time. It's all ready for you. The notation says it's totally complimentary. Have you been in one of our Tower Suites before?" We both shook our heads, while Annie signed the credit card slip.

"The special-access elevators are around to your left.

You're in 7b and there's access from both the seventh and eighth floors. Most guests go in on the higher level first, because that's where they'll keep their luggage. Do you need restaurant reservations or any other assistance at this time?"

I looked at the room key. It was old-fashioned and made out of metal, in the church key style. I was surprised. "I thought most quality hotels now have magnetic keycards so you can change the lock with each new guest. Don't you have that here?"

"We do in all of our other hotel rooms," Marie answered, "but so far not in the Tower Suites. It's a system problem, because we need the doors on two separate floors to use the same key. So far the engineers haven't figured out how to do it. But we're working on it and it should be changed shortly."

"But that way," Annie concluded, "anybody who hasn't turned in their key to 7b for the past several years still has a current key."

"That's true," Marie conceded, "although we've had extremely few problems with that sort of thing. But be sensible about it. Lock your doors with the deadbolt and chain when you're inside and use the safe in the closet to secure your valuables. Do you have any other questions?" After receiving additional head shakes, she continued, "Okay then, enjoy your stay at the Golden Nugget."

On the hallway off the eighth floor, we saw double doors for rooms 8a, 8b, and more on the right, and single doors labeled "7a Chambre," "7b Chambre," and more on the left. I opened the door and Annie went in first. The lights were already on.

"Ooh, this is lovely!" Annie exclaimed. "Shannon said it'd be perfect and she's right." She shrugged out of her jacket and asked me to hang it up along with mine. "The closet's probably over there somewhere," she said waving her right arm vaguely toward an opening in the wall on the left.

I went through that opening and found I was entering a squared-off U-shaped area with me at the bottom. To the right I could see the Jacuzzi on a balcony overlooking the main part of the suite, so I didn't figure the closet would be that way. Going up the left arm of the U, I found a large glassed-in shower, a room with two toilets in it, and a mirrored closet on either side of a four-foot hallway.

I hung up the jackets, then immediately removed all my clothes and threw them on the floor of the closet. Took me a full six seconds or so. "Annie, come quick! You've got to see this," I ordered. She came running, shrieked when she saw me, and eagerly wrapped her arms around my neck, kissing me. We sank to the carpeted hallway with her on the bottom. She still had on all her clothes, but that was too damned bad. I lifted the front of her skirt and was on top of her in nothing flat. I have a faint recollection that I noticed at this point that she was indeed a natural redhead.

No finesse or tenderness here. Only need. There was a runaway locomotive inside me that had to get to the station. She held me tight and whispered, "Take me, Chris. Hard! I'm all yours." She might have said more. I don't remember.

It was over almost immediately, as I erupted with a loud groan. I lay there immobile, struggling for breath. I was in no hurry to run off anywhere, as she stroked the back of my hair.

Although I was definitely on cloud nine, I was embarrassed at how quick it had been. I'd had so many dreams about what our first time would be like. Slow. Lingering. Sensual. Never did I imagine it would be slam bam thank you ma'am.

In about a minute she said, "Don't go very far, but you're squashing me. Whoever designed the carpet padding in this hallway didn't allow for its occasional use as a love nest." I rolled off her and immediately started apologizing.

"Oh, Annie. I'm sorry. I wanted it to last forever and make sure you were satisfied first and for you to have the best birthday present of your life. I ..."

She stopped further apologies with a finger to my lips. "Hush, darling, everything's perfect. I seem to recall you took care of me very nicely a few hours ago, and I'm pretty sure I'm responsible for you being in such a state of urgency. I've no desire to change a single second of our trip so far. Even the rocks turned out to be fun. Just lie quietly for a while and hold me." She snuggled in so her back was to my front and she held my arm across her chest.

Ecstasy.

Quick as it was, this was my first full-scale sexual adventure since Paula and I broke up. Although early sexual adventures with Paula were quite memorable, it'd been fifteen years ago. I didn't want Paula's memory to show up this weekend. It just did.

After about ten minutes, I asked her. "Did it occur to you that you might be overdressed for this party? I may have *had* you, but I've never *seen* you. And I've been looking forward to that."

She giggled and we both untangled and got to our feet. She stood directly in front of me and even dressed, I was fascinated by the view. I've always enjoyed the braless look, and I'd never seen Annie that way. She lifted both her arms lazily over her head and invited me to assist her. Instead of removing her shirt, I reached under and gently cupped a breast in each hand. "Sure," I said. "With what would you like assistance?" She smiled and took off her own shirt.

"Luscious," I said as I looked at her chest. Truth be known, I would have said something like that no matter *how* it looked. If there was ever a time that it paid to invest in a woman's self-confidence and keep the mood flowing, this was it. But, in fact, Annie's breasts were symmetrical and well-shaped, with evenly colored, round, one-and-a-half-centimeter-diameter areolae surrounding eight-millimeter nipples. She started to unbutton her skirt and I squatted down to untie her tennis shoes. As her skirt fell, it totally obstructed my view of the shoelace and totally eliminated any thoughts I had about her shoes. My eyes were at ground zero, and the pungent aroma of mingled love juices was overpowering. My train of thought had just lost its caboose! I picked her up and carried her to the bed. As I walked along, her arms were around my neck and she whispered, "I don't care who does it, but my shoes and socks have *got to go*!"

I laid her on the bed, kissed her gently on the lips, and continued attending to her footwear. I was going rather slowly, enjoying the view. Her pelvis was slowly rising and falling as she lightly stroked herself with two fingers and I couldn't take my eyes off that.

"Linger all you like, if that's what you really want," she told me hoarsely, "but my personal choice right now would be to go directly to the missionary position. I've got my own fire that needs your help to put out. Please?"

Needless to say, the shoes and socks were off in record time. As I moved into position, she reached to put her arms around me. Although I'm not always successful at aiming when neither person is using a hand for guidance, this time I went in on the first try. "Nice shot," she approved.

"Nothing but net," I boasted, echoing a popular television commercial.

Even though I'd had an orgasm 15 minutes previously, I was still quite excited by the entire situation and her moving against me was highly stimulating. I was afraid that if I moved with her, I might finish before her—especially since I wasn't used to her sounds and didn't know how long I'd need to hold off. Would she do this for three minutes or 33? I just wanted her to finish first.

And she did. It took her about eight minutes and there was no doubt when she was through. She tightened up all over and let out a long loud groan about two octaves lower than anything I'd heard from her before. She kept her eyes shut for at least a minute, lying perfectly still while I gently moved in and out. She opened her eyes slowly. “That was delicious. Thank you. That’s my best birthday present ever. And anything you like now is okay with me.”

I had no desire other than to continue what I was doing with Annie. After a few more minutes, my body picked up speed and my second explosion of the night rocked us both. It wasn’t the huge release that I experienced the first time, but the fact that she came first made it more satisfying. I vaguely remember her getting up to turn off the lights. I don’t know how I got under the covers.

Friday
February 11, 2000

A doorbell was ringing. And it didn't sound like *my* doorbell. I sat up, figured out I was at the Golden Nugget, and heard Annie downstairs talking to someone. I staggered into the bathroom and found my toiletry kit laid out with a note alongside. "After you clean up, put on a robe from the closet and come downstairs to a very happy woman." It was unsigned. The handwriting looked similar to some I'd seen before. Though it seemed to be more flowery this time for some reason, I didn't have to wonder who left it.

Before jumping into the shower I went into the toilet area. I'd never seen a room with two side-by-side toilets and I had to check this one out. Turned out one was a bidet, which I'd heard about. As I sat on the toilet I experimented with the faucets on the bidet. Water spurted up from the center—and you could regulate the temperature and the force of the stream. It was easy to tell it was used for hygienic purposes, primarily by women I suppose, but it seemed pretty messy. Oh well. Luckily, we were in Vegas and not Paris, and there was toilet paper on the wall.

When I emerged from the shower, I noticed that my "very happy woman" had snuck in, left a cup of steaming coffee, then disappeared again. When I went to find the aforementioned garment, I discovered a note from the hotel management saying I was welcome to use the robe and I could purchase new ones in the gift shop, but taking this one home with me would result in a charge of $150 on my credit card. No problem. I had a robe at home and wasn't planning to rip anything off. I'd already received the first installment of the only prize I wanted this weekend, and it wasn't costing me any money, but this robe *was* nice. It was expensive, thick cotton with an embroidered gold "GN" over the left breast.

It was only 7 a.m. when, clean and freshly shaven, I descended the spiral staircase to the main area of the suite. Annie extracted the almost-empty cup from my hand and gave me a big kiss and some tight hugs. Light breakfast fare of granola, fresh fruit, yogurt, muffins, and coffee was all laid out.

"They'll have a version of this for free down in the tournament area, but I'm not ready to share you just yet. Hope you don't mind," she said.

"I'll let it slide this time, especially if you lean over every now and then and let me look down the front of your robe. What time did we go to sleep last night?"

"We got to the hotel a little before eight, so it must have been nine or so when we finished with the festivities. You conked out almost immediately and didn't budge when I got up at six and took a long shower. I didn't know how long you'd sleep. I didn't expect the room-service waiter to ring the doorbell and for that to wake you up. I feel great today! How about you?"

"Pretty rotten, actually. It's been three whole minutes since anyone has kissed me and I'm feeling very neglected."

"Oh dear, we can't have that." She came over, untied the sash to her robe, and sat down in my lap. She pulled my head down to hers and vigorously intertwined her tongue with mine. With my left arm I supported her back and with my right hand I explored her chest. After thirty or so seconds she asked, "Feeling less neglected yet?"

"A little. I might need another dose of this medicine in the very near future, however."

"Okay, overall I'd say that's a good sign." She stood up and returned to her chair on the other side of the dining room table, fastening her robe along the way. "But I'll have to cut off your medicine for 15 minutes or so. We need to talk about our plans for the day. We have a tournament round at 10 a.m. and I thought we might want to get some clothes on before then.

"I'll play the first round of the tournament," she continued, "so all you have to do is to sit behind me, observe how it all works, and yell "*Come on, Annie!*" every few minutes. Don't take this as a challenge, but I don't think it's possible to yell too loudly. The rounds are 30 minutes each and our second one is at two this afternoon. I'm thinking that you'll play the second round. By the time you've sat behind me for the morning round, you'll be an expert. You'll see."

"Okay," I said. "That takes us to ten-thirty. What happens then?"

"We go to the High Limit Slot Salon and check out the availability of the $5 9/6 Jacks machines. There are three overlooking the elevators and three or four overlooking the crap tables. If we can find a game relatively distant from cigarette smokers, I'll sit down and start playing—under your close supervision, of course."

"I'm sure I'll be able to help you a lot," I commented dryly. "But mostly I'll be your bodyguard as we carry off all your winnings. It's none of my business, I suppose, and you don't have to tell me, but how much money did you bring to gamble with?"

"I have about $150 on me. Think that'll be enough?" She saw my eyes open wide in disbelief, then continued. "I've got a line of credit here for $10,000, and if I need more than that, which I doubt, it's easy to get more since I've got a good history of paying. Did you ever take out markers at blackjack?"

"I didn't personally, but I saw it done all the time at the tables, so it's not a surprise that they do it in the slot department too. Although I hadn't really thought about it until now."

"My plan is to average 400 points a day and we'll be here three days. It doesn't matter if we put on exactly 400 points today or not, as long as we earn 1,200 points over the course of the weekend. Even though the suite will cost 3,000 points, I'm going to pay for much of it with accumulated points rather than what we earn this time.

"Together we'll decide on what to do about lunch. Some of the events provide food in the tournament area and some don't. I'm not sure about this one, but we'll find out when we show up for the first round. I've made dinner reservations for eight o'clock tonight. I assume you can tolerate Italian food with singing waiters?"

I nodded my acceptance of almost anything she wanted to do, and she continued. "Somewhere along the way we have to get a player's card for you too. And I'll talk to Shannon and find out if they're full up for next month's event."

"You've mentioned Shannon a couple of times. Is he or she your host?"

"Shannon's a 'she' and yes, she's a host. Here at the Nugget they trade off between hosts rather seamlessly, but I suppose she's my main one."

"Are there any other Golden Nugget employees I should know about?"

"Gee, there's Myron, and Bruce, Lynn, Linea, Phyllis, and a slew of others. You'll eventually meet them all and you'll like them. They put a very heavy emphasis on friendliness around here."

"That's good. Sometimes a guy can die of loneliness in his own room in the mornings."

"Poor baby! If you can hang on, the cavalry's coming to keep you company. But let me first tell you about Kelly and the Bally Belles."

"Sounds like some sort of a lounge act."

"I guess it does at that. Kelly Flynn is a treasure. He emcees a lot of these events at a lot of different casinos. His personality and sense of humor will dominate the sessions today and the event tomorrow night."

"Sounds like fun. Who or what are the Bally Belles?"

"They're a group of women—all married housewives, I think—who help run these events. As near as I can tell, the primary job requirements to be in this group are to be real friendly to the customers and to pay enough attention to detail to make sure everything in the tournament is run according to the rules."

"Why are they called the Bally Belles?"

"That's just my name for them, I guess. They used to work for the Bally Systems corporation when Bally provided this 'slot tournament assistant' service. I heard that Bally got out of that business and now one of the girls in the group runs the service instead."

"Are there a lot of these women?" I asked. "It doesn't seem like it would take that many people to run a tournament."

"More than you think. Some casinos try to run them with a skeleton crew and it shows. I'm not sure how many of the Bally Belles there are, but I know three of them by name. Heidi is the tall blonde who's drop-dead gorgeous. I think she used to be a showgirl. Cindy has dark hair and is medium tall. And Lynn is the short one with dishwater-blonde hair."

"Can't wait to meet them, but right now I'm feeling neglected again. Is my 15 minutes up yet?"

"I'm not sure," she said. She came and stood in front of me. I loosened the belt of her robe. Still sitting, I put my hands on her butt cheeks and nibbled on a breast. She caressed my shoulders while I suckled and said, "I need to start putting clothes on if we're going to play. I can be ready in about ten minutes, but that's only if you don't mess me up any more. You planning on letting me loose anytime soon?"

"Can't promise," I mumbled. "My mother told me never to talk with my mouth full. Sometimes I obey her."

By 7:40 we were heading down the elevator. I told her, "I'd very much like to hold your hand as we go out in public. But you know these people and I don't, so if that makes it awkward for you, I'll resist the urge."

"A little awkward, but I'll get over it. I like the idea of holding hands with you."

At this hour, all the machines were empty, so Annie

selected the first machine we came to in the High Limit Salon. "This one's perfect. It's on the corner so we can get you a chair to pull up without monopolizing an extra machine. Go get a slot club card while I fetch some money. If you get back before me and the cocktail waitress comes by, get a bottle of water for me, please, and whatever you want. I usually tip 50¢ or a buck a drink, but you can do whatever you like."

"Yes, ma'am!" I saluted and set off for the 24 Karat booth.

I ended up back at the machine in five minutes, and it took Annie another ten to return. "I really like this place, but it takes *so* long to get a marker. None of the other casinos I go to takes half as long. Every time I come and it's been more than two days since my last marker, they have to call some executive over to remove a hold from my account. I don't know why that's necessary here and apparently nowhere else, but it's time-consuming. Thanks for the water. Why don't you pull that chair up right next to me and we'll get started?"

She inserted two $100 bills into the machine, which converted the money into 40 credits. "Why two bills?" I asked. "Why not one? Or 10, for that matter?"

"The reason I don't put 10 bills in is that turns into 200 credits, and the machine only holds 239 before it spills tokens into this compartment over here. Since we'll be playing in multiples of five coins each time, for practical purposes it means that the machine is fine with 235 or fewer credits, but spills at 240 or more. You'll see. With normal luck, it should happen several times this weekend.

"Putting in one bill at a time would be fine too, but it kind of breaks your rhythm every time you insert bills, so I put in two bills at a time as sort of a reasonable compromise. You may have noticed I put some bills into the spill compartment. On the short machines like these, called slant tops, the spill compartment is off to the side. On the taller machines, called uprights, like those over there, the spill compartment is actually a spill tray. They serve the same purpose."

"Is a slant top better than an upright?"

"That's usually not a decision factor because each casino will have it only one way. I'll play either, depending on what a particular casino has. If you're going to be playing a long time, the slant tops are more comfortable, because you can rest your wrists on the machine itself rather than having to hold them up. Anyway, there are exactly eight $100 bills in the spill compartment, which makes an even $1,000 when you include the two bills I've already inserted into the machine. I'll keep feeding them in as needed, and only count them when I'm done or I need to add another $1,000. I find that I can remember $1,000 units, but remembering every time I put in $100 is quite cumbersome. I'll record the total win or loss at the end of the session. When we get back home, I'll show you the computer listing of my gambling results."

"Although nothing you said so far seems that complicated, it seems like you have *every* nuance of video poker figured out. Do you?"

"Hardly," she laughed, "but I do tend to do things systematically and the same way every time. That comes from being a computer programmer, I suspect, because if you do things the same way every time, you don't have to worry about dropping something out. But I'm always looking for ways to improve how I do things. It wouldn't surprise me if this weekend you say something that triggers some change."

"Interesting. And as you said, talking about something that turns you on can't be all bad for me."

"Smart guy. This is where I put my slot club card, and information is displayed right next to it. Can you read it from there?"

The reader said, WELCOME ANNIE YOU HAVE 10,422 POINTS. This information flashed once. Then, other information, COUNTDOWN 15 SESSION 0 replaced it.

"I can see it easy enough, but I'm not sure exactly what it all means."

Annie recorded the number of her existing points in a small notebook, then remarked, "Perfect. Not that it surprises me, but you're a good student and you're not shy about telling me what you don't know. Each point is worth 50¢, so I have $5,211 in the bank, so to speak. I can figure this in my head, because multiplying by 50¢ and dividing by two come out to the same number. I'll cash in 3,000 points to pay for the Tower Suite for three days, and they'll give me $1,500 for those points. Since I expect to earn 1,200 points on this trip, I'll still have plenty left for us to enjoy our next several visits in the Tower Suites too. I haven't asked you about the trip in April yet, and I suppose I am being presumptuous, but I've already made the reservations. The Tower Suites book up fast."

"Presume away. Why did you write down the ten-thousand-plus figure and what do countdown and session mean?"

"It's just the starting position. Since I want to earn at least 1,200 points on the trip, I know I need to keep going until my point total reaches 11,622 points, which is my current point total plus 1,200 more. It takes $75 to earn each point. Since each coin on this machine is worth $5, it takes 15 of those coins to equal $75. Each hand takes five coins. I'll press 'max coins' and you'll see the countdown go from 15 down to 10." She did, and I did. We then looked at the hand that was dealt. K♥4♠K♦9♣4♥. The machine dinged.

"That noise indicates that you have some paying hand. It sounds the same whether it's a pair, two pair, three-of-a-kind, or whatever. Up in this area at the top you can see 'Two Pair' lit up, which tells you what the paying hand is. A lot of beginners hear the ding, see the kings, and don't also hold the second pair. A very expensive mistake. So we'll hold both pairs and hope for the best."

She did and drew the 6♣. "Are you disappointed that you didn't get the full house?" I asked.

"It obviously doesn't please me," she told me. "It's an extra $175 every time I end up with a full house rather than two pair. I know that I'll only connect four times in 47, or about once every 12 times I draw to two pair. Eleven out of twelve of these draws won't succeed. No big deal. We'll play 3,600 hands on my card and 3,000 on yours on this trip. I don't live and die by the results of every hand. If I just miss a straight flush worth $1,250 or a royal flush worth $20,000, I definitely feel a twinge. But smaller hands don't really affect me much. Let's try another hand." The machine dealt K♠9♣3♠7♦4♠.

"Hold the king," I said, and it didn't improve. From A♣K♥J♣T♦4♠ , I told her to hold AJ. Annie nodded her head and drew three cards, ending up with a pair of aces.

"Now look at the reading of the slot club card," she said. It said COUNTDOWN 10 SESSION 1. "We've played four hands so far. Here's an easy test. After we play one more hand, what will the countdown read?"

"Let's see. The countdown will be five and we'll still only have one session point. After an additional hand, the countdown will be back at 15 and the session total will be two. Our current score of 35 is the result of starting with 40, winning 10 on a bet of five, winning five on a bet of five, then losing five twice."

"Perfect!" she enthused. "It's not too hard once you get the hang of it. Let's do some more."

We played this way for a while, until our credits went down to zero. Annie inserted two more bills into the slot and kept going. This didn't seem to be a big deal to her. Those two went too and she inserted two more. As we got down to almost zero again, she connected on four sevens and we smiled at each other as 125 credits racked up. On the very next hand she hit four kings for another 125 credits and the coins started spilling.

"Very nice! At times like this it seems like such an easy game," I remarked.

"It always does when you're winning." She pointed at a big cabinet about 20 feet behind. "Why don't you bring some racks so we can stack these coins? We'll need three of the black ones. They're usually in the center drawer."

We loaded up the racks before continuing. Each of the racks had three rows. Each row held 20 coins, equaling $100. Since 125 $5 coins adds up to $625, we totally filled two racks and had five coins in the third. "Do you want me to change the coins for bills at the cashier back there?" I asked.

"No. Some people like to sell the coins back as they get them, but I feed them back in as the credits go down to zero. Since they only put four racks of coins, which total $1,200, into the machine hopper when it empties out, if we keep selling the coins, they have to keep filling the machine. It doesn't matter money-wise, but every hopper fill takes five or 10 minutes, depending on how busy the floorpeople are at exactly the moment you need one. If I keep feeding the coins back, far fewer hopper fills are necessary."

"Are you *sure* you don't have every nuance worked out?" I asked, partly in amazement. "Let's keep going."

For whatever reason, Annie's machine turned very generous. In the next several hands she got a couple of full houses for 45 coins apiece, then along came another four-of-a-kind and the coins started spilling into the tray again. The machine ran out of tokens and a floorman named Carl came over to fill it up. Before opening the machine door, he removed Annie's card and inserted his own, removed his, then put hers back in. He then went away for five minutes and returned with four black racks full of tokens and another employee as a witness. After the fill we racked the coins, and I noticed the card reader displayed COUNTDOWN 5 SESSION 0. "What happened to our points?" I asked.

"Nothing. They're still there. It's just that they've been moved to our cumulative balance and our session count starts over again. That's one reason why I wrote down the original figure, so I can tell how much we've played. We'll check our total points before we leave to go to the tournament, but since we're not going to be anywhere near 1,200 points by then, the exact total is irrelevant at this point."

"Irrelevant? It really doesn't matter at all?"

"I don't think so. Whether we have 100 points and have 1,100 to go or 400 and have 800 to go, it's just a temporary stop along the way. We're going to be playing several hours this trip, but I don't think it's going to be a problem or even an unpleasant experience getting the hands played."

By the time we were ready to go to the tournament, Annie was ahead $925 and we'd put 215 points on her card. "We'll play at a faster rate when we're not talking about so many hands," she told me.

While we stood in a line to get a tournament machine number, several of the Golden Nugget employees recognized Annie and greeted her warmly. When Annie said "And this is my friend Chris," they all welcomed me too. She was right. This was a friendly place. Annie pulled a pink heart with the number "4" on it from a red silk bag, so she'd sit at that machine for the first round.

On long tables near the reception area were fruit, pastry, coffee, and juices for the taking. Although we'd had plenty upstairs, that was two hours ago, so we each grabbed a muffin and some juice. At 9:55 the guy on the microphone said, "Ten o'clock players. It's time to start finding your seats." This must have been that Kelly guy she was talking about. She said he was funny, and he'd sure dressed for the event. He was wearing a pink Cupid outfit, with a big red heart over his left breast. I figured that any guy who could wear that costume *had* to have a sense of humor.

I found a chair directly behind where Annie was sitting and held her purse as requested. "We have a tradition here at the Golden Nugget," Kelly was saying. "I want you to turn to the player sitting next to you, look them square in the eye, and say, 'Sorry, but you're playing for second place.'" Most of the players did this, and everybody smiled.

"I hope you've all noticed my outfit today. Especially the big red heart." Kelly walked around so everybody got a look. There was scattered applause. "I'm sure not many of you had any idea last night that today you'd see an overweight man going around with a *heart on* all day." That got a big guffaw. Perhaps some of the people were slightly embarrassed by the risqué double entendre, but no one complained out loud. I guess anything goes in Vegas. At any rate, it certainly broke the ice and everybody was glad they were there.

"All you do is hit the blue button," Kelly continued. "You can do it while sitting down, standing up, or you can hit it with your elbow. I don't care. Just don't stop hitting it for thirty minutes and you'll do fine. But if you're not hitting when the reels aren't spinning, you're hurting your chances to collect the money at tomorrow night's award dinner, right here at six o'clock. In the rare event of a machine malfunction, what you do is quickly glance at the score of the person on your right and the person on your left. Whoever's score is higher, push them out of the way and continue on their machine." We all laughed again. "Actually, this is not a problem. The Golden Nugget has top-notch technicians to fix such situations. Too bad they were all busy and we got Stephen instead." Everyone laughed again as Stephen, wearing a navy blue shirt that said 'slot tech' on it, smiled and shook his head. What could he do? "But if you have any malfunction, just raise your hand and we'll get you squared away immediately. If there are no questions, it's FIVE, FOUR, THREE, TWO, ONE, HIT THE BUTTON!"

Everyone started banging away. Maybe half of the players had one or two people directly behind them rooting them on. "Come on, Annie!" I yelled. At the exact moment I yelled, Kelly was passing by and I was loud enough that he turned, looked right at me, and spoke in a voice that was a Johnnie Carson imitation.

"And that's a very lovely handbag you're holding today, sir. It goes so well with your eyes. Although I must say that the next time you carry a navy purse, perhaps you should consider not wearing black shoes. You can do so much better." I laughed along with everyone else as Kelly walked away looking for someone else to skewer.

The tournament machines had three spinning reels. Players hit the blue spin button and all the reels spun for maybe five seconds, then they'd stop in order, left to right. The big symbol was a flaming trio of sevens. If you matched three of these triple-seven symbols in a line, you'd score 1,500 points. There were also single sevens and three of them were worth 500 points. When you mixed sevens with triple sevens, it was worth 100 points.

You had single bars, double bars, and triple bars. I think a set of single bars was worth 60, double bars 90, and triple bars 120. A mixed set was worth 20. Matching bars with sevens was worthless, and sometimes the reel would land between symbols and you'd score nothing there too. Probably 20 times in every round, each player would experience triple sevens on the first reel, triple sevens on the second reel, then some useless symbol on the third reel. Heartbreak.

Players got to rest a little. Triple sevens across entitled you to 20 or so seconds off as the machine racked up the credits. But even the triple bars for 120 allowed you a couple of seconds if you wanted. It didn't take long to figure out how much rest you got. Meanwhile, you could see the score go up. If you knew you got 100 credits for mixed sevens, you could rest until the score got up to 80 or so, then start banging away again.

Annie was right. It was easy. I could play it as well as anybody else in the second round. Meanwhile, Annie's score was climbing nicely. She had maybe six sets of triple sevens in the first ten minutes, whereas about two seemed to be average for everybody else. Her machine was the first one to turn its light on, which, I figured out, meant she got to 10,000 points.

"Come on, Annie!" I yelled. "Triple sevens!" And when she'd collect on a set, I'd call "Back to back!" One time she did manage to follow one set of triple sevens with another set, but otherwise my back-to-back urging went unfulfilled.

Kelly didn't say a lot over the mike, and most of what he said was either useful information or gentle teasing. He knew almost everybody's name and let people know he noticed them. "John, I see you're in your usual position of bringing up the rear," or "Esther just hit triple sevens back to back and is screaming like she has a mouse loose in her panty hose."

He spread his teasing around, but Annie's machine was really close to Kelly's home base where he had a chair and a bottle of water. I suppose I was boisterous enough that Kelly had to come by and say something else. "Excuse me, Annie, but by any chance do you owe money to the guy sitting behind you? He seems *awfully* interested in you winning this thing."

Annie responded with a smile, "Not money. But I do owe him something else."

Kelly nodded his head at me and said, away from the microphone, "Nice going. You're clearly doing something right."

Annie broke 20,000 points with more than 15 minutes to go. Nobody was close. And then her machine died. She kept hitting the button, but the scoring combinations were few and small. With ten minutes to go, she had only increased her score to 22,000 points. It was still a decent score, but other players had more. "Come *on*, Annie!" I encouraged. Her body language made her state of frustration clear. But then her back-to-backs came and she was jumping up and down hitting the button.

"Two minutes to go," Kelly announced. "If you haven't made your move yet, now might be a good time." Annie was at 33,000. I could only see half of the machines, but hers was the top score in sight. I was hoarse, and whenever Annie turned around and I was moving my arms, I probably looked like I was riding a horse. I was having a good time.

When the machines stopped, Annie's score stood at slightly over 37,000. I walked around and saw one score at 38,500, but otherwise Annie was in second place. I had to stay behind the restraining rope, but encouraged from afar with, "Attawaytogo, Annie! You could win this sucker!"

"Make sure you don't leave your machine until you sign the official score sheet," Kelly instructed over the microphone. "One of our charming assistants will be by momentarily."

Heidi was the one to take the scores from the row Annie was in. As Annie had said, Heidi was a knockout, and any unbiased judge would rank her beauty considerably higher than Annie's. But the only judge who counted was me and Heidi came in a distant second. Poor girl. "That's a real nice score," she told Annie when she came around. "Good luck in the second round."

"Thank you," Annie said, ducked under the rope, and gave me a hug. "You must be my good-luck charm. Think I'll keep you around."

"I'll take that as a sign that you're getting smarter every day. Do you want to go upstairs and celebrate?"

"The deal was that I'll say yes to whatever you want, so if you insist, we can go upstairs. But I really would like to go play some video poker. It turns me on to do that and I don't think you'll find having a turned-on lady on your hands is such a bad thing. Besides, we haven't won anything yet. There's another round and it's all luck. It seems to me that you can't win a tournament in one round—but you surely can lose one."

"Okay with me," I yielded. "Going along with your agenda has worked pretty well so far. No reason to fix what's not broken."

Instead of placing $1,000 in the tray like she did before, Annie started with $925. "That way I don't have to add this morning's score to the new one. I just have one accumulated score going."

"Do we want to keep playing on your card or should we start playing on mine?" I asked.

"Mine, I think. I haven't seen Shannon yet, so I don't know whether or not they have openings for next month. If we're playing to get you into the April tournament, which is a much smaller event, we'll probably play less."

"You're the boss."

"But it's okay with me if you play on my card while I supervise," she told me.

"I'd like that. I'm really hot to trot. They don't mind if you play on somebody else's card?"

"You're not supposed to. But with me sitting right here and us obviously together, it won't be a problem."

I made sure Annie's card was in and started by putting $125 into the machine, leaving an even $800 in the slot. In five minutes the $125 was gone. I put in another $200 and it went fast too. As did the next $200.

"Perhaps you should play instead of me," I said. "You obviously did much better than I did."

"Nonsense. You've played every hand correctly so far. I'd have played exactly the same and had exactly the same score. Keep going."

I got a little play out of the next $200, but not much. I inserted the final $200 in and said, "There goes all of the profit."

"Not to worry," she told me. "These are normal sorts of swings. They're just faster than you're used to, because video poker players play more than ten times as many hands an hour as blackjack players do. That makes the score go up and down much faster."

The machine must have had pity on me, because I got two separate 4-of-a-kinds in the next five minutes. All of a sudden my credits were up to 220. "Wow! Eleven hundred dollars! I guess I'm a pretty good player after all."

"You *are* a pretty good player," Annie told me, "but you're no better now than you were ten minutes ago. Just because you hit a couple of quads doesn't make you a good player any more than the fact that the machine was eating your lunch meant you were a bad player. It's just the normal swings of the game."

"But I *feel* smarter now."

"Yes," she agreed. "That's part of the rush of gambling."

I then hit a full house and 45 coins started to fall into the spill tray. "I'll get some racks," Annie said. "But if the coins stop spilling before I get back, please wait."

"Don't trust me yet?"

"Well, I haven't seen you make one misplay in over an hour, but a lot of tricky hands haven't shown up yet on the machine. It'll be awhile before I'm confident enough to let you play with my money unsupervised."

"No problem."

"I hope so." She left to collect some empty racks. "You know, Chris, it isn't about lack of trust about the important things like honesty, faithfulness, and integrity," she continued when she returned. "It's just that it'll take time to evaluate your skill level. That's all. Call it a business decision rather than a personal one."

"I know." I started to play again and watched the credits go south. In 20 minutes I was down to 20 credits. "Wow. A thousand bucks. Just like that."

Annie smiled. "Yeah, it's no fun when that happens. But get used to it. It'll happen every trip."

I then hit four kings and was up to 140 credits. And then that total started to erode. My credits dwindled down to 30 when I hit two full houses in a row to get me over 100 credits again.

"Is this a pretty normal session?" I asked.

"Sort of. The ups and downs are typical, but we've been ahead the whole day. Many times that won't be the case. Sometimes with this much play we'll be down $2,000 or $3,000. And sometimes you'll hit a royal and be up $20,000."

"I guess you're telling me that a whole lot of different things could have happened and it still would have been typical."

"Right. To have typical results you need to play maybe a million hands. Within that million will be extremely profitable short terms where you might hit two royals in the same day. There will also be extremely costly short terms."

"My trouble is understanding how you cope with those extremely costly short terms. Seems to me you need a lot of faith in the fairness of the machines and the accuracy of your system to keep going when you've lost, lost, lost for a long time."

"I'd call it 'confidence' in the numbers rather than 'faith' in any sort of mystical power, but I agree with the thrust of your statement. It might come from trusting your guru, I'm not sure. In your case, you're following in my footsteps. And I'm supremely confident that the numbers work out. The fact that you think I'm bright, knowledgeable about gambling, and committed to winning might make it easier for you to determine my confidence is well-founded than if you had to figure it all out from scratch."

"And if I merely thought you a beautiful partner to share a love nest?" I teased.

"Then you'd have to determine for yourself whether you can deal with the financial swings." Apparently Annie was still in her lecture mode, but then she added, "Of course, you just may have a big smile on your face while you're discovering this information."

"Yes, you certainly know how to put a smile on my face." Unbidden, Paula's memory popped up again. I couldn't remember any smiling moments during our last two years together. "It's 12:50 and our session is at two. Let's go check out what kind of food they have in the tournament area."

"Sounds good," she told me. "Hit the cash-out button." She pulled her card, put it in again, and announced that we'd accumulated 612 points so far. And we were ahead $975, which meant we were up $50 since the first tournament round.

We both went to the restrooms to wash our hands. The casino uses some kind of light machine oil so the coins slide in and out of the machine smoothly. It causes all sorts of dirt to stick to the coins, and your hands get quite black when you rack the coins or feed them back into the machine. I discovered I wanted to wash both before *and* after I urinated. I didn't want to touch myself down there with that black gunk on my hands.

On the way to the tournament session, I told Annie I was having a great time learning about gambling—in addition to experiencing the best Valentine's Day present any guy could ever want.

"I'm glad," she said. "I just love this game, and you liking it too means a lot to me. Thank you."

We got to the tournament area forty-five minutes early, in plenty of time for the two o'clock session. They had a decent lunch spread as they'd promised earlier, and we each grabbed plates and made our selections. We sat down at one of the tables and I questioned her about the upcoming session. "It didn't look like there was any skill other than continuously hitting the button. When to rest seemed pretty obvious. Is there more to it than that?"

"Not really," she replied. "But there's one place where people can mess up. If the first reel stops on triple sevens and the next reel stops on triple sevens, I've seen people stop hitting the button in anticipation of the long rest they'll get as soon as the third reel lands on triple sevens. But lots of times the third reel lands on something that leaves you scoreless. If you've stopped, it takes a half second or so to start back up again. That could cost you a roll.

"What I do is stop pounding when the reels start spinning and rest while the first reel stops. At just about the time the second reel stops, I start pounding again. So I'm always pounding when the third reel stops and I don't miss a beat. If it turns out that it's a good score and I can rest, I do. On the scores worth 1,500, I watch the credits add up and start pounding when they get to 1,450 or so. I shift periodically from the right hand to the left hand so I don't tire myself out. And I always congratulate people on either side of me when they hit something good. Spreading good vibes around makes it more fun, because people usually respond in kind."

"I guess you could lose quite a few spins by not paying attention," I surmised. "That could make a difference."

"It'd be hard to lose more than one spin unless you fall asleep. It takes maybe six seconds for the reels to stop spinning once they begin. Losing a quarter or half a second a few times won't add up to more than one spin. And usually one more spin won't matter. But it *could*. And as long as you're trying to win, you might as well give it your best."

This made sense. She hadn't provided me any earth-shaking insights, but it allowed me to feel more comfortable. She couldn't know for sure how much I'd picked up and neither of us wanted to drop down a place or two because of a preventable mistake.

A woman approached us from across the room, "Hi Annie! Welcome back."

"Hi Shannon. Nice to see you again. This is my friend Chris George. Chris, this is Shannon."

"So you're the lucky guy that Annie's told me about. Are you having a good time here?"

"Super. We've got a good first round in the tournament, we're ahead in the casino, and we're ..." I cut myself off in the nick of time, just before blurting out something really stupid.

"And we're really enjoying the suite," Annie laughed and finished the sentence for me as I blushed a fine shade of red at what I almost said.

Shannon smiled. "I'm happy for you. So you think you might want to get in the tournament next month, Chris?"

"Definitely."

"Well, we can swing it if you give us some play. Have you gotten your 24 Karat card yet?"

"Yes," I said pulling it out and showing it to her. "I haven't started playing yet, but yes, I plan to put on 1,000 points."

Shannon wrote down my card number. "Very good. That'll make it easy on me to get you in. Let me know if there's anything you need." We chatted a bit more and she left. I'd had versions of this same conversation with several other Golden Nugget employees. I could learn to like this!

"Two o'clock players! If you haven't picked your machine numbers for your round yet, go and see Linea or Diane and they'll fix you right up." I recognized Kelly's voice easily by now. I hoped he'd saved a few good zingers for the second round.

I drew machine number 17 and Linea commented dryly, "I hope you don't mind being the net in a ping-pong match." To my look of utter confusion, she merely responded, "You'll see. Good luck."

When called, I took my seat and Annie sat on a chair directly behind me as close as the restraining rope would allow. "If you're worried that Kelly might ignore you this time," Annie told me, "you can hold my purse again. It'll be more fun this time. There's *money* in it."

I gave her a thanks-but-no-thanks look. The player seated on my right set down two cups of coffee and a bottle of water. I had no idea who he was, but I said, "Good plan. Terrible to risk dying of thirst in a slot tournament." I guess I was in a pseudo-Kelly mode. I hoped this guy wasn't offended by a smart-ass comment from a stranger.

He looked at me for a moment and must have decided my gibe was intended to be friendly. "In fact, these tournaments bore me. Shirley likes them, though, so we do them. That's her on the other side of you."

"'Shirley,' you say? You wouldn't be Bob Dancer by any chance, would you?"

"That's me," he said sticking out his hand. "Have we met?"

"No, we haven't. Chris George. You're a hero to my girlfriend, so you've been required reading for me. I'd never heard of video poker until recently, but thanks to your 9/6 Jacks or Better report and your *WinPoker*, I'm getting there."

"Glad to hear it. Although I did make some suggestions along the way, *WinPoker* is predominantly the work of Dean Zamzow. I use it all the time myself and I'm fortunate to be associated with it. Who's your girlfriend? Do I know her?"

As I turned around to point out Annie, I found her staring right at us. She couldn't hear what we were saying, but she knew exactly who I was talking to and seemed a bit star-struck. She waved timidly and Bob and I both smiled back.

"She's a doll," Shirley chimed in. "I've seen her before but I don't think I've ever spoken to her. Have you, honey?"

"Nope. Shirley and I are planning to eat at Stefano's tonight, Chris. If you two don't have a better offer or show tickets or something, why don't you join us? Our reservations are for seven o'clock."

"After the round we'll check with Annie, but I'm pretty sure we'll be happy to."

As Kelly was giving some preparatory remarks for the second round, Shirley reached across me to Bob and said, "Let's make a one-dollar bet on the round. Shake on it." Bob shook her hand.

Kelly, used to everyone being quiet while he spoke, noticed something was going on and walked up directly behind Bob. "Excuse me, sir. I was telling these nice people about how they could win their share of $32,000. Was I speaking too loudly for whatever you had to say to your wife?"

Shirley squealed and covered her mouth with her hand in embarrassment. Bob didn't back down, though. "We're having an important negotiation about whether or not we should have a one-dollar side bet on this round. Would you mind keeping it down a little bit, please?"

Teasing a guy like Kelly when he had a microphone in his hand was the equivalent of a man in a wheelchair waving a red flag at a charging bull. A one-sided contest, to be sure. Dancer might as well have printed up a sign reading "target" and pinned it to his forehead.

But for whatever reason, Kelly didn't go for the kill.

He merely said, "In that case, I hope she wins," and continued with his instructions as he walked away.

"I do too," Bob said to me under his breath. "Shirley got 33,000 in the first round and if she repeats it, she'll get some money. I had 25,000, so I need a miracle. It usually takes 65,000 or 66,000 to get to tenth place, and that's all they're paying this time. And don't let this rattle you, but you'd be well-advised to scoot your chair toward me. Shirley is a lady with sound effects when she gets triple sevens."

"FIVE, FOUR, THREE, TWO, ONE, HIT THE BUTTON!"

I started banging away with everybody else. Shirley got triple sevens across right away and squealed, "Yes! I'm gonna win!" I kept hitting the button with my left hand while I used my right to scoot my chair over closer to Bob. It didn't do a lot of good, though, as she next screamed, "Back to back! Yes! Kiss your dollar goodbye, honey!"

My machine started slowly. After three minutes I had 400 points while Shirley had almost 4,000. She was jumping up and down; I was concentrating on making sure I hit the button. Bob looked bored, sipped his coffee, and kept hitting the button. He'd hit a few sets too and his score was actually a little higher than Shirley's, although his points came a lot more quietly than hers did.

Kelly came by and stood directly behind Bob and me. He put his microphone behind his back so what he said wouldn't be amplified, bent down, and said quietly. "I've got 23 minutes to come up with the perfect come-back for you. Don't think for an instant that you'll go unpunished for what you said."

"Yep. Paybacks can be a bitch," Bob laughed. "Have you met Chris George, Kelly? He's Annie's friend."

"Glad to meet you, Chris. I remember commenting on your accessories this morning," Kelly said with a smile as he moved on.

"Oh. That was you he got," Shirley said. "We were on the other side and couldn't see who he was teasing. He nails everybody sooner or later. His wife Jennifer is a real sweetie, too. We love them both. Ooh, I see your machine has come alive, Chris. That's the third set you've gotten in the past couple of minutes."

"Come on, Chris!" Annie urged. "Back to back!" Every time I hit something good I turned around and winked at her. She was watching intently with fingers crossed on both hands. At the 20-minutes-to-go mark, I had 9,000 points, Shirley had 11,000 and Bob had 12,000.

Shirley hit another set of sevens, screeched, stood up and ran around to Bob's chair, saying, "I want to see your score." Bob playfully covered up his score with his right hand. She tugged at his arm unsuccessfully. When that didn't work she tickled him on his right side with both of her hands. Bob dropped his hand to protect himself and Shirley got a peek at his score. "Hoo-wee! I'm ahead." Then she ran back to her chair and was in position by the time the 1,500 credits had finished accumulating.

"She cheats," Bob told me. "It's an abusive relationship."

"Yes," I agreed. "A clear case of assault. Let me know if you need a witness in court after you have her arrested."

"Thank you very much," he deadpanned. "I'll keep that in mind."

At 15 minutes to go I was at 14,000. If Bob was right in his predictions of the score necessary to place, I'd need 28,000 at least. I was on target, but had no cushion to spare, and maybe Bob's prediction was low. I'd already seen how the machine could turn cold for a few minutes just for spite. I kept hitting the button furiously. I don't suppose it matters how hard you hit the button, but it felt like I was doing more that way. "Come on, Chris!" Annie kept yelling behind me.

At eight minutes to go I was at 22,000. Hanging in there. Still possible, if only the machine kept responding. "Come on sevens!" I found myself yelling.

"What's your score, Bob?" Shirley asked.

"I might have 34,000," he replied. "What's your score?"

"Don't believe him, Shirley, he's barely got 21,000," announced Cindy, one of the Bally Belles.

"We caught him lying again," reported Lynn, another of the same crew.

"Damn," says Bob. "Shirley's got spies everywhere."

"Thank you, Cindy. Thank you, Lynn," Shirley sang happily. "Us girls have got to stick together. I'm winning. Hoo-wee!"

Twenty-six thousand. I was getting there. "Triple sevens," I heard Annie plead.

"Less than two minutes to go," Kelly announced. "Don't give up. Keep tapping to the end. Your machine might turn around. That is, unless you're Bob Dancer. In that case, your score is so pathetic you have no chance in hell of a recovery. To add insult to injury, you've also lost a buck to your wife."

With one minute to go, I had 28,200, Shirley had 32,500, and we were both pleading with our machines. Bob had 24,000 and turned around to tell Kelly, "Not one of your better zingers, you know. You must be off your feed today."

"Don't press your luck. I'll have the microphone tomorrow night too."

At the end of the round, the Annie-Chris-team scores added up to 66,220, while Shirley had 66,340. "Probably both get $1,000," Bob predicted. "We won't know for sure until they make the announcement tomorrow night."

I introduced Bob and Shirley to Annie and we firmed up the seven o'clock date. Shirley agreed to call and get the reservations switched from two tables for two to one table for four. "I love Stefano's," Shirley cooed. "I think it's my favorite restaurant in town."

"Hey look, Bozo," Cindy tapped Bob lightly on his shoulder with her clipboard. "You have to sign the score sheet."

"Why? What happens if I don't?"

"Then you can't win anything."

"I won't win anything anyway."

"Then sign it because I said so and quit giving me a hard time."

"Was I ever married to you, Cindy?" Bob asked while he signed the score sheet. "Your tone of voice sounds so familiar."

"You wish." She filled out my score, had me sign, then did the same with Shirley. "Hey. You and Chris have good scores and might win something. Not like some people I could mention." She tried to look sternly at Bob, but only managed to crack herself up. "See you guys next month."

"She likes you," Annie said to Bob after Cindy went off to take down the next person's score. "So does Kelly."

"That's because Shirley and I play with each other and let them play too. It makes their job more interesting. Now if you'll excuse us, we're each going to try to hit a royal flush before dinner. See you at seven."

"That was fun," I said, turning to Annie. I laid both my forearms on her shoulders and stared her in the eyes. "And now what I'd like to do is to go upstairs and play with you. How does that sound?"

"Like a very good idea."

We sat on opposite sides of the Jacuzzi, which was overflowing with bubbles from some bath prep Annie had brought from California. "I was thinking we were going to get a nice soak last night. Somehow I miscalculated," she said with a smile.

"I assume you'll be able to get over your disappointment," I said. "Did you bring any lubricant?"

"Well, yes, as a matter of fact," she answered. "Is this the start of some special request?"

"Oh no, nothing like that. There might be one down the road sometime, but right now I'm blissfully happy with just plain mama-and-papa sex. I was merely thinking that we're subjecting parts of our bodies to a whole lot of friendly friction, so to speak, and I'd hate for either of us to remember this weekend because we're sore. Since baths tend to remove natural lubrication anyway, I just thought of it now."

"How considerate of you," she said. "Actually, I packed a couple of different kinds. I was super-lubricated last night, but I figured I'd start using some today."

Just then the doorbell rang. I was surprised. I certainly wasn't expecting anyone. "I ordered chocolate-covered strawberries and some Bailey's from room service, We'll be playing tonight, so I don't want to drink much, but a sip or two would be nice. Would you be a sweetie and put your robe on and go down and get it? I put a $5 bill on the table for the tip."

As I was signing the check, Annie shrieked, then there was a big splash of water. I was alarmed until I heard her laughing out loud. The room-service guy took the $5 and left quickly.

"What was that all about?" I asked as I got back upstairs. "What was so funny?"

She laughed again. "Well, I figured I was being clever. The way the mirrors are situated around here, I could see what you and the waiter were doing if I sat up extra tall. When I did, I saw he was looking right at me. And if I could see his eyes, then he could see my chest. He saw you in your robe and probably figured that if he looked up, he might get lucky. Those room-service guys must know *exactly* how the mirrors work and where to look."

"Are you angry about it?"

"Oh no," she smiled. "There were enough bubbles sticking to me that he couldn't have seen much. Plus, Vegas is filled with places where women half my age take it all off, so I suspect he's seen bigger and better lots of times. Still, I bet every male who works for room service will soon hear about the redhead in room 7b."

"I don't see how that's possible."

"What do you mean?"

"Well, I've already figured out that you're 29 years old. Half your age would be 14 and a half. Even in Vegas, you're not going to find naked dancing girls that age."

She laughed. "Silly me—forgetting how old I am! I was thinking I was 36. Thanks for reminding me that the best ten years of a woman's life are between 29 and 30. But don't tell my boss. He thinks I never make mathematical mistakes."

She poured a shot of Bailey's into a glass and handed it to me. She peeled the stem from a strawberry, put the morsel in her mouth, and presented the other half for my pleasure.

I did, and lingered there. We'd kissed before, of course, but always with the uncertainty of how far along Holly Bennett's list we'd get. Now, finally, there was no more of that uncertainty, so we could just enjoy the pleasure of kissing. I pulled her onto my lap and we just kissed and kissed. There was some idle touching of various parts of each other, but mostly it was just passionate necking. I liked it immensely, and apparently so did Annie, who didn't find any need to suggest another position or activity.

Eventually, after two shots of Bailey's and two-thirds of the strawberries, we got out of the tub and dried each other off. "Your wish is my command," she said, "but if you don't have anything specific in mind, I suggest you let me lead the way."

"Lead on, MacDuff," I said. "Who was MacDuff, anyway?"

"That's also a conversation for another day," she smiled, happy with herself for remembering her response to a similar question on Christmas Day, now a month and a half ago. "Now close your eyes," she ordered, as she started to direct me using the same hands-on technique she employed to steer the car last night. "Now stop here and keep your eyes shut."

I could feel my legs against what I figured must be the bed. She let go of me, and I could feel the bed move as she climbed on. For about 20 seconds, nothing happened. The suspense was killing me. I didn't know what was going to happen, but I was pretty sure I was going to like it. My erection was complete and I didn't even know exactly what for.

She started to lubricate me. At first I wasn't sure how or why. And then I felt both of her hands on my buttocks and I knew she was using her mouth. Ooh! Paula had barely kissed me there a few times and then pulled away. During my collegiate philandering, I'd experienced oral sex many times. But that was 15 years ago and I'd forgotten how good it felt. Annie was slowly and gently moving up and down the length of me. "Oh, that's nice," I said, "but I need to lie down."

As we lay down, Annie kept her mouth moving. I was swept away by the excitement and lasted barely longer than I had the first time last night. Usually, in my sexual experience, I'd been the one making sure my partner was satisfied. This weekend I was finding out that it's pure pleasure to be on the other side.

"Thank you, darling," I told her. "You're absolutely the best."

"You're welcome. And I've never had a more-fun weekend either. The alarm is set for 6:20. Let's nap until then."

Friday
February 11, 2000

"You guys seem so much in love. Almost like a new love affair, but not quite," Shirley observed as we were seated at Stefano's.

"Something like that," I said. "Maybe we can give you a better answer next time."

"Okay. We'll take that as an extremely gracious way of saying none of your damn business. Are you enjoying your trip to Vegas so far?" asked Bob.

"Oh, yes. We're winning at the machines, possibly scoring at the tournament, and the room we have is truly mind-boggling," I responded.

"Oh, I know," enthused Shirley. "Our courtship took place largely in the suites at Treasure Island and the Mirage. They aren't nearly as nice as the suite you're in this week, but they were beyond our previous experiences and we had a wonderful time."

"Are you up a lot on the machines?" Bob asked. I nodded, but Annie shook her head.

"Not really," Annie replied. "We've played a little over 600 points and are up about a grand, not counting cash-back. We plan to play 1,200 points on my card and 1,000 on Chris's. We've really just started."

"Isn't being $1,000 ahead significant?" I asked.

"To give you an idea," Bob answered, "Shirley and I played 1,800 points between us and lost $3,800, although that will be reduced by $900 worth of slot club cash and probably $1,000 from the tournament. Still, every hand was played perfectly. It just wasn't our turn."

"This is my first video poker gambling trip," I said. "Perhaps I haven't experienced Reality 101 yet."

"You will eventually," Bob said. "You seem to have a

good tutor. It's okay to take some time to learn, especially when you enjoy the learning process. I'm still in the learning mode, and I've been doing this for over five years."

"I *am* enjoying it," I said. "Annie tells me your strategy is perfect. Frankly, my mathematical tools aren't sufficient to evaluate her analysis. Is it really true that there are no errors in the report?"

"Interesting question," Bob replied. "I'm convinced the strategy is perfect. It's been out three years and no one has told me there's an error, at least in Jacks or Better. But even though that's true, I'm about to improve on it."

Annie spoke up, "Okay. I'll bite. How can you improve on perfection?"

"In the way the information is presented," Bob told us. "I've been working with a man named Liam W. Daily, who is very innovative. The Dancer / Daily advanced strategy is identical in how to play the hand as the Dancer Professional Strategy in the report that you read, Chris. But it only takes about half as many lines to display. And hand categories simply disappear with no loss of information."

"I don't understand how categories can go away at no cost," I said.

"Good question," Bob said. "Here's how. Take 4-card straights and 3-card straight flushes. On the chart you've been studying, there are five separate entries for these straights. That is, for four high cards, three high cards, two high cards, one high card, and no high cards. With me so far?"

"Sure."

"And there are eight separate entries for 3-card straight flushes, depending on the number of high cards and the number of gaps."

"That many?" I was surprised.

"Yes. In the report, listing those takes thirteen lines. And the highest straight flushes are higher in value than the lowest straights," Bob said. "It takes quite a bit of practice to keep that all straight."

"I agree," I said. "How is the new way different?"

"It says ST4 is greater than SF3 +1," Bob said. "Letting the "plus 1" part of it go undefined for now, what this rule says is that *every* 4-card straight is superior to *every* 3-card straight flush that can appear in the same five cards."

"But how can that be correct?" Annie asked. "The first strategy says that sometimes a 3-card straight flush is higher than some straights and the second one says otherwise. How can such opposite presentations both be accurate?"

"That's the beauty of Daily's discovery," Bob said. "A straight flush combination like queen jack nine, which is the most valuable one, simply cannot appear in the same five cards as, say, a nine, eight, seven, six 4-card straight. It would require at least six cards for all those to appear together. So, since it can never happen, we don't need to allow for it in the strategy. In every case where a 4-card consecutive straight and a 3-card straight flush *can* exist in the same hand, the straight is more valuable."

"That's slick!" Annie exclaimed. "As a computer programmer, I can appreciate the difference between a program being written so it works and it being written elegantly. Is this strategy close to being ready to publish?"

"Very soon," Bob said. "We're producing four different strategies for five different games all at once, and redefining notation as we go. Liam, Anthony Curtis, who's the publisher, and I are all sticklers for accuracy. This is going back and forth innumerable times. But enough of shop talk. Let's look at the menu. I'm hungry."

"I love the lamb chops here," Shirley enthused. "Bob usually has one of the fish dishes. And we usually go for a salad or soup with it. We skip the appetizers, because we're being good at avoiding fried foods, for now at least. But we're in no hurry at all, so if you want an appetizer, go ahead. We don't drink, but I've heard they have a pretty good wine list here if that's your thing."

Annie spoke for both of us, I guess, when she said,

"We're hitting the machines again in an hour or so, so it's no alcohol for us. I think I'll have the veal special that the waiter told us about, and a Caesar salad. How 'bout you, honey?" she said.

I was about to answer, but Bob spoke up first. "Thanks for asking, sweetheart. I'm having the salmon." We all laughed. He continued, "On the off chance she was referring to you, Chris, what are you going to have?" I ordered osso bucco, not exactly sure what it was, but I was in an adventurous mood.

"Oh good!" Shirley exclaimed. "Everyone is having something different. I put in dibs for a small taste of each."

Just then the waiter took the order, and Bob told him that we wanted it on two separate checks.

Annie asked Bob, "Are you guys playing more than one event this weekend?"

"No," he answered. "Sometimes we do, but it has to be two very lucrative events for us to try both. Part of our enjoyment of these events is staying in the nice suites. What's the fun of having a nice suite here and at the Mirage the same weekend, and running back and forth between them so we're frazzled? This way, we can enjoy visiting with friends we know at these events and enjoy the moment."

"Or people we've just met," Shirley added. "Also we love to dance, so we generally choose the events with dancing at their award banquets."

"And Shirley never forgets to remind me of it," Bob said with affection. "She makes sure our dance shoes are always packed in our casino-weekend luggage."

The waiter brought salads for Bob and Annie and soup for me. Shirley waited for her entrée. Except that Shirley insisted on having a bite of each salad and a taste of the soup to hold her over until her food came.

"Chris and I are taking dance classes. It takes such a long time to get good, and tomorrow is our coming-out party, sort of. We've danced socially before only among people who didn't know us. I'm a little nervous about it."

"Don't be," Shirley said. "As long as you two enjoy each other, it doesn't really matter how good you are. What kind of classes are you taking?"

"West Coast Swing classes at the Swingtime Dance Studio in Bellflower," I contributed.

"Really! Phil Adams is wonderful," Bob enthused. "I took probably four hundred hours of lessons from him."

"Wow!" I exclaimed. "That's a mess of classes. Either you're a very slow learner ..."

Bob laughed. "Well, I'm not Fred Astaire, but I got hooked on Phil's classes in both swing and Texas two step. Through much of that period I was single and not in the space for a relationship. Dance classes are safe sex, so to speak. Also, it really helped my self-confidence."

"How so?" Annie asked. "You don't seem shy now."

"I got to be a good enough dancer that I could go up to the prettiest unattached woman at any dance club or party and know there was a good chance she'd accept my invitation to dance and enjoy herself when she did. That's how I captured Shirley. Asked her to dance one night."

"Yep," Shirley added, "and now he can't get rid of me. We should swap partners at least once tomorrow night."

"I'd like that," said Annie.

"I don't know," I hesitated. "We're only halfway through the first intermediate class. I'm not sure we can keep up."

"Don't worry about that," Bob said. "You rotate partners in class and adjusting to each new partner is part of the fun. For example, I'll start off slowly to get Annie used to my lead. I'll do basic West Coast patterns like the underarm turn, lock whip, side pass, and tuck turn, and see how it goes. If she follows pretty well, we can try something more complicated. If she doesn't, we won't. But we'll have a good time and that's really all that counts.

"Plus, Shirley is a lot of fun and is expert enough that she can follow just about anybody. Besides, if you refuse you'll break her heart."

"Oh, please don't break my heart, Chris!" Shirley pleaded. "Please please please!"

We all laughed. "Okay. Having a broken-hearted woman on our hands wouldn't be a good thing. You've got yourself a deal," I said. "But I'm worried that Annie may like your dancing better than mine."

"She well might, but even if she does, I'm sure she knows better than to admit it. If she ever did let on, it just might break Shirley's heart."

"Oh please don't break my heart, Annie!" Shirley pleaded again, this time clasping her hands together like she was praying. "Please please please!" This cracked us all up. "Besides," Shirley continued, "changing partners is fun, and you're welcome to enjoy dancing with Bob, Annie. I've seen the way you and Chris look at each other. I've got nothing to worry about. Plus, Dan will probably dance with you too."

"Who's Dan?" I asked.

"Dan Williams is the new vice president of slot operations here," Bob explained. "He might well be the highest-ranking Golden Nugget executive at the party, although sometimes the president shows up. Dan just moved here from Mississippi and he *loves* to dance. His wife is still in Mississippi getting their house sold or something, so Dan will dance eight or ten different dances, each with a different woman."

"Yes," agreed Shirley, "dancing is just plain fun for him and he doesn't hit on any of the women. Once he sees Annie out on the dance floor with both of you guys, he'll probably ask her himself. And if he does, Annie, say yes. You'll be glad you did."

At this point, music started and all the waiters started to sing the old Dean Martin song, "That's Amore." Many of the diners sang along or swayed with the music, and the brief two-minute performance was greeted with rousing applause.

"That's my favorite part of Stefano's," enthused Shirley. "They do maybe one song an hour and sometimes they're in Italian, sometimes in English, and sometimes half-and-half. The tall waiter who shaves his head and the short maitre d' have been around forever and are the ones who get into it the most."

Later, during coffee, Annie asked Bob, "I'm going to be subsidizing Chris's play. While we've already figured out a game plan, we've never done it before and I'm curious for your thoughts. Are there any pitfalls to be concerned with?"

"Maybe," Bob answered. "You need to have a definite plan to handle the W-2Gs. If you're playing a $5 9/6 Jacks machine, you'll get a straight flush worth $1,250 every 9,000 hands and a royal flush worth $20,000 every 40,000 hands. You may not hit one of those this trip, but keep this arrangement going and these jackpots will come. The casinos give the W-2G to the person playing the machine, not the person putting up the money.

"You can fill out a 5354 tax form and give it to the casino. That authorizes them to give you the W-2Gs for Chris's jackpots, but most casinos don't stock the form and the IRS office will probably be closed until Monday. You can agree to assist each other with taxes a year from now, you can switch seats before they get there and hope they turn a blind eye, or you and Chris can beg for mercy with the casino managers, saying it's all your money anyway and he's going through a messy divorce and if a W-2G shows up it could really complicate things. Most casinos will fall for that one, I suspect. They don't want to be the bad guy in these situations, but they're on the hook whether they want to be or not. If the IRS or the Gaming Commission decides to punish them, it could be a stiff fine. The two of you should probably talk about these things beforehand.

"Also, some people have been known to take shots. Let's say you put up $1,000 and Chris hits a $20,000 royal. Nice thought so far, right? But whose money is it? One interpretation is that it was all your money and the jackpot should be yours. Another interpretation is that you were lending him the money, so he should give you back the grand and keep $19,000. Are you sure you trust each other enough so these problems won't arise? A $20,000 jackpot is enough to turn some people into real assholes and forget handshake agreements. Don't think that I'm insinuating anything specifically about either you. I barely know you. But you asked about potential pitfalls and those are the ones I see."

"Thank you very much," said Annie. "I'm sure things will be fine. I'm not concerned about Chris turning into an asshole. He's the most trustworthy guy I've ever known."

Shirley wanted somebody to share a tiramisu for dessert with her. Everybody else was pretty full. "Don't worry about keeping this promise to her," said Bob. "Just make it. Once the dessert is here, she won't care whether you have a bite or not. It's just that she feels guilty ordering an entire dessert for herself."

"Okay, Shirley," I cooperated, "subject to the caveat that Bob said it was okay to lie about this, I'll share a tiramisu with you."

"Oh goody!" Shirley exclaimed. Bob and I ordered coffee and Annie ordered hot water with lemon.

We finished, signed the checks, left a tip, and said our goodbyes. As we walked to the machines after, I said to Annie, "That was not only enjoyable, it was informative. Anything Bob say about the W-2Gs that makes you want to change the plan?"

"Not really. I think our agreement covered all of the points he brought up," she told me. "But I'm glad I asked him. He might have brought up something I hadn't considered, and if he had, I'd have wanted to get it clear with you ahead of time before it bit us and caused hard feelings somehow."

We went downstairs to continue playing. The machine we played earlier was busy, so we went around the corner to some others. "Are these the same?" I asked. "They look a little different."

"The ones we played earlier today were by IGT, which stands for International Game Technology, I think, and these are by Bally Gaming. Slightly different button placement, different sounds, and different card graphics, but as near as I can tell they're exactly equivalent and I'll take either one. These Bally machines are older and more prone to hopper jams, but the IGT machines are pretty close to the dice pit, which is likely to be smoky and rowdy on a Friday night."

"I'll take a hopper jam over cigarette smoke any time."

"Me too. Actually IGT dominates the market and I play their machines in most other casinos, so I'm used to their look and feel. But at the Nugget, where the machines are placed is the dominant factor in my decision, so I mostly play the Bally machines."

"Works for me," I said. "Do we play on your card, mine, or both side by side? You're the boss."

"Why don't you play on my card while I supervise. Let's finish up my 1,200 points before starting on yours. If you continue to play well tonight, tomorrow we'll let you play without me hovering."

"Okay," I replied. Since we were up $975 so far, I fed $175 in bills into the machine and Annie placed $800 into the spill slot to keep our running total easy to manage. I got to play all of nine hands. One time I got two pair; on the other eight hands the machine gave me nothing at all. I put in another two bills and lost that quickly too. In about half an hour, I was down $1,975. "It was more fun when we were up a thousand instead of down a thousand."

Annie laughed. "Don't worry about it, really. We've got a long way to go. Keep it up. These are simply normal swings."

"Okay, Boss Lady," I responded, as I inserted two more $100 bills. For whatever reason I started to get full houses and flushes and even four jacks. I got it up to 220 credits and commented proudly, "We're back to zero. I feel rich!"

"Cute. Not being down feels good, but it's way too early to celebrate. You've earned 65 credits so far and we're planning on putting a total of another 500 on my card tonight, then another 1,000 on your card tomorrow.

More important is that you're playing well and I haven't seen you make one error in the 600 hands you've played this afternoon and tonight."

"So you're proud of your student?"

"Remember about fishing for compliments," she said grinning. "But yes. I'm really proud of you. I have no doubt that you could master this game if you put your mind to it."

Her praise felt nice. "Would you like to play some, or maybe rotate back and forth somehow?"

"I'm happy doing it this way. Are you still alert and having a good time?"

"Oh yes. I'd like to keep playing." I hit the deal button and received 5♦Q♥7♦4♦J♠. I was sure holding the diamonds was correct so I did, but I always gave Annie a chance to speak up before I hit the draw button. To our great surprise, this time the 3♦ came out first, followed by the 6♦. The machine said "Straight Flush" and music started to play. Annie and I whooped and kissed. "What now?" I said, very excited.

"Now you're going to experience your first W-2G," Annie said. "If you like that jackpot music, that's good, because you'll be hearing it for the next ten minutes or so. If you'd rather not hear it, one of the nice features of a Bally machine is that you can hit the red change button and the music will turn off." I did and the music disappeared. "Here comes the floor lady. Why don't you let her tell you what to do?"

A lady in a maroon jacket came up. Her name tag said "Sherrna." "Congratulations," she said, "you've got some money coming. I'll need a photo ID and something with your Social Security number on it." I gave her my driver's license and my Social Security card. "This'll work fine," Sherrna said. "I'll be back."

My face was probably flushed. I'd never won anything this big before. "Do I have time to go to the bathroom?"

"Nope, you've got to hold it all night," she kidded. "Of course you can go. I'll be right here."

"Will you save my place?"

"I'll think about it."

When I got back to the machine, Sherrna still hadn't returned. I asked Annie, "I assume a tip is appropriate when I get paid. But how much and to whom? After all, it's your money I'm talking about giving away."

Annie smiled. "Ten bucks feels about right on a jackpot of this size. At least two people will be here to pay you. Somebody in a blue-green jacket is a little higher up the food chain than the people in the maroon jackets and you can tip either one or both. I don't think the maroon jackets share tip money with the blue-green jackets. You can ask and they'll tell you. If it's somebody in a suit who has you sign the tax form, at most places they can't accept tips, so you'd give it all to Sherrna."

A lady in a blue-green jacket with a nametag reading "Silke" came up, returned my ID, and politely asked for my signature. "Congratulations," she said. She gave me a copy of the tax form and told Sherrna to go ahead and pay me.

Sherrna counted the $1,250 into my hand and I asked her how tip money was shared. She told me that all tip money was pooled, but that she and Silke were in different tip pools. "Fine," I said as I handed her a $10 bill. Thinking I was being clever I said, "Why don't you tear this in half and put half in your pool and half in Silke's?"

Without skipping a beat, Sherrna said, "Sure, no problem," promptly ripped the bill in two, and handed half to Silke—who shrieked in disbelief. "That's what you asked for, isn't it?" Sherrna said innocently. "We're taught to give the customer whatever he wants whenever possible." As they walked away, Silke was laughing while shaking her head and Sherrna had a huge grin on her face—apparently quite proud of herself.

"Good show," Annie said after the two women left. "I'll bet they tape the bill back together again, turn it in for fives, and make sure the money gets into the right place. But they'll probably laugh about it for days. Meanwhile, why don't you see if you can earn another one of these tax forms?"

We played some more, had coins spill into the tray, and fed them back. When we decided to call it quits for the night at 400 points for the session, I was down $450 plus the $10 tip. "Not bad at all," Annie declared. "I'm rather proud of myself for turning you on to this sport. I think you're a natural at it."

"Thank you, but I lost. It's tough to use the yardstick of 'did I make any mistakes?' rather than 'did I win or lose?'" We were in the elevator heading up to the suite.

"I know. So let's put a different spin on it. Other than gambling, do you feel like a winner this weekend?"

"Are you kidding? I've been dreaming of holding you in my arms all night for a few months now. This has been a milestone weekend."

"At the risk of dangling for a compliment, doesn't that make you feel like a winner?"

"Oh yes!" I concurred, pulling her into my arms. "All of a sudden, our video poker score seems pale in comparison."

Inside the suite, I shaved again just in case. We showered together and climbed into bed naked. It was delightful being next to her, and I quickly became erect. But it was sort of a mild erection, very unlike the throbbing monsters I'd had yesterday and earlier today. I gave her a long kiss and told her, "Annie, these have been the best two days ever, and I'm really looking forward to the rest of the weekend and the rest of my life. But right now I'm not particularly horny. If you have any special requests, tell me and I'll do my best to satisfy you. But if it's my choice, I'd rather skip the lovemaking for now and replenish my sexual energies overnight. That way we'll be able to resume our wonderful sex life with full vigor tomorrow. Is that okay with you?"

"Of course. We're flesh-and-blood lovers, not sexual athletes. I'd much rather wait until you really want me again. I have the funny feeling that you won't make me wait too long. And if by any chance the mood strikes you in the middle of the night, I'm right here and the answer is yes."

We kissed awhile and drifted off to sleep. Both of us were available to the other, but neither pressed the issue. The day had been a satisfying feast. There was no need for any dessert.

Saturday
February 12, 2000

I woke in the morning full of energy, a full hour before she did, and quietly got out of bed so as not to wake her. I donned my robe and quietly went down the spiral staircase. I plugged in my laptop computer at the bar in the corner. It was tucked under the loft where Annie slept, so the light there had little effect on the darkness upstairs. Any of the other lights downstairs would have had a bigger effect. I started practicing with *WinPoker*. I was hooked. My dreams hadn't been about Annie as much as about Annie and me hitting a royal flush. About pairs becoming full houses or four-of-a-kinds. About 3-card straight flushes filling in. Annie was definitely in the picture. But she wasn't the entire picture.

When Annie awoke, she came downstairs and gave me a big hug. That definitely aroused me, but what I really wanted to do was to go play video poker. We dressed and went for breakfast at the Carson Street Café, the Golden Nugget's upscale coffee shop. The VIP line pass here worked the same as the one we had at the Luxor, and we were seated in the coffee shop within five minutes of leaving our suite—even though there was probably a half-hour line full of non-VIPs.

The waitress brought coffee right away and returned in a few minutes to take our order. "So," Annie said with a gentle smile after the waitress left, "it seems that video poker is now in your blood."

"It is. I actually dreamt about playing video poker last night. That surprises the heck out of me. After all, here we are on a honeymoon of sorts, and I'm dreaming about you and me doing something with our clothes *on* rather than with our clothes *off*. Amazing!"

"So you're bored with my body already?" she teased.

"Not by a long shot. You tired of mine yet?" I teased back.

"It's okay," she laughed. "I'm glad video poker is another passion we share together. If you don't mind, I'd like to review some of the tricky Jacks or Better hands before we go out and play. It'll get our focus right where it should be."

"Good idea."

She wrote down A♠K♥Q♣J♣ and asked me how to play it. "It's a misdeal," I said, proud of myself. "You need five cards in a hand."

"Very good. Now tell me the correct play for every possible fifth card in the deck."

Before I could answer, the waitress brought my omelet and Annie's yogurt and granola. She saw we were studying. "I see a lot of folks studying gambling over their meals. I think some of them even think they can beat the house. Can you believe it?"

Annie smiled. "I don't know if we can or not this trip, but we're certainly going to try our hardest."

"Well, good luck to you, then. I hope you win a bundle."

When the waitress went away, Annie tapped the paper where she had written out the problem.

"Okay," I began. "There are twelve cards in the deck that will pair one of the cards shown. If any of them is the fifth card, you keep the pair. There are four tens in the deck where you'd keep the straight. If you draw the 8 or 9 of clubs, you'd keep all three clubs. If the fifth card is any other nine or any other club, you keep all four cards shown. With each of the other possible cards, you hold queen jack."

"Perfect!" she exclaimed. "Same thing on this one." She wrote down the A♥K♥T♥4♥. I knew from earlier tests that when she wrote down "T," she meant "10."

"Okay. If it's the queen or jack of hearts, you keep the top four cards, throw away the four, and pray like hell." I smiled at the image I was creating. "If you draw any other heart, you keep all five cards. If you draw any queen or jack that isn't a heart, or any ten, you hold all four cards shown. Anything else and you hold the top three hearts. Perfect again?"

"Nope, you missed something important."

I hadn't been writing things down, so I wasn't exactly sure what I had said. When I shrugged, she said with a smile. "It's something you know, but just forgot to say. If the fifth card is another ace or king, you keep the high pair."

"Oh yeah. Damn. I knew that. High pairs are better than every 3-card royal or 4-card flush, so long as it isn't a 4-card straight flush."

I wasn't angry with her for her nitpicky test. Just a bit irritated at myself for not getting credit for something I knew. "Give me another one. Please."

"Okay. How about when you're dealt a suited king ten. When do you hold the king by itself?" I got that one right. "Now give me the entire set of rules for when you have two unsuited high cards with a ten suited with one of them. When do you hold the high cards and when do you hold high-card ten?" I scribbled a chart that looked like this:

A	KT	AK
A	QT	Depends on flush
A	JT	JT
K	AT	KA
K	QT	KQ
K	JT	Depends on flush
Q	AT	QA
Q	KT	QK
Q	JT	QJ
J	AT	JA
J	KT	JK
J	QT	JQ

Since Annie knew the subject matter, she could see immediately what the columns meant, even though I didn't label them. The first column was the unsuited high card. The second column was the suited high-card-ten combination. And the third column was the correct play. The "depends on flush" notation referred to whether one of the other two cards in the hand belonged to the same suit as the ten.

"You get an A-plus!" Annie beamed. "You seem to know this stuff cold. Things must really be clicking in your brain. I knew you could do it."

"Then I've got a Jacks or Better puzzle for you," I said. "It's a fair question, though it's tricky, and I bet you won't get the right answer."

"A bet, huh? Before I hear this puzzle, what do I collect if I win the bet, and what do I have to pay if I lose? Bob and Shirley bet a buck with each other, but I don't really think they pay off when they lose."

"Oh, you'll like this. If you get it wrong, there's no penalty, because you're already making my dreams come true this weekend. But if you get it right, I'll recite the poem I've written for you."

"You wrote a poem for me? How sweet! No guy's ever done that before. I promise I won't demand one every day if you tell it to me now."

"No deal. You're right about the not-every-day part, but you have to get the puzzle right first. Here it is. In what hands in 9/6 Jacks do you have a choice in which cards to hold while making the best possible play?"

"That's easy," she responded. "None. Every hand in 9/6 Jacks has a unique right answer."

"Wrong. I've come up with two distinct kinds of hands where that's not true. There might be more, I don't know. But at least two. If you want to hear the poem, you'll have to find them both."

"How long do I have to get the right answer?"

"How soon do you want to hear some poetry?"

"And it's not some recycled poem from Holly or Paula or someone else?"

"Nope. Brand new. Inspired by you. And you'll know

it's true, because it's about West Coast Swing and I didn't even know what that was when I dated anybody else."

"I don't know right now, but I *will* figure this out."

"Your poem will be waiting. In the meantime, I think I hear a royal flush calling to us. Do you hear it?" I cupped my hand to my ear.

Annie nodded as she signed the check and I left a few bucks on the table for a tip. "Why don't we finish off your card and then start on mine. Okay?"

"Sure, but I want you to know that your puzzle is bugging the hell out of me."

"Thank you very much. I'll take that as a compliment."

She spanked me lightly on the butt, then happily took my hand as we marched off to try our luck again.

Some cigarette smokers were playing the Bally machines, so we were back on the IGT. Annie sat down to play first and inserted the two bills. "Let me say the way to play the hand out loud and that way you can correct me if I'm wrong," I suggested and she agreed.

I found myself announcing my choices in a sort of video poker shorthand. On a hand such as K♠Q♠ and three hearts to a straight flush, I'd say "Hearts" if the straight flush had no gaps, like 456, 567, or others, and I'd say "High cards" if the straight flush had at least one gap, such as 235, 457, or 589. As long as the phrasing gave a unique answer, Annie and I figured it was fair.

On one hand, J♣8♥6♠5♠2♠, the correct play is to just hold the jack. The two-gap straight flush with no high cards is the lowest-valued eligible hand in Jacks or Better; anything else is superior. In this case, even the single high card was better. So I directed, "Hold the clubs."

"Wrong," she said, and then, "whoops, you tricked me. Smart ass!"

After a while, the hand K♥Q♠T♥T♠J♦ came along. I said, "Hold the straight," and tried to say it in a voice that didn't betray anything unusual. In fact, however, this was one of the hands in Annie's puzzle. You could hold the king, queen, and jack with the ten of hearts or the king, queen, and jack with the ten of spades. Both were equivalent. Both were right. It was tricky to be sure, but that shouldn't bother Annie.

She was up to the task. "That's one of your special hands, isn't it?" she asked. "Or is this a third type you hadn't considered?"

"Very good," I praised. "You're halfway home to a poem. Hey! That kind of rhymes too. Anyway, the other type of hand is approximately just as tricky. We had one once yesterday, though not yet today."

"I want a hint," she demanded. "I've been so nice to you this weekend that surely I deserve one."

"Hmm. I can't argue with that logic. This is the best weekend of my life so far. Okay, here's your hint. The hand will delight you when it comes."

"That's it? That's the whole hint?"

"Yep. Although if you want to go upstairs and be nice some more, maybe I can think of a better hint."

She looked at me and smiled. "If you're hot to trot, we can cash out right now. But I'd still like a bigger hint."

"Okay. But even when you get the right answer, I'll only give the poem to you when we're both upstairs naked. Agreed?"

"That almost sounds kinky. But I agree. Now, what's the hint."

"The hint is that the *last* hint was actually a pretty big one."

"Really? That the hand will delight me when it comes? *That's* a big hint?"

"Yep. Anyway, let's play this hand." Annie held the four-card straight, including the ten of hearts, and hit the draw button. She drew a red nine for a straight and promptly hit the cash-out button.

"Why'd you do that?"

"Because I figured out the answer to your puzzle and I'm ready to get naked and listen to some poetry. I know I have the right answer, because your hint makes a lot of sense."

"So how'd we do on the play?"

"We put 94 points on my card, we're down $25, and I'm horny. Let's go."

Sometimes it just doesn't pay to argue with a woman.

Up in the room, for some reason, we both decided not to say a word. We were giggling and enjoying ourselves, but not speaking. We were both naked and in bed when I broke the silence as I ran my fingers up and down over her entire chest—from her neck to the top of her pubic hair. "Well, my lovely lady, would you like me to quell the fire raging within your pretty little body or would you like to hear some poetry first? I must warn you, however, that while you've claimed that you know the remaining answer to the puzzle, you've yet to reveal it. And while I'm quite willing to ravage such a tender young morsel as yourself without hearing the solution, a thousand horses couldn't drag this poem from my lips until you yield the correct answer."

She pulled my head down, kissed me, then maneuvered so that I was flat on my back and she was straddling me while facing me. She pinned my hands down. She was actually pretty strong, but I was stronger. Of course, I was interested in loving her, not fighting her, so I let her have the upper hand at the moment.

"You're a crazy goofball," she told me, kissing me again. "The answer to your puzzle is a dealt quad. If you're dealt, for example, four kings and a three, holding all five cards is one option or just holding the four kings and discarding the three is another option. They're different plays, but both are worth 125 coins. And you're right that it is a delightful experience to be dealt four-of-a-kind. Great puzzle, but I want a poem and I want it now! Is it written down somewhere or can you recite it from memory?"

"I can recite it. And it's just a limerick. Do you know what a limerick is?" I teased.

"I think so. Is it a five-line verse where lines A, B, and E all rhyme with each other and C and D also rhyme with each other?"

"Yes, Miss Smarty No Pants. What else?"

"Most of them can't be told in church, and the most famous one relates to Nantucket."

"That's good. I'm truly amazed by your knowledge of erotic literature. Are you sure you're ready?" I asked. She nodded her head up and down like a little kid about to get a piece of candy. We were both enjoying this.

At the party tonight when we dance,
You will know from my amorous glance,
My side passes, distracted,
Sugar pushes, impacted,
'Cause I'll want to get into your pants.

She laughed in surprise and delight at the last line and effused, "That's cute and corny and I've never had a poem inspired by my body before. Thank you, darling. Thank you. You're my best Valentine's Day present ever too! Now, about that raging fire you were talking about ..."

While still pinning me down, she started kissing me on the lips. Soon her grip loosened, then disappeared entirely, and it was just two people making love. No unusual positions, nothing earthshaking at all. Just good old-fashioned vanilla sex. Lots of kissing. Lots of pelvis-to-pelvis grinding. And a big release for both of us.

It was wonderful.

Five minutes later, when our breathing had returned to normal, more or less, she whispered, "What do you say we nap for a half-hour and then go down and get some more W-2Gs?" I gave an unintelligible mumble that I suppose she took for agreement.

Saturday
February 12, 2000

"I'd like to take a walk before we go play," I told her. "I've got somewhere in mind and I'd like it to be a surprise. It's outside, so you might want to wear your jacket."

I'd looked up florists in the Yellow Pages and there was a shop less than a mile away on Fourth Street. It was a joy to get out of doors and stretch our legs. The temperature was in the low fifties and clear. Downtown Las Vegas isn't exactly a glamorous place. A lot of down-on-their-luck street people hang around. I didn't feel that Annie and I were in peril, but I was alert just the same. Even without a genteel ambience, though, nothing could dampen my fine mood.

When we got to the flower shop, I told Annie that I wanted to buy some flowers to enhance her outfit for tonight. She teared up a little, got very quiet, and wandered about the shop in a daze. We decided on a wrist corsage because her dress was rather delicate. And we got a matching rose for me to wear on my lapel.

On our trip back to the Golden Nugget, I reflected that I'd been in Vegas almost 48 hours and hadn't given a *thought* to playing blackjack. It's funny how sometimes your life can change in a major way so quickly.

It was shortly after 2 p.m. when we showed up in the high-limit room again. My internal clock was a bit off due to the nap following the morning delight. We'd finished off the fruit basket that was waiting in our room Thursday night, so we grabbed a few finger sandwiches from the food offered for free to the high-limit players. Otherwise, we decided we'd wait until the six p.m. awards banquet before eating again.

We still weren't quite finished with her points, so we

continued to play on her card. We had our choice of machines and chose a Bally game this time. I sat down, inserted her card, and slipped two bills into the acceptor. The first hand was K♥T♥9♠3♦4♥. "One of the exceptions," I noted, automatically holding the king by itself. Not that it mattered this time, as I drew a Q722 of mixed suits for no payout whether I'd held the king or the king ten.

"I'm sure you're smart enough to memorize these hands. But I encourage you to keep practicing on the computer. Part of it is a matter of seeing what's there when the cards are in random order. If those same cards came out king nine three ten four, it might have been harder to see. As much as I've played, I still miss some hands sometimes."

"Okay," I promised and hit the deal button again. A♥8♠T♠K♦Q♠. I had to think for a second, because this was one of the tricky hands that we hadn't reviewed. It's a close play whether you go for the highest four cards or the spades. I correctly held the spades, and promptly drew a red jack and a black four. "Would have had the straight if I went the other way," I groused.

"I know," said Annie, "but I don't think it does any good to worry about such things. You were going to hold the spades as long as I had any vote in the matter, so what would've happened if you didn't is totally irrelevant."

In the first hour we dropped $2,000. "I want to change machines," I announced.

"Don't bother," she said. "The next hour will be different than the last hour whether we change or not. It really doesn't matter."

"I still believe we should change," I insisted.

"No. It doesn't change anything relevant," she told me firmly.

"Then what's the difference?" I asked. "If it doesn't matter one way or the other according to your theory, and it *might* matter according to mine, then why doesn't that add up to making a change?"

"Because I'm the boss."

"This is about who's in charge?" I retorted, perhaps too quickly. "You are. You know more about this game than I do. Maybe more than I ever will. But you told me you wanted someone to stand up to you. Now you're getting all prissy when I do."

"But it's just a waste of time!"

"Seems to me that we could have moved one seat over much more quickly than continuing to argue about it."

"All right!" she finally agreed, exasperated. "Move over if that'll make you feel better."

"Thank you, Annie," I said quietly and leaned over to give her a kiss. She kissed me back, but her heart wasn't in it.

The hard feelings over the spat didn't last long. In another ten minutes or so we were laughing. Over the next three hours we went up and down and ended up dropping another $400 after the seat change, making us very close to even *if* Annie collected $1,000 from the tournament and we included the cashback for the points earned. Also, we'd finished Annie's 1,200 points and put 200 on my card. Including the sensations over the weekend, I figured I was a million or two ahead. Annie wanted to fix her hair for the party, so we got back to the suite around five. She showered first, then started to make herself up, while I showered and shaved.

We hadn't mentioned the jewelry I was supposed to make for her, but I knew she remembered it. I laid the necklace right next to her dress, which she'd spread out on the bed. I had her belt still tucked away, but she wouldn't be wearing that tonight. When she saw the necklace, she was thrilled.

"It's more delicate than I thought it would be. And it's perfect. I sure lucked out in hooking up with a jewelry maker. Thank you, darling."

"You're welcome. And I'm sorry this birthday present is a bit belated. I got distracted."

"I forgive you," she smiled.

When we got down to the party, the doors were already open and Bob and Shirley were on the dance floor. "Over here!" Shirley called. "We saved you two seats at our table. As long as Chris isn't going to break my heart." A live five-piece combo was playing a song that sounded familiar, but I couldn't quite place.

We smiled, sat down, and took it all in. Bob and Shirley were doing the Texas two step, I think. Neither Annie nor I knew that dance, and the music wasn't the right tempo for a swing, so we just watched. They knew a lot of patterns, were smooth, and were enjoying themselves noticeably.

The next song was "Up on the Roof" and Bob and Shirley broke into a cha cha. Since a cha cha is another on the long list of dances we didn't know, we stayed put. Bob came over. "Hey, you two. This song is a pretty good tempo for a swing. It's a little slow, perhaps, but close enough, especially for intermediate dancers. There may not be a lot of songs you can swing to tonight, so you might as well get while the getting is good." They went back to their cha cha and Shirley nodded encouragement as we made our way out on the floor.

Annie looked beautiful. Her dress matched her hair, which accentuated the speckles in her jewelry, and the skirt was full so it lifted gracefully whenever I spun her. I was totally smitten just by watching her and knowing she was with me. There's a song by somebody called "Lady in Red" about a man loving the way his wife looked in a red dress. I knew exactly the way he felt.

Red was the dominant color among the dresses tonight, being a Valentine's Day dance and all. But nobody else had flowers. Since we were younger than most of the players who go to the Golden Nugget, I suspect we reminded some of the older folks of high-school kids at a prom. But that was okay. It was a very special night for both of us.

When the song ended, the band broke into the old Motown hit, "I Heard it Through the Grapevine." Bob came over, took Annie's hand, and said, "See you later, Chris."

Shirley took my hand and said, "Poor guy. You're stuck with me. Let's show 'em how to do it." I led the steps I knew from class and Shirley followed like she was dancing on air. My mind registered that Shirley was wearing a bra, that she was long and lean, and she felt very different in my arms than Annie did. I experienced a slight sexual twinge that surprised me. Shirley was 15 years older than me, happily married, and was merely being friendly. I was as happy as could be with Annie, and here were those twinges nonetheless. I didn't mind, actually. I didn't plan to act on them, but it was gratifying to get them. Dancing is fun!

I didn't have many patterns in my catalog, so when I finished what I knew, I started over again. Shirley kept smiling all the way through. On the way back to the table, she said, "You have a good lead. You'll need to take more lessons, but you have potential. It's fun dancing with you." That was very nice to hear, and I thanked her both for the dance and the compliment.

A waltz started and Bob and Shirley popped up again. Annie and I sat there holding hands. A man I hadn't seen before came up and asked me if he could dance with Annie. I looked at Annie, who was pushing her chair back in order to stand up, so I said, "Sure." At the end of the waltz, the man brought Annie back to the table and started to leave.

"Don't forget, Dan, you owe me one too!" Shirley called after him. Dan smiled and nodded agreement. "That's Dan Williams," Shirley told me. "He's the slot director or something like that, a great dancer, and a nice guy. I'm sure Annie is having a good time so far tonight."

Annie was a little flushed and nodded. "I'm with my best guy and other people are going out of their way to show me a good time. What more could a girl ask for?"

Shirley responded, "She could ask for $1,000, that's what. And if you do win, both of you should go up when they call your name. They'll take your picture and mail it to you. It's a fine memento and it'll last a lot longer than the $1,000 will. The money will be thrown into the pot and lose its identity. But the picture can last for years."

"Won't they mind?" I asked. "Officially, the entry was in Annie's name."

"They won't mind at all," Bob said. "They celebrate winners in this town. They know that most players lose most of the time, but if they can have a memorable time when they *do* win, they'll keep coming back and not mind the losing trips so much. So the casino makes sure they treat the winners like kings and queens. That's what makes this town go round."

"Queen for a Day," Annie announced. "Not too shabby."

"King for a weekend," I responded. "That's not too bad either."

The band broke into "Mustang Sally."

"That's another swing," Bob announced. "Battle stations, everyone!" We all laughed as we walked to the floor. Annie and I did the steps we knew over and over again and had huge baboon grins on our faces.

After the dance I asked Bob, "Where's Kelly? I thought he'd be here."

"He will be. But he only shows up just before it's time to give out the money. He may have another event or two to do tonight. It's possible that there's a Rio party starting at seven and an MGM starting at eight and he'll do all three. They'll feed us and get us primed and Kelly will be the main event. Somehow, he'll make a spectacular entrance. He's a talented guy, as I'm sure you've noticed."

A little later Bob asked Annie if she'd like to try a Texas two step. Annie said she'd try, even though she'd never done one. As they were walking to the floor, Dan took Shirley by the hand. He leaned over and in a conspiratorial whisper told me, "I've got to grab Shirley when Bob's not looking. He dances with her so much, you'd think he *owned* her or something." Shirley and I laughed.

Bob and Annie looked pretty good. Sometimes they were in standard dance position, sometimes side by side, and sometimes Bob was going backwards. There were several different arm positions and they seemed to flow gracefully from one to the other. Bob kept talking to her the whole time and Annie kept smiling.

When they came back, I asked Annie what Bob was saying. She laughed. "He kept saying, 'Right left right.' He'd let me step on my left foot uninstructed and then say, 'Right left right' all over again. I told him he was one hell of a conversationalist."

"Did he ever say, 'Left right left?'"

"Never. That's the man's footwork, I think." She then leaned over and kissed me. "Thank you so much for being here tonight, darling, and thank you for being a good sport about other guys dancing with me. I'm having a wonderful time and I'll make sure you feel like 'King for a Day' in just about an hour from now."

She was wrong, of course. I pretty much felt that way already.

The drummer started a steady roll and the lead singer announced, "And now, ladies and gentlemen, the Queen of Hearts herself, Kellisa!" The band launched into, "Here she comes, Miss America," and Kelly came strolling in, in full drag. He was wearing a slinky red dress—size extra extra large, I imagine—with a considerable amount of makeup. He carried a red patent-leather purse with matching one-inch heels. The crowd burst into thunderous applause. He strutted around the room and several of the guys tried to pinch him in the ass or squeeze his fake boobs. He'd slap their hands away with a falsetto, "Oh, you silly goose!" Bob got up and asked him to dance, but Kelly hit him with his purse and said, "Get away from me, you masher!"

Eventually, he sat down on a stool in front of the band, microphone in hand. Everyone quieted down and the air was full of anticipation. Nobody knew what he was going to say, but everyone expected it to be good. "The problem with wearing panty hose," he told us in his normal voice, "is that when you fart, it rolls all the way down your leg and almost knocks your high heels off." Everyone roared. "And don't let anyone tell you differently: These industrial-strength bras aren't built for comfort," as he squeezed and adjusted first his right breast and then his left.

"Show us some leg, Kellisa!" one of the players shouted.

"You animal!" he said in full falsetto. "Room six-fourteen. Immediately after the party." We laughed again. In his normal voice again, he added, "I hope he has a good time in room six-fourteen. My wife and I will be at the Rio."

Kelly then introduced the Golden Nugget employees. He called up all of the hosts, one after another. I'd met Shannon and Miguel, but none of the others. I listened closely, anticipating making many future trips to the Golden Nugget.

"Next month's invitational slot tournament is called 'Spring Fling' and it takes place from March 17 to 20. I suggested we call it the 'Vernal Equinox' tournament, but for some reason they vetoed my idea. It just doesn't pay to be 'ed-gee-cated,' I guess. If you'd like to be here, keep using your 24 Karat Club card when you play and talk to one of these hosts. Now you clowns get out of here." The hosts sat down to some applause, while Kelly continued with the introductions.

First up was "Dancing Dan Williams," the Vice President of Slot Operations. The biggest cheer went up when he introduced Phyllis "Boom Boom" Bryant, an older black woman who seemed well-liked. I wondered how long he had been calling her "Boom Boom." It seemed an unlikely moniker, but with Kelly, I guess anything went. Kelly had us applaud the band, whom he called "Billy and the Heartaches." Kelly then introduced "The *dynamic* duo of these slot tournaments, also known as the *dysfunctional* duo of these slot tournaments, Myron Kuchman and Bruce Herman."

Finally, he announced, "We are now bringing to the stage the 10 winners of our 'Hearts and Flowers' tournament. We know that, frankly, most of you have no chance in hell of hearing me call your name tonight, but at least try to pretend that you're excited for the lucky winners.

"You have to have a little luck to win these tournaments, so in tenth place winning one thousand dollars, with a score of 65,920, John and Sue Luckman." The band broke into a song and the Luckmans made their way up to the stage. The band played on as Myron and Bruce each gave John a handshake and Sue a hug. The photographer shot a couple of pictures of the winners along with Bruce, Myron, and Kelly. Everyone was smiling—except for Kelly who was vamping in outrageous poses.

Shirley was bouncing up and down and turned to Annie, "That means you and I each get at least a grand. We did it!"

The music stopped as Kelly made the next announcement. "In ninth place also for $1,000, with a score of 66,220, if you have to drive a car, you might as well make it a Ferrari. And if you have to have a Ferrari, it might as well be an Annie Ferrari." The band broke into another song. Annie grabbed my hand and tugged to make sure I was coming along too. I didn't know any of these people, but a lot of them were applauding. Myron and Bruce shook my hand and hugged Annie and we had our pictures taken. They handed Annie an envelope and we returned to the table.

"In eighth place, also for $1,000, beating Annie by 120 points, with a score of 66,340, a regular Golden Nugget visitor and our favorite dancing girl, Shirley Dancer! And you can bring that Bob guy along, too, if you really have to." As they made their way up, Kelly said into the microphone using his falsetto voice again, "Please don't try to kiss me again, Bob. You just don't know when to quit." Bob laughed along with everybody else.

We were sitting close enough to hear Bob say to Kelly, "That's a much better zinger. I figure we're even now." Kelly laughed and nodded his head.

"At least until next month," Kelly said deviously.

The calling of the seven additional winners followed the same format. We didn't know any of them, but Bob and Shirley knew at least two and called out congratulations.

Pretty soon it was, "From all your friends at the Golden Nugget, we wish you Happy Valentine's Day, good luck, and good night."

Bob said, "The band plays another three or four songs. Our evening isn't over yet," as he and Shirley headed back to the dance floor. Soon Annie and I joined them, along with two or three other couples.

When it was over, Bob and Shirley said goodbye to the band, came over, and started to change their shoes. They have special dance shoes, I guess. There was something bothering me from yesterday, so I decided to ask Bob about it. "How did it happen that you and Shirley were seated so close to each other at the tournament? That seems like a long shot."

"Not so long. I reached into the bag and pulled out eight hearts with numbers on them. I quickly looked for two that were close to each other. Right next to each other would have been better, but I didn't draw them this time. I got 16 and 18 and handed them to Linea."

"Isn't that cheating?" asked Annie. "I thought it was supposed to be a random draw."

"Of course it's cheating," Bob replied, "but it doesn't hurt anyone. Every time they scold me, slap my hand, tell me not to do it again, and give me the numbers I picked anyway."

"So it's victimless cheating. Is that what you're saying?" Annie asked.

"Yes. The only purpose of the cheating is to have Shirley and me sitting close to each other, and they know that. I have no idea which machine will be hot this round. It was totally random that you were the guy who sat between us, but we're glad it happened that way. It was fun meeting you two and who knows, it might be the start of a nice friendship."

"Are you going to be here at next month's event?" Annie asked.

"I don't think so. There's a lucrative giveaway at the MGM Grand for only a few invited guests, and they're letting us stay at the Mansion. It's too good to pass up."

"What's the Mansion?" I asked.

"It's a separate building with the MGM's 29 high-roller villas. The villas are maybe 29 times nicer than the Tower Suite you're in this week," Bob replied. "Interested in seeing it?"

"Oh, yes," Annie replied. "I've heard of it, but I've never seen it."

Bob wrote down his cell-phone number along with Shirley's. "Call me on the Friday afternoon you're here at the Nugget. If our plans haven't changed, and I don't expect them to, we'd love to have you join us for breakfast there Saturday morning. How does that sound?"

"Wonderful!" Annie gushed. "Thank you. We'll look forward to that."

We said our goodbyes and they left. I turned to Annie. "Hey, Miss Queen for a Day. Ready for another bubble bath?"

"Sounds good. And maybe we don't need to give any room-service guy a peek this time."

Upstairs, Annie washed her makeup off as we waited for the Jacuzzi to fill. I got in first, then Annie came over and sat down on my lap. "This weekend was supposed to be my gift to you. I had no idea it would turn out to be such a nice gift for me too."

"I planned it that way, you know."

"Yeah, right. Why don't you shut up and kiss me?"

We necked for a while, and there was no doubt in either of our minds where we were headed after the bath. Still, I had something to talk about first. "Annie, I want to say something to you. It's so important that I want to say it before we get carried away again."

"Okay. What is it?"

"It's about saying, 'I love you.' Neither one of us has spoken those magic words yet, although we've come close, and I've known for some time that they were appropriate to say, at least for me. I keep aching to hear you say them, for a lot of reasons, but also because it's a lot easier for me to say 'I love you, too' than it is to be the first one with the declaration."

Annie had her head on my chest, crying softly and clutching me tightly. I'd come this far, I had to finish the job. "I love you, Annie. And I wanted you to hear it with the lights on and not merely in the heat of passion, though I'm sure you'll hear it then too."

Then we just held each other, both of us lost in thought. She'd have to find her own way to say those words, if she ever did. I wanted her to say them, of course, but if she never did and the relationship stayed the way it was now, I could live with it. I knew she still had a lot of pain to work through, and I didn't know whether or not saying "I love you" got close to the pain. But I felt better. It wasn't a secret I was hiding from her; after all, actions speak louder than words. Still, I felt a huge release from just saying it.

"I've had enough of this bath for now," she declared. "Have you?"

It wasn't a question that needed answering. When we were dried off, she looked me in the eye and told me, "Chris, thank you for saying that. I've wanted to hear it. But for now, I've got so many feelings tumbling in my heart that I don't know what to say. You're the only guy in my life and I want us to be together for a long time, but I need to wait on the rest of the words for a while. Okay?"

"Sure. There's a country western song by Clint Black that says something about love being something that you do rather than something that you say. I'm content with the way you show me every day that you love me. It's a far better thing to have the actions without the words than the words without the actions."

"Thank you, darling. Now please take me to bed. I want you."

"I'm looking forward to seeing if I can get you off just by kissing and licking, Annie. Do you mind if I try?"

"You always ask such tough questions," she responded huskily.

In bed, I lowered my mouth to her left breast and laid

my left hand gently onto her mound. What with the kissing and fooling around in the hot water and then the words about love, I figured she wouldn't need any more foreplay. I knew I didn't. Even though I just had my hand lying there and wasn't doing anything extra to increase the stimulation, she was moving against my hand and starting to breathe heavily. I moved my head into position, fingered her gently, and just watched—for the moment, just a voyeur. But a happy voyeur, as she was groaning and moving.

I was totally out of practice; oral sex wasn't part of life with Paula. But hell, I figured that if I was gentle, and she kept moaning and grinding against me, those would be good signs. And if she instructed me to do it different, all the better. I moistened my lips and placed them right at the top of her vaginal slit. I extended my tongue and started probing.

Annie lay motionless for two minutes, other than stroking the top of my head with her fingers. Soon, though, she came alive and started bucking. Up and down and side to side, while holding my head in place. I was doing my own grinding away against the bed sheet. For once, I wasn't concerned with whether she climaxed first or not, figuring I could keep my tongue hard even if the rest of me went soft. I think she was groaning louder than me, but it was hard to tell.

I came first. I didn't say anything, not wanting to distract her from what she was doing. I kept my tongue going exactly as before and within a minute or two, she tensed up completely and screamed "YES!" Then she dropped her hands to the bed and lay perfectly still, other than breathing hard. I kissed her a few more times down there, then scooted up, placed my head on her tummy, and just basked in the pleasure sweeping over us both.

After ten minutes or so, I got up and aligned her body with the bed. She was dead to the world, almost, as I turned out the light, lay down next to her, and pulled the comforter over us. "I can still take you if you like," she mumbled. But I knew she was talking in her sleep.

Sunday
February 13, 2000

I awakened at 4 a.m., refreshed after seven hours conked out. Annie was snoring softly and I crawled out of bed carefully so as not to disturb her. I went downstairs, cranked up the laptop, and started practicing on *WinPoker*. I called up room service and ordered approximately the same breakfast we had our first morning, except I told them to have the server knock gently on the downstairs door rather ring the doorbell.

Still, Annie came down at 4:20, naked and sleepy. We enjoyed a long passionate kiss together. I told her I loved her and really liked the view, but unless she *really* wanted the room service staff to talk about the redhead in 7b, she'd better go put on a robe. She said she was going to take a shower but would love some coffee when it arrived.

At 4:25 I carried a cup of coffee upstairs and left it on the bathroom sink. I dropped my robe and entered the shower with her. She was a little surprised by, but happy with, the intrusion. She was shampooing and I just enjoyed watching. Nothing particularly unusual in the way she did it, I suppose, but I'd never seen her do it before. As with any newly sexual relationship, there were so many private things she did that I knew nothing about. And it was all fascinating.

We got out and she sat on the counter drinking her coffee while I shaved.

"Do you have any sexual fantasy still unfulfilled this weekend, Chris?"

"Not really. But I'd enjoy some more oral sex. Both ways. It's been a long time for me and it's very exciting."

"Oh goodie!" she squealed. "Me too."

I finished shaving and she gave me a big hug. "We've

never done it first thing in the morning," she said. "Do you have the energy and desire to give it a try? I could help you get hard."

And she did. And I did. And we did.

And this time we didn't wake up again until about nine. As we worked on the muffins, yogurt, and fruit, I said, "What's on the agenda for today?"

"We have to put 800 points on your card. That will take us four hours if we play one machine together, or two hours if we each play on our own machine. I think you're ready to play unsupervised. Officially, check-out is at eleven, but getting a late check-out is no problem at all. And that still lets us charge meals to the room."

"There's something I'd like to do that we haven't had time for yet."

"What's that?"

"I think I'd like to play a little blackjack. See how it feels after so much video poker. Do you mind?"

"Of course not. Don't be silly. You can do whatever you want. Actually, I enjoy playing video poker by myself. So why don't I play on your card while you play blackjack? Whoever finishes first can go and find the other."

"I don't know. Think you're good enough to play on my card unsupervised?"

"I'll try really, really hard not to make any mistakes."

"Okay. Sounds like a plan," I told her and gave her one of my cards. "Do we have to do anything special for the late check-out?"

"I'll take care of it." She went directly to the phone. She told whoever she spoke to that we wanted to leave at six. "I don't think we'll actually be that late," she told me, "but it's nice to have the room in case one of us feels neglected before we go."

"Good idea," I told her. "I wouldn't want my organ to shrivel up from under-usage."

"I wouldn't want that either," she told me as we left the room holding hands.

When I sat down at the blackjack table, the pit lady

came over and asked if I wanted to be rated. I said, "Why not?" and handed her my slot club card.

"Unfortunately, this doesn't do any good," she explained. "The pit and slot departments have totally different systems. If you give me your driver's license, I'll have them make up a card for you." I shrugged and agreed. I wasn't too worried about my average bet, because I knew that whatever I earned at the blackjack table couldn't touch the full comp in the Tower Suite.

Playing blackjack was different for me this time. Since I'd learned one type of video poker essentially perfectly, it seemed like I was throwing away money not playing blackjack the same way. And there was no doubt in my mind that I couldn't count like Annie could. Besides, after playing $25 a hand for 600 hands an hour at video poker, playing so much slower for lower stakes wasn't nearly as exciting as it used to be.

After about an hour and a half, I'd had enough. I was up $80. When I retrieved my card, I was told that I could have a brunch buffet if I wanted one. "We put on a good Sunday brunch."

I shook my head, said, "Not this time, thank you," and went off to find Annie. She was playing on the IGT machine side with an open seat next to her. I sat down.

"Hello, pretty young thing," I said. "Want to mess around?"

Annie recognized my voice and gave me a big welcoming smile. I'd spoken loudly enough that my words caught the ear of some people passing by and they turned to watch. Playing to the crowd, I said, "I've got 45 minutes before my wife comes back. Do you have a room?"

Annie's expression darkened immediately and completely. She clenched her teeth and said forcefully in a very quiet voice, "*Do not joke about that. Ever!* Infidelity is not a laughing matter. *Do you understand?"*

I lifted my arms in surrender. "Sorry. I was just trying to make you smile. I guess my joke was in bad taste."

"Yes. Very bad taste," she spat out angrily, turned to

her machine, and continued to play video poker. I waited quietly, hoping it would blow over shortly. I hadn't seen this darker side of Annie. The entire incident struck me as making a mountain out of a molehill.

Still, I hadn't been exaggerating earlier when I told her this was the best weekend of my life. Even with this kind of unexpected explosion, I believed her to be a prize and I was lucky to have her. I didn't regret my profession of love last night. With time, I figured these blowups would be rare and short-lived.

In five minutes she started talking to me as if I'd just sat down and nothing untoward had happened. "How was your blackjack game? Did you win?"

"A little. But it's not as much fun as it was when I thought I was a good player. I used to think the comps I could get playing blackjack were pretty spiffy. After this weekend, though, I see how much better comps are for video poker, and playing this game with an advantage is within my capabilities."

"It is, and pretty soon you won't be afraid of the possibility of a $10,000 loss. You'll see that the chance of that happening is pretty slim."

"I hope so. So how are you doing here?"

She pulled out my card and put it in again. It showed I had 483 points. Since we each could play 200 points per hour, we'd have less than an hour and a half apiece of play. "I'm up about $2,000 today. I hit a straight flush."

"Nice! I'm ready to play too. If we both play, I don't suppose it matters where I sit."

"Actually, it does. The index on the cards is in the upper-left corner of each card. If I sit on your right, I can see your cards perfectly. If I sit on your left, I can't see your left-most card."

"Is it necessary for you to see?"

"Not usually," she said, "but you may have a question about a hand, and if you do I'd like to be where I can see."

"Do you want me to work out of my own $1,000 stack or should we share?"

"You can use the same pool of money that I'm using, because this entire play counts as being on your card. I have $1,000 of profit in my purse, a few hundred dollars in the spill tray, and some racks of coins here from a spill. Plus some credits on the machine. It's all 'community property' in a sense. You take over this machine and I'll sit on your right."

"Neat! It's nice to know that I've been playing so well so far today."

"Yep," Annie smiled. "Every hand perfectly so far."

It took almost two hours to earn the rest of my 1,000 points. We each spilled coins and had our hoppers run out of money at different times, and it took longer getting them filled than Friday and yesterday. Sunday mornings aren't busy times in the casino, which the casino staffing reflects. Each time the floorman, Carl, came by to fill up our hoppers, he mentioned that he was really running. "Sometimes it's like that," he said, "and sometimes we just stand around. You never know until you show up at work."

Our net for the weekend was -$1,725 when playing on Annie's card, +$2,750 on mine, plus $1,000 for the tournament, plus $600 in cashback on her card and $500 on mine. She wrote all of these figures down and asked me to follow her to the 24 Karat Club booth. "I need to check out. It's not rocket science, by any means, but I think you should be aware of what's involved."

At the booth, Annie gave her player's card and driver's license to the attendant, Jenny, and told her our room number, that we'd been here for three nights, and would like to use points to pay for it.

Jenny pulled up Annie's account number on the computer. "Three nights is 3,000 points, and for that you get $1,500 in cash."

"Yes, that's exactly what I was expecting." While Jenny was filling out the requisite forms, Annie wrote "+$3,125" on a slip of paper and told me it was the bottom line.

I took her pen and wrote "+$80—blackjack" and showed it to her. She smiled and gave me a big hug.

Jenny filled out a form to send to the front desk, I think, to cover the charges on the room and gave Annie one voucher for $1,000 and another for $500.

"Not done yet," Annie told me as we walked the twenty feet to the casino cashier. Annie used the slot club vouchers and $8,500 in cash to pay off the marker she took out at the beginning of the trip. As we waited for the cashier to bring the signed marker stamped "PAID," Annie asked me if I was hungry yet.

"Not for food," I told her, "but I would like to go see what you've got hidden under your blouse. I have such a short memory."

She smiled. "I haven't played hide and seek for a long time."

Hide and seek was not what I had in mind. I hadn't worked everything out yet, but I thought some sort of master-slave game was called for. I'd never played such a game before, but no woman had ever volunteered to do whatever I wanted before either. I might never have this chance again.

When we got to the suite, I stood behind her, wrapped my left arm around her and held her left breast in my right hand. "You are my slave," I said in the deepest voice I could muster. "Do not say a word."

"Don't hurt me," she reminded me of the rules.

"*Quiet*!" I ordered.

I extracted the slip from a pillow and placed it over her head. "Stay," I commanded.

"I don't know what 'stay' means."

"*Quiet!*"

I went into the bathroom and got the hair clip she'd worn yesterday. I clipped the bottom of the pillowcase around her neck. She still had plenty of breathing room, and it wasn't at all tight around her neck, but it was tight enough that she couldn't see out the bottom of it.

I then unbuttoned her blouse and took it off. Then her bra. "Place your hands on top of your head, and don't move," I instructed gruffly. She did. I still didn't have a plan for how to continue, but my non-plan was getting me hard. I removed her skirt and panties. Her slip-on shoes went too.

I then removed all of my clothes. I got close to her and she could feel my erection touch her. I sidled around her body, keeping that one point of contact, so she couldn't be sure what orifice I was going to eventually enter. Truth be known, I was only interested in her vagina and mouth, but she didn't know that. At least not yet. And maybe a little uncertainty would add to the situation. We'd see.

Again ordering her not to move, I lubricated myself with K-Y Jelly and positioned a straight-back chair so it was a few feet behind her. I sat down, pulled her backwards, and entered her vagina. Between her own lubrication and what I added, I slipped in easily. I rocked back and forth inside her, her toes sometimes on the ground and sometimes not. I used her breasts for hand holds. Once she started to take her hands off her head, but I told her not to.

Surprisingly, as exciting as this was to me, it was even more so to her. After three minutes, she started moaning. Although this was a strict violation of my orders for her to remain silent, I decided that part of the game was over. In another three or four minutes she had a screaming orgasm, and not the Bailey's, Cointreau, Galliano, and Kahlua cocktail.

Although I was strongly aroused, I wasn't close to coming. For whatever reason, I need to be on top facing down for that to happen. So I removed her hood, picked her up, laid her on the bed face up, and entered her in the normal fashion. She lay immobile, as was her post-coital habit, and I murmured "I love you" over and over again as I moved in and out.

After almost a dozen orgasms in the previous three days, it took me awhile to finish matters, especially since she wasn't counter-thrusting. For a while, it wasn't even important to me whether I came or not. But eventually, I got a second wind and climaxed.

We cuddled for a few minutes, until Annie decided she was hungry and said she wanted to go to the California Pizza Kitchen restaurant right there in the hotel. Although I was more in the mood for a snooze than a snack, after I showered and dressed I felt great.

I ordered soup, she ordered salad, we got an eight-inch pizza to split, and she told me she'd never had that kind of sexual experience before.

"Did you enjoy it?" I asked.

"If you need to ask that, you weren't paying much attention," she responded with a smile. "And you? Did you enjoy it?"

"If you have to ask that, you weren't paying attention either."

"Actually," she said, "it was a bit confronting to me. The idea of bondage brings up trust issues, plus I wasn't sure where you were going with it. Nothing you actually did was that much of a stretch, but thinking about what you *could* do or *might* do made me uncomfortable."

"You figured you didn't really know my sexual desires all *that* well, so you were taking a huge risk? And that bothered you?"

"Yes. But I certainly liked the way it ended up."

"Me too."

Over soup and salad, she asked me. "So you never played these games with Holly or Paula or anybody?"

Oh shit. I didn't want to go anywhere *near* there. I'd already accidentally found a sensitive spot earlier today. I didn't relish finding another.

"Do you need to know? I hope not. I've had pleasant experiences with other ladies in the past. If I start to focus on good times between me and them, it deflects my attention from me and you."

"You're right," she agreed. "I'm sorry for mentioning it."

"Actually," I said, "Bob taught me Friday night how to answer the question: Who's better at sex? Holly, Paula, or you?"

"Really? Was I there?" she asked. "The only thing I remember that was at all related to sex was Shirley begging you not to break her heart."

"You were there. I'm sure you heard him. You just thought he was talking about something else. So did he."

"Okay, remind me. What did Bob say?"

"He said that you and Paula aren't in the same five cards," I answered triumphantly. She was smiling, but still had no idea what I was talking about.

"He said the only time an exact ranking is important on a strategy card is when two options can occur simultaneously. There was no competition between you and Holly 22 years ago, or you and Paula 10 years ago, or you and anybody now. So rankings are totally irrelevant."

"So you really think that's the reason that Bob and Liam W. Daily are publishing a new series of strategy cards?" she asked me, shaking her head. "I bet both of them will be amazed to find this out."

"Perhaps that wasn't foremost in their minds," I conceded, "but it's a good point nonetheless."

"Agreed," she said. "Let's finish up here and hit the road."

The freeway back to California at the end of a weekend is never a picnic, but Annie knew about a road called Industrial that we picked up about a mile south of the Golden Nugget. It wasn't a shortcut distance-wise, but it was definitely a shortcut time-wise. It paralleled I-15 for several miles and moved much faster, even allowing for some traffic signals. We picked up the highway quite a bit south of the Strip and it was moving better by the time we got on. Probably saved a half an hour or so that way.

"So how was your weekend?" she asked playfully as we drove along.

"Pretty much the same as always," I replied. "How was yours?"

"Same-o same-o."

"Okay. So we got those lies out of the way," I said. "Where do we go from here? We have something special going and I, for one, am in favor of keeping it going. How do we do that?"

"I'm not sure," she said, "but I think we're on the same

page. I'm not ready to move in with each other, but I hope maybe someday."

"Sounds right," I said. "First things first. Your place or mine tonight?"

"Neither," she said, "or maybe the right answer is both. I need to work long hours the next few days to make up for taking off Thursday afternoon and all day Friday. And tonight I need to get focused on work again so I can show up running in the morning. But I'd like to spend Wednesday night together after class. How's that?"

"I guess. Not my first choice, but everything considered I'm still a lucky guy. Tomorrow is officially Valentine's Day. I guess you could say we've already had the best Valentine's Day possible."

"I agree. And Primm's coming up. I need to use the facilities and I'd like to change drivers. You mind?"

After our break, Annie said, "You said you cut gemstones. Does that include diamonds?"

"I don't cut diamonds. I took some classes in it back at the GIA, but I don't like to do it. If I decide one of my creations needs some diamonds, I'll use precut stones."

"Why don't you cut diamonds?"

"Several reasons. Diamond-cutting requires different equipment and skills altogether than cutting colored stones."

"Colored stones?"

"All gemstones other than diamonds are collectively called 'colored' even though some of them are colorless."

"I see. I was hoping we didn't have to get into a discussion on racist remarks."

I laughed, "On the contrary, the jewelry business cuts across all nationalities. And for me personally, I've been around athletes all my life. Although a ballplayer occasionally makes a racist remark, it makes big news when he does because it's so rare."

"Is that why you never got engaged to Paula? Because you hate diamonds?"

I ignored the first question and addressed the second. "It isn't that I hate diamonds or anything like that. But well-cut ones are readily available. If I want to use them in some of my pieces, I buy them."

"What kind of stones do you usually use?"

"Malachite, mostly. It's green and striped, and there's a big variety. If you had twenty 1-inch square malachite pieces, you'd be able to tell them apart. If you had twenty 1-carat diamonds, they'd all look the same."

"Really? Identical?"

"To the uneducated eye, yes. If you have a strong enough loupe, every diamond is different. Sort of like every snowflake is different. But unless you look very closely, they all look alike. One reason women fall in love with jewelry is that their piece is unique."

"So you think women love malachite more than diamonds?"

"They love them for different reasons. Diamonds sparkle. And they cost more. Some women prefer affordable uniqueness."

"If you use malachite so much, why'd you use heliotrope for me?"

"Strictly for color reasons. When I saw the color of your hair and eyes, it reminded me of the stone. Heliotrope isn't used much for jewelry, and I never worked with it before I met you."

"So do you like heliotrope now?"

"The stones polished up nicely, but I really don't know how they'll hold up to wear. We'll have to see. The stones weren't expensive at all, but I really like the way they look on you."

"I do too," she said, squeezing my arm. "I like them a lot."

"You keep showing your appreciation like you did the past few days and you just might find yourself getting a sizable jewelry collection over time."

We drove the rest of the way home while listening to music—each lost in our own thoughts. It had been a turning-point weekend.

Tuesday
February 15, 2000

The next day, Monday, was totally wasted. How I could suffer from jet lag when we didn't fly, Vegas is in the same time zone, and I had a nap every day, I didn't know. But I slept until noon and didn't get much done the rest of the day. I did make the 5 o'clock Body Pump class and worked on finishing up some jewelry pieces in the evening, but that was about it. I went to bed early, exhausted.

Tuesday morning a phone call from Richard woke me up. He told me to get up and he'd call me back in ten minutes. When he did, Meg was on the line too and they sounded excited.

"Miamoto's lawyer called and said they have financing and if we like they're willing to close today. He wants a $10,000 discount, but that's still $15,000 more than it was two weeks ago," Richard told me. "Meg and I think we should do it, but you have a vote too."

"How would this work?" I asked. "We have to figure how much inventory he wants to buy, among other things."

"He'll deposit an extra $400,000 for inventory," Meg answered. "He wants to come over at one o'clock this afternoon to decide what he wants. Both Miamoto and we believe that we can get it all resolved in a day and a half and he'll be able to open on Thursday. What he doesn't want, we'll keep in the safe at your house until we figure out what to do with it. I'm sure my father's store can take a lot of it."

"What about my supplies and equipment? It belongs to the partnership, but I want to keep it. I do plan to stay in the business, you know," I said.

"Meg and I came up with a formula that seems workable. See if you can live with it. Midnight last night was the cutoff point. You can decide what you want to offer to Miamoto for sale. Any already-made jewelry that you want to keep, you can buy from the partnership at wholesale. Whether he buys it at wholesale, or you do, doesn't matter to us. Any work-in-progress, we'll come up with a fair price together. All supplies, including precious metal, stones, soldering supplies, whatever, we'll price at cost. Any equipment costing under $100, such as tools, vises, clamps, and the like, you can keep for free. For the more expensive things, like the safe, sander, grinder, we'll charge you half whatever we paid for it if it's less than 10 years old, and it's yours to keep without charge if it's over 10 years old. The things we didn't pay for, including your new microscope, remain yours. Anything we left out?"

I thought about their offer. It was clearly one based on expediency, but there was a considerable amount of trust and affection among us, and it sounded to me like whatever we hadn't covered could be handled amiably enough.

"Okay with me. I can get my things here organized and over to the store by one, assuming the escrow company says they have his check. May I have special dispensation to leave by 5:30 tomorrow whether we're done or not?"

"What for? Got a hot date?" Richard asked.

"Dance class with my sweetie."

"I thought you said your dance class was on Tuesday," Meg said.

"It was for the beginner series. But now, drumroll please, I'm in the intermediate series."

"I don't see why not," Richard agreed. "Anyway, we all have work to do before one. Let's hop to it."

"Yes sir!" both Meg and I answered at the same time. I saluted the phone. I don't know what Meg did.

Wednesday
February 16, 2000

I was pretty wiped out before meeting with Annie. Miamoto and his wife were knowledgeable about the value of jewelry and clearly chose the best pieces for their $400,000—including all of those of mine that I showed them. We had additional pieces worth $125,000 on our books. Miamoto said if we wanted to be done with everything he'd offer us $80,000 for the rest, but we'd have to take a personal check.

Richard, Meg, and I went for a walk to discuss the matter. "I'm fine either way," I told them. "I'm set up to sell stuff on eBay. We may or may not do better."

"My heart's set on being done with this," Richard admitted, "I say take the money."

"Okay," said Meg, "Though it does seem like we're being awfully cavalier about $45,000."

"Some of the pieces are slightly flawed or part of unmatched sets," Richard said. "They chose well. Probably $80,000 is a fair price for what's left."

"Sounds like we're agreed, then," I said, then looked at Meg. "I haven't come up with a final value for my stuff, and I kept several of my best pieces, but we can work that out tomorrow. That sound right?"

Richard and Meg nodded.

"Do we have a bottom-line number yet?" I asked.

"No," said Richard. "Let me add stuff up tonight and give you a better idea tomorrow."

"Sounds good." I left to get cleaned up for dance class.

Wednesday
February 16, 2000

"I'm no longer a jewelry-store owner," I told Annie as we started to drive toward Bellflower. "If that's why you were attracted to me, you may have to reconsider."

"Hmm … A guy has his way with me, then renounces his former life," she concluded. "Can't say I'm surprised." I'd told Annie that the sale of the store was pending. The fact that it went through two weeks early was a small surprise, but she knew it was coming.

"Silly me!" I laughed. "I hadn't realized how intimately your intimacy was involved in the process until now."

"Now that you're rich and unemployed, have you decided what you want to do when you grow up?"

"I've never known that for sure," I told her seriously. "Maybe I never will."

"Fair enough. But without examining the big picture completely, do you see the sale of your business affecting your small picture very much?"

"I don't think so. My part of the business was to create jewelry and sell at the store and on eBay. The new owners seem to like my jewelry and I just got a big order from a new buyer. My sister-in-law Meg will be running her father Ike's store—you've heard a little about both of them—and she wants to sell my pieces there."

"So you'll actually be busier since you sold the business?"

"I'll continue to be as busy as I want to be, I suspect," I answered. "The biggest changes in my life recently, though, don't involve jewelry. The biggest changes involve you and video poker."

"I know I've been a change in your life. But I didn't realize that that video poker might be a major part now too."

"It was fun. I won. I was thinking about moving to a warm-weather locale, anyway, so now Vegas is on the list. Video poker is something you and I can do together. The comps are awesome. Feels like a no-brainer to me."

"Interesting," she said. "All your reasons are good, except the one about you winning last weekend. That's a pretty lousy reason."

"It is? I thought that was a principal reason that you like the game."

"Nope. I go to Vegas and play video poker because I mathematically expect to win in the future. Whether I won or lost last weekend in particular is essentially irrelevant."

"I guess I don't quite understand or believe that yet," I said. "My score on any particular weekend is something solid. 'Mathematical expectation' sounds like mumbo jumbo to me."

"Do you want me to try to explain it in everyday language?" she asked. "It's something I believe in strongly. And understanding the concept is essential to playing a winning game."

"Sure," I said, "but not tonight. I've had a very intense few days evaluating jewelry and negotiating with the new owners. I'm ready to turn off my brain for a while. Why don't we go hiking this Saturday and you can explain it to me then?"

"That'd be fine," she told me. "Plus, we're already here."

Tonight's class was largely a review of the swivels we learned last week. I'd vowed to practice them in Las Vegas, then totally forgot to do so. Something about a lady in red, I think. This week they came easily. We also learned a slightly different syncopation to sometimes add to a sugar push.

As we drove home, I asked Annie if class seemed any different tonight.

"Every week there're differences, but this seemed about the same. Why do you ask?"

"Well, for the past two months, dance class has been part of my master plan to get into your pants," I admitted.

"I know that," she said, "and it was part of my master plan to let you succeed eventually. Are you saying you're no longer interested?"

"Definitely not! I'm very much looking forward to being with you tonight. But before, there were always questions in my mind about if, when, and would it be good. Now, I know, and like, the answers to those questions."

"I like them too," she said, "and I understand what you mean. But I still enjoy going to class together and hope we can continue, even though it isn't strictly necessary, according to your master plan."

"No danger in me wanting to quit," I said. "They'll be calling us Fred and Ginger before long."

Wednesday
February 16, 2000

I was expecting a wonderful sexual experience like I had at the Golden Nugget. So much for expectation.

Annie's body was still delightful and totally available to me, but it seemed like she had no sexual energy. Instead of being the hot mama before she climaxed and the dead log afterwards, she was a dead log from the start. I didn't let this stop me. I wanted and needed this.

After my release, she drifted off to sleep, while I laid there quietly, and wondered what went wrong.

Thursday
February 17, 2000

In the morning we showered together, then she shooed me out the door. "I've got to get focused for a meeting," she explained. "I'm going to the step class from 6:30 to 7:30. Do you want to eat dinner together after that?"

"Sure."

I looked at her questioningly, searching for some explanation about her lack of interest last night, but she just said, "Good. I'll see you then," and turned back to getting ready for work. Oh well. I guess I'd find out tonight.

Plus, Richard and Meg were coming over at one to inventory what I had at the workshop. I needed to get ready for them. Fortunately, I didn't need to go far. The one-minute walk in the cool air was refreshing.

I'd been thinking about how to do this. I'd started an Excel spreadsheet and listed the items. I weighed the precious metals I had in the various levels of purity (such as 10-karat gold, 12-karat gold, 14-karat gold, 18-karat gold; plus similar breakdowns for silver and platinum) and also the base metals. I stacked the stones by type and grade and input an estimated value. I listed each of my completed pieces with a wholesale price. I had stamps and other mailing supplies that were paid for by the company; these I assigned the actual price paid, rather than any discounted price, because they hadn't been used. I gave a value to my workbench, scales, computer, safe, grinder, and a few other items. The rest I figured fell into the under-$100 or older-than-10-years category.

Both Meg and Richard went through the list. I'd been trusted to include everything, and I had. It added up to a little more $60,000. "This looks good," said Richard. "Is there anything you had a question about whether or not to include?"

"Yes," I answered. "GGG paid for the cable modem to be installed for the computer, special lighting in this room, and the installation of the security system. Obviously, I need to pick up the monthly charges now, but do I need to reimburse you guys for those installation fees?"

Meg looked at Richard, and answered, "We're okay with letting them go. As well as you starting to pick up those charges effective March 1 instead of February 15. Anything else?"

"Part of my assets is the ready market that Miamoto and Ike are providing to sell my stuff. Plus, I learned about eBay on company time. Do I owe you anything for that?" I asked.

"I don't think so," Richard said. "Meg and I consider it a fair trade for how much you contributed to GGG while it was alive."

I thanked and hugged them both. "So then, how does this all add up?"

We went over the books in an approximate way. We still had accounts payable and receivable, not to mention a big tax liability. Richard asked if I needed money immediately and I said no. He wanted our accountant to figure everything out before distributions were made. He said he was pretty sure that my share would be more than a quarter-million after taxes and after keeping the $60,000 worth of supplies. "Sounds good," I said. "Great, actually."

I went to the kitchen and brought out an ice bucket with a bottle of 1993 Pol Roger champagne and three glasses. "Would you care to do the honors, Richard?" I asked.

"Sure. I've never heard of this kind of champagne before. Is it good stuff?"

"Probably too good to waste on someone who can't tell the difference," I teased. "But enjoy it anyway. I love you both, and we all did well with GGG."

Richard sipped his and proclaimed it excellent. Meg finished her glass in four swallows and asked for another. I intentionally only had one bottle for the three of us. I wanted to avoid Meg getting drunk if I could. Richard and I both knew that if we didn't drink up, our share would be gone pretty quickly, so the entire bottle was polished off in almost no time. Not my favorite way to enjoy champagne, but today it was fine.

Thursday
February 17, 2000

This was my fourth time in advanced step class and by now I understood the patterns. I was dragging by the end of the class, but that was mostly because I took the Body Pump class first. If I'd had no plans for the evening, I probably would have just gone to bed early after such a workout. But I had a dinner date with Annie and who knew what afterward. So I took a shower and was ready to go. A new vegetarian Indian restaurant had opened up on Pico Boulevard that Annie wanted to try.

"Indian as in Bombay and Calcutta or Indian as in Native American?" I asked.

"The former, although I don't know which particular region of India the owners come from," she told me. "A couple of people at Rand have eaten there and liked it."

"Why not?" I told her. "Let's go."

Pico Boulevard is a major east-west thoroughfare in Los Angeles, running roughly parallel to the Santa Monica Freeway between the Pacific Ocean on the west and the Harbor Freeway on the east. It was named for the Pico family, major landowners back in the days when California belonged to Mexico, and this particular restaurant was about a mile west of the San Diego Freeway.

After we ordered, I asked her if I'd ever told my Pico Boulevard anecdote. She said she hadn't heard it, so I began.

"A friend of mine named George spent a couple of years in Chile in the Peace Corps in the late 1970s. Most Americans pronounce the name of the country like it rhymes with 'silly,' but George pronounced it like it rhymed with 'relay.' That made his story about Pico sound authentic to me. While in Chile, George met and fell in love with a local señorita. He wooed her, married her, and brought her back to Santa Monica to live."

"How'd that work out?" asked Annie.

"Not so well. Too much difference between Southern California and the mountains of Chile. But that's a story for another time. Right now I want to tell you about Pico. It seems that the word *pico* in the part of Chile where George was stationed is a slang term for 'penis.' Probably like cock or prick. Not extremely vulgar by itself, I suppose, but that would depend on how it was used."

"I suppose," said Annie dryly. "Go on."

"When George brought Maria to Santa Monica, he drove her around to give her the lay of the land. The suburbs of Los Angeles must be quite different from what she was used to. But when they came across the street called Pico Boulevard, it struck them as hilarious, as it would us if we went to Chile and drove along a street named El Calle Cock, or something."

"Okay," Annie said, not amused so far. "They're laughing at a phallic name. What next?"

"Now it gets good. They come across a restaurant called Señor Pico's, and of course, they *have* to go in to see what it's all about. It turns out to be a rather upscale Mexican restaurant. They're hungry, so they decide to eat there. They're ready to conclude that while it's sort of cute about the name, it's really no big deal."

"That's my conclusion so far," Annie informed me. Her tone told me it would be a good idea to get to the punch line quickly.

"And that's when their margaritas arrived. They picked up their drinks and noticed the napkins underneath advertising the specialty of the house—ta da—El Pico Grande. Now the hilarity broke out all over again. They had to order this, of course, and it turned out to be an oversized burrito with everything on it. When the check came, they wanted to know if they could order a hundred napkins to go. They decided that they had to send some back to Chile.

"The manager came over and asked about the request. George and Maria told him, apparently in Spanish because it was funnier that way. The manager laughed and gave them as many napkins as they wanted. That year, George and Maria's Christmas letters back to Chile were sent with a napkin—but with no explanation. George said they got quite a few colorful letters back and had fun with it for six months."

Annie laughed finally, "You're right. That *is* a cute story, although I suspect it's funnier to a man than a woman. Whatever happened to George and Maria?"

"I actually don't know. When I first met George he was dating a lady named Sandra, and whatever happened between him and his ex was never mentioned. Other than this one story."

Our food came. There was a lentil dish, another with cauliflower and potatoes, and still another one with onions and chick peas. The first one was spicy, and the other two weren't. Different, yet tasty.

"I'd like to talk about our lovemaking last night," Annie addressed the subject that had been on my mind all day.

"Okay," I said. I wasn't sure where this was heading and I didn't want to comment until I did.

"You probably noticed that I was a bit subdued," Annie said. "Were you wondering why?"

"Yes. I didn't know if I'd done something to offend you, or if maybe it had nothing to do with me at all. Perhaps you were extra tired."

"Being tired might have been part of it," she told me, "but mostly I think it was being home."

"What do you mean?"

"My work requires me to figure out difficult problems. And I'm good at it. I frequently immerse myself in the problem before I leave work, think about it while I'm preparing to go to sleep, and by morning I sometimes have a handle on the solution."

"I see," I said, though I didn't really.

"This makes me an extremely valuable employee to

Rand, but probably not much of a lover," she said quietly.

"Well, it happened for the first time last night. How can you be so sure it will be a regular event?"

She shrugged. "It was that way for the last two years with Tony. I was hoping that with a new and exciting lover, things would be different."

It occurred to me that this might have been one of the reasons Tony strayed. If he did. No way I could mention this. I was just grateful she was available when I came along.

"Do you think sleeping in my bed might yield a different result?" I asked.

"Maybe. I don't know. But I'd certainly like to try that."

"Well, you're welcome to stay tonight," I told her. "But I'm too beat to perform. If you could stand just being held and putting put off the sexual experiment until tomorrow night, then you've got yourself a deal."

Saturday
February 19, 2000

Annie spent both Thursday and Friday nights in my bed. Thursday we just went to sleep. Friday turned out to be a repeat of Wednesday: She was very still while I moved in and out. She didn't hurry me or make me feel like she resented what I was doing, but neither was she an active participant.

On Saturday morning I tried an end run around her sexual hang-up. Annie and I drove to the old Sullivan Canyon trailhead. It actually began in the middle of an upscale housing development off of Mandeville Canyon in Pacific Palisades, but some years ago the trailhead was completely blocked off. Some activists periodically remove the impediment to maintain their right of way, but then others block it back up again. This morning we examined whether we could get around the most recent blockage.

"No way," said Annie. "That's too formidable a fence."

"Perfect. This is exactly what I want." She raised her eyebrows in an unspoken question. "You'll see," I told her.

The next canyon over to the west is called Rustic Canyon and I knew where that trailhead was, so that was where we went. For the first mile and a half, we held hands while we walked quietly down the trail. Then I led the way, single-file, up a little-known horse trail that goes up the side of Rustic Canyon, then down into Sullivan Canyon. No signs say "Welcome to Sullivan Canyon," but I knew were we were and told Annie.

"Okay. So we're in the place that we're not supposed to be able to get to. Now what?"

I pulled a blanket and a bottle of champagne kept chilled by a cooler sleeve out of my backpack. "May I buy you a drink?" I asked.

"Sure."

We sat down and sipped champagne. "It's very nice, but what's the occasion?"

"Can't a guy do something nice for his special girl?"

"Sure. And thank you. But you must have a motive. Are you trying to seduce me?"

"Yep. I read somewhere that candy is dandy but liquor is quicker."

"You think that getting me drunk will solve my sexual passivity?"

"No. That's not it at all. The champagne is mainly to help us both relax a little, and to give me a little time to tell you I love you. The real secret is we're out here in the middle of nowhere and no one will come by and bother us. There's nothing here to remind you of work."

"You think that'll do it?"

"I don't know for sure. And you don't have to do anything that feels uncomfortable. But I'd very much like you to sit on my lap and let me kiss you. Maybe things will progress from there, and maybe not. Either way's okay with me."

She set both wine glasses and the half-empty bottle on a nearby tree stump and came over. She didn't sit on my lap, but she sat on the ground with her back to me, and leaned back so I could cradle her in my arms.

I kissed her gently. "I love you, Annie. Very much." We kept kissing while she unbuttoned her flannel shirt. Underneath she wasn't wearing a bra today, which surprised me a little. Her shirt had been loose enough that I hadn't noticed. I thumbed her nipples until they were both erect and firm. "Let's get naked," I suggested shortly after I heard her moaning quietly.

I didn't have to ask twice. Even from the start, her kisses had been reminiscent of the way they'd been last weekend. After ten minutes of kissing and fondling, she was breathing rapidly. I pushed her back and lowered my mouth to her sex. She held my head with her hands as she thrust into my mouth. In short order I heard the screams that I so loved in Las Vegas.

Giving her a minute or so to fully enjoy the throes of her orgasm, I entered her. In a little while, she told me, "I'd like to be on top. Is that all right?"

I pulled out and lay down face up. She squatted over me so that the only part of her that was touching the ground were her fingers and her toes, and the only part of her that was touching me was the part that mattered. It was wonderful. It was effective. After less than three minutes of it, I was done. I expected her to come and lie beside me for a while. She didn't. "If this were June, I'd be ready for a very tender post-coital cuddle," she told me. "But it's February and I'm cold. I'm going to get some clothes on."

After I dressed too, I filled up both our glasses and we clicked them together in a triumphant toast.

"You're looking rather smug," she told me. "Are you proud of yourself?"

"I think so," I told her. "I do feel like a winner. But as you probably noticed, it wasn't me competing against you, but *with* you *against* a common enemy. Sort of like playing video poker from a common bankroll and hitting a royal flush."

"More like a dealt royal! And thank you. I'd become resolved to the fact that I wouldn't reach orgasm again until we were back in Las Vegas. Sometimes it's nice to be wrong."

"The original reason we came up here was to talk about mathematical expectation," I reminded her. "Although I must say this discussion went better than that one would have."

We finished our champagne, brushed off the blanket, and repacked it in my backpack. We walked along hand in hand, more stroll-like than hike-like. "Did you wonder why I suggested you be on the bottom?" she broke the silence.

"I didn't analyze it. At the moment the most important thing to me was to keep the ball rolling downhill, sort of.

There were a variety of ways that would have been acceptable to me at that moment."

"Yes, and I would have been willing to do a lot of different things to keep that ball rolling for you too. If we'd been on a mattress, I would have let you continue. But this ground is too hard and the blanket is too thin, so you lying on top of me was simply too uncomfortable."

"You think packing in a waterbed next time would be a good idea?" I asked.

"That'd be perfect. Do you love me enough to do that?"

"Probably not," I told her. "I guess I had to break the news to you sooner or later."

She laughed and hugged me. We walked along quietly for another 10 minutes or so.

"Sex was a lot better today than last night, wasn't it?" she asked.

"Of course. When you come first, it makes it a lot better for me. But last night wasn't terrible, by any means. If my choice is between last night and today, I'll take today for sure. But if my choice is between last night and sleeping by myself, I'll take last night. Every time."

"It might be that way most of the time," she told me.

"In that case, I'll still want to sleep with you. We'd probably make love once or twice a week and I'd try to figure out ways to get you to Vegas more often. When we get there we'll make love five or 10 times in the same weekend."

"I could live with going to Vegas more often."

When we got back to the condo, she told me. "Nothing went according to plan. We didn't get our talk about video poker and we didn't end up with any aerobic exercise to speak of."

"I agree. All in all, a perfect day."

Monday
March 6, 2000

I was showering at home after my morning Body Pump class. I'll clean up at the gym if I'm going somewhere immediately afterward, but I prefer my own space where everything is in its place. I've participated in team athletics for too many years to be uncomfortable around a bunch of naked guys, but I'll take privacy given a choice.

I heard the shower door being opened, but I was in the middle of shampooing, so I couldn't see. This was *not* good. Either someone had broken in or Annie figured out the code or … That was when I felt Annie's hands caress my butt. Very nice. Reminiscent of her sexual appetite in Vegas rather than here. As I rinsed the shampoo out of my hair, I felt her reach around to gently squeeze my cock. How promising! That's when I felt her chest on my back.

"What the hell?" I sputtered. That was *not* Annie's chest. This one was very large and very soft. I turned around and tried to focus my eyes and saw Meg was readying herself to put a liplock on my recently fondled phallus.

"Whoa, whoa, whoa, Meg! Stop! I can't do this!"

Shower floors aren't known for their traction, especially when they're soapy with shampoo. I grabbed her wrists, but she was struggling. "Please, Chris! I need a man so bad! Richard has ignored me for three weeks. I'll do whatever you like. Just *please*! Help me get off." Even in the shower I could smell the wine on her breath.

It wasn't voluntary, but I was becoming erect. There was something about being stroked, then wrestling, with a naked woman that does that to me every time. Meg kept struggling so as to occupy my hands, but her eyes were glued to my increasing tumescence. "Chris, it's lovely. And so much bigger than Richard's. Let me suck it. Please! I'll let you come in my mouth."

"No, Meg! No!"

I didn't want to hurt her physically so I just held her by the wrists. Eventually, she stopped struggling. When she quieted down, I grabbed both of her wrists with my left hand, turned off the water with my right, then opened the shower door and stepped out. I wasn't quite done with the shower, but there was no way I could remain in that close space with both of us nude and her horny and drunk and me hard and uninterested. When she followed me, I tossed her my robe and told her to put it on, which she did, fortunately, although she didn't tie the sash and my eyes kept finding their way to look at her pubic hair, even though I didn't want them to. I wrapped a towel around my waist even though I was still erect and pushing the towel outward.

"Chris, I can see with my own eyes that you want me. Why do you pretend otherwise?"

"Meg, this is not going to happen. Not now. Not ever. Do you understand?"

"But I need a man. Real bad! If I can't have Richard or you, I'll have to find somebody else. And you're so big. Please."

"Stop it, Meg! I wish you wouldn't go looking for another guy, but I can't control that. All's I can control is to make sure it isn't me. Now go put some clothes on." I left the bathroom to do the same myself.

In a few minutes she was fully dressed. "You're not going to tell Richard about this, are you?"

"Meg, your husband carries guns and has a jealous streak a mile wide and you want to know if I'm planning to tell him you and I were naked together? Get real."

She looked contrite.

"Meg, this is your last chance. Next time the lock on my door will be changed. We're not business partners anymore, so you don't need to be here. You and Richard are still family and I won't lock you out just yet. But any more ..."

She nodded and left.

I knew I was bigger than Richard. It wasn't that Richard was particularly under-endowed, it was just that I was noticeably larger for some reason. In the high school football locker room, I remember him being teased about the size of his manhood. He'd been humiliated. I'd always believed that that was why he started owning guns in the first place. Dad was never a hunter or a gun enthusiast, so Richard didn't inherit or learn the desire from him. I remembered several small comments through the years that a man with a gun who wasn't afraid to use it didn't have to take shit from anyone.

When Rosalind Meacham told me back in college that I was a bigger-and-better man than Richard, I'm ashamed to say it gave me some satisfaction. That feeling was short-lived. She must have told Richard that she liked my dick better than his, because he nearly killed me before he told me that Rosalind was *his* girl and I should stay zipped up and out of his way. That was the first time he'd had a loaded gun in his hand with me in the same room. He never pointed it directly at me, but I got the message. I told him I would never see or call Rosalind again. And I never did.

Now Meg's observation that I was larger than Richard just made me sad. It was an irrelevant comparison. Meg was totally mistaken if she thought that Richard and I were in the same five cards of her hand. Her brief 'victory' of copping a feel was gained by subterfuge and would never happen again. There was absolutely no competition between Richard and me in the sex department, anyway. I'd never make love to Meg, and Richard would never make love to Annie. Or whoever else was down the road love-wise for either one of us.

Meanwhile, Ike and Annie were both coming over later, so I dried the water on the floor and went around to make sure Meg hadn't left any hard-to-explain mementos of her visit. I sat down and sighed. Meg might be the biggest reason of all for me to leave Los Angeles.

Monday
March 6, 2000

When Ike arrived for our monthly chess match, Annie and I were practicing the reverse whip pattern Phil taught us last week.

"I'm very sorry," Ike told me. "I guess I got confused on the date. I didn't know you'd have company."

"Come in. Come in. You're right on time. This is Annie, who wanted to know exactly how sexy this senior-citizen jewelry-store owner was. I asked her to visit with us for ten minutes or so, and then she's going to go do something else. Ike Herman, please meet Annie Ferrari."

Ike kissed Annie's hand and said, "Miss Ferrari, I'm sorry. My adopted son Chris lied about you. He told me you had one except, but I can tell at a glance that this couldn't possibly be true. It's a pleasure to meet you."

Annie curtsied, giggled, then hugged Ike. "Oh, Ike, you are so gallant. Chris told me you were sexy, but he didn't tell me you were *this* sexy. Ooh la la."

I went to the kitchen, opened a bottle of Mirassou Showcase Selection Chardonnay, and poured three glasses, including a less-than-half-full glass for Annie who'd told me she had to work on figuring out an algorithm tonight. But introducing Annie to Ike was a reason to celebrate. When I returned, Ike was on the couch, telling Annie a story, while Annie was seated about four feet away and leaning toward him in a gesture that signified interest.

"Hey Ike, I saw her first. Annie and I've been taking dance lessons and I want to show you what we've learned."

"She thinks I'm sexy and now I have to see you all over her with your hands? What's this world coming to?"

I turned on the original Louis Prima, "Just a Gigolo—I Ain't Got Nobody," figuring Ike would recognize the song from years ago, and Annie and I showed off our moves. Ike tapped both feet in time with the music and watched us intently.

"You two are too young to remember that song when it first came out, but I remember hearing it maybe 40 years ago. Louis Prima used to perform with Sam Butera and Keely Smith at the old Desert Inn. I know I heard it in Las Vegas, and maybe on the Ed Sullivan Show. My wife and I were married in 1955 and we always used to watch that show on Sunday night."

"Did you go to Vegas very often?" I asked Ike.

"Maybe once a year. I was a real piker at gambling. I'd never take more than $25 to gamble with. All my spare money went back into the business. But my Esther liked the shows. Even the ones with Buddy Hackett and the dirty words. Oy! She worked very hard in the store, so every year I'd take her for a few days."

"She sounds like she was a lot of fun." Annie said.

"She was. Especially just after hearing Buddy Hackett!"

Annie waited a few respectful minutes before saying, "Ike, I've got to go. It was a real pleasure meeting you. I'd like very much for all three of us to do something together someday soon."

Ike and I both stood as Annie rose to leave. "If ever he doesn't treat you right, you tell me. He's still not for me too old to take to the woodshed."

Annie looked back and forth between us. Ike was 5'7", slightly slump-shouldered, and weighed a not-too-fit 160 pounds. I was 30 years younger, 6'1", weighed 190, and had the body of an athlete. "That I'd like to see. Do I have to be telling you the truth when I say he isn't treating me right? It might be worth fudging a little to see you do this."

"Oh yes. You must tell the truth. It's very important."

"Well, then, I'll have to wait, because so far he's always treated me well." She gave Ike another hug. "But I'll keep your offer in mind. Enjoy your chess match."

"A lovely woman," Ike told me after Annie left. "She has good manners and a fine sense of humor. You've done well. You've not introduced me to any woman since Paula. This one serious?"

"Pretty serious, although the better I get to know her, the more excepts I see, obviously."

Ike shrugged. "Except for you and me, who's perfect?"

"True. Other than the excepts, I think I'd do well to keep Annie around for a long time."

"What do you two do with each other, other than things that would make me blush to hear about?"

"We're taking a dance class together, as you know. We met at the gym, where we both go regularly, and also like to go hiking in the hills. Annie's a mathematical genius and knows how to win in Las Vegas. We've been there twice so far and we're going back at the end of next week."

"Last time you asked me about investing your money, and now you tell me you're going to Vegas a lot? Is this a change of direction? It's your money and you can do what you like, but this doesn't sound like a good way to accumulate wealth."

"You're right, but it's not like it sounds. The last two years, Annie's won $30,000. It's not a huge amount of money, but it *is* a win and not a loss. Plus, they treat us like royalty there. And I wasn't exaggerating about Annie. She *is* a mathematical genius, and gambling is applied math."

"And you really believe this? That you can win in Vegas? I've heard that many of the taxicab drivers in that town, and waiters in restaurants, and blackjack dealers originally came there thinking they could beat the house. And most of them lost all their money and their dreams. I'd hate to see that happen to you."

"So would I. Actually, I'm not quite convinced about the money yet. Annie's been subsidizing my gambling until I'm comfortable with the financial swings."

"Really? She's paying for you to gamble? Why on Earth would she do that? Are you a gigolo?"

"Ike, if you can look at Annie and tell me you'd think she'd need to pay men to have sex with her, I'm going to recommend you have yourself checked for cataracts. She believes she has the financial advantage, and she's smart enough to figure it out exactly. She plays for big stakes and knows that they'd scare most people. So she's willing to take the risk, and the gain, until I'm ready to do it myself."

"So she's not after your money? Don't forget that you now have substantial assets, and many women are willing to spread their legs to get a share of the good life."

"She told me she bought her condo outright, and I know that they went for $450,000 two-and-a-half years ago when I was looking. She must make real good money at Rand, and other than her BMW, I haven't seen anything she owns that I'd consider an expensive toy. And she has cash on hand to gamble with. I'm comfortable she's not a gold digger.

"Right now, I can't lose in Vegas. Of course, I can't win either, but that's fine with me. All I have to do is learn the game until I'm an expert, live with being treated like royalty, and spend quality time with the woman I love. Things could be worse."

"Much worse. Now bring out your board. I'm going to beat you twice in a row tonight just for spite. You were wise waiting until you bowled her over with your charm before introducing her to me. You wouldn't have stood a chance."

Sunday
March 12, 2000

I'd remarked one day to Annie that I'd grown up in North Torrance, about halfway between our condos and Swingtime. She asked to see my old haunts, so today we were driving there.

"I guess I don't know what your father did."

"He worked for aerospace companies," I explained. "They called him an engineer, but he was an engineer who rose through the ranks. With a wife and two sons, he never got his degree. I don't know if you remember, but in the Cold War days in Southern California, the aerospace giants lived and died by Department of Defense contracts. Entire divisions of tens of thousands of people would lose their jobs overnight sometimes."

"That must have been tough."

"It was. All the fired engineers, secretaries, technicians, and whatever else would scramble to find other jobs if they could. And then a year or two later, another contract would come along and the companies would go hiring everybody they could find. Dad worked for Northrop, Douglas, and TRW—more than once at the first two."

"Hard to raise a family on undependable income, I bet."

"I'm sure, but pretty well the family life was insulated from it. We lived in a modest apartment complex and Mom and Dad banked a third of his paycheck whenever he was working. Mom worked part time and all of that was banked. When the layoffs occurred, they dipped into savings and Dad took any job he could get—even pumping gas sometimes.

"Dad strongly believed in athletics. Since we couldn't afford a place with a backyard, he found an apartment directly across the street from Alondra Park playground. So we always had ball fields and organized activities close by. I stuck to the athletics. Richard played football in the fall, but in the summer when they'd have an acting club, he'd do that. He was never the lead, but he got pretty strong supporting roles."

I exited the 405 Freeway at Redondo Beach Boulevard and turned left. Redondo Beach Boulevard is a major thoroughfare, running northeast to southwest, although its entire length is less than ten miles. But since it runs diagonal to several other streets, it's often the best road to take.

Along the left as we traveled northeast was the Alondra Park golf course. I remembered the 20-foot fences—intended to keep stray golf balls inside the course. A little farther, on the right side of the street in a row of two-story apartments almost indistinguishable from each other, I pointed. "The third one from the end. Upper floor, in the back. It's been over twenty years since I lived here full time, and I don't come look at it very often. It was kept up a lot better back then."

I pulled into a parking lot for Alondra Park playground across the street and we got out of the car. We strolled along the path hand in hand and I looked the place over. "They have lights on the two largest baseball diamonds now. I wonder when they were installed."

"Does it look any different otherwise?"

"The whole place seems smaller than it was, but it's probably just that I'm bigger and have seen more places. This playground used to be a very large part of my world."

"Were all your schools nearby?"

"Yes. The elementary school is no longer there, but North Torrance High School is less than a mile away. We walked to and from every day for four years."

"Were your high-school days happy for you?"

"I'd have to say yes. I was a jock, first string in both baseball and football. Our baseball team won the league and advanced three rounds into the all-Los Angeles

County inter-league playoffs in my junior year. We didn't go all the way, but I was enough of a star that I got scholarship offers from several schools. I picked UCLA because that was where Richard went, and I was close enough to Mom and Dad to visit regularly."

"Did Holly Bennett live nearby?"

I laughed. "Her family lived about a mile south of the high school and we lived north. Holly was my first real girlfriend, but we only went all the way twice. Arturo and Kyle only scored once each, so I felt proud that I was twice the man they were, even though I still don't have a clue why she picked me for the special treatment. Anyway, I hadn't thought of her for years until recently, and that was just the fact that you made me wait so long."

I kissed Annie warmly. "I love you, Annie. I'm not carrying Holly around with me as ancient baggage. You shouldn't either."

We held hands as we went back to my car. "You hungry?" I asked.

"A little."

"May I talk you into fast food, if it's *good* fast food?"

"What specifically?" she asked as I turned right onto Redondo Beach back toward the freeway.

"Have you ever tried Tito's Tacos?"

"You mean that place near us where the one Washington Street becomes two? I've passed by it many times, but never gone in. There always seems to be a line, day or night."

"That's *exactly* the place. It's on Washington Place right off the freeway, and you're right that there's a Washington Boulevard less than a quarter-mile from there. I haven't eaten there in several years, but when I was a ballplayer at UCLA, I probably went there more than 50 times. And maybe 20 times since."

"What makes it so special? Obviously, the fact that there's always a line speaks volumes about its popularity."

"I'm not positive of everything they do. They use beef chunks in their tacos and burritos rather than ground-up burger that most other taco stands use, and I'm sure they use fresh vegetables in their sauces. When I was raised, Richard and I ate Campbell's soup a lot. I got to like it. When I became an adult, I discovered Progresso Soup. It was far thicker and tastier. When I later tried Campbell's, it seemed watery and flat. Tito's is to Taco Bell and Del Taco what Progresso is to Campbell's."

"I'm not sure that's much of an endorsement. They're still both canned soup. But what the heck. Let's try Tito's."

Since the day was nice, the normal 10-minute line was 15 minutes instead. I ordered an all-beef burrito with a Diet Pepsi, and Annie ordered a taco and a cup of water. "This is tastier than I thought it would be," she commented. "Is it like you remember?"

"Now they use Pepsi products and when I was in college they used Coke. And inflation has kicked in a little on the prices. Other than that, it tastes the same. And that's a good thing. I'm glad we're here."

"Me too. Thank you for sharing your past with me."

"What about your past, Annie? I know you went to graduate school at Ohio State, then moved out here. Where did you grow up?"

"Let's change the subject, Chris."

I recognized the set of her jaw. Whatever had gone on in Annie's past, she had her own 20-foot fence around it to keep it all in. Maybe a 40-foot fence.

Wednesday
March 15, 2000

We'd settled into a routine of sleeping together three or four nights a week, including sex about twice a week, but it always included Wednesdays after class and I was really looking forward to it tonight. Annie hadn't climaxed since Sullivan Canyon three and a half weeks ago. We'd tried oral sex, on-the-floor sex, and her-on-top sex. Sometimes in my condo and sometimes in hers, but she just couldn't loosen up enough to reach orgasm. Still, it didn't seem to affect her cheerfulness or her desire to be with me. And overall, I too was content. Spectacular sex is the stuff that dreams are made of, but having okay sex regularly and a good friend all the time was a huge improvement in my life. I could live with her excepts.

As we started to drive to dance class, she told me, "We still haven't had that talk about the difference between actual results and mathematical expectation. I think that maybe it's still festering underneath somewhere and it'd be good to get it out in the open. Especially since we're leaving for Vegas tomorrow."

"Okay," I told her, "but I don't think I'd call it 'festering.' You helped me start a record of my gambling for the year. I have an Excel file called Gambling Log 2000, and I have entries in it for my two trips. I'm ahead so far. There's no reason to assume I can't keep doing it."

"On the contrary," she told me, "there are powerful reasons. The results from any one trip are largely luck. You being ahead now is just a fluke."

"Why a fluke? I played every hand correctly."

"So did Bob and Shirley, and they *lost* that weekend. Do you really think you played better than they did? If you lost and your score was negative so far this year, would that mean that there was no reason to assume it would ever be positive?"

"Well, no," I admitted. "I tend to be an optimist."

"Being an optimist probably makes you more interesting to me as a boyfriend. But being a realist is more sensible when it comes to evaluating gambling opportunities. Being ahead or behind is an interesting historical fact, perhaps, but it doesn't give you any insight into what games to play, where to play them, or even if you're a favorite to continue to be ahead or a favorite to give it all back."

"And mathematics tells you these things?"

"Absolutely," she replied. "I can calculate the return on any video poker game and the correct play on any hand. And the return from the slot club. The 0.67% we're getting from the Golden Nugget is the highest return in Las Vegas at the moment. Three years ago that was the standard on the Strip, but no more. The Golden Nugget is the only one left."

"And that's why we play there. I understand that. But I'm ahead even without the slot club."

"Yes. For 3,000 hands. Luck is pretty dominant over such a short time period. But if we start going more regularly, you may well play 100,000 hands this year. The money a slot club returns is important."

"And the tournaments as well, I suppose?"

"Of course. I don't particularly care whether I win $20,000 in a drawing or a tournament or by hitting a royal flush. They're slightly different tax-wise, but my accountant worries about that. I just try to hit as many jackpots as I can."

"You've been ahead at video poker for two straight years. Do you predict you'll be ahead this year?" I asked.

"I think so, and I hope so. Roughly, I'd say that if I play 50,000 hands this year, it's about 70-30 that I'll be ahead. If I play 100,000 hands this year, then it'll be about 80-20. If I lived in Vegas, played full time, and got in a million hands a year, I'd say the chances I'd be ahead would be around 98-2."

"So the more we go to Vegas, the more money you get and the more orgasms you get. Sounds like you'd be in favor of going every weekend."

She laughed. "We might get tired of so many orgasms after a while. Ya' think?"

"Maybe someday," I said. "I'm not close to that point yet."

"Good," she said. "Me neither."

This week's dance class was a sugar push that included a hip roll. West Coast Swing is a sexy dance, first inspired by the dancing of hookers, at least that's the story I've heard. I couldn't tell you where these prostitutes go dancing and make up sexy new moves.

To do the dance well, you have to be willing to make a spectacle of yourself. Annie and I got into it pretty well, but then again, we were both physically fit, generally happy with our bodies, and getting laid regularly. Many of the others in the class were in nowhere near the same situation. Rotating your pelvis all the way forward and in a circle all the way back is not something that 'nice' people have a lot of practice doing. And many people who believe that they don't have a particularly attractive body will attempt to hide it, not flaunt it.

It was confronting for many of the students, to say the least. Even more so when Phil, working with the ladies, told the guys, "Stand over there for the best view." He said it playfully, but there was obviously method in his lechery. He knew that the best dancers have an attitude of, "I'm sexy, damn it!" even if they're 80 pounds overweight and ugly enough to make paint peel. Anyone who wished to succeed in this dance had to operate within that frame of reference.

On the drive home, Annie asked me if I'd been practicing Jacks or Better. I told her that I'd practiced several hours. I'd used the "Hard Hands" feature of *WinPoker* in the Advanced Training Mode section and set it to 0.1. That limited the computer to dealing hands where the expected value between the best play and the second-best play was less than a tenth of a coin. "I got lots of practice with the close hands," I told her. "I think I knew it a month ago, but I've reviewed everything and I'm now very confident."

"Excellent! That's a smart way to go about the winning process. You're certainly treating gambling at video poker a lot more seriously than you treated gambling at blackjack."

"Thanks to you. You set a good example and gave me a wake-up call. I'm grateful."

"Have you decided whether you want to gamble with your money or mine this time?" she asked. "Or maybe half and half or some other ratio? It really doesn't matter to me. Pick what's best for you."

"I'm still going to go with yours," I told her. "After the sale of the shop, my personal net worth is considerably in excess of a half-million dollars. Still, losing ten grand in one weekend would upset me a lot."

"Not a problem," she told me. "To change the subject, I've got a special sexual request for you tonight."

"From the outset, I can tell you that the answer is probably yes," I said expectantly, even though I actually had some doubt. After all, I'd been on a roller coaster with her so many times. "What exactly is it?"

"It's sort of a please-don't request," she said. "Although I'm looking forward to sleeping with you tonight, I'd really rather we not make love until we get to Vegas—or maybe at least until we get into the car on the trip to Vegas. If you can save your sexual energy until I can enjoy it too, I think it'll be better for both of us. I promise it'll be another spectacular weekend."

So much for really looking forward to tonight. I was disappointed, and it would be a bit of torture sleeping with her without entering her, but sometimes you have to give a little in order to get a lot.

Thursday
March 16, 2000

The energy level at the start of our drive to Vegas was different than it had been five weeks ago. There was still plenty of sexual tension, to be sure. Our relationship was still very new, physically speaking. But "very new" is not at all the same as "about to do it for the first time after aching for it for months." Of course, since we had reason to expect a lot more sexual fulfillment in the next three days than we'd had the last five weeks, we were both upbeat. This time we took the Lexus, with Annie starting out as the driver.

She was wearing the same skirt, tennis shoes, and socks as before. Her top was pink this time and not a tank top. It had zippers up each side. Down each side, actually, because to close it you zipped down and to open it you unzipped up. I'd never seen a top like this before, and it *demanded* exploration.

I reached over and scratched her tummy gently—partly to get a sense of her willingness to play as before. She didn't say anything, but kept her eyes firmly on the road with a smile that could only be called "expectant."

Through her blouse, I cupped her right breast. "I'm really looking forward to holding you and kissing you all weekend long. It's such a joy for me to wake up in the morning with you right there."

She responded with a sound somewhere between a purr and a moan. Unzipping the right side of her top was a two-handed affair. I tried it with one hand and couldn't get the zipper up. But with two hands it was short work. I considered unzipping both sides but we were in traffic. I was less concerned with Annie's modesty than with the guy in the next lane over paying more attention to getting a free peek than driving safely. A large proportion of guys are forever in the mood to see one more woman's body. Always. And causing a car accident didn't sound like a good idea to me.

When I tweaked her nipple gently through her bra, it was already well-defined and erect. I moved two fingers to the center of her bra and tugged. She wasn't exactly sure what I meant at first, but soon figured out that I was asking her to move her torso forward. When she did, I unhooked the bra and gently pushed her back to the full upright position, as they say on airplanes.

I enjoyed Annie's breasts more than I thought I would. They still retained a lot of their girlish shape and firmness. A benefit of smallness, I suppose, her youth, and not being a mother. But mostly I liked them because when I caressed them, *she* responded. At least when I did it either in Vegas or on the trip to Vegas. Her breathing accelerated and became shallow. Last month she asked me to transfer my caresses to her below-the-belt areas right away, but this month she encouraged me to stay exactly where I was. It didn't appear she was close to losing control, but she was enjoying herself.

Eventually, I decided it was time to move on. I reached under her skirt, touched her leg, and was immediately surprised. I was expecting to feel skin. After all, I'd noticed that she had on her tennis shoes and socks, although I guess I didn't look closely enough. Now I felt nylons—or maybe they were silk stockings. I glanced at her foot on the accelerator and she was still wearing tennis shoes and socks. I never imagined she'd be wearing both socks *and* hose. I looked over at her and she was smiling.

"Surprise!" she sang. As I moved my hand up her leg, I discovered that these were not panty hose at all. These were stockings, and she was wearing some sort of garter belt. Interesting!

"You are full of surprises today," I said. "What a special treat for me. Thank you."

She beamed at the compliment. I don't know why bare

inner thigh after moving your hand over stockings seems a lot more erotic than feeling the same leg without the stockings, but it does. This was a revelation to me, because no woman I'd ever been with had worn stockings with a garter belt. "Any chance we could pull over for a quickie?" I asked.

Annie giggled and shook her head. "Keep your pants on, tiger. At least for a little while longer. But I must say, I like the way you're growling. I'd set the cruise control, but there's still too much traffic."

I kept my hand in constant motion all over her leg, gradually inching my fingers toward the eventual goal. When they got very close, my fingers followed the shape of the garter belt. I wasn't surprised to learn she was wearing nothing underneath the garter belt. I lightly tickled the tips of her hair down there. As her breathing shallowed a bit more, I took the steering wheel in my right hand. Soon she wanted more. She reached under her skirt, grabbed my fingers in hers, and together we worked toward getting her off. She knew exactly what she wanted and I was there to add a little extra spice. I kept my eyes on the road, steered carefully, and watched that she maintained proper speed. Other than that, I let her have her way with my fingers. I saw no reason not to.

As she started to groan I kept watch on our speed. But she was able to keep that constant even though she shut her eyes tightly. Before her breathing slowed down, she gave me back my hand and took the wheel again. "Well!" she gasped. "That'll keep a smile on my face for a few hours."

"Mine too," I agreed, then I put on a CD. It was a collection of country-western love songs by various artists. It really hit the spot. After that played, I put on a collection of R&B artists singing love songs. Though the styles were totally different, the emotions generated while listening were similar.

At Barstow we switched drivers, same as we did last trip. I was expecting her to start fondling me, but instead she just turned on another CD. At the end of the CD we were within sight of Mandalay Bay, the first major casino on the south end of the Strip. She leaned over and stroked me over my pants. "Did you think I forgot about you?" she asked.

"I wasn't sure. I remember being a little bit uncomfortable with it last month, but was looking forward to feeling uncomfortable again."

"Good. I have the wheel. Show me what you've got!" She smiled as I unzipped. She took my organ in her hand and began steering with the joystick again. "Actually, there were two separate reasons why I took longer to start this time. First, you're a wimp and begged me not to do it so much last time."

"Guilty as charged," I confessed. "What's the second reason?"

"Because I want you to get excited, of course, but not *that* excited. As I recall, last time it took you less than 12 seconds to finish having your way with me once we were in the room."

"You insult me!" I objected. "I am such a considerate lover, I'm almost positive it took me at least 18 seconds. Possibly even 20."

"Maybe you're right," she said as she steered me off at the first Charleston exit this time, "but what I'd really like is to come first. I know I had a head start a few hours ago, but I'm ready for seconds. Do you think you can hold off long enough?"

"I'll have to think about it," I said as I drove up Main Street, "Maybe if you could wear nothing but your hose and garter belt?"

"I'll have to think about it," she teased as she steered me right onto Bridger, then two quick lefts into the parking garage. I was wondering if the same guy would be there getting an eyeful of Annie getting a handful. He was in the booth, but as we pulled in he was taking money from somebody leaving the lot, so he didn't notice us this time.

Although I was still bulging, this time I knew my jacket

was long enough to hide the evidence. It was the same jacket as last month, but I'd been so discombobulated then that I didn't figure it out until later.

Marie met us at VIP check-in. I wasn't surprised that she remembered Annie's name again, but was very impressed that she remembered mine. For this weekend we were in 7c. "Is that any different from 7b?" I asked. "That's the one we had last time."

"The two rooms are mirror images of each other," Marie replied. "With 7b, the stairway circles down the right side of the suite as you look from the bedroom loft to the parlor. In 7c, the stairway circles down the left. The furniture in most of the Tower Suites is the same, with some small differences in a few cases. The suites on the other side of the hallway are a little bit larger and the view is totally different, of course, but we've never had anyone complain about the suite you're in being too small."

"And you won't," chimed in Annie. "It's the nicest hotel suite I've ever stayed in."

"Yes," concurred Marie, "most of our guests are thrilled when they get to stay in a Tower Suite. Do you need help with your luggage?" We shook our heads. "Then enjoy your stay here and good luck."

When we entered the suite, Annie handed me the jackets as before and pointed me toward the closet. "Don't get lost in there this time," she admonished with a smile.

When I returned from the closet, she'd removed her top, skirt, and tennis shoes and was digging in her luggage for something. I started to remove my clothes and by the time I'd stripped she was actually putting on some red patent-leather high heels. The effect of a beautiful lady in stockings, red garter belt, and red shoes was extremely striking. She stood up and asked, "You like?"

"I'm not sure yet. Walk around so I can see," I said while sitting on the edge of the bed.

She grinned, twirled like she did in dance class, and walked around a bit.

"I think it's time to practice your hip roll," I told her.

She obliged, giggling. Then she came over and held my erection gently. "I'll take that as an indication that you like the shoes." She released me, then spread out on the bed with her legs apart.

"Take me, Chris. Now! Please."

"Umm. With pleasure." I mounted her and rejoiced in her excitement. In our condos she was a passive lover. In Vegas she was a dynamo, wanting to please and wanting to be pleased. It was a lot more fun for me to be thrusting when she was eagerly reciprocating. I'd experienced it so many times last month in Vegas, but only once since. This was bliss.

I got lost in the loving. I didn't want to, but I couldn't help myself coming before she did. Although disappointed in myself, I kept at it. I rolled off her, continued kissing her, and used my fingers to keep her stimulated. As she had done in the car, she grabbed my hand and guided my fingers where she wanted them. She was more forceful with herself than I would have been. In another minute or so, she released with a scream, went rigid for a brief second, then totally relaxed.

"Thank you, darling," she said as she snuggled up close. She didn't mention me coming first and I wasn't going to either. "Let's nap for a few, then go play some video poker. And if you want some more of me later, there's a good chance that can be arranged."

"Sounds good, but I'm planning on dreaming about hitting a royal flush."

In 45 minutes or so, I woke up with her in my arms. I found myself aroused, and so I moved my head to her breast and started gently nuzzling her there to see if I could generate any interest. She lazily stroked my hair and said, "Can we save this for a few hours? If we make love again now, then you'll probably want to sleep all night. And I'd rather go downstairs and gamble some beforehand. Okay?"

This wasn't a tough decision for me. Video poker in Las Vegas is what turned this lady on. And when she got turned on, I got rewarded big time. Plus, I liked the game too. "Sure. Let's shower first and hide the evidence of our hanky-panky. I'll bet you a dollar I get a W-2G before you do."

She'd brought $5,000 in cash with her. We knew she had about $4,000 in cash on account from her 8,000+ accumulated points. She'd collect $1,500 when she checked out, and we were each only planning on earning in the 1,000- to 1,200-point range. In addition this tournament was more lucrative than the last one and we'd collect at least $100 apiece even for bottom-of-the-barrel results, and possibly more. This added up to at least ten grand.

"It should be more than enough," Annie surmised. "On my worst weekend ever on a $5 machine, I lost seven thou. We'd have to both lose pretty badly to exceed the cash we have to play with. And if we do, there are always markers and I have my checkbook. No problem."

"I've decided I want 10% of my action," I told her. "By that I mean 10% of my win if I win, and 10% of my losses if I lose, after calculating the return from the slot club. It's a trivial amount, but it helps to keep me focused."

"Sure," Annie agreed. "It's sort of like my small bet on the Super Bowl. But let's clear up the 10% in cash at the end of the trip, so we can still think of the money in your slot club account as belonging to me. It's easier to keep it straight that way. Your 50% from anything you cash at the tournament won't be affected by this."

When we got down to the high-limit slot area, the IGT machines were occupied with other players from the tournament, but two seats were available on the Bally machine side. We sat down, each inserted our own card, and started to feed money. We had two separate stacks of $1,000 so we could keep our individual scores straight.

Sherrna came up and greeted us. "Just so you two are aware," she said, "the machine Annie's on hit a royal two hours ago and the one Chris is on hit yesterday. Some players want to know this kind of thing."

"Why?" I asked.

"Some players feel the machine has to catch up for the royal by taking from the next few players."

Annie smiled. "Thank you Sherrna. But I don't think that matters. Everything I've heard from writers I respect says it's totally random when the royal comes. And I guess I'm willing to put my money where my mouth is. Or maybe that's put my money where Bob Dancer's pen is."

"Was there any aftermath when you tore the $10 bill in half last month? I've thought about that several times in the past few weeks."

"Nah," Sherrna replied. "Silke told everyone about it, of course, but she said it in a way that she thought it was pretty quick thinking and kind of funny. The money got to where it was supposed to go, so nobody got upset."

"That's good. We thought it was funny, too," said Annie. "Maybe we'll hit a royal and we'll see if you have the nerve to tear a $100 bill in half."

"Oh I do," said Sherrna. "I definitely do. Now go ahead and hit a royal on my shift and tell me to tear a $100 bill in half. Please."

"Nothing would make me happier," said Annie, "except for doing it twice."

"She's like that," I told Sherrna. "Once is never enough." We all laughed.

We started to play. I hit four jacks within the first half-dozen hands. Annie hit a set of nines a few hands later. "This is going to be a very lucrative session," I predicted.

I was wrong. Within ten minutes, both of us were feeding more $100 bills into our respective machines. A few minutes later, we were feeding still more bills. After about two hours with neither of us hitting another quad, I told Annie I was ready to quit for the night. She agreed. I was stuck about $3,000 and she was behind $2,000. Each of us had earned around 300 points so far. While we were cashing out, we discussed food. There was a fruit basket in the room, and we decided it'd be better than a full-fledged meal in a restaurant. There were also four large bottles of Evian water and a bottle of Bailey's when we arrived, which Annie had requested from Shannon.

"That was fun," Annie said as we each had a shot of Bailey's and some fruit. "Thank you for going down to play tonight."

"What do you mean that was fun?" I asked. "We lost our entire cash-on-hand and we've only finished a fourth of our play. I know we can always get a marker tomorrow, but I was hoping to win. I could think of a lot of words to use to describe the experience, but 'fun' wouldn't be on the list."

"I like to play," Annie said. "I think it was Nick the Greek who said that while playing and winning is best, playing and losing is second best. I'm glad I got to play.

"Sure, I like to win, but the fun is in the *playing*. I *like* the decision-making. I *like* the feeling you get when you hit a big hand, or even just miss one. The losing sessions, like what we just went through, make the winning ones so much sweeter when they happen. These losing sessions are part of the whole experience. Get used to them. Embrace them, even. To me, the losing sessions aren't so bad and the almost-inevitable net winning is such a sweet thing that it all adds up to a great time.

"Of course, we'd still be the favorite without Stefano's, the California Pizza Kitchen, Kelly, and dance parties. Even if you didn't include the Class A sex, this would be the best place in the world for me. Are you really so sure you're not having a fun time?"

"Well, when you put it like that," I conceded, "yeah, you're right. It's just that $5,000 has disappeared. And even though only $300 of it was mine, I'm in a little bit of shock. That's all."

"I understand, believe me," Annie said. "It takes awhile to get used to these swings. Which is why I'm glad I'm here during your first losing sessions. When it comes to gambling, I'm the 'older and wiser' one. Part of my satisfaction with you is to be your guide and introduce you to this sport—including the ups and the downs."

"Oh thank you, old, wise, and sexy one." I said kissing her. "Wanna take a Jacuzzi?"

"What? We just took a shower three hours ago. We can't be that dirty."

"Sorry," I said, hanging my head. "I didn't realize that you had a time limit on getting naked, wet, and close ..."

Annie smiled. "Well, when you put it *that* way, I'll run the water."

As the bath filled, we unpacked our things and laid them out for the weekend. While I shaved, she washed her face, then poured some bath prep into the water and adjusted the temperature.

In the tub, Annie sat on my lap. Even though I was bummed out by the money, she was smiling broadly. "I feel *fantabulous*! Las Vegas, video poker, and you! What could possibly be better than that?"

Her enthusiasm was infectious and soon I had no thoughts whatsoever about money. "I have a special sexual request this weekend," I told her.

"Oh really!" she said. "I didn't see any whips or chains in your luggage. Is it kinky?"

"I'm not sure if it's kinky or not. And you can say no. But I've never seen a woman totally shaved down here before," I said as I placed my hand in her lap.

"Really? Not even in a porno magazine?"

"I don't think so. I haven't seen any of those since college and I don't specifically remember any pictures like that. And certainly never up close and personal."

"I've never done it myself," Annie said, "and I've had girlfriends tell me that it's itchy growing back. But it might be a kick. Okay, tell you what. If you write a special poem for me for tomorrow night, we can do it then. Is that an okay price?"

"A bargain. Would you trust me with the razor?"

"What? *You* want to shave *me*?"

"Yes please."

"We'll see."

"I'd at least like to watch."

I'd soaped up a washcloth and was gently cleansing her entire body. "I'm getting just about ready to inspect the merchandise in its before state. And it'll need to be a very close inspection—including sight, smell, touch, and taste."

"You're such a goofball!" she said with a laugh. "You might as well check out the sound while you're at it. Enough about me. Now you stand up and I'll wash you. I just might want to do a little exploration of my own."

She pulled the plug on the water, got out, and started gently scrubbing me when I stood. She held the wash-cloth under clear running water and used it to rinse me off. As I became erect, she put me in her mouth for about five seconds. She stood up and said, "I just had to see if I did my washing job thoroughly."

She pulled me to the bed using her customary "handle." She lay down face up on the bed with her head in one corner—inviting complete access. "Inspect as long as you like. I've already come twice today and I'm not sure how rambunctious I'll be. But anything you like is okay with me."

And inspect I did. With my fingers, eyes, lips, and finally, briefly, my tongue. She purred at the attention, but her body was almost perfectly still. When she was sufficiently lubricated, I moved up and entered her the traditional way.

She was more responsive than her "California" mode, but, as she'd warned, hardly rambunctious. After a few minutes, she whispered, "Please go ahead and finish, darling. I feel great just the way I am."

Well, since she said please …

Afterwards, she asked, "So, Mr. Sleepyhead. Are you still grieving over the loss of the $5,000?"

"Easy come easy go," I muttered as I drifted off into dreamland.

Friday
March 17, 2000

The alarm erupted at 8:30 a.m. and neither one of us stirred until it went off. We snuggled together in bed for ten minutes, then arose and started getting ready. I'm faster in the morning than Annie is, so I went downstairs and practiced on *WinPoker* while I waited. I played almost 100 hands without error and she still wasn't down. I then remembered that I had to come up with an acceptable poem by the end of the day and hadn't started yet. I put the computer away and tried to think of words that rhymed with "Vegas," "Nugget," "tournament," and "video poker." "Poker" was easy, as was "Annie", but I didn't have much luck with the others. Her request had actually taken me by surprise, although it probably shouldn't have, and so far, I didn't have any good ideas.

We both had 10 o'clock tournament sessions and this time we ate a Continental breakfast in the tournament area. Myron and Shannon came up and said hi, as did Kelly. He was wearing a golf shirt with "Spring Fling Golden Nugget March 17-20, 2000" silk-screened on it. Several of the players were wearing the same shirt. I guess they gave them away at the welcoming reception the night before.

"They let you off easy costume-wise this time," I observed.

"Sometimes I get lucky." Kelly responded.

"Do you resent having to wear costumes?" I asked.

"Oh no. Not usually. The costumes are fun, but they do require a lot of extra effort. The only time it's a problem is if I'm doing several events back to back and the same costume doesn't work everywhere. When that happens, usually they'll all settle for me wearing a tuxedo."

"How many types of costumes have you worn?" Annie inquired.

"Hundreds, I suppose. My wife takes snapshots and we've collected some outrageous photos through the years. Good luck today," he said as he went off to chat with some of the other contestants.

One couple we hadn't met before, Jim and Sandy, joined us at our table. They'd been at last month's event and remembered us dancing. They lived in El Paso and were considering taking dancing lessons together. They said we'd inspired them. "It was clear that you were still in the learning process, but obviously you were enjoying it immensely. We're checking out studios near where we live. What kind of dance were you doing?"

"It's called West Coast Swing," Annie told them.

"Do they do it in Texas?" Jim asked.

"I really don't know. Sorry," said Annie.

"I'm pretty sure they do some sort of swing dancing all over the country," I chimed in, "but it wouldn't surprise me if there were some regional differences. Bob and Shirley Dancer also do the Texas two-step, and surely they do *that* dance in El Paso."

"They danced more two-steps than swings at the party last month," Annie recollected. "That would probably be a good dance for you to start with. It wouldn't surprise me if it's the dance we take up next."

"Really?" I said. "Not that I'm complaining or resisting the idea, but Annie's never mentioned that to me before. But it does seem like a versatile dance you can do almost anywhere."

"Yes. And mostly I don't think it matters where you start as long as you're in the same class together," Annie said. "El Paso has a large Mexican population, so they must do a lot of Salsa there. That might be a good dance to learn if you like that music."

"We've taken weekly group classes for about three months," I chimed in. "And I took five more before Annie started going. I never would've believed that I could take lessons 17 times, or whatever it is, and still obviously be a beginner, but that's the way it is."

"I like the people we've met since we've started dancing," said Annie. "We've met all the people in class, since we rotate. Last month we got to know Bob and Shirley better because of the dancing, along with Dan Williams, and now you. We can't know for sure who'll turn out to be a good friend and who won't, but I'm sure that some will."

Sandy, a well-groomed woman wearing a lot of silver and turquoise jewelry, poked Jim in the ribs. "That does it. We're starting dance classes next week."

Jim adjusted the silver and coral bolo on his string tie as he looked over at us. "You two are like a tag-team commercial for the Start Dancing Today organization, if there's such a thing. But I think you're right. It'll be good for Sandy and me. Thanks for the pep talk."

"Ten o'clock players!" Kelly's amplified voice boomed. "If you haven't selected your machine, now is a very good time. Linea and Diane will be glad to set you up."

Annie and I went to get our machines. This time we were picking yellow bunny rabbits out of an Easter basket. Annie picked machine 19 and I grabbed three numbers, hoping to find one close by. But none were and I wound up with machine 5. We told Linea that we hadn't picked up our shirts yet and asked how we could get them.

"We'll have them at the afternoon sessions. You each are entitled to two shirts. Unfortunately, we're down to Large and Extra Large, so unless Annie is looking for a nightshirt, they'll all be too big for her."

"That's way too big for Annie," I said, disappointed that my girl had to miss out on a freebie.

"I don't figure I'll lose any sleep over that disappointment," Annie said with a smile. "I have lots more shirts from Las Vegas special events than I'll ever be able to wear. It's time for Chris to start his collection, so we'll get all four of the shirts in Large."

"I bet I could unload these on eBay," I mused.

"Really?" said Annie. "I never thought of that. How

about some with dates from 1998 and 1999 that have never been worn?

"Shouldn't be hard for me. I sell stuff on eBay all the time."

"Oh good," Annie told me. "You've just created the possibility of an empty drawer for me. This is a case where less is more. Thank you very much."

When it came time to take our tournament seats, I found out I was seated next to Sandy. I'd just met her, but it was still nice to have a familiar face nearby. Jim pulled up a chair right behind her and wished us both luck. I was excited about this. Who knew? I might win first prize.

On the other side of me was a heavyset man named Archie who didn't seem particularly enthusiastic. I asked him if he'd played in many of these tournaments.

"Probably 100 of them," he told me. "I've won once, come in second twice, and had various other in-the-money finishes."

"That's all? Out of 100 tries? And you still bother?"

"Sure. My results are fairly typical. After all, if most of these tournaments have 150 people in them, I don't figure to win more than once every 150 times on average. I don't show up unless the tournament is worth $200 or more in equity. Sometimes I win a lot more, and usually nothing at all, but I always enter when the casino offers a profitable situation. It's a numbers game. Keep showing up and sooner or later something good will happen."

That was pretty much the same song that Annie and Bob sang. I started to consider that they were all on to something.

"Welcome to the Spring Fling slot tournament at the Golden Nugget," Kelly was saying. "Since you're all winners to us, every one of you will be taking home at least 100 smackeroos. Not bad if you ask me. And some of you will be taking home a lot more." Kelly went through the preliminary instructions one more time. I was surprised how he could give the same information as last time, only make it just different enough that it was still interesting. This time he had us shake the hand of the person next to us and say, "Welcome, fellow winner." And then it was, "FIVE, FOUR, THREE, TWO, ONE, HIT THE BUTTON!"

I still had zero points after my first ten spins, but then the machine kicked in and I got back to back-to-back-to-back triple sevens for 4,500 points. The machine took a few spins off to catch its breath, then delivered another set of triple sevens. "Back-to-back one more time!" I urged.

"Greedy son of a bitch, aren't you?" commented Archie. He had 1,800 points, while my meter registered over 6,000.

"Yep! The more I get now the less I have to get this afternoon."

My machine kept cooperating and I surpassed 10,000 points with 23 minutes to go. Ride 'em cowboy! Heidi came by and complimented my score. "Are you allowed to go to machine 19 to tell Annie that my machine is kicking butt?"

Heidi smiled. "I don't see why not."

My credits kept accumulating nicely and I got back-to-back triple sevens again. I reached 20,000 with 16 minutes to go. Cindy came by and said, "Annie says her machine sucks, but she's rooting for you." I guess Heidi had passed the word and the Bally Belles were in the business today of passing messages.

"Fifteen minutes to go," Kelly announced. "Some of your machines are still asleep. But don't stop hitting the button. Many times have we seen machines turn around and come alive in the last ten minutes or so."

My machine was still overachieving. I left 30,000 in the dirt with 11 minutes to go. "You're doing great," Lynn told me. "I've seen maybe five scores ever above 45,000. You're on track to be number six."

In another few minutes Kelly was at it again, "With less than nine minutes to go, I'd like to announce that John Luckman has finally broken 10,000 points. He always manages to make it tough on Sue to make up for him in the afternoon. Eleven o'clock players, if you'd like to select your machine, go and see Linea and Diane."

I passed 40,000 with four minutes left. Sandy had 24,000 and Archie had less than that. I could hear Annie's occasional "Come on Chris!" in the background. I suspected she was receiving regular updates and knew I was doing spectacularly.

"Less than two minutes to go. It's all up to you. Don't quit now," Kelly urged.

My machine ran out of steam near the end, but I still ended up with 43,440. It was a fantastic score—especially considering the second highest score in the entire session was under 38,000.

"Make sure you don't leave your machine until you've signed for your score. One of our friendly ladies will be by shortly."

When Cindy came to get my signature, she was very encouraging. "People win the whole thing while averaging only 36,000 or so. You have a big cushion. Try to hang on to it."

"I will!" I said excitedly. "You can bet on it."

Annie had slightly over 29,000, which was average. "My hero," she exclaimed as she greeted me with a big hug. "That's a great score."

"If you've got talent, you just can't hide it," I boasted. Then I cupped my hand to my ear. "I think I hear a royal flush calling my name. Do you hear it too?"

"Yes, but I'm pretty sure it's calling *my* name," she responded. "Let's go."

"Yes, let's," I concurred. We found two empty machines on the IGT side. I held them both while she went to get a marker. I noticed Archie was playing a $5 8/5 Jacks or Better machine with a $42,000 royal flush next to us and I asked him if that was a good game to play.

"Percentage-wise, it's slightly better than 9/6 Jacks with the standard royal. It turns out to be a *great* deal if you hit the royal, but you lose much faster on this game in the short run. You probably get seven full houses and seven flushes an hour, and each one of them returns $25 less on this game than your game. Since I'm going to be playing six or eight hours this weekend, that's about $2,000 extra I'll lose by playing this game that I wouldn't have lost by playing 9/6 Jacks. To some people, that's important.

"Plus, it's a lot more difficult and the strategy changes as the royal goes up. For example, at this level you hold a suited jack ten over a jack ten seven. But you still hold a jack ten eight over a jack ten. Unless you've practiced at various levels, it's hard to know when to make which adjustments."

I wished him luck and greeted Annie as she returned with $5,000. As before, she and I each started with $1,000. We put two bills into the machine and left the other $800 in our spill trays. She returned the other $3,000 to her purse.

We started to play and did better than we'd done last night. When I was dealt the hand A♥K♥T♥5♥Q♣ I told her. "Yes I know the book says to play all four hearts, and I will. But I don't like it. Doesn't it bother you to make such a play?"

"Not really. Drawing two cards to the suited AKT only becomes a $20,000 royal once in 1,081 times, and that's worth only $18.50. Giving that up and greatly increasing your chances for a $150 flush from three percent to 19% more than makes up for it."

I drew the 3♥ and watched the 30 credits rack up. "Paid off better this time," I commented.

"You can't know that unless you also see the next card," Annie said.

"If you ever decide to learn Double Bonus or another game where flushes return 7-for-1 rather than the 6-for-1 they return in this game, you'll hold a 4-card flush in preference to a 3-card royal most of the time. It'll get so holding all four hearts on a hand like this is second nature to you."

We played on. I connected on two 4-of-a-kinds in short order and coins spilled into the tray. "This is more like it," I grinned as I went to get the racks.

Annie started with a pretty interesting hand,

K♦Q♦J♦T♦5♣. "This might be a royal," she said as she held the diamonds. "Wish me luck." I wished her luck and she drew. The machine locked up and the music started playing.

Archie had heard Annie, and then the music. "Wow!" he exclaimed. "That's pretty cool. Twenty thousand big ones. Congratulations, whoever-you-are."

"Thank you. I'm Annie, and I wish it were a royal. I actually drew the 9♦ rather than the A♦, so I get $1,250 rather than $20,000."

"I wouldn't throw it back," said Archie.

"Okay, you talked me into it," Annie said with a smile. "Not that I know *how* to throw it back and try again. Twelve hundred and fifty dollars is still a nice jackpot."

While waiting to sign her W-2G, Annie said. "For this tournament we have to allow time for lunch, because it isn't included. I vote for the California Pizza Kitchen. We'll leave at 12:45, okay?"

I nodded. By lunch time, I'd put an additional 400 points on my card and Annie only had about 350, because it took awhile for the straight flush to be hand-paid. For the day, I was up $950 and she was up $250, not including cashback. Because we were running a bit late, she went to the restroom while I got us seats in the restaurant. "Order me a bowl of the soup with tomatoes and beans in it, a small Oriental chicken salad, and bottled water," she requested. "You'll have time to wash up after we order and before the food comes."

Our VIP line pass gave us priority seating at the restaurant and I actually had the order in before Annie returned. I left to clean up and told her on my return, "I got a verse worked out but I'm having a little problem with the rhyming. Perhaps you can help.

Some people drive a car.
Some people drive a truck.
If you were only here,
Together we would kiss.

"I think it's missing something," I said as innocently as I could. "Do you have any suggestions?"

"I suggest you've got to do better than that or I'll remain happily hairy for at least one more day."

After lunch we strolled over to the tournament area and picked our machines. This time I was on 15 and Annie was on 2. "You guys can peek at each other if you like," Linea commented.

There were a total of 32 machines. Machines 1-8 backed up to machines 9-16 with machine 1 opposite 16, 2 opposite 15, etc., so Annie and I basically faced each other on back-to-back machines. I collected my four golf shirts and got ready to hit the button.

"You've got a good chance to win this thing," Annie said. "But whatever place you end up, you're still my bestest guy in the whole world."

"That's worth a lot, although I do wonder if being your bestest guy is as good as being your most favoritest."

"Two o'clock players, it's time to take your seats!" Kelly's voice boomed. We found our seats and sure enough, we could look at each other through the gaps between the machines.

"Hey lady," I called through the gap. "You want to go mess around?" Annie grinned and looked pleased with the way her life was going.

"The party tomorrow night starts at seven p.m. in this room. We have limited seating and people who have extra guests with them would like tickets. If you're not going to be using one or both of your tickets, please turn them in to a host so somebody else can appreciate all my funny lines." It was just like Kelly to put a different twist on a mundane announcement. "FIVE, FOUR, THREE, TWO, ONE, HIT THE BUTTON!"

I started hitting the button anxiously. First place was $15,000, second was $7,000, and third was $3,000. I figured I had about a 75% chance or so of ending up with one of those prizes. My machine was starting slowly, but I wasn't worried. Machines regularly go through cold spells.

With 20 minutes to go, though, I had only 6,000 points. Heidi came by and tapped me on the shoulder. "Come *on*, Chris. You can still do it." Annie and I were keeping each other posted and I knew she had about 12,000. Normally she'd be bouncing up and down with her score, but the fact that my machine wasn't cooperating dampened her enthusiasm.

"Don't stop hitting your button," Kelly urged everyone. "It's nice to see that Sue Luckman is trying her hardest even though John put her in a hole with his pitiful score this morning." I couldn't see, but I suspected that John was seated right behind Sue and was enjoying the ribbing.

I got two sets of triple sevens in about five spins, so I started to like my chances again. "Maybe I can still salvage a good score," I said to Annie. But then my machine died again and with ten minutes to go I had only 14,000 points. Annie had 26,000. I hadn't even considered the possibility that she could outpoint me sufficiently in the final round to erase my 14,000-point head start, but now that didn't seem so farfetched.

I knew that last time, 66,000 was needed to get tenth place, which paid $1,000. To reach that, I needed 22,560. With two minutes to go, I had 20,000 and Annie had 33,000.

"Less than two minutes to go," Kelly said. "I know you're tired and want to give up. But keep going anyway. One extra spin can make a difference. The finish line is almost here. HIT THE BUTTON."

I ended up with 22,400 and Annie had 35,300. Overall, I beat her by a little. We figured that we'd both get at least $500, the prize awarded from 11th to 25th place, and there was a slight chance that one or both of us would get $1,000. It wasn't what we were hoping for, but all and all not bad for an event where we had a small advantage at the machines, a lovely suite, and as Annie had said, "Class A sex."

As I signed for my score, Lynn commiserated.

"Too bad. You had such a good score in the first round

and then the machine just got cranky. We see it all the time, but I know it's painful."

"Hey, it's not all bad," I said. "At least I've got four golf shirts." Lynn laughed and took down the next person's score.

Annie signed her scorecard and came over and gave me a hug. "I'm sorry, darling. I know you were hoping to do better. But there's nothing you can do about it. Sometimes the machine cooperates and sometimes it doesn't. What would you like to do now?"

"I'm pretty much open," I responded. "We need to play some more, but we're well over halfway done and we have until Sunday morning. How 'bout we go for an hour-long walk, then go upstairs for some Class A?"

"Not bad," Annie said as we headed up the elevator to get our jackets. "I should call Bob and Shirley first and see if we still have a breakfast date. Where should this walk take us?"

"This isn't the best place in town to go for walks, but back and forth to the flower shop should be okay. How would you like a rose? I figure that might help me get a favorable poetry review."

Annie laughed. "I'd forgotten about that. How's it coming anyway?"

"I already have a poem that should bring out the Schick. I'm trying to improve on it, just in case."

"Just in case what?"

"Just in case you're so attached to your short curlies that you become a hardass about whether or not the poem is good enough."

"Well," she responded. "Last time I checked I *was* rather attached to them, or maybe they were attached to me. It just might require one hell of a poem to unattach them. Is it another limerick?" We were both pretending this was a serious discussion we were debating and were doing so quite straight-faced. But the sheer absurdity of it was actually enjoyable.

"Sort of," I replied. "It has five lines and lines a and b

rhyme, as do lines c and d. Line e, however, rhymes with c and d rather than a and b. And for rhyming purposes, it refers to where we are now as 'Vegas City,' but it's definitely about us and our relationship. Any fair critic would definitely order up the Gillette Foamy immediately after hearing it." We were inside the suite now.

"Ooh, I can't wait," she clapped her hands together while jumping up and down. Her little girl act reminded me a little of Meg's, but Annie's turned me on, as opposed to Meg's which scared the hell out of me, thinking about possible consequences. "Poem me now!"

"I can do that," I said, "but you're currently overdressed to hear one of my poetic masterpieces. And if you get appropriately unclad, we might not get our walk today or maybe not even call Bob and Shirley. What's it going to be?"

Annie went and turned on the water to the Jacuzzi. Unbuttoned her blouse. Came over and kissed me. "How about you buying me a rose tomorrow?"

"Hmm. Let me think about it." I started to take off my own clothes.

The tub was halfway full by the time we were both undressed. Annie sat herself cross legged in the middle of the bed. She summoned me by slapping the bed beside her and bouncing up and down. "Hurry up. Poem me. Poem me."

I sat down next to her, held both her hands in mine, and recited:

Last night in Vegas City
I was with a lady pretty.
When she held me tight,
It felt so right,
I'd like to do it again tonight.

She kissed me and giggled. "It's cute, and I like your chances for tonight. But it does seem to be a rather lightweight composition for such a major reward. I'm not sure."

"Well, let me remind you that you've been promised a rose to somewhat compensate for the lightweightness of the composition. Also, I suggest you make a decision rather quickly if you don't want the Jacuzzi to overflow."

Annie shrieked, ran in to check the tub, and turned off the water. Then she came back into the bedroom with a smile. "No harm done, although it's probably a good thing you didn't go three verses. The water's a little too hot, so let me call Bob."

"Don't tell him what you're not wearing. You don't want to break Shirley's heart."

In a few minutes she reported, "We're all set for nine a.m. Now mind you, I haven't entirely made up my mind yet, but let's soak and discuss the logistics of this. Just in case."

"Is it fair for me to stack the odds in my favor?"

"In what way?"

I went to my luggage and brought out a wrapped package. "To celebrate your unfleecing," I told her.

"You were probably going to get to see me in all my hairless splendor anyway. But whatever this is, it's too late not to give it to me. What is it?"

She opened the box to see a heliotrope necklace that exactly matched her earrings. It was a more substantial piece than the strung beads I'd given her last month. "Ooh. This is lovely. And a totally different style than the last one you gave me. I'm building up a sizable and one-of-a-kind collection. Thank you." She came over and gave me a big kiss.

"You're welcome. It's too bulky to wear with your Valentine's Day dress, but a lot of outfits you could wear would take this, I think. Like your current one."

Annie went to the mirror and tried on her necklace. "It's too bad you think my current outfit needs accessories. I thought you rather liked it."

"Fishing for compliments again? Actually, your current outfit is quite to my liking, other than being in need of a tonsorial treatment. Why don't you unhook your necklace and I'll check the temperature of the water."

"What kind of treatment?"

"Tonsorial. It refers to the barbering process."

As I eased myself into the tub, she had a ton of questions: "Do you have a fresh blade? Plenty of shaving cream? Do you think it will hurt? You'll be careful, won't you?"

I responded, "Look, Annie. Do you seriously believe that I would want to incapacitate that part of your anatomy in any way?" She shook her head. "You know I'm in heaven when you're my sex goddess. You can depend on me being as careful as possible."

"Okay then. But I'm not ready to get out of the tub just yet."

We decided to lay a pillow in the center of the bed, place some towels on top of the pillow, then position her face up on the pillow. This would give me complete access while I barbered. There was a mirror on the ceiling, so she could sort of see what was going on. I convinced her that it was more important for me to see clearly than for her.

I hadn't really thought about it before, but most of the hair isn't very close to the vaginal lips. Shaving the hair wasn't difficult. I considered letting out a loud, "Oops! Damn! I'm really sorry, Annie," but I wasn't sure she'd think it was funny. I decided to do it right when I was finished. That way she couldn't change her mind about letting me complete the deed.

When it came time to shave close to the edge, it wasn't a problem for a guy who shaves close to his own lips every day. Soon she was bare as a baby. Her vulva stood out far more prominently than I'd expected. I'd only seen such a sight hidden behind pubic hair before. Now it was very nicely obscene and I was quite turned on by the view.

"Is this going to take much longer?" she asked.

I was finished, but the devil in me decided now was my opportunity to be funny. I wished I'd taken some of Richard's acting classes. I touched her with the razor and gasped, trying to inject alarm into my voice, "Oh no! I didn't mean to, Annie! I'm so sorry."

She sat up instantly. "What happened?" She saw me giggling and realized I was pulling her leg. "Oh, you monster! Let me see what you did." She ran into the bathroom, looked in the mirror, and shrieked. "I guess I never knew what it looked like. I hope you like it, because it'll be awhile before it grows out. Of course, I can always wear my new necklace if you think this outfit needs to be accessorized."

I took her in my arms. "I like. I like. And I think it's a good idea to go back to the bed so I can show you exactly how much I like."

So we did. And I did. And we napped a few hours until dinnertime.

When we were dressing later, I inquired. "Are you in more of an eating-dinner mood, or a video poker mood, or a go-getting-you-a-rose mood?"

"Let's go play. We should be able to completely finish in three hours or so. Then we can eat and then I'd like to go to the Venetian, get you a slot club card, and put some points on it. I'll explain over dinner. We don't have reservations, so I suspect that Stefano's and Lillie Langtry's are out. But there's always the buffet, coffee shop, or California Pizza Kitchen again. You choose."

"I'd have to say that the Pizza Kitchen sounds the best. There are still a lot of interesting things on the menu we haven't tried. Let's go back there."

This time two adjacent Bally machines were open, so that's where we sat and checked our points. I'd accumulated 745 points for the trip so far and Annie had 684. We could average about 200 points per hour on these machines. Of course, if we hit a royal or two, it would slow things up a bit.

The Bally machines overlook the bank of elevators where a large number of hotel rooms are located, not including the Tower Suites. There must be Golden Nugget offices up there too, because we saw a lot of casino executives using the elevators in addition to the hotel guests. Dan Williams alit from an elevator, noticed us, and came over to say hi. He remembered Annie's name and needed to be reminded of mine—but he seemed sincerely interested in learning it. "You gonna save me a dance tomorrow night even if I hit a royal?" Annie asked.

"Count on it, and it's okay with me if you hit two. It's not *my* money, after all," he responded with a smile.

"I plan to hit one tonight too," I spoke up. "But you don't have to dance with me to prove you're legitimately happy."

"That's the best news I've heard all day," Dan answered. "I've got a meeting to go to. Good luck and I'll see you tomorrow night." He left.

We set about playing. Most of the hands were second nature, but I still needed to pay attention. On one like A♣K♥3♣J♦4♣, I had to think about it a bit before I was sure that it was right to hold the clubs. But if the king and the jack had both been the same suit, then I'd have held the honor cards over the clubs. It wasn't *that* difficult, but I needed to concentrate in order to get each hand right. The challenge in video poker was not learning how to play the hands, at least to me, but seeing all of the possibilities and extracting the maximum from each deal. I decided to ask Annie about this later.

Although we'd talked about hitting a royal flush every session, it hadn't happened yet. I ended up winning $250 for the evening and Annie ended up losing $1,300. For the entire trip, I was stuck $1,750 and she was down an even $3,000. We'd each earned $600 in cashback. She'd collect $1,500 from spending the points on the suite, while I'd let my points stay in my account. We figured to each make $500 or $1,000 from the tournament. Not counting what was going to happen at the Venetian, we'd probably go home with less money than we started with. Annie wasn't worried about it, and I was actually cash ahead, thanks to Annie's generosity. My half of the $500 or $1,000 tournament result would more than compensate for 10% of the loss from playing.

While waiting for our pizzas to arrive, I told Annie that the challenge to video poker seemed to be staying alert enough so you didn't make any stupid mistakes.

"Yes," she agreed, "that's the way it is for me. In no other area of my life do I need to keep doing the same thing, precisely, over and over again. In programming you need to be precise, but every programming assignment is a little different. Here the assignment is always the same. Just play perfectly. That's all. It's not that hard, but it's not that simple either."

"It feels a lot different to me this time than last."

"How so?"

"Last month I was in a learning mode and everything was new. I was a real sponge for information and it was a lot of fun. Now I'm convinced that I know the game and the real challenge is to just do it perfectly."

"Yes. Kind of like my new necklace."

"What do you mean?"

"I don't know how much different it is for you to mount the heliotrope to gold fittings and attach the mounted stones to gold chain, but whatever you needed to learn about that, you figured out when you made my Christmas earrings. For my necklace, there probably weren't any new challenges. But you needed to concentrate to see that each of the attachments was completely correct."

"Yes. That's a good analogy. Creating the same jewelry pieces over and over again can be boring. But I take pride in doing a good job. I think that bodes well for my video poker future. Even though gambling is exciting, playing correct video poker is very repetitious and I'm sure many people don't have the personality to handle that."

The waiter brought me a Thai chicken pizza and Annie a goat-cheese-with-roasted-peppers pizza. Eight-inch pizzas here were pretty small, and even Annie could almost finish one by herself. We figured that if she ate three-fourths of hers and I ate the rest, plus my own, it should be quite sufficient.

"Tell me about the Venetian," I prompted.

"It's a brand new casino and their slot club returns a half-percent if you earn points in even multiples. Officially, it returns only 0.4%, but you get this bonus every few thousand points worth 0.1%. For people who play the stakes we do, it's no problem as long as we're sensible about when we stop for the day. I played there when they opened and they've invited me to an invitational drawing in two weeks. I thought we'd go by and see if we could play enough to get you an invitation too."

"Is a half-percent such a good deal?" I asked. "After all, 9/6 Jacks or Better returns 99.54% and I'm already getting a taste of the swings. One mistake could wipe out the entire advantage."

"True," she said, "except they have probably four or five of the top 15 restaurants in town. I mean, this pizza is good, but sometimes dining at a four-star or five-star restaurant is fun. At their tournament, I'd like one super meal. The rest can be at the Grand Lux Café, owned by the Cheesecake Factory, which is their low-end eatery, but still definitely a quality restaurant. Quite a bit fancier than the Carson Street Grill here, in my opinion.

"Plus, they're giving away $75,000 to the invited guests. I suspect everybody will get a drawing ticket for some fixed amount of play, perhaps $2,000 or $5,000, and then probably they'll award the money Saturday night. I estimate the drawing adds well over a quarter-percent of equity, although you never know for sure, because it's hard to judge how many tickets are in the barrel. At a minimum, it'll be a better-than-even game in a nice hotel suite. We'll have at least one scrumptious meal and some more Class A. But maybe you have something more interesting to do with your time."

"Not likely. Count me in," I said. "Part of me is a little uneasy. Now that our play at the Golden Nugget is over for this trip, even though I accidentally won due to your largesse, I feel relieved. It's like I've dodged a bullet, almost. Voluntarily subjecting myself to a possible loss seems unnecessarily risky to me."

She smiled. "You still believe that the casino will always win in the long run. The only way to get by that one is to play and win. It'll take you some time, but you'll eventually end up with the same gut belief I have. I believe that the Venetian presents an *opportunity*. You seem to believe that it presents a *possible disaster.* If you're afraid, I won't insist, but I do think it's a good idea."

"I'm going to trust you on this one," I said, "misgivings and all. I assume we'll be playing $5 Jacks or Better again, right?"

"No. Although they have that game there, they shortchange the straight flush. Instead of giving you 250 coins for a straight flush, they give you 239— which adds up to $1,195 and is under the W-2G threshold. That nicety robs you of a small bit of equity.

"Instead, we'll play $2 Triple Play. You'll play three separate hands at the same time. It's actually a lot more interesting than the machines we've been playing. You'll see."

"Are we playing five coins per hand?"

Annie nodded at my question.

"Then we're talking about $30 per hand. I'm *still* scared of $25. Is your bankroll sufficient to handle this?"

"I think so. Triple Play is new and there's still some debate on exactly how much bankroll you need, but the consensus is overwhelming that Triple Play takes less than twice the bankroll than single play of the same amount. So the game you'll be playing would take about the bankroll of a $3.50-per-unit-bet game, if one existed. It's actually quite a bit less than a $5 game."

"Do you make any strategy adjustments when you're playing three hands at once rather than one?"

"Absolutely not. Trust me, if there were strategy changes, we'd be having a lot longer discussion. I'm a girl who believes in playing every hand perfectly."

"Sounds good to me," I said, leaving a $5 tip for a $25 tab. "Why don't you sign for the check while I go up and get our jackets? Do you need anything else from the room?"

She shook her head and I left.

Friday
March 17, 2000

On the drive over to the Venetian, I told Annie I would still keep my 10% share of the additional gambling.

"That's fine. And thank you for making it super clear up front so there's no possibility of a misunderstanding later."

We got two cards in my name at the Venetian and found a $2 Triple Play machine with 9/6 Jacks on it. In Triple Play, you're dealt five cards on the bottom of three hands. Whatever cards you select are automatically held on all three hands. When you draw, you draw from three separate decks to the same hand. Annie was right. It was a lot more enjoyable, especially when you were dealt a paying hand or a hand with a lot of potential. Dealt three-of-a-kinds, for example, were a lot more exciting. Instead of improving to quads two times in 47 tries, you had three separate chances at the 2-in-47 improvement. And even one quad (for $250 on this machine) or one full house ($90) felt like a pretty nice hit.

Side-by-side machines weren't available, so we traded off every 10 minutes. We lost $2,000 in the first hour and Annie said to keep going. We lost another grand in the second hour, and then I connected on my first royal flush ever. I'd drawn two cards to K♠Q♠T♠ and ended up with a royal flush in the middle row and two pair on the top row for a total of $8,020. I lifted my arms in a "touch-down" gesture and Annie and I both yelled. It called for a kiss, of course.

"How does it feel to hit your first royal?"

"Almost as good as Class A," I answered, "but not quite."

"Right. If someone said you could choose between

having an extra $8,000 and one more orgasm, you'd take the sex. Sure you would."

We both grinned.

When the attendant came to take my ID, Annie asked for $5,000 in a strap and an empty strap. She intended to take the loose $3,000 from this jackpot and add it to $2,000 in her purse to fill up the second strap. When the attendant went off to take care of this, Annie went off to search for a host. She brought back a man named Chris Corona. He and I agreed that we could remember each other's first names easily enough.

Annie told Chris that this was my first royal flush ever and asked if I could get an invitation to the special event for two weekends from now. "He won't need a room," Annie told him, "because he and I will be staying together."

"That actually makes a difference," Chris informed. "The event isn't full, but the hotel is sold out. This way, we'll be getting an extra player at essentially no additional cost to us, and my bosses like that tradeoff. Are you comfortable putting $50,000 through the machine this weekend? If so, it'll be easy for me to put you in."

Since we'd already put through $25,000 in the first two hours, and the royal put me way ahead, it was easy to commit to another few hours. I didn't know if we'd do it tonight or tomorrow, but we had plenty of time before we left on Sunday. "Count me in," I said.

"And can you set us up for a meal for two at Star Canyon for 10:30 for that Friday night? No smoking? And put a bottle of Bailey's, a large fruit basket, and five liters of Evian in our suite? I promise you we'll both play enough so you'll have no problem justifying any of that. I already have a Piazza Suite reserved in my name. Just add Chris's name as a 'share with.'" Annie seemed to have this system down to a tee.

Chris smiled. "Can do." He backed up a step to make way for the floorpeople. "It seems as though my colleagues want to give you some money. If you want to hit another royal tonight, that's okay too. Good night and continued good luck."

"Chris!" Annie called after he started to walk away, and both Chris and I looked up. "Host Chris, I mean. I'm tired, so I'm going to have player Chris drive me back to our room at the Golden Nugget. He'll play some more tomorrow, so don't check to verify that he kept his side of the deal until tomorrow night." Chris nodded and left.

After we were paid, I looked at my watch. "Do we cash out now? You said we had to make the amount even to get the full half-percent."

She checked. "It looks like 12 more hands. Then we'll cash out. But instead of going back to the Nugget, I'd like to walk across the street to the Mirage. My host there works evenings from six to two, so he's there now. I've heard they just changed their slot club. I want to make sure."

As we walked across the street, I remarked that we were now up for the trip. "It feels good. Especially because the only reason I was up was because of your generosity in giving me a full 50% of the tournament win. Now we're both up and I like it better that way."

"Me too, but don't spend too much time counting your money," Annie advised. "Every day it's a different amount and some days will be up and others down. You haven't gone through a losing streak yet, but you will. Just know that you're on the right path and enjoy the ride."

At the Mirage, we walked to the Club Mirage booth. Annie's host, Harry Sullivan, greeted us. When Annie inquired about the change in the slot club, Harry responded, "To earn the higher rate, you now have to play $25 or higher video poker machines or any slot machine, but if you do that we still return the same rate as we've done for years." Annie said we wanted to get a card for me anyway, but we weren't sure we'd play tonight.

"We can each afford that game financially," Annie told me. "But there's no way in the world you can emotionally handle the swings just yet. And I don't think I want to subsidize both of us on $25 machines. I think we better stick to the $5 game for now."

I agreed. "*Now* are we ready to go back to the Nugget?"

Annie smiled and grabbed my hand as she led me toward the door. "What's your hurry, Big Boy?"

"I've already collected on a financial jackpot tonight. I'm in the mood to go collect on another kind."

"Don't forget. You still owe me a rose."

"I certainly intend to keep my promise and get you the rose. But if I didn't, what would we do? Glue the hair back on?"

"No," she answered. "We'd just have to shave you down there. And I'd promise to try very hard not to let the razor slip."

"What color rose did you want?"

Saturday
March 18, 2000

We set the alarm for seven so we could join Bob and Shirley at the Mansion. We were supposed to meet them outside of Wolfgang Puck's restaurant and they'd escort us past the security station.

"Have you played at the MGM Grand?" I asked Annie.

"Never. I don't know of any 9/6 Jacks game there less than $25, and I didn't think the slot club paid all that much. But they must have something good to interest Bob. This could be educational."

"Do you know where Wolfgang Puck's is?" I asked.

"No. But I remember that there are overhead signs everywhere in the MGM giving directions. We'll find it easily enough."

When we got to the restaurant, Shirley greeted us with hugs. This surprised me a little, but who was I to complain? "Bob's up in the villa finishing an article, so I'm your tour guide. Get ready for a treat."

She walked us through a 15-foot-wide hallway. Nicely decorated, but nothing spectacular. Two security guards seated at a corner nodded at Shirley as we passed. "If they didn't recognize me, we wouldn't get any farther than here."

The hallway turned right. Now the furniture all looked like antiques, and every ten feet or so was a table with some orchids. We lingered at several of the orchids while Shirley enthusiastically shared what she knew about them.

We passed an open door on the right. "That's the restaurant and we have reservations for 9:30. You might want to peek in. It's pretty elaborate."

An understatement. There was so much to take in: the chandelier, the bar in front, the polished wood tables.

What caught my eye, though, was golden nautical rope going up several columns from floor to ceiling. "Regular, heavy-duty, nautical rope that was hand painted with 24-karat gold leaf is what I've been told," Shirley said.

I know 24-karat gold leaf when I see it. I estimated $250,000 worth for this one restaurant alone, though that could be low.

A man walked up to us and addressed Shirley pleasantly. "Good morning, Mrs. Dancer. Did you decide to come down a little early for breakfast?"

"No. We're still aiming for 9:30. It's just that we had to pass by the restaurant on the way to our villa and I'm showing it off to my friends."

"Very well. May I get you something to drink while you're looking? Perhaps a Mimosa or Bloody Mary? Or fresh orange juice maybe?"

"I think orange juice would hit the spot," said Shirley. She looked at us and we each agreed instantly.

When the waiter went off, I asked Shirley. "Do we tip him now? If so, I'd like to cover that."

"You don't need to. Bob and I take care of that at the end of our stay. But if handing him some money would make you feel better, go ahead."

At the back of the restaurant was a large walk-in wine cellar. "There's supposed to be a $9,000 bottle in there. I hope you're not thirsting after it. Our comps aren't quite at that level."

"Well, you're a pretty stingy host," I commented, "but we'll get over it." Annie elbowed me.

Leaving the restaurant, we went outdoors. Or so it seemed. We were in a 5-acre garden, with a greenhouse-style roof about five stories high—trees, flowers, benches, peace, with a huge fountain in the center. Three gardeners were tending the grounds. Including the two security men at the entrance, we'd seen about 10 Mansion employees, in about five different styles of uniforms, and no guests. This was an amazing place.

"Do you smell the citrus trees? They grow several

kinds in this atrium to purify the air. And now, I've got a puzzle for you," Shirley said as we crossed the courtyard. "Look at the hinges on the big doors we are going to enter and tell me whether we should push or pull. I hate trying to solve puzzles, but I like giving them to others. Hee hee."

The door didn't have any visible hinges that provided a clue, to me anyway. "I'm going to guess that we pull on the door," I told her.

"I don't know," Annie said. "But I agree it's a fine puzzle."

"You're right, Chris. It pulls rather than pushes." Shirley said. "I'll let you do it, because it's heavy. There's a lot more to see here, but now let's go up to the villa and fetch Bob." We walked under a huge chandelier, original artwork on the walls, and rooms and hallways going off in several directions.

Shirley led us to an elevator and inserted a magnetic room key. "This elevator is for three villas only. There are two villas one flight up and the entire top floor is a super-large villa. We've already passed a few of these banks of dedicated elevators, and some ground-level villas each have their own private swimming pool. We are only at the lowest level of villa. But it's still far far nicer than anywhere else we've ever been."

The elevator opened out onto a wide hallway, decorated in antiques, with several arrays of fresh flowers. And this was only for the enjoyment of the occupants of two villas? The villa itself was maybe twice the size of the Tower Suite. To the right was a huge sitting area with elaborate, one-of-a-kind furniture, and more original artwork on the walls. A 15-foot dining-room table was included. A huge fruit bowl full of exotic fruits and a freshly made cake that hadn't been touched. Shirley took us out onto a 30-feet-long balcony overlooking the atrium. We passed a full kitchen on the way to the bedroom.

The bedroom was as big as the sitting area, dominated by a poster bed. It hadn't been made up since Bob and Shirley awoke, but the down comforter seemed twice as thick as the one at the Golden Nugget. At a large desk, Bob was typing away on his laptop.

"Hey Chris, Annie. Glad you could join us. I'm just finishing up here and I'll need about three minutes. Why don't you let Shirley show you the bathroom? I suspect you've never seen anything like it."

Really? The bathroom? What could be so spectacular? I soon found out.

It was quite large, mainly constructed of marble and granite. The Jacuzzi was actually smaller than the one at the Golden Nugget, more of a one-person relaxing tub, but it had a tilted high-definition television, so you could watch while you were soaking. There was also a small TV over by the magnified lighted shaving mirror. I guess one couldn't be expected to survive with only one television in one's bathroom.

"The floor is heated, as is the towel rack," Shirley bubbled, relishing her tour-guide role. "You can easily fit five people into the shower, if you're the friendly type, and please don't consider that as an invitation, and it includes a sauna. The robes you have at the Nugget aren't bad, but they don't compare to these. We get four complete sets of Bvlgari toiletries each day and they all go in my suitcase."

For breakfast, we went down to the restaurant and sat at a table that was in the "outdoor" courtyard. "We could have had them serve breakfast in the villa upstairs, but we didn't know what you wanted. Plus, I love this atrium," Shirley told us.

Although I ordered my normal omelet with dry rye toast and coffee, it was a whole different experience here. It was a marble rye and the coffee was probably a French-roast blend. The silverware was real silver. The place settings were fine china.

"Thank you so much for inviting us," Annie said. "I had no idea something like this even existed in Las Vegas. This is really its own little world. Wow!"

"Until four months ago, the Tower Suites were probably the nicest ones we'd been in—although we've been in some very nice suites at the Mirage and Venetian as well," Bob said. "This is our third visit to the Mansion and we're still blown away by it."

"Are you comfortable telling us what games you play here, Bob?" Annie asked.

"Sure. No problem. It's just ordinary $25 9/6 Jacks."

"I've heard the slot club pays only 0.39%, which adds up to 99.93%. Obviously you're here and staying in the Mansion must be worth a huge amount psychologically, but I'm surprised you're playing a game that adds up to so little," Annie pressed. "And if it's none of my business, that's okay too."

"It's a very complicated system here at the MGM Grand. I'm still learning about it and it keeps changing. Are you comfortable playing $25 machines?"

"Funny, Chris and I were just talking about that last night. For now we've decided to stick to the $5 machines, but it wouldn't surprise me if we moved up relatively soon."

"Okay. When you're ready for the bigger machine, ask me again and I'll tell you. For now, just know that I think it's a *lot* more lucrative than the Golden Nugget, which has a generous club of its own."

"Do they have any $5 machines worth playing?" I asked. "Right now, even these make me nervous, but I suspect I'll get over it."

"They have $5 8/5 Bonus progressive machines. This is a game that starts out at 99.17% when the royal is at $20,000. When the royal increases to about $24,000, it returns the same as 9/6 Jacks, although it's much harder to play. Usually the royal is less than that, so overall it's not such a good deal."

"I saw Archie yesterday playing 8/5 Jacks or Better progressive at the Nugget. He said there were quite a few adjustments to make. Is 8/5 Bonus as tough as 8/5 Jacks?" I asked.

"Archie knows what he's talking about. The two games are similar in many respects," Bob said, "but most of the breakpoint numbers are different. Still, if you could learn to play one of the progressive games well, you could learn to play the other."

Shirley had her own story to tell. "Check out the floor to the restaurant when you leave. It's all Italian marble tiles, hand-laid by Italian artisans. Apparently, it took a few months longer than they expected and the workers were getting testy, wanting to go home, needing to work around the gold-leaf appliers, the air conditioner sometimes needed to be turned off, and what not."

"I can see how they could get testy," I said. "What then?"

"They started regularly cursing in Italian. The head man here, whose real name is Bob, but I'll call him John because I don't want you to think this happened to my Bob, gave them instructions every day through an interpreter. And he was constantly on their case telling them he needed the job done perfectly and needed it yesterday. Understandably, many of the curses were directed at John—or maybe John's mother.

"Anyway, when they were finished, John started talking to them *in Italian*. He'd understood every curse, even the ones about him and the moral character of his mother. I think those are fighting words in Italian."

"Oh dear," said Annie. "What happened then?"

"John let them sweat about it for a little, then broke out laughing. He said he understood the working conditions were sometimes unpleasant, thanked them for a job well done, and forgave them for the insults."

That seemed to be a good time to go our separate ways. We thanked Bob and Shirley profusely and they both walked us to the entrance of the Mansion, with Shirley pointing out a few more things she'd skipped on the way in.

Saturday
March 18, 2000

Annie and I decided to leave the Lexus parked at the MGM and walk up to the Venetian. "If we run out of time on the way back," Annie told me, "we can take the monorail. It cuts off about half the walking and drops us off right near the car."

As soon as we got to the Triple Play machine, a cocktail waitress came by and I ordered two waters. It's impossible not to notice that these ladies must have been hired for the size of their implants, which the uniforms are meant to display and accentuate. When the waitress set the water down in front of us, my eyes were inexorably drawn to her chest. I wasn't horny. I didn't want this woman. But not looking would have been impossible.

I looked over at Annie and she seemed very angry. "Enjoying yourself?" she asked bitterly. I recognized the set of her jaw. I decided not to comment, hoping her black mood would disappear as fast as it arose.

It didn't. Previously, each time Annie got angry over something that seemed a trifling matter to me, she was fine again in a few minutes. This time though, she sat next to me and followed the game, but she didn't say anything more.

It took me two hours to finish my points. Although our score went up and down, we lost about $2,000 over that time. The game was interesting, though I felt tense with Annie not talking. It's a very different feeling having three chances at every hand. Starting with two pair, for example, it's still 4-out-of 47 chances to complete turn this into a full house, now I had three separate 4-out-of-47 chances.

Finally, I asked her a video poker question, hoping it

would bring her out of her funk. "Does that mean we now have 12 out of 47 chances?"

"No. I'm pretty sure the Binomial Theorem is the appropriate mathematical tool to figure it out, but I've never done it," Annie answered. "It shouldn't be too hard using Excel on your computer. I can show you when we get home."

Now she seemed to be the same old Annie. Like the two hours of gloom had never happened.

"Between us we're about even for the weekend," I observed.

"Maybe financially, if this turned out to be your last weekend of play ever," Annie replied, "but you now have invitations at both the Nugget and the Venetian, and each of them are worth hundreds of dollars. Plus, now that you've seen the Mansion and listened to Bob talk about $25 machines, you're probably not so nervous about playing $5 machines as you were."

"You're right," I admitted. "I guess we're *way* ahead from playing in Las Vegas this weekend."

"By the time we get back to your car, I'll be hungry. We've earned plenty of comps at the Venetian, and of course an unlimited amount at the Golden Nugget. I also have some across the street at the Mirage, but I think I want to save them."

"Why?"

"When you play at the level we do, you generate essentially unlimited food comps as long as you keep playing. But with the new slot club at the Mirage, it's possible I'm done there. So whatever comps I have there I'd like to hoard—to be spent on something I can't get elsewhere. Today, we can get good meals here or the Golden Nugget, so it seems a waste to spend limited comps on lunch."

"I see what you mean. I'm not tired of the food at the Golden Nugget by any means. And since that's already paid for with the room comp, I'd rather not touch my comps at the Venetian, so I have more next time."

"Okay. I vote for the Carson Street Grill. Let's start back."

"And let's stop by the florist shop on the way. I owe you a rose."

"Oh yes. I hadn't been thinking about that, but I would have remembered. Smart of you not to forget." She was completely back to her normal self, as near as I could tell: clever, hugging me, enjoying life.

"After lunch," she told me, "I want to rest before the party."

"A 'Class A' rest?" I asked.

"If you like, my insatiable one. Your wish is my command."

"Ooh," I sighed, "are you sure you don't want to rest *before* lunch?"

"Yes, I'm sure. You want to make sure that my moans are from pleasure and not hunger, don't you?"

"Do you want a chivalrous answer or an honest one?"

I pulled the car into the florist shop. My plan was that Annie should grab a rose and then we could rush back to the suite for the good stuff. But Annie was of a different opinion. She smelled several flowers and compared all sorts of features from one to another. She probably sensed my impatience. She came over and said, "Relax, darling. I'll see to it that you're completely satisfied back at the room whether we go now or in 15 minutes—whether we eat lunch first or not. Promise. But I *like* flower shops. I just want to take in the experience. Okay?"

What could I say? I was embarrassed for being so selfish, but worse, for being *caught* at it. "I'm sorry, Annie. Take as long as you like. And did you see these yellow and red ones over next to those gladiolas? They have a really unusual color combination."

Annie couldn't decide among the prettiest ones, so we picked out several. Before we got in the car again, she gave me a big hug and said, "Don't be too contrite about wanting me so bad. I *like* it that way. That's a big part of the reason why you're here, you know."

I felt better immediately. "Yeah, I do know that. That's a big reason I'm here too. And I can even keep a lid on it until we eat."

At the restaurant, we both ordered chicken Caesar salads. "What did you think of the Mansion?" I asked Annie.

"Awesome. I'm glad we got blown away by the Tower Suites *before* we saw them. That way, we were blown away *twice*, instead of just once."

"Do you think we'll ever play enough at the MGM to be invited to stay there?"

"It's possible, but you've got to learn to accept a lot more risk first. A $25 machine means that sometimes you'll lose $20,000 or $30,000 during a weekend. And it seems to me they won't let you stay in the Mansion unless you play these machines a *lot*. Which means that sometimes you'll have those losses back to back."

"Wow! The thought of a $5,000 loss scares me. I can't even comprehend one for $50,000. Do you think I'll ever get there?"

"I don't know. We can gradually approach it and see how it goes. Maybe you can take 50% of your action in two weeks instead of 10%. A couple more trips, you'll take all of your action. Maybe a few after that, you can subsidize my play. I don't need your financial help, but we should find out what that much risk does to your psyche."

"You think the MGM slot club is good enough?"

"Oh sure. Bob didn't tell us the details, but clearly he thinks it is. If and when you're ready to play such a big game, we can find out the finer points then."

We finished our salads, signed the check, and left the tip. "I don't need to stay at the Mansion to be happy, Chris. I wouldn't turn it down, of course, but if it scares the hell out of you to play that big, we don't need it."

Fifteen minutes later, during our shower, Annie asked, "Any special requests? Or are you willing to just take it as it comes?"

"I'm willing. I'm willing. It's better for me when you come first. So what would *you* like?"

"I'm in the mood for some regular meat-and-potatoes loving. Let's go."

It doesn't have to be fancy to be good. Afterwards, she said, "Now rest up so you can take me dancing tonight."

"Anything you want," I muttered as I drifted off into contented sleep.

After napping for a few hours, we got up to dress for the awards banquet. Annie had another new dress, emerald green this time and absolutely stunning. I was downstairs practicing *WinPoker* when she came down to model. She spun and her full skirt floated gently outward. "I like my new necklace, but I already had the dress and the colors don't go with each other. Next time, I'll have an outfit where I can show off the accessories you made for me."

"That'll be fine."

"You like the dress?"

"I don't know yet," I said. "I need to check something. Come here." She did, with a smile, and I moved my hands underneath her skirt and kept them there. "I need to see what kind of underwear you have on. You know, for modesty reasons, in case your skirt flies up while we're dancing."

"Oh yes," she agreed. "I understand. Strictly for modesty reasons. I'm so lucky to have you assist me in this way. But you've been checking for over two minutes now. Thoroughness is a virtue, but just how long does this modesty check take?"

"I'm not sure. I'll have to let you know." But I removed my hands anyway and kissed her warmly. "Annie, you look lovely. I'm sure you'll be the prettiest lady there tonight."

"That's the plan," she agreed. "Now let's go down and dance the night away."

The band was the same as the month before and they nodded like they recognized us as we walked onto the dance floor. We danced the half-song that was remaining after we got there and stayed on the floor in case the next song was a suitable tempo. There were four men in the band and a female singer. All of them were probably Annie's and my age or older, except for this young black horn player who was exceptional. I'm not sure who the band leader was. Although the woman sang lead on over half the songs, each of the men took a turn too, while the others sang backup. The horn player didn't sing, but I remembered from a month ago that he did a dead-on Kenny G solo.

The next song was "Under the Boardwalk," a good beat for us. Dan Williams came to the dance floor and did a cha cha with Sandy, the lady we'd met yesterday. We were the only two couples on the floor, but it was early; I expected more dancers after a drink or two. Annie and I'd learned three more 10-second patterns than we knew a month ago, plus I remembered the swivels this time, so now it took a little longer for us to go through our entire inventory of steps. But we still could do them all a couple of times in every dance. I figured I'd have to take lessons for at least another six months before I could go through an entire dance without repeating myself.

After the song, Myron took the stage and welcomed everyone to the party. He told us that while they usually have a catered meal, tonight was going to be buffet style and that they were going to call us up table by table. "In the meantime, sit back, relax, have a drink, and enjoy yourselves. We're happy you're here tonight."

Jim and Sandy were at our table. We introduced ourselves to everyone else and somebody brought up scores. With both of us being a little under 66,000, Annie and I had the top scores at the table. "We're hoping for a thousand apiece, but think that's probably out of reach," I said. "We'll see."

"We have 61,000," said Jim, "We might just sneak past the cutoff for $200 instead of $100."

"We have 53,000," said a man we just met named Tex. "The big advantage to a score like that there's no mystery about how much you're gonna get."

His wife muttered, "Big advantage. Huh! I'd take the uncertainty any day," and everyone laughed.

Tex seemed to enjoy being the center of attention for a moment. "People always think I was born in Texas because of my name. But it's just not true." Everyone waited patiently for the punch line to what seemed like an oft-told joke. "I was actually born in Louisiana, but I refuse to let people call me Louise."

Tex's wife looked like she'd heard that one a million times, but Tex got enough chuckles that he continued. "My wife and I went to hear Jerry Seinfield at Caesars Palace last night. We were at a table with another couple. I put out my hand and said, 'Howdy. Where y'all from?'

"The woman looked at me and gave me a very snotty, 'We're from a place where we don't end sentences with prepositions.'

"So I replied, 'Excuse me for not realizing that. In that case, where y'all from, *bitch*?'"

We all laughed and Tex seemed primed to provide the entertainment all night, but apparently decided that three laughs in one minute were enough. The band broke into "Moon River" and Dan came over. He looked like he was about to ask my permission to ask Annie to dance, but she was already on her feet and walking toward him. My permission, obviously, was superfluous.

Afterwards, the band broke into a song we could swing to, so Annie and I danced again. When we got back to the table, everybody was gone. "Time for the buffet, I guess," Annie concluded.

We got our food and I kept one ear on the music. If it was close to a swing tempo, we were on the floor, having a good time. One time when we returned to our seats, Tex toasted us with his glass of beer, "Mighty fine dancin', folks."

Sandy leaned over and said. "You've convinced us. We're going to take dance lessons."

"If your experience is anything like mine," I said, "you'll be glad you did."

The guitar player in the band said, "And now we have a very special guest. Please turn toward the doorway on your right and help me welcome Kelly the Rabbit!" The band struck up the "Bunny Hop" and in hopped Kelly in a bright-yellow floppy-eared rabbit costume with a big cotton tail, sort of reminiscent of pajamas a two-year-old might wear. The Bunny Hop is a conga-style line dance where you kick to the right twice, kick to the left twice, then hop once forward, once backward, and three hops forward. Kelly was doing it solo, but he had all the moves down and it took him maybe five verses to hop his way to the front of the room. Everyone in the room was laughing and many were giving him a standing ovation.

Handed a microphone, Kelly said, "If Hugh Hefner calls and wants me to be a bunny in his mansion, tell him I already have a job that pays better." He then fired off a few one-liners.

"How do bunny rabbits surf the Web?" When nobody got an answer quickly, he said, "They use a *hare net*." The drummer gave Kelly a rim shot while the crowd groaned. Next he took on a pseudo-Oriental accent and said, "Confucious bunny say that anyone who want fat rabbit to pay him prize money should make a point to laugh at jokes."

Kelly then asked, "What kind of music do bunny rappers listen to?"

Somebody yelled out "Hip hop music!" The crowd applauded whoever got one of Kelly's riddles.

Kelly turned to the band leader and said, "Take a note. Last question too easy.

"How about this one? When bunnies want to get across town quickly, how do they do it?" Nobody knew this one, so he said, "They use the *rabbit transit system*." Another rim shot. More laughs and groans. "Confucious bunny also say that anyone who thinks jokes will get better probably mistaken."

I looked around the room. Everyone's attention was riveted on Kelly. He was being booed and heckled in a way that indicated he was well-loved by all.

"And now for the *last* bunny joke ..." Kelly paused,

allowing those who wanted to applaud this to do so. Quite a few did, although just as many laughed. He saw a food server and said, "This is so stressful. Do you have any *hare tonic* you could bring me?"

The woman looked confused as the crowd laughed. She shrugged with an expression that said, "I'll bring you whatever you want, but I have no idea what that is."

But Kelly didn't skip a beat, "Maybe a *rabbit punch* would be nice." More laughter. The woman handed him a bottle of water. Kelly took a swig and quipped, "Close enough." Finally he posed, "What kind of information is found on a bunny rabbit's family tree?" Nobody could figure it out in time. "Their *heritage*."

People applauded Kelly's little monologue. Henny Youngman he wasn't, but he certainly put people into a good mood. Not that he needed to do much to get them into a good mood. We were all there to collect money.

As he had done last time, Kelly first introduced the hosts, the event crew, the band, whom he called "Janice and the Springboards" this time, Dan Williams, and Phyllis "Boom Boom" Bryant. And just before he gave out the money, he introduced the "two funny bunnies of the Golden Nugget, Myron Kuchman and Bruce Herman."

"Everybody here won money tonight," Kelly announced, "but the ten names I'm going to call up front won more than the rest of you. In tenth place, with a score of 66,320, and worth $1,000, we have Sam Arden."

While we waited for Sam to go up, I turned to Annie. "We were both under 66,000. Oh well."

Sam wasn't there, apparently, so Kelly continued. "This is very good. All unclaimed money goes to a great cause. Specifically, the Big Bunny Retirement Fund. In ninth place, with 160 points more and also worth $1,000, we have John and Suki Yamamoto. John and Suki live in Hawaii and are regular Golden Nugget visitors. It looks like finally Suki got lucky." John and Suki were effusive winners and they came up and had their pictures taken with Myron, Bruce, and Kelly with a weird expression on his face.

Kelly announced the rest of the winners, then had everyone else collect their money in groups based on the initial letter of their last names. While he called letters, the band kept playing and Annie and I danced as many of the songs as we could. Annie and I each got the $500 we were expecting. Then the party was over. It was still early and we'd napped and eaten. "What now," I asked.

"Let's drive to Treasure Island and explore," Annie suggested. "I haven't checked their machines in a while. They might have added something."

At Treasure Island they had plenty of 9/6 Jacks machines for $5 and higher. Checking out the High Limit Slot room was the first thing she did, but she then checked each unoccupied machine at every bar.

"Do you play here?" I asked. "Seems they have the same games as the places you do play and it's not a bad hotel. Not as nice as the Mirage, but certainly acceptable. I remember Bob and Shirley saying they played here during their courtship."

"They cut their slot club return in half not long ago. Now it's only 0.33%, and when you add that to the 99.54% of 9/6 Jacks, there's still a house advantage."

"Do they have promotions like the other casinos?"

"Sure. But not enough to make up for the lesser slot club. As long as other casinos have juicier slot clubs, I'll play with the better odds. If nobody had a better club, Treasure Island would be acceptable, because the promotions have value. But just barely. A 0.33% difference is $50 an hour difference on a $5 machine. Playing eight hours each trip means that it costs an extra $400 to come here than play at the Golden Nugget. Why bother?"

"I noticed you checking out the Deuces Wild games. What pay schedule were you looking for?"

"The one that returns 16 for five-of-a-kind and 10 for a straight flush. It returns a little more than 9/6 Jacks and sometimes you'll find it in a casino that just reduced its slot club. If that game were added here, it would just about halve the difference between the old slot club rate and the new one, and would put the casino in the running again. I didn't find any this time, but I walk the floor of several casinos every few months. Since it's still early, let's check out Caesars Palace. On the way out of town tomorrow morning, I'll want to check out Bally's and the Luxor, unless you have any objections."

"Not me," I said. "I'm a sponge for new knowledge about this game."

Back in the suite, we cleaned up and climbed into bed. She snuggled up and kissed me. "This was a perfect day. I'm going to want you to nail me big time in the morning. If you're up to it again tonight too, that's fine, but I don't think I can come again today."

"I don't know if I can either," I told her, "but dancing with the prettiest girl in the whole place excited me. Don't know where we'll end up, but there's only one good way to find out."

I lay on top of her with my mouth on her left breast and my fingers gently massaging each of her buttocks. As I moved my mouth to the other breast, she started rubbing her fingers through my hair and began pushing herself against me.

Then she started directing my head southward. I lingered a bit at her belly button, where she squirmed because it tickled, and kept pushing. When my mouth reached her shaven pubis, she stopped pushing and held my head exactly where she wanted it to be. I was familiar enough with her sexuality to know that she was very close. So I just kept doing what I was doing and let her move against me until, contrary to her earlier prediction, she reached her goal.

After a minute for her to recover, I moved up, covered myself with Vaseline, and eased into her. She lay still while I enjoyed myself. She gently held me and whispered, "God, Chris! I can't believe what you do to me. I've never had so many orgasms in my life."

"Me neither," I said after having my own.

Sunday
March 19, 2000

In the morning we did it again before breakfast. Nothing spectacular, but even ordinary sex in Las Vegas was very special.

We stopped at a couple of casinos on the way out of town to check out the games. Annie found that nothing significant had changed since the last time she'd scouted. We hit the freeway about one, which was early. Although a considerable number of cars shared the road, it wasn't as crowded as last time.

"If we wanted to come here more often," I asked Annie, "are there enough good games and promotions?"

"Before we even consider it, I think you need to learn another game or two. Probably your best bet is 10/7 Double Bonus. I have Dancer's report on that game at my condo. Take it and study it."

"Is it much different than Jacks or Better?"

"Probably two-thirds of the hands are played the same, but there are some major differences. It's a much more difficult game than Jacks or Better, but with the report, the computer, and your study habits, you'll be fine."

"Does the game pay as well as Jacks or Better?"

"Better, actually. It returns more than 100% all by itself, so the slot clubs at the casinos that have the game don't pay as much. And the casinos that have these games aren't as glamorous as the ones on the Strip. I wouldn't take you to the Orleans for one of our first Class A weekends, but it'd certainly be a satisfactory destination some of the time—especially during double points."

"You also have a Dancer report on Deuces Wild. Should I learn that game too?"

"Probably not, but take it anyway. Deuces Wild returns well over 100%, but you can only find it for quarters and only in Las Vegas. Playing quarter Deuces perfectly, even with a good slot club and double points, your earnings potential is $10 an hour or less. Since you have the bankroll and knowledge to play $5 games that return $30 an hour even before you include the value of promotions, you don't need to learn Full Pay Deuces Wild.

"After you've mastered Double Bonus and have played it for a couple hundred hours, you should probably read what Dancer has to say about Full Pay Deuces Wild, then construct your own strategy for the version of Deuces Wild with a pay schedule 16-10-4-4-3-2-1. I'll give you my strategy for that game, but it's not perfect. Mine is better than the strategies published by anybody else so far, but if you're going to be playing for real money, you'll probably want to do better."

"Why that game?"

"I think it's the coming thing in Las Vegas. It returns 99.73%, but you'll probably see it as additional casinos reduce their slot club."

"What else should I be doing if I want to keep getting better at this game?"

"You've got to be reading what other people write. Dancer writes about video poker in *Casino Player* and *Strictly Slots*. You should also look at some video poker bulletin boards on the Internet, supported by video poker players who send each other emails back and forth. What you do is read them all at first to discover who's knowledgeable and who isn't. Then you read only the ones who know what they're talking about. Then only about subjects you're interested in. Video poker in Mississippi probably isn't relevant to us at this point, so no matter who's telling how good or bad the games are in Biloxi or Vicksburg, it's not worth your time. But keep these emails in a folder and if you ever decide to go there, you'll have some insight about what you'll find."

"Anything else?"

"Nothing that I can think of now," she replied. "But

tackling Double Bonus will keep you busy for weeks. It's a complicated game."

"Okay then, I've got another question. I guess I've accepted that you lose most of the time you don't hit a royal, but that when you hit a royal you profit enough to make up for a lot of losing sessions. I hit a royal, but we didn't end up winners. What happened?"

"A couple of different things happened. First of all, you were playing on a Triple Play machine, where royals aren't worth as much. They still pay you 4,000 coins, to be sure, but your initial bet is 15 coins rather than five. On a single-line machine, the payoff is 800 for one. On a Triple Play machine, the payoff is only a third of that. This is balanced by the fact that on Triple Play machines the royals show up three times more quickly. Over thousands of hours it all works out the same, but during the short run the peaks and valleys on a $2 Triple Play machine are generally smaller than those on a $5 single-line machine.

"Another way to look at it is you hit the royal on a $2 machine and took the loss on a $5 machine. What happens on the largest-denomination machine you play generally swamps what happens on the smaller-denomination machines. This is a normal situation whenever you play machines of different sizes."

"I must say that if my professors in college had been as pretty as you, I'd be a perpetual student."

Annie smiled, reached over, and turned on some music. We rode quietly the rest of the way.

When we got home, she told me she needed to refocus on work, so it'd be best if she slept alone. But she gave me Dancer's Double Bonus report. "It might help you fall asleep," she told me.

Wednesday
March 22, 2000

At dance class we worked on hip rolls again. It wasn't quite so intimidating this time, as everyone had had a week to get used to it. But this week, in addition to practicing the same sugar push as we had last week, Phil taught us how to add the hip roll at the end of an underarm turn. That was when I realized that dance steps are sort of like building blocks. Part of being a good dancer is mastering each of the basic components, then putting them together in various combinations.

On the drive back, Annie told me she wanted to check how my Gambling Log 2000 was coming.

"Are you sure you're not an auditor for the IRS?"

"Actually, that's one of the reasons it's important to make sure we're doing it consistently," she told me. "I think you should be entering all of the results where your slot club card was entered, whether or not I was bankrolling the action."

"Is there a big difference whether it's entered on my gambling log or yours?"

"Probably not," she told me, "but right now you're plus, thanks to the $8,000 royal. If we both enter it, then we're going to end up with more taxable income than we need to. If you have it all under your name, then the slot club records provided by the casino will be consistent with your records. You probably won't be audited, but you may be, especially with the sale of your business this year. You want to be able to pass an audit if it comes."

"Right, and that *is* how I entered the records," I told her. "I noticed it was *fun* to write down plus scores in the gambling log. Recording that I lost at the Golden Nugget wasn't particularly enjoyable. Recording that I won at the Venetian was pretty cool."

"I know," Annie said. "For me, I have to make a point to do it every time, win or lose. When I started out recording my results, I found that sometimes I'd keep losses in my head in some sort of a to-be-entered-later compartment. It was very easy to let these go long enough that eventually, I wasn't sure any more. I then had try to reconstruct the results and I was nervous about being caught by the IRS."

"Have you ever been audited for gambling?"

"Once, but not recently," she answered. "I'm not positive it's true, but rumor has it that all the W-2G records blew up in the Oklahoma City explosion a few years ago. Plus, the past couple of years, the IRS has been spending so much extra time getting preparing for the Y2K problem that it hasn't been concerned about auditing gamblers. The consensus over the Internet is that this free ride is about to change."

"Did you enter any fudge factor on your tax returns to take advantage of this relaxed scrutiny?"

"Not me," Annie said with a laugh. "I'm pretty sure I handle my taxes more scrupulously than many other people do. It's not so much that I'm such an honest virtuous person. It's mostly that I'm a chicken and hate the idea of being caught and punished."

"But if they weren't auditing gamblers, didn't that reduce the likelihood of being caught?"

"Yes, if the rumor was correct. But it's impossible to know if it *was* correct, plus I didn't hear it until after the fact."

When it was time for bed, Annie was back to her available-but-not-active mode. I didn't understand it completely, but it didn't seem to be a problem that needed fixing. Having frequent sex with a beautiful woman, even though she might be passive sometimes, clearly wasn't the worst thing that could happen to a guy.

Saturday
March 25, 2000

Richard had requested I go hiking with him—guys only and not too tough—because he had things he wanted to discuss with me now that the sale of the business had finally gone through. I told Annie that we could go out to dinner tonight, but I'd be spending the day with Richard.

I decided to take him to Point Mugu State Park, about 20 miles up the coast from Santa Monica, a 15,000-acre chunk of the Santa Monica Mountains immediately adjacent to the Pacific Ocean. Although the park contains some challenging trails, it also has long stretches of essentially flat woodlands. It's peaceful and relatively unused.

As soon as we started driving, he showed me his shoulder holster. "I've got a Glock 17. It's almost the same as the military-issue Glock 18, but not quite. There've been some lunatics in these hills preying on hikers sometimes. I want to be prepared. Anyone who messes with us will be sorry."

I'd never heard of lunatics in these specific hills, and I strongly preferred that Richard leave his gun at home, but arguing about it wouldn't do any good.

We got on the Santa Monica Freeway headed west, which would become Pacific Coast Highway heading north along the shore.

"I think Meg's cheating on me," Richard came right out and said it. "I don't know what to do about it."

Uh oh! This was not a discussion I wanted to get into, with or without a precision pistol between us. Still, part of being a brother and friend means that you're available to each other whenever you're needed. For now, I didn't say anything and he kept talking.

"I don't know for sure. But I think so. You two ever

made it with each other?" he asked nonchalantly. No beating around the bush today! He'd had to have been planning this question for a long time. Maybe this was why he brought the gun.

"Absolutely not!" I told him emphatically. "I haven't even fantasized about Meg since you two were married, what, eighteen years ago now? At the time it was less than a year after we fought over Rosalind Meacham. Remember her?"

Richard nodded as I continued. "I learned that lesson well. When it comes to women, Richard, you don't share. You'll never have to worry about me in that regard.

"Plus, Meg's like a sister to me now. Believe me, I'm immune to her charms. A lot of sexual attraction is exploring what's new and different, and I've known Meg almost half my life. She is definitely *not* new and different to me at this point."

Richard didn't say anything for several miles. Trying to figure out if I was telling him the truth, I suppose. Although I didn't foresee this conversation at the time, I was now enormously relieved I'd turned Meg down both times she threw herself at me. Even though I was telling the complete truth, I was still sweating. No telling how I'd feel had I been lying. And whether I was telling the truth or not wasn't as important as to whether Richard *believed* I was telling the truth.

"What makes you think she's messing around?" I asked. "Have you seen overt clues or do you just have a feeling?"

"It's a feeling. What really makes me suspicious is that she's tickled pink to be working for her father now rather than me. I think she knows it'll be easier now for her to step out undetected."

"Has it ever occurred to you, my dear older brother," I asked him gently, "that working for you hasn't been a bed of roses for her? You're a control freak, you know, and when you're around, you're the iron-fisted boss. You look at every guy in the world as a potential home wrecker.

I would think that I'm the guy you could trust most in the world about anything, and you're even suspicious of me! You've had her under your thumb for so long, I don't wonder that she's relieved to be out from under that pressure."

"You think that's all it is then?"

"I don't know. I've never seen her with any guy other than you. I've always felt the reason she drinks too much is because of the grip you have on her. She's never said anything like that to me directly, and it's just a guess on my part. I might be totally wrong," I told him. "It's hard to know all the reasons somebody else does anything."

"Sounds to me like you're defending her," Richard told me sourly.

"Why shouldn't I? She definitely pulled her weight at GGG. She worked long hours and was excellent with the customers. You couldn't have made the sales she did. Neither could I. Without her and her father, there wouldn't have been GGG to start with. But don't get me wrong. I'm your brother and friend and will remain so whatever happens between you and Meg."

"If Meg and I split, would you remain friends with her?" Richard asked.

"I didn't know you were even thinking about splitting, and if so, I'm sorry. I haven't given that possibility a single moment's thought. There's no way she and I will ever become romantic friends whether or not you're still in the picture, but if she wanted me to visit once a year or so? Why not? Like I said, she's been like a sister to me—especially since Ike and I are so close. And whatever differences you two are experiencing have nothing to do with me."

When we arrived at the park, I tried to change the subject. I didn't want a depressed Richard on my hands all day, especially a depressed *armed* Richard, if I could help it. "Kind of opposite to your situation, I suppose, but I'm getting in rather deeply with Annie." Fortunately, he bit.

"You mentioned her to us just after Christmas. Things progressing nicely since then?"

"Very. It wouldn't surprise me if you got to be a best man in the next year or so."

"Really? You never told me that with Paula and you were with her for a long time. What's this Annie look like?"

"She's a few years younger than me. Divorced. Petite. Trim. Red hair combed back away from her face. Laughs like an angel."

"Does petite and trim mean she's got tiny tits?"

"They're smallish, I suppose, but proportional to her body type. I think they're rather shapely. Not deficient in any manner from my point of view, and I suggest that's the only point of view that matters in this because you, for one, are never going to see them up close and personal."

"Okay," he conceded. "I guess Meg's big ones haven't brought me any everlasting happiness. What do you guys do together other than enjoy her smallish tits?"

"We both work out a lot, and we've come up into these mountains several times, and we're learning West Coast Swing together, and we've been to Vegas three times and are planning to go again next weekend."

"Is she smart enough to play blackjack?"

"Actually, she's a master at it. Not only does she count cards, she keeps two or three separate counts going at the same time. But she's taught me video poker, and it's a much better game."

"What makes it better? You've always told me that machines are all luck and the only people who play them are too dumb to play blackjack. Sounds to me like this petite and trim red-haired honey has got you pussy-whipped."

"Maybe so," I said, ignoring his bait. "She's definitely convinced me to look at gambling differently. She's a mathematical genius, and uses computers, and wins. Our strategy is simple enough that I can play 100% perfectly, although it took me 20 or 30 hours of reading and practice to memorize it the first time and I still regularly review it. The casinos throw enough extra stuff at you that the knowledgeable players actually have an advantage."

"You going to move to Vegas and make your fortune?"

"I'm not ready to become a full-time gambler," I told him. "But I wouldn't mind moving to Vegas and doing it more often than I do now. Right now the only thing keeping me in L.A. is Annie, who's got a good job and has given me no sign that she wants to quit. Now that the store's gone, I can set up my gem business anywhere. All selling on eBay requires, assuming you can produce something to sell, is access to a computer and a post office. I'm sure jewelry stores in Vegas would sell my stuff.

"The lease on my condo is up in three weeks, so I've got to come to some decision quickly. I think Annie and I are ready to live with each other, somewhere, although I haven't asked her specifically. Maybe tonight's a good time to do that. And I'll find out how committed she is to staying in L.A."

We chatted some more as we hiked. Richard told me his teaching degree was still considered valid, but he needed to take some refresher courses in a variety of subjects, because techniques had changed a bit. It'd take him about a year of full-time class work to get his certification up to date, and he thought the classes offered at UCLA Extension would qualify. He was meeting next week with the Los Angeles Unified School District people to see what his chances for employment were once he finished a year more of classes. "Pretty good, I think. The school district is losing teachers faster than they're recruiting them."

"So you'll teach general education elementary school?"

"Probably. I'd like to teach drama, but this close to Hollywood, drama teachers are a dime a dozen."

"Can you live on what they'll pay you?" I asked.

"Oh, sure. Remember, even after taxes, Meg and I'll together receive well over half a million dollars from the sale of GGG, and we had some money from before. Plus, her dad will probably leave us a bunch. How much do you need? I bitch about her sometimes, but I don't think

I'll ever leave her. I might kill her, but I'll never divorce her," he told me with a smile, apparently proud of his little joke.

"Richard, you're going to get a piece of brotherly advice whether you want it or not. I know you well enough to know that was a joke. But you own guns and have a well-known jealous streak. It's not smart to kid about such things. If she ever winds up dead in circumstances that are anywhere near suspicious, statements like that could come back to haunt you."

"Point taken," he said. "And you're right that it was strictly a joke."

"And as long as you're taking my advice, you're going to need to clean up your act to succeed as a teacher. Your mouth is far too comfortable around 4-letter words for most schools to tolerate. And evaluating your female students on the basis of bra size is about as dumb as it gets."

"You're right, but knock it off. I've had about as much of you telling me what to do as I can take for one day."

With that, we decided to head back toward home, stopping off at a seafood restaurant on the water in Malibu for a late lunch. Although it started off with a sweaty subject, the day ended up pleasantly. We hadn't had many of the "brother-bonding" days since Richard's marriage and we promised to do it more in the future.

Saturday
March 25, 2000

When I got home, I listened to my phone messages before calling Annie. There was only one message, and it was from her.

"This is Annie, you son of a bitch!" The voice was familiar, but the venom could have killed me. "Don't you ever, *ever*, talk to me again!"

What the hell?

I tried to figure out what could possibly have triggered such an outburst and I came up empty. Oh well. Whatever it was had to be a misunderstanding. I had no doubt I'd be to clear it up easily enough after an hour or so of coldness. I could picture the set of her jaw. But these things had always blown over quickly enough before.

I called her back. She wasn't there, so I left a message. "Hi sweetie. Just got home and heard your message. I don't have a clue what you're angry about. Are we still on for dinner? I love you. Please call me."

I left a similar message on her cell phone. I knocked on her door and got no response. I couldn't tell if her car was in its garage or not, because the door was closed.

I left two more messages a few hours later. She didn't return any of them.

Monday
March 27, 2000

I'd left more messages Sunday morning and none were returned. Last night, she didn't show up for dance practice. I called her office and her phone was answered by Isabel, the department secretary. This was unremarkable in and of itself. Annie usually took her calls directly, but several times when she was in the middle of an important project, she forwarded all her calls to Isabel. I'd never met her, but we recognized each other's voices.

"Is this Chris?" Isabel asked.

"Yes."

"I have a message for you that Annie asked me to read exactly."

"Okay. Go ahead."

"You are a lying bastard. Never try to contact me again. About anything. If you do, I'll have my lawyer get a restraining order against you. Stay away!!!!" Isabel had to tell me about the four exclamation points at the end.

"I really have no idea what this is all about," I pleaded, on the verge of tears. "Did she give you any clues other than the note?"

"She told me not to answer any of your questions, although I can't believe you don't understand why she'd do this. I'm sure she has a very good reason and you know exactly what it is. If you want me to read the message to you again, I can do it. Otherwise, good day."

I had Isabel read the message and I copied it down word for word, including all of the exclamation points, and then hung up. I poured myself a glass of wine and read the note again. And then another glass of wine. And then another.

Sunday
April 9, 2000

Someone was shaking me. I looked up from my bed and saw Meg and Richard standing over me. "What the hell happened to you?" Richard demanded.

"Nothing. Why?"

"Why? Your whole place is littered with empty containers for Trader Joe's frozen burritos and about three cases of empty wine bottles. You haven't shaved in a month and you smell like hell, that's why," Meg told me. "And you're having a bad hair day."

"Annie left," I told them.

"Left? Waddaya mean left? Where'd she go?" Meg asked.

"I don't know," I said. "I don't have a clue."

I heard Meg ordering Richard around. "Get him into the shower and I'll see what I can do about cleaning up some. We've got to get him to eat something other than frozen burritos."

I'm stronger and more athletically fit than Richard, but I was in no mood for a fight. I let him drag me into the shower. When I got out, he gave me a sweatshirt and some jeans. "Put these on. You're going with us whether you want to or not."

They took me to a restaurant called Souper Salad, or something. All-you-can-eat salads and soups. "If all you've been eating is burritos, your intestines must be messed up. Salad is what you need. Eat!" Meg ordered.

"Daddy called and told us to come check on you," Meg told me as I was eating my first helping of salad. "He said you always call him the first week of the month to set up a chess match. You didn't. Nor did you answer your phone. He was worried about you."

After three helpings of salad and some water with lemon wedges, I started to feel a little better.

"When did she leave?" Richard asked when Meg was off getting a refill on salad.

"The day you and I went hiking. I came back ready to talk about moving in together either here or in Vegas, and she left a message saying to never call her again. She won't return my calls, and her secretary at work read me a very explicit message threatening me with legal action if I try to contact her."

"Wow. That was two weeks ago yesterday. And you've been nowhere other than Trader Joe's since then?"

"Guess not."

Meg came back and joined us. "So what's the deal? Are you still figuring she's going to come to her senses and call you or have you given up on her?"

"With the letter from her lawyer, I don't think there's anything I can do," I answered.

"Lawyer? What lawyer?" Meg wanted to know. "What'd he say?"

"Not he," I answered. "She. Sheila R. Finkelstein, Attorney at Law, with a Beverly Hills law-firm address."

"I stand corrected. What did *she* say and when did she say it?"

"I don't know the when exactly. It was a few days after I fell into the bottle. I answered the door to somebody who wouldn't stop knocking and ringing the bell and found myself signing for a registered letter."

"This is like fuckin' pulling teeth," Richard said. "What did the letter say?"

"It was all in legalese. But basically it served official notice that I was to leave Annie alone forever and ever. And if I didn't, awful things would happen to me."

"Well, little bro. What are you going to do now?"

Good question. I'd been happy enough wallowing in my grief, self-pity, and disbelief. But now that Richard and Meg had found me, I had a feeling they wouldn't let me stay there. Especially not when Ike found out about it. "I don't know," was all I could muster, and I started to tear up again.

"You've been talking about getting out of Dodge. That your lease is about up."

"Yeah."

"You want some advice?" Meg asked.

"Do I have a choice?" I asked, with a small smile.

"Good," she responded. "You're getting your sense of humor back. And no, you don't have a choice. If your relationship has evaporated or imploded or whatever, there's nothing for you here other than Richard and me, and the road and the phone go both ways. Besides, I've been trying to get Richard to take me to Vegas for years. You living there would be a good excuse."

"I don't have anywhere to live there." It all sounded like so much effort, and I had no energy for anything.

"Duh. So find a place. I've got to work this week, but Richard doesn't have anything pressing to do that I know of. Do you?" Richard shook his head. "So you two go and find a decent enough place that you can stay in for two months, six months, whatever. While you're at this new place, search for the house you want. Even if you don't set up your lapidary workshop until you've got a permanent place, it's no big deal. You have hundreds of salable pieces. Hook yourself to eBay. Take your stuff around to local jewelry stores there and see who wants it."

"She's right," Richard chimed in. "You've got plenty of money, so taking a few months off is a luxury you can afford. And sitting around here drinking yourself into oblivion won't bring her back. Time to move on. Can you leave in the morning to go to Vegas?"

"I don't know," I answered, with an embarrassed smile. "I have to check my To Do list."

"Yeah, right," Richard said. "I'm sure you've been checking your list regularly the past few weeks."

"Actually," I said, "I better just stay in bed tomorrow. Without any wine. It'll take a little while for the hangover to go away. I'll try to go to the gym tomorrow. Does Wednesday work for you?"

"Sure, that's just as good for me."

"Plus, I think I want to go see Ike tomorrow night. He's always had pretty good advice. I could use some now."

"That's good," Meg said. "I don't know what Daddy will tell you, but he'd be really hurt if you used this as an excuse to cancel the chess match. Do you want to sleep at our place tonight?" Meg asked. Even in my foggy state, I could tell these were the words of a friend and not a horny woman. "Even though I changed your sheets and took out the trash, your place smells like a wino's been living there."

I agreed. Before I went to bed I gave Meg a big hug. "Thanks, sis. You've been a big help." Then I hugged Richard and said, "You too."

"That's the first time you've ever called me sis," Meg told me. "It sounds nice. And you're welcome."

Tuesday
April 11, 2000

I'd spent the whole next day getting my place and my body functioning again. There were phone messages from Phil Adams wondering why we'd missed dance class, and another from Chris Corona at the Venetian wondering why we hadn't shown up for the giveaway, and a few from Ike reminding me of our chess match. But none from Annie or her lawyer. I guess they hoped I would just dry up and blow away.

I noted that I'd accumulated two W-2Gs so far—one for $1,250 and one for $8,020. Annie had told me she would take care of the taxes. I also had the accumulated cashback at both the Golden Nugget and the Venetian that were officially Annie's money. Netting these things out still meant that she owed me money, if not an explanation. I really didn't care. The loss of Annie was so crushing to me, the fact that she owed me a thousand dollars or so was small change. I'd have paid *lots* more than that to have things back like they were.

I planned to keep playing video poker. I might run into Annie there in some high-limit slot salon, but I rather doubted it. From what she told me about her breakup with Tony, she was willing to give up a gambling game in order to avoid seeing her ex. I wondered what game she would take up next.

I showed up at Ike's home at 7 p.m. "Where's my barbecued pork?" he asked.

I looked down at my hands. They were empty. "Guess I forgot. I'm sorry."

"Never mind. Let me get my jacket. I'm taking you to a fish house. Fish is supposed to be brain food, and that's what you need right now."

Ike drove me to a Red Snapper restaurant. I asked him to order for both of us because I didn't care. He ordered the halibut special, rice pilaf, salad with ranch, and a Diet Coke.

"So how long do you plan to feel sorry for yourself?"

I shrugged, so he tried again.

"You want I should go bomb her house? Will that help?"

"No no. If you killed her, she wouldn't be able to tell me *why*. That's all I want to know."

"Nonsense. I'm sure you want more than that. Once you find out why, you'll want to know what you can do to fix it. To make life happy-ever-after again."

"Probably," I conceded. "As near as I can tell, I didn't do anything to deserve this. I don't know what she *thinks* I did, but whatever it is, I didn't do it."

"Well, you recognized her big except right from the start. I told you it was nothing to worry about and then it bit you in the butt. I was wrong. I'm sorry."

The waiter brought our salads. Ranch dressing wasn't my favorite, but since I forced Ike to choose for me, I suppose I deserved whatever I got.

"Do you want me to go talk to her for you? She impressed me as a woman with good manners, so she'll probably at least talk to me. Maybe she'll tell me what your big crime was."

"Thanks, Ike, but no. It wouldn't do any good. The vitriol in her voice on the message machine. The four exclamation points in the message relayed through her secretary. The no-ifs-and-or-buts letter from her lady lawyer. She clearly doesn't want to reconcile. Her mind is made up."

"Okay. You're probably right. The question remains. What are you going to do now?"

"Richard and I'll go to Vegas tomorrow to find me a temporary place. In a few months I'll find a permanent place and set up my business again. I'll be fine."

"You planning on gambling? I'm worried about you. Especially now."

"What do you mean?"

"Even if you were right about having a slight edge over the casino, that presumes you're at your best. You're not. You didn't bring any food along tonight. That's the first time you've forgotten in 17 years."

"A freak accident. It doesn't signify a trend. I'll be okay."

"Maybe. Maybe not. You've trashed your health in the past two weeks. Burritos and wine, I think Meg said. Yes? How many times have you worked out since Annie left? How many times have you been hiking? Or gone to dance class? Or practiced gambling on the computer? What else haven't you been doing? Your eBay auctions ended 11 days ago. You put those things in the mail yet? You think the lady in Dubuque who bought one of your rings gives a shit that you've been having with your love life a tough time?"

"Okay, okay, Ike. You've made your point."

We paused for a minute while the waiter served our fish and refilled my Diet Coke.

"So tell me. When are you going to go gambling again?"

"What's the answer you want from me?"

"Something like the following: After you've joined a gym in Las Vegas and worked out at least twice. After you've had at least ten normal meals and are going to the bathroom regular. After you're square with your eBay accounts. After you've unpacked enough things to live for two months. And after you've practiced on the computer. If you want to gamble then and you think you have the edge, go right ahead."

I knew he was right. "Okay, Ike. I promise," I told him meekly.

"What are you going to do about finding a new girlfriend?"

"Nothing. I'm still dreaming about Annie. I'm in no position to consider any other woman."

"That's a good boy. Rushing into things again usually doesn't last."

"What else, Ike?"

"So! You'll call me every Tuesday night until I tell you

otherwise. You need somebody to talk to and it'll be awhile before you develop a circle of friends in Las Vegas."

"What else?" I was really touched.

"It was a guess on my part. Do you really have eBay mailing to do?"

I nodded.

"Then go home and get it packaged tonight. You and Richard can stop by the post office on your way out of town tomorrow. Your reliability on eBay is like a credit rating. If you screw that up, it's tough to get it squared away again."

"Thank you, father." I'd never said that before. His eyes told me he noticed, and was moved. "What about our chess match?"

"Not tonight. As much as I look forward to our matches, son, you have something more important to do tonight. But you owe me. Thursday night, after you've arranged things in Vegas, come and get your *tuchus* potched. And don't forget my barbecued pork!"

Wednesday
April 12, 2000

My criteria for a place to live in Vegas were as follows. The place had to have at least two bedrooms. It had to be in a safe neighborhood. It needed to be air-conditioned and well insulated against the Vegas summers. And I wanted only a 3-month to 6-month lease. When Richard and I got there, we exited at Flamingo and randomly headed east. We picked a Century 21, the first real-estate office we saw, and asked if they had any properties for lease. They did. The second place I was shown was acceptable and I signed the papers at about four o'clock.

The agent, an Oriental woman named Kim, said to let her know when I was ready to start shopping for a house. She noted that I seemed physically fit and told me that she and her husband belonged to a nearby Gold's Gym, which offered 3-month memberships. "It's at a higher monthly rate than the annual signups, but it lets you work out until you decide where you finally want to live. It'd be expensive and inconvenient to sign up for a gym membership in this part of town if you end up in Summerlin, say. Gold's has several gyms in town, but they're not everywhere."

I was impressed by Kim's thoroughness. I told her I'd definitely contact her when I was ready to buy and asked for directions to the nearest storage facility that had air-conditioned units. I rented one, starting the following Saturday, to store the furniture that wouldn't fit into my temporary condo.

"You going to show me this video poker crap while we're here?" Richard asked.

"My mind's not on gambling right now," I told him.

"Right now I'm thinking of logistics for the move. After I get moved in, come back and stay as long as you want, with or without Meg, and I'll show you everything I know."

"Sounds good. Let's grab a bite to eat and head home."

Saturday
April 15, 2000

Although Richard and I packed for two days, I hired some professional movers to load up a truck and haul my things to Vegas. Richard and Meg decided to caravan to Vegas with me, help me unpack, and see a bit of Sin City. For the first half of the trip, Meg rode with Richard. But in Barstow, she switched cars and rode with me the rest of the way. Richard was more than willing to have Meg bend someone else's ear for a few hours.

Meg asked me when Annie disappeared. I told her it was the same day that Richard and I went hiking. She thought about this for a while. Then she exclaimed, "Oh my God!"

"What?"

"Is Annie a small lady with red hair?"

"Yes. Why do you ask? You seem very distressed."

"I might have screwed things up for you royally. I was drinking and don't remember for sure, but maybe."

"Tell me," I ordered.

And she did.

"That doesn't make any sense, because she doesn't know the code." I thought it through out loud. "But if somehow she figured it out, it might explain things."

"We can't discuss this in front of Richard, you know," Meg warned. "He totally wouldn't understand. But I think I ought to at least try to tell Annie what I think happened. You do still love her and want her back if you can get her, don't you?"

"I think so. She's a prize, but an explosive one. Call her at work on Monday and see if she'll have lunch with you. And if she does, call me back and tell me what happened."

"Oh, Chris. I'm so sorry. I had no idea."

"I know you didn't do it on purpose, Meg. The good news is that at least there's a possible explanation, not to mention some reason for hope, whereas for the last three weeks there's been neither."

"What if she won't see me?"

"Then set up an appointment with her lawyer. Sheila Finkelstein from Beverly Hills. I don't remember her middle initial, but how many can there be? You can find her in the phone book, I'm sure. She'll at least listen to your story, although she may charge you a couple of hundred bucks for the privilege. Pay it. I'll reimburse you. Then, maybe she'll pass along your story. It's worth a shot."

Wednesday
April 19, 2000

I was dressed in shorts and a T-shirt, unshowered and unshaved, while I worked to put my new home together. It would only be short-term, and many boxes would remain packed, but I still needed to have some semblance of order.

The doorbell rang and I almost didn't answer it. I didn't know anybody in Las Vegas except for the Dancers and a few casino employees, none of whom would be likely to help me unpack. Besides, I had a bunch of work to do and wasn't in the mood for the Welcome Wagon folks or Jehovah's Witnesses. But I answered it anyway.

It was Annie. Dressed in the green and red outfit that knocked me over back at the Luxor. Including the new belt and *both* necklaces. "May I come in?" she asked meekly. I nodded.

She came into my arms and we just stood there holding each other. I must have smelled pretty ripe, but she didn't let go. I'd thought about this possibility nonstop since Meg figured out the plausible explanation. I wanted her desperately, but I couldn't handle a yo-yo relationship that might disappear again in the blink of an eye. I held her, but I was wary.

"I really screwed things up," she admitted.

"No shit, Sherlock! Here I am the happiest guy in the world, thinking forever-and-ever thoughts, believing you're thinking some version of the same, and all of sudden my world collapses and I don't even know why. I still don't know the details, although Meg called me up yesterday afternoon and told me you two met for lunch. Come on in and sit down. Can I bring you a glass or water or wine?"

"Maybe wine would be best," responded Annie. She

sat down on my sofa amid the chaos of packing boxes. I brought her a glass of wine and some water for me. Then I sat down on the other end of the sofa. And waited.

"The keypad to your door was always a challenge to me. I was intrigued that no matter how closely I watched, when you entered the code on the keypad, your fingers moved so quickly that I couldn't figure it out. But I kept watching. One night shortly after our first trip to the Golden Nugget, we went back to your condo after drinking a little bit. You had your right arm around me, so you punched in the code with your left hand, slowly, one finger at a time. This time I easily made out the code to be 3840, and as you know, I'm good at memorizing numbers. And the alarm was those same numbers backwards."

"Why did you want the key code to my condo?"

"Nothing sinister. Mostly it was the challenge of figuring out a puzzle. But once I did, then it was a question of what to do with the information.

"When you and Richard were off hiking that day, I figured it was the perfect time to sneak a gift into your condo."

"What gift? There was nothing when I got home—except your message."

"It was a photograph of when you and I went up on stage to get the $1,000 at the Nugget. Remember? They took pictures and sent me one. It's actually a pretty cool shot, as long as you can appreciate Kelly in drag with a god-awful pseudo-sexy expression on his face. Anyway, I got a copy made and framed it and was going to leave it on your pillow. Only my plan got sidetracked."

"I think I know what happened. But tell me anyway."

"Well, I entered the code, opened the door, and saw this naked woman, with a bottle of wine, drunkenly wandering around like she owned the place. It was Meg, but at that time I'd never met Meg. Of course, I immediately flashed back to when I found Tony and Betty Boobs together. My worst nightmare was happening all over again.

"Naturally, I fled back to my own condo and tried to

figure out what had I'd just seen. This woman was obviously not a cat burglar who'd broken in. She had to be there invited. And she was naked. And intoxicated, I didn't have to use all my brain cells to figure out why. I was convinced that you'd lied to me about being with your brother, and that instead you were having a tryst. That despite your protestations that you liked me and my body, you were just like every other guy and went for the D-cups every chance you got. I figured out that the code, 3840, stood for your favorite bra sizes."

I just sat there, not saying a word, shaking my head in disbelief that she could believe these things about me.

She continued, "But I didn't want to hear any more lies from you. After all, I'd caught you red-handed, or so I thought. I didn't actually *see* you there, of course, but I could easily infer your presence. When you called me that night on your cell phone, sounding all chipper and trying to hide your guilt, I realized that you could've been calling from anywhere. And that I'd been a sucker. And any explanation would be a lie and I didn't want to hear it. So I cut my losses before I was hurt any more.

"As you surmised, I'd been thinking forever-and-ever thoughts about you too. Until I caught you cheating. Or rather, what appeared to be cheating. And then I convinced myself that I was lucky to find out the truth before it was too late. Even though I cried myself to sleep for weeks and changed gyms and gave up dance class and missed the Venetian invitational and decided to give up my favorite gambling game again, I knew deep down that I'd made the right choice.

"And then Meg called out the blue, identified herself as your sister-in-law, and asked to meet me for lunch. I agreed reluctantly, not knowing that she was the mystery woman. When I saw her, I recognized her, although she looks a lot different with clothes on. She asked me to stay for at least five minutes to hear her out, and then I could go if I had to. I said okay. Five minutes.

"As soon as Meg's glass of wine came, she downed

it like it was water and ordered another. Obviously, something was eating at her big time. Or she was a wino. Or both. She showed me her wedding pictures to prove who she was. Although you both looked younger than you do now, it was clear she was the bride, you were the best man, and that you and the groom share a family resemblance. 'Okay,' I told her, 'you're married to Chris's brother. Go on.'

"She said that among other things she'd been the courier between the store and your place, which is why she knew the code. She said she really loves your Jacuzzi. Since you and Richard were out together, and Richard was packing his Glock, and she was worried Richard was complaining to you about her, she needed to relax. She said she wasn't planning on getting drunk, just to have a few and enjoy a long bubble bath. She said she vaguely remembered seeing me open the front door, but was pretty far gone by that point and couldn't figure out how anybody would have your code. So she figured it was her imagination and didn't say anything until you jogged her memory last week.

"Everything she told me clicked with the facts I'd either heard from you or had seen with my own eyes. Of course, they were opposite to the conclusions I had drawn. I asked her if she knew how you'd selected the door code, and she told me it was Richard's and her phone number and you wanted to make it easy for her to remember. I asked her if you and she had ever had sex together. She said she twice tried to seduce you by being naked when it was just the two of you in the condo, and both times you emphatically turned her down. Is that true?"

I nodded, and Annie continued. "I asked her if you'd said anything about me. She told me that you'd never shared much about your personal life, but that she and Richard had been told that I was the one and you hadn't the foggiest idea why I left. She said you went on a two-week bender and decided to move here because with me gone there was nothing keeping you in L.A. Is that true, too?"

I just looked at her.

"She told me that she thought you were one of the good guys. She gave me your address. She said that it was my choice whether I contacted you or not, but she at least had to tell me the truth about what had happened. She called herself a semi-drunk with other problems as well, but said she was loyal to her family and friends and you were both. She said she couldn't live with herself knowing that she had screwed up something important for you without trying to fix it as best she could.

"I remember testing you at the Mirage to see if you could handle it if I proved you were wrong. Well, this time I was wrong. Big time. I'm here to apologize. I'm very very sorry. I really misjudged you. I love you. Completely. Do you still love me? Can you forgive me?"

I sat there a long time, staring at my feet. I'd longed for her to tell me she loved me, but when she finally did, it didn't feel right. Thoughts were tumbling through my head like clothes in a dryer without Cling Free. I took deep breaths and let them out slowly through pursed lips, trying to get my heart rate under control. I didn't want my voice to quiver when I finally spoke. Eventually I was able to tell her, "Yes, I still love you, but there's a lot we need to talk about. Right now I need a shower. Will you excuse me for 15 minutes or so?"

"Do you need your back scrubbed?"

"Maybe later. Let me figure out some stuff. I'll be back shortly."

Wednesday
April 19, 2000

It took me closer to a half-hour to return. Annie's smile was both welcoming and uncertain. I didn't blame her. I wasn't sure myself what I was going to say. And even if I figured out what to say to Annie, I still didn't know what I'd say to Ike. Telling him that Meg liked to come over to my condo and take her clothes off wasn't going to happen. Ever. And if I didn't tell him, what could I say was the reason Annie came back?

"Annie," I began, "I'd like nothing better than getting back together with you. But if you disappeared again I'd be even more devastated. And right now the dread of that devastation looms much larger than the anticipated joy of a reunion. Before I can go full speed ahead, I need to make sure the brakes work. As near as I can tell, I didn't do anything to deserve what happened. Yes, I can see how things looked suspicious to you, but I could have explained it away in 30 seconds, given half a chance. But you refused to even give me that chance.

"For whatever reason, Annie, you have this bug up your ass about how you always need to be on your guard, lest you lose your guy to a big-chested woman. It's irrational. At the Venetian, I watched a cocktail server put down a bottle of water in front of me and you went on tilt! Any guy who sees that much breast flesh right in front of his eyes is going to look. Including me. Doesn't mean I'm not happy with you. Doesn't mean I'm thinking about cheating on my promises. Doesn't mean anything other than it's impossible for a guy not to sneak a peek. Yet you wouldn't talk to me for an hour. If we get back together, we'll see plenty of cocktail waitresses at various places. And some of them will be well-endowed. I don't need to be punished for looking. It's not a crime or something a healthy male should need to apologize for.

"I don't know how to solve this problem. But until it's behind us, there's this very sharp axe hanging over me. I'll never be able to relax."

Annie sat there awhile, and then spoke quietly. "After Tony, several girlfriends urged me to get counseling. They could see quite clearly that I wasn't rational. But I put it off. It was easier for me to give up on men than to face the truth. And then you came along."

Tears streamed down her cheeks. I ached to hold her, but I just sat there.

"I know that most problems don't go away by themselves. Let's say I went to a counselor for a while and started to overcome my fears. Would you still want me as a girlfriend?"

"Of course. I don't expect everything to always be perfect. But I at least need some sort of assurance that if you ever decide to run away again because of something you think I've done, you'll let me discuss it with you, if only to verify that I deserve your wrath for what you think I'm guilty of."

"Sounds fair. I'm truly sorry for what I put you through, as you know."

"I know you are," I said. "But sorry doesn't cut it. It was the worst time of my life. You going to counseling is a good first step. But there's more."

"Okay," Annie said with a sigh. "What else?"

"I've been ready to leave Los Angeles for some time. It was just a coincidence that you served me with legal papers the same time my condo lease was up, but there were other reasons as well. The business sold, as you know, so I've got plenty of cash. I can sell my jewelry anywhere. And I've loved Las Vegas for years and, thanks to you, I think I can play here with an edge.

"In other words, when your lawyer served me, I put my car into goodbye-gear and there's no reverse. I plan on living in Las Vegas for the foreseeable future. My guess is that a long-distance romance wouldn't prove satisfactory to either one of us. So if you think you want to be with me, you've got to move here. This particular place is too small, but it's temporary. I have a three-month lease while I look around for a house to buy. A place to settle down. I'm staying."

"Wow. That's a big one, but I understand. You already know I like my job in Santa Monica. And I'm not crazy about Las Vegas in the summertime. But I also love you very much. This sounds like something I should talk to my counselor about. In the meantime, would it be all right for me to come visit you, at least semi-regularly, to see if we can heal some of these wounds?"

"Yes. I'd like that very much."

"One nice thing about you living in Vegas," that mischievous smile crossed her face, "is that Vegas is the only place I can relax enough to enjoy sex. When I visit, we'll probably have good sex all the time. Starting now, if you'll have me. Please, Chris. Please?"

It didn't solve my problem of what to tell Ike. I'd have to work on that one some more. Besides, she did say please …

To Be Continued

Note on the accuracy of the novel

The title *Sex, Lies, and Video Poker* was originally chosen by my editor *par excellence*, Deke Castleman. I rejected it as being too much of a rip-off of the Academy Award-nominated movie, *Sex, Lies and Videotape*.

But the name grew on me. When I cursed Deke for creating a name that I couldn't let go, he smiled and said, "The best title is frequently a derivative." Since "derivative" is so much better than "rip-off," I decided I could live with it. One problem with the title is that while the novel deals with both sex and video poker, it doesn't deal with lies. At least not very much. Oh well. I apologize. I *still* like the title.

In many of my articles, I write in the first person, which is Bob Dancer. In this novel, I'm writing in the first person, but that person is Chris George. Chris and I are not at all the same person, and Annie has very little in common with Shirley.

The major characters in this novel—Chris, Annie, Ike, Meg, and Richard—are completely fictitious and not based on any specific person living or dead, although the way Chris and Annie attack the winning process is typical of successful players. The workers in the Los Angeles Jewelry Mart are made up, but the description of the buildings, the shops, and the ethnic separation there is accurate. The specific players named at the Golden Nugget, other than Shirley and Bob Dancer, are not real. I took liberties with the location and employee names of the restaurants in Southern California. Otherwise, most of the characters in this book are real. I used their real names, and their words and actions are what I think they'd be if they actually found themselves in these situations.

The hotel suites of the Golden Nugget and MGM Grand are accurately depicted, although the problem with keys at the Golden Nugget's Tower Suites has been solved by now. The slot clubs at the casinos are fairly presented as of early 2000, which is when the novel mostly takes place. Each of these slot clubs has become less generous in the intervening years, primarily because players are become more knowledgeable about video poker.

The Golden Nugget has more slot tournaments than any other casino I know about. The ones described in the novel are fictionalized, yet representative.

The Bob Dancer Reports are now out of print, but they've been superbly superceded by the Bob Dancer/ Liam W. Daily *Winner's Guide* series. There are numerous products geared toward teaching you how to play better video poker available at www.bobdancer.com.

Making Shirley and me characters in my own novel was a kick. I've no doubt that some readers will enjoy this with me, while others will criticize me for it. Shirley is accurately portrayed here. She's a delightful part of my life and I enjoy her little idiosyncrasies. The toughest character to describe was myself. I probably ended up with a fair depiction of "Bob Dancer on a good day."

Video poker remains a beatable game. While slot clubs today are less generous than they were in 2000, probably more players are net winners at video poker than at any other casino game. The methods described in the book (limit yourself to the highest playing games, learn to play every hand accurately, learn the ins and outs of slot clubs, and take advantage of casino promotions) are your roadmap to success.

I wish you many royal flushes. The Golden Nugget remains one of Shirley's and my favorite places to play.

Bob Dancer, March 2004

Other Fine Video Poker Products from Bob Dancer

Million Dollar Video Poker
by Bob Dancer

Bob Dancer is the best-known video poker player and writer in the world. In just six years, after arriving in Las Vegas with a total bankroll of $6,000, Bob and his wife Shirley won more than $1 million in a six-month period playing video poker. His book, which recounts the events of those six years with stories about his meteoric ups and downs, has many lessons for players of all skill levels. Video poker is one of those rare casino games that can be beaten by a talented and informed player, and Bob explains how he did it. Never before has a top video poker professional shared so many of his winning secrets.
$16.95

Video Poker Winner's Guides
by Bob Dancer and Liam W. Daily

All *Winner's Guides* cover both strategy and non-strategy aspects of play that are important for winning. Readers learn through the presentation and explanation of basic principles that take them through four levels of strategy.

Volume 1—Jacks or Better (including 9/6, 9/5, 8/5, 8/5 with quads = 35, and 8/5 Bonus) Second Edition: $18.50

Volume 2—Double Bonus (including 10/7, 9/7, and 10/7 with straight flush = 80) $16.50

Volume 3—Full Pay Deuces Wild (also including—"pseudo Full Pay Deuces Wild") $16.50

Volume 4—NSU Deuces Wild (including 16/10/4/4/3 "Not So Ugly" and 15/9/4/4/3 "pseudo NSU") $16.50

Volume 5—Pick'Em Poker $10.00

Volume 6—Double Double Bonus Poker $16.50

Volume 7—Joker Wild (expected publication date early 2005)

Bob Dancer Presents *WinPoker*
Created by Zamzow Software Solutions

This software comes with 25 of the most popular video poker games in the casinos, including 9/6 Jacks or Better, 8/5 Bonus Poker, 10/7 Double Bonus, Joker Wild, Deuces Wild, Double Double Bonus, Atlantic City Joker Poker, Pick'Em Poker, and more. No other software compares for graphic quality, pre-loaded games, accuracy, and ease of use. There are also several variations of the new multiple-hand games, such as Triple Play.

Version 6.0–$29.95

Video Poker Strategy Cards
By Bob Dancer and Liam W. Daily

Excellent companions to the Dancer/Daily *Winner's Guides*, these video poker strategy cards may be the best strategy cards ever devised for any game. Four strategy levels take you from beginner to advanced, all on one six-panel tri-fold pocket-sized card. The "Beginner" strategies alone will improve almost anyone's play, while those who graduate to the "Advanced" strategies will be playing virtually as accurately as a computer. Carry the cards with you into the casinos and refer to them while you play. 9/6 Jacks or Better, 10/7 & 9/7 Double Bonus, Full Pay Deuces Wild, Kings or Better Joker Wild, Two Pair Joker Wild, Double Double Bonus, Pick'Em Poker, 8/5 Jacks & 8/5 Bonus, and 16/10 NSU Deuces Wild.

You can purchase all these products at 10% off at www.bobdancer.com.